SUGAR

SUGAR

SERESSIA GLASS

HEAT | NEW YORK

HEAT

An imprint of Penguin Random House LLC
375 Hudson Street, New York, New York 10014

This book is an original publication of Penguin Random House LLC.

HEAT and the HEAT design are trademarks of Penguin Random House LLC.
For more information, visit penguin.com.

Library of Congress Cataloging-in-Publication Data

Glass, Seressia.
Sugar / Seressia Glass. — Berkley trade paperback edition.
p. cm. — (A sugar and spice novel ; 2)
ISBN 978-0-425-27520-7 (paperback)
1. Erotic fiction.   2. Love stories.   I. Title.
PS3557.L345S84 .   2015
813'.54—dc23
2015016679

PUBLISHING HISTORY
Heat trade paperback edition / November 2015

PRINTED IN THE UNITED STATES OF AMERICA

10 9 8 7 6 5 4 3 2 1

Cover photo by hotdamnstock.com.
Text design by Kelly Lipovich.

Penguin
Random
House

*To "The Guy," my guitar hero,
who inspires me more than he'll ever know*

ONE

Charlie O'Halloran had a plan, and today was the day to set it in motion.

The plan? Get Siobhan Malloy to notice more than his sandwich order.

He hadn't stopped thinking about her since the day he'd delivered a floral order to the café instead of one of his injured couriers. The order was for her business partner, thank goodness. He'd been struck dumb by the blonde goddess in the "Everything Nice" T-shirt from the moment he'd seen her. Realizing that the café she co-owned wasn't that far from his office just off the downtown square, he'd begun doing something he hadn't done in nearly three years: take lunch out of the office.

He didn't visit the café every day because, stalker much? However, there was nothing wrong with stopping in once or twice a week to sample the day's specials, get the lay of the land, and covertly ogle the woman he very much wanted to get to know better.

Not that Siobhan noticed. She had never said anything beyond the standard customer–server interactions, but he hadn't minded since she treated everyone the same—friendly to customers, warm to coworkers. She didn't flirt, didn't encourage attention from men or women. No rings, though that could have been because of her job. Still, the lack of a visit by a significant other piqued his interest. It made him wonder if she had someone in her life, and whether the answer was by choice. Made him wonder if her choices and reasons were anything close to his.

He would have abandoned his reconnaissance mission altogether if not for her coworkers, the baker, Nadia, and the cashier, Rosie. He'd thought he'd been subtle, but obviously not subtle enough. Nadia had boxed up a catering order for him one morning—it had been market research, not stalking—then smiled, told him Siobhan's full name, and informed him that Siobhan handled their lunch business and had an excellent soup-and-sandwich combo that would be good for a group lunch.

The very next week he'd ordered the suggested catered lunch and as Siobhan packed it and Rosie rang it up, Rosie had quietly mentioned that Siobhan was single. With that information, de facto blessing, and meal in hand, he'd beaten a strategic retreat. Strategic because he'd done his homework. The Sugar and Spice Café had been in business for just under four years and had mostly positive reviews on the various social sites from both business and college customers. There was a gaping hole in its business model, one that he could help with. At the very least it would garner him face time with the lovely Siobhan. At the most, he'd get the girl and the business.

No other outcome was allowed. Charlie would use his brains and his charm to get what he wanted. Neither had failed him before. He had no intention of failing now. Not when it came to the gorgeous woman who'd made it impossible for him to even think about anyone else.

Yes, blonde-haired and blue-eyed described her, but that was like describing the ocean as water. She was pinup model beautiful, complete with the look that said she could be on a retro calendar winking at him while astride some missile or painted on the tail of some World War II bomber. Her hair gleamed like woven gold with sun-streaked strands of platinum. Her eyes changed depending on what she wore, transitioning from the bluest blue of a perfect summer sky to the dusky deep blue of evening, a color change so startling it made him wonder if she sometimes wore contacts. If so, they worked for her. She was doll perfect, if you like dolls with an hourglass figure of full breasts and hips he ached to hold on to.

He pushed back from his desk, then glanced ruefully down at his lap. Yeah, Junior usually piped up whenever he thought about Siobhan, which seemed to be continuously. It was his own damned fault for being too wrapped up in work to take time for anything else, especially a woman. Most especially a woman who would expect to take priority in his life.

He couldn't meet that expectation and rather than lead anyone on, he'd decided to abandon dating altogether. Even when he found someone just as career-focused as he was, there were other factors that usually made his relationships come to an end sooner rather than later. One-night stands and quick hookups had fulfilled the need for a while, but even those became monotonous. It was just easier to go without.

Yet something told him that Siobhan was different, could be

different. She took her career as a business owner just as seriously as he did. Yet she also took time for her friends. She was driven, but not blindly so. Her capacity to care was evident and hinted at her ability to be compassionate and understanding. All of that, and independent enough to not need to be with him every moment of every day. And with curves that went on for days, she had a body built for sex and a life designed for commitment-free intimacy. She was perfect for him.

He just had to convince her of that.

———

Jealousy was a bitch, and the bitch had claws.

Siobhan tried to choke it down as Nadia whistled while she kneaded dough. After everything Nadia had been through in the last few years, she deserved her happiness with her sexy professor, Kane Sullivan. They'd been back together for two months now, and Siobhan knew her partner spent as much time at Sullivan's beachfront condo as she did the townhouse above their café.

It wasn't even the love that suffused Nadia's face that caused the bright gouge of envy. Okay, it was that too. But the fact that Nadia was obviously and repeatedly reaching the Big O courtesy of someone else was enough to turn Siobhan's blue eyes green.

She couldn't even remember the last time she'd gotten laid. It had been before she and Nadia had set up the café in Crimson Bay, that much was certain. That was four years ago. Before that, they'd both spent time in a drug rehabilitation facility in Los Angeles and trying to figure out their next steps. No sex while in treatment. Prior to attending court-mandated rehab, what had she done?

Gone on a downward spiral that had culminated with her breaking her husband's heart, alienating her daughter, and making sure no one in her family would ever speak to her again.

Siobhan blew out a breath. Yeah, she was pretty sure her vagina had spontaneously re-virginized. After more than a five-year drought, your body forgot certain things. The weight of another body sliding against it. The feel of someone else's fingers thrilling, teasing. The heat of a hot mouth sliding over her breasts, her clit.

Okay, she hadn't forgotten. Memory and fantasy kept her pretty busy most nights. If she needed a thrill, she had plenty of opportunity when she performed with her burlesque troupe once a month. She liked letting the music transport her, liked moving into that other mindset that allowed her inner sex kitten free rein. Too bad there weren't any decent prospects in the bevy of admirers that hung around after the shows.

"What's wrong?"

Siobhan blinked, bringing the kitchen back into focus. Nadia had moved from kneading dough to shaping it into loaves. "Nothing's wrong. How's that new organic flour working out?"

"Pretty good. The flour takes the powdered matcha well, and people are raving about the green tea cakes. I think we should make the mill our regular supplier."

"Good to know. Their sourdough is pretty good too. We've gotten a lot of compliments on the Crimson Bay-L-Ts."

Nadia wiped her hands clean on the towel she'd thrown over one shoulder. "You're not going to distract me with business talk, Sugar," she said. "That's the second time you sighed in as many minutes. Talk to me."

"There's nothing to talk about."

Nadia trained her dark gaze over Siobhan's features, and she did her best to appear blithely unconcerned. Nadia knew her too well though. "That's the problem, isn't it? Nothing's happening, when something should be. Between the two of us, you've had more chances to get laid than I did. You should take a couple of those guys at your shows up on their offers."

"The guys who hang around after my burlesque shows are either creepers or frat boys," Siobhan retorted. "Neither of which are high on my list of prospects. I may be dateless, but I'm not desperate." Not yet.

"So does that mean that you do have a prospect list?" Nadia brightened. "I thought I'd have to get you and the other girls to draw straws at the next Bitch Talk session. Not that I want Audie to even think about the opposite sex right now." She shuddered.

Ah, a change of subject. "How is Audie doing, by the way?"

"Holding her own. The assistant district attorney told her that they've set an arraignment date for her assault case. I told her I'd go with her."

"We'll all go." Outwardly, Audie appeared to have recovered from her assault, but Siobhan knew something like that could scar a person and those scars could bury themselves deep. Audie had almost irrevocably burned her friendship bridges in the aftermath, but she'd worked with a crisis counselor to come through more or less better than she'd been before. "We'll support her."

"She knows that. And I support you, which is why I'm not going to let you keep changing the subject."

"I'm not changing the subject," she protested, and even she heard how weak of a protest it was. "There's no subject to change."

"Whose fault is that?" Nadia settled her hands on her hips.

"You're miserable, Sugar. And your misery is self-inflicted. Come join me on the dark side. You know we have excellent cookies."

Rosie stuck her head through the swing door. "There's a hot guy out here asking for the owner."

"Your turn," Nadia said, turning Siobhan toward the door. "I know for a fact that my hot guy is still at work. If you'll take care of our mysterious hot guy, I can finish up these loaves."

Siobhan pushed through the swing door then stopped short, barely catching the door in time. Double-espresso shot, Crimson Bay-L-T was back. The first time she'd seen him was when he'd delivered flowers for Nadia four months ago, and the way his long muscular legs had filled those navy blue bike shorts was seared on her mind's eye—and had starred in a couple of late-night fantasies. He'd returned numerous times since then, though regrettably not in biking gear. This time he wore dark khakis with a pale green oxford bearing his company logo instead of the aerodynamic bike shorts and T-shirt, and he carried a leather satchel instead of a fanny pack. She tried not to feel disappointed that she didn't get the pleasure of ogling his muscles. He was still heart-poundingly gorgeous and nice to look at though, one of those guys who could look good in any-thing, thanks to the chiseled jaw, expressive blue-green eyes, and the artfully tousled honey-blond hair.

Though the business-casual attire hid it, she remembered all too well how his lean and fit body had filled his shorts and shirt. He looked to be a man who enjoyed activity, all sorts of activities, in-timate and public. And young enough that those activities probably involved jet skis and kegs and strippers.

Siobhan smoothed her apron, then stepped around the counter, unaccountably glad that she'd forgone the standard work attire of Sugar and Spice T-shirt and jeans for the fifties-style pink, teal, and white apron she'd created that complemented her retro pink pedal pushers, teal button-down over a white camisole, and teal sneakers.

For a moment he stared at her blankly, as if frozen. Then he smiled, and damn, that mouth. His mouth promised all sorts of wicked delights. It was a mouth that said it knew how to kiss and do all sorts of other things to please a woman. It said this guy and I, we know what we're doing when it comes to sex and we know how to deliver on everything we promise.

Good Lord. Siobhan blinked, attempting to gather her composure. It had been too long since she'd had sex with someone besides herself. Her immunity to the opposite sex was woefully out of date.

Maybe it was the talk she'd just had with Nadia. Maybe it was her own internal monologue for the last couple of months. Or maybe, just maybe, the man standing before her with the smile full of promise was the cure for what ailed her.

"Hello. Siobhan Malloy, Sugar and Spice Café. What can I do for you today?"

TWO

ᔕᕦᑕᔆ · ᔆᕦᑕᔆ

"Hello," he said, sticking out his hand as Siobhan approached. "I'm Charlie O'Halloran with Crimson Bay Couriers. And the questions is, what can I—or rather, what can my company—do for you today?"

"What is it that you thi . . ." Her voice faded as his hand engulfed hers, her breath stolen by the warmth that snaked up her arm and went straight to her chest. Was this what a heart attack felt like? The tingling, the shortness of breath, the painfully hard nipples? Okay, maybe not the nipple part, but everything else.

"Do you have a few minutes, Ms. Malloy?" O'Halloran gave her that smile again. He had to know it was a weapon of mass seduction. Even she, with her scarred-over heart and dormant libido, wasn't immune to its charm.

She glanced around the café. He'd timed his visit well; their regulars knew what time they closed up shop, and the few stragglers who did come in were choosing to-go orders from whatever was left.

"Of course, Mr. O'Halloran," she said, gesturing to the out-of-the-way table they used for their Tuesday talks. "And please call me Siobhan. We don't stand on formality around here."

"Siobhan. What a beautiful name." He pulled out her chair for her, then took the seat opposite. "Please call me Charlie."

"Charlie." At least he didn't give her the tired line about beautiful names for beautiful women. Point to him. Then again, he probably didn't have to use pickup lines. All he had to do was lean forward, stare into a woman's eyes as if she were the most important thing in the universe, and give that smile that promised to let her in on the secret.

Siobhan wasn't about to let him add her to his string of conquests. She wasn't some college coed or innocent. She'd seen too much, done much more, and pulled herself through to the other side. His charms wouldn't work on her, as powerful as they were. In fact, maybe it was time to show him that an experienced woman had a charm of her own.

She smiled at him, knowing her cheeky grin revealed a pretty potent set of dimples. "What can I do for you, Charlie?"

His smile dimmed slightly, no less potent. "I'd like to discuss a proposition with you. A business proposition."

Figures. Courier boy was a salesman, and a slick one at that. She smothered the minute disappointment that he wanted her business instead of her and tilted her head at him. "Are you interested in my sweet treats, Charlie?"

He blinked for a moment, then caught himself. "Actually, yes. You're surrounded by several businesses and government offices, and I'm sure you get a majority of your business from them, with spikes in sales from students around exam time."

So he wasn't stupid. Neither was she. "Go on."

"I noticed that you offer light catering services with twenty-four hours' advance notice," Charlie continued, withdrawing one of Sugar and Spice's brochures from his portfolio. "But your catering is pickup only. I believe there's a missed opportunity there, and that's where Crimson Bay Couriers can help."

Siobhan leaned forward, intrigued despite herself. The café's catering business was small, but not because of lack of interest. Their foot traffic was the center of their income stream and they used it to build rapport and repeat customers. They had regulars that they knew scheduled weekly meetings, and they managed their inventory down to the last cookie, tracking which days they had a spike in sales and why. Nadia would sometimes deliver baked goods for some of their regulars using her MINI Cooper, but that wasn't often and didn't include any lunch orders.

"You want your courier company to take on delivery service for Sugar and Spice?"

"Yes, initially." He handed her a presentation folder whose cover bore the logo *OBS* of stylized lettering with the tag line *Support at the speed of business* in red and navy and the phrase *Sugar and Spice Café Delivery Proposal* in bold, black lettering. "It's something we've done for other local eateries. We would add Sugar and Spice to our food delivery family and interface our website with yours. The customer would place the order through our website and we pass the order to you after payment. On top of the charges you normally have for your items, Crimson Bay Couriers would add two: One is a delivery fee to help defray any operating costs, including fuel if a motorized vehicle is used. The other is a mandatory tip for our courier. The details of how the payment would be dispersed are included in the proposal I gave you. We also offer other services that have proven beneficial to other local small business in the area."

Curious, she flipped through the proposal. His bosses had done an impressive job, offering up their client list for references, detailing the projected increase in revenue for the café, what the projected profit-loss calculation would be, and a list of other services including web design and social media marketing.

"You've presented an impressive proposal, Mr.—excuse me—Charlie," she said, closing the proposal and placing it on the table. "I'll have to discuss it with my partner before I can provide any sort of response."

"Of course. I wouldn't expect anything else. My contact information is in the proposal packet. If you have any questions about our services, anything at all, please feel free to call."

"I will." She shook his hand again, and it was like lightning striking twice as that same current of awareness snaked up her arms and energized her body.

He turned his wrist, and instead of shaking her hand he held it, his fingers tangled loosely with hers. Strong, callused fingers that denoted a man used to working with his hands, used to hard work. Would she feel the same electric current if those fingers stroked over other parts of her body, like her breasts, the small of her back?

Shocked at the direction of her thoughts, she attempted to pull her hand free of his. He tightened his grip instead. "Charlie?"

"You're so beautiful," he said then, his tone dazed and wondering. "I don't think I've ever met a woman as beautiful as you."

"How many women have you used that line on?" she asked, but couldn't muster the heat she wanted to interject into her tone. Not when he looked at her as if she'd just appeared out of a fantasy. His fantasy.

"A couple," he admitted, "but I didn't understand what that meant until now. I should have saved it for you."

She was only human. It was perfectly all right for her to take a little feminine satisfaction in knowing that she'd had an effect on such a handsome man, even if nothing would come of it. Nothing *could* come of it.

Still, she had to know, so she asked. "Is this how you charm all your clients, with a combination of business smarts and flirting?"

The smile he gave her was at once indulgent and self-deprecating. "But you aren't my client yet, Siobhan."

She took a deep breath. He was a stranger. Sure he came in an average of once a week, but they'd hardly said two full sentences to each other before now. He shouldn't have said her name like that, all soft and sweet as if they'd just awakened from an exhausting bout of lovemaking. As if he knew her, and liked what he knew and wanted to know more. No, he shouldn't have said it like that, and she shouldn't have reacted the way she had, melting at the sound and the yearning it evoked in her.

"You think I'm going to be your client?"

"I think you know a good business opportunity when you see it," he told her, his smile deepening. "I think you'll at least discuss it with your business partner, do some due diligence. Sugar and Spice Café has successfully been in business for nearly four years, which is a lifetime in restaurant terms. That says a lot about the business and the people who run it."

His confidence was strangely attractive. On anyone else, that confidence would have been off-putting. But with that open, easy smile and the "just between you and me" tone, his self-assurance drew her like a moth to a flame.

"Be that as it may, don't you think your overt flirting is offensive?"

"You're not offended." He squeezed her hand, reminding her that he still held it. "You're curious, intrigued even. Wondering if I can back up all the flirting."

"Can you?" she asked, then immediately wished she could take the words back.

"You should find out for yourself." He leaned forward, lowered his voice. "Let me take you out on a date."

Damn the trill of pleasure that swept her bloodstream! It betrayed her resolve, her need to ignore every wish but one, to have her daughter back. "I'm sorry, Charlie. I don't mix business and pleasure."

"That's not true," he insisted. "You're surrounded by friends here. Your business partner is your best friend."

"That's different."

"How is it different? Is it different because you don't look at your friends and imagine yourself kissing them the way you do when you look at me?"

Her nipples tightened. God, when was the last time she'd felt any of this? Anything close to this? She couldn't remember, but it had to have been years. Years.

"Charlie, this is highly inappropriate. What would your boss say?"

"I don't think he'd have as big a problem with it as you think he would. As for whether or not it's inappropriate . . . maybe, but do you think it's wrong?"

Oh hell yes, it was wrong. It was multiple levels of wrong. Because now, thanks to him, all she could think about was kissing him, touching him, *everything him*.

She shook her head, trying to distance herself from him, from the things he was resurrecting for her. Things she wasn't sure she was equipped to handle any longer, if she ever had been.

"Siobhan. Give me one good reason, outside of the potential business relationship, why going out with me would be a bad idea."

"I can think of one major reason."

"Which is?"

She sighed inwardly. "I'm older than you."

"So?"

"So?" she repeated. "What do you mean, so? It's a big deal!"

He shook his head. "Not to me."

"Well it is to me!"

"Age ain't nothing but a number," he retorted. "How old are you?"

"I'm thirty-five."

"And I'm thirty," he told her, shrugging his shoulders. "That's only a five-year difference. You make it sound like you're old and decrepit and past your prime." He gave her a long, slow perusal, teal eyes alight with appreciation. "Which I can tell you, you most certainly are not."

He'd stolen the words right out of her mouth, leaving her without an argument. "What am I then?" she asked, wanting to know how he saw her. Not that what he thought of her mattered.

"I think you're retro sexy, like a pinup," he said, sincerity flooding his tone. "You remind me of cotton candy—fun, indulgent, a sweet treat. But I bet you're also a habanero hottie on the inside. Yes, sugar and spice, just like your café."

Flummoxed and flustered, she could only sit and stare at him. Why her, why now? She wasn't ready for anything like this. She doubted she'd ever be ready for anything like this. For all her bitching and moaning to Nadia and to Charlie that she was too old for the relationship dance, she was honest enough to admit to herself that she didn't feel that she deserved anything like this, an opportunity like this, even though she wanted it. Not with Charlie, though. Not really.

She'd made a mess of her life before. She'd ruined her daughter's childhood, destroyed her marriage to her high school sweetheart. Did she really deserve another shot at relationships, when the ones she'd had were still in tatters?

"Siobhan." He turned their hands so that he could press a kiss to the back of her hand. As kisses went, it was tame, chaste even, but she felt it all the way to her toes.

He stood. "Whether it's for business or pleasure or both, I look forward to hearing from you. My contact info is in the proposal."

He left. She remained seated, stunned, aroused, and very confused. It was a state that continued when she opened the portfolio to retrieve his business card. As she read it, she realized what *OBS* stood for: O'Halloran Business Solutions. Charlie O'Halloran wasn't a courier or salesperson for Crimson Bay Couriers.

He was the owner.

THREE

"So, Hottie McHotterson has brains to go with all that brawn," Nadia joked as she closed the cover on the business proposal. "Your boyfriend sure is full of surprises."

"I'm not going to rise to your bait." Siobhan joined her business partner at the small round table tucked into their office. "But thanks for reading the proposal and letting me close the café before you started in with the innuendos."

"Are you going to take his bait?" Nadia asked, wiggling her eyebrows suggestively. "I gotta say, that's some mighty fine bait."

"Can we talk about the proposal?" Siobhan asked, wishing she'd selected a stronger tea than the rosehip currently steeping in front of her. "I'd like to know what you think about it."

Nadia checked the brew strength of her own pot of tea, a mild rooibos. "I'm glad to know that your potential Mr. Right Now was doing more than stalking you. He did a very thorough background on our business."

Siobhan decided to let the "Mr. Right Now" quip pass without comment. She didn't need to encourage Nadia more than she already had. "Apparently, Crimson Bay Couriers is just one of the companies under the O'Halloran Business Solutions banner. It looks like they have an answer for anything a small business could need."

"I think his proposal is sound," Nadia said. "Definitely something we need to consider."

"Actually, we have considered it. We just didn't have the infrastructure and overhead necessary to implement it."

"True." Nadia tapped on her tablet, pulling up their business plan. "McHotterson's proposal would enable us to branch out into delivery and onsite catering without a hardship investment on our part. It's a way for us to bring in more business without having to resort to extending our hours and potentially destroying the balancing act we have with inventory. If we start planning now, we could be ready to launch it when business picks back up in the fall."

Summer was their slowest season. Not only was traffic light because attendance at Herscher, the college that anchored the town, went to less than forty percent capacity, but most tourists to their seaside town spent their time on the boardwalk, not the town square. Gatherings on the square, like concerts and movie nights, were usually at hours when the café was normally closed. They ran a skeleton crew and summer hours to offset the light business, opening at eight during the week and operating nine to noon on Saturdays.

While upping their income was always at the forefront of their minds, neither wanted their quality to suffer. Thanks to their stints in rehab, both had become control freaks. Though they both had assistants, neither would turn their kitchen duties over to anyone else in order to expand their service hours, and both had learned the hard way that burnout wasn't pretty.

"Maybe we could do a trial period with them, and reassess at the end of the contract," Siobhan mused. "It would be like having a soft opening. We'd tell a few of our business regulars about the delivery option and see how it goes."

"Good idea. In the meantime, we'll work on overhauling the website. I did a little tinkering a few weeks back, but it was mostly to keep myself occupied." Nadia's tone dimmed, and Siobhan knew she was thinking of the breakup she'd had with Kane before both had come to their senses. "Anyway, McHotterson's included an upgrade in one of the options package. Seems like his company is a full-service provider, and the client list is impressive. Like I said, your man's got a good head on those gorgeous shoulders. You should find out if he has a good head beneath those khakis."

"You're not going to let it go, are you?" Siobhan said with a long-suffering sigh. She knew Nadia's heart was in the right place, but she didn't need her business partner to become a relationship evangelist trying to convert her friends' lives into sexily-ever-afters, no matter how nice it would be to get it on the regular.

"Just consider me your sex cheerleader," Nadia answered with an unrepentant smile before launching into a cheer. "Get S-O-M-E— Siobhan is next, just wait and see!"

"Good grief, you're fucking impossible!" Siobhan exclaimed, laughing despite herself. "You should be completely focused on your sexy professor. Stop worrying about me."

"I wouldn't call it worry." Nadia poured tea into her mug, then added a healthy dollop of local wildflower honey. "I know you have a full life. I know you're in a good place. That doesn't mean that I think it's okay that you're just treading water."

"What's that supposed to mean?"

"Emotionally you're just keeping your head above water, not trying to move forward. I wouldn't push you if it wasn't for the fact that you want more."

Siobhan concentrated on preparing her own mug of tea. She decided to ignore the treading water remark. "What makes you think I want more?"

"Because you have the biggest heart of anyone I've ever known, outside of my dads. Because you're at your happiest when you're caring for someone else."

"Yeah." Siobhan snorted. "My track record is just awesome on that."

"I'm not talking about your daughter or your ex-husband. I'm talking about how you helped me get through rehab. I'm talking about how you helped me stay clean for the last four years. How you had my back when I faltered. How you helped Audie when she tried to push everyone away. How you staged a cookie intervention when I almost ruined things with Kane."

Nadia reached over, wrapping tea-warmed fingers around Siobhan's suddenly icy ones. "You have an incredible capacity to care, Siobhan, and I'm grateful you care for me and all our friends. I'm just saying that maybe it's time to care for someone in a different way—especially someone who can care for you in a way the rest of us can't."

Damn. Siobhan tried to force a sip of tea past the lump in her throat. "I'm not ready to fall in love."

"I didn't say anything about falling in love," Nadia said gently. "I don't think you're ready for that. But there's nothing wrong with falling in lust. Particularly when you have a prime young stud apply for the job of fantasy maker."

"You think he's too young for me?"

"I don't care how young he is, as long as he's legal." Nadia's gaze sharpened. "Did he tell you how old he is?"

"He's thirty."

"Excellent! That means he's exactly what you asked for!"

"I didn't ask for him!"

Nadia cocked her head. "Are you sure? You said most guys interested in you are either fraternity guys or too old for you. Hottie McHotterson is a responsible thirtysomething who owns his own company. He's also very interested in you. He's hot, responsible, hot, a business owner, hot, good-looking, charming. Did I mention that he was hot?"

Siobhan fought a smile. "You might have mentioned it once or twice."

Nadia cocked her head. "You don't think he's attractive? I know he doesn't look anything like Mike."

"That's a good thing, though." The mention of her ex-husband always caused a shaft of guilt, but at least the pain had lessened over the years. "I'm glad Charlie doesn't look like Mike. Charlie's surfer-god gorgeous, with the most amazing lashes I've ever seen on a guy. And those eyes! God, Nadia—when he looked at me, I knew I had his complete attention, like I was the best thing he'd ever seen. Like he knew the world's biggest secret and wanted to let me in on it. It was flattering."

"Sounds like he made quite an impression on you."

Blood heated her cheeks. "You won't believe what he said!"

"What?" Nadia leaned forward with schoolgirl eagerness. "What did he say?"

"He called me retro sexy."

Nadia laughed. "He nailed you good. Not as good as the naked mambo, but retro sexy fits you. Given your whole burlesque-rockabilly vibe, I'd say retro sexy is a good description of you."

Siobhan shook her head, still dumbfounded over the most bizarre sales pitch she'd ever participated in. "Do you also say I'm cotton-candy fun covering a habanero-hottie center?"

Nadia's eyes widened. "He said that to you?"

"He sure did," Siobhan answered, then blew out a breath. "Right before he kissed the back of my hand."

"That must have been some kind of hand kiss."

"I melted," Siobhan admitted. "I seriously fricking melted because a guy kissed my hand. My hand! How pathetic is that?"

"I don't think it's pathetic at all," her partner said, her voice understanding. A dreamy haze filled her eyes. "When Kane kisses my hand like that, I tend to get all melty too. There's something to be said about a guy who can be charming like that without it feeling cheesy."

"I was feeling a lot of things, but cheesy definitely wasn't one of them!"

Nadia waggled her eyebrows. "Were you thinking about what it would be like to ride his surfboard?"

"Nadia!" Siobhan barely refrained from spewing her mouthful of tea. "Good grief, your mind has gotten dirty since you've been bumping uglies with the professor. I can't believe you said that!"

"Why? Because it's true?"

"I . . . It's . . ." Siobhan shook her head, unable to protest in the face of Nadia's blithe demeanor. "Okay, I thought about it, all right? How could I not with him sitting there being all gorgeous and charming and smart? I'm not dead!"

22

"No, you aren't, and I for one am glad you've finally realized that. What you are is out of practice. Personally, I don't think there's anything wrong with taking your blond hottie out for a test run. Especially since he's volunteering."

"He asked me out on a date, so I guess that means he's volunteering."

"What?" Nadia's mouth dropped open. "How do you save that little tidbit for last? What did you say?"

"I came up with reasons why I shouldn't," Siobhan admitted. "He shot every one of them down."

"Hot, charming, smart, and persistent," Nadia said, ticking off each word on her fingers. "I hope you said yes."

"Um . . . He kinda left me sitting there with my mouth hanging open."

Nadia cackled. Her friend and business partner actually cackled. "You are three seconds away from wearing your tea instead of drinking it," Siobhan warned. "This isn't funny!"

"Of course it is," Nadia insisted, but wisely choked back her laughter. "You, my dear friend, are the only thing standing in your way. He's interested. You're interested, no matter how much you pretend you're not. You should go for it."

The idea of "going for it" both intrigued and scared her. "So you don't think it's a conflict of interest? If I decide to go there, I mean."

"I'm not worried that you're going to screw over the café, if that's what you're asking." Nadia balanced her teacup between her palms. "I also don't think Mr. O'Halloran would sabotage our business if things go sour between you two—which I totally don't think will happen. He's a businessman, and his business is right here in Crimson Bay. This is a small town, and the community is pretty tight-knit. We can certainly vet his credentials. He did include a client list for just that purpose."

She picked up the presentation folder. "Professionally speaking, we need to do a trial run at the very least. Personally speaking, you do too. Let's see what happens."

Butterflies danced in Siobhan's stomach. What would be the harm in having a fling, especially with someone like Charlie? She and Nadia had worked their asses off to make the café a success, and like Nadia had said before, they deserved personal lives. As long she and Charlie both took business seriously, there was no reason why there couldn't be a little pleasure had along the way.

"If we do this, there's got to be rules."

"Of course there should be rules," Nadia agreed, then grinned. "In fact, I think you should wear that schoolmarm outfit from your show when you tell him the rules. He'll agree to whatever you say."

"You're impossible."

"I'm enabling. At least when it comes to sex." Mischief danced in Nadia's eyes. "If you'd like to borrow my copy of *The Perfumed Garden of Sensual Delights*, I'd be more than happy to pass it on— with the best positions highlighted."

Siobhan laughed. "You and the naughty professor moved on from medieval sex manuals already?"

A blush colored Nadia's cheeks. "You could say I've graduated to the master class now."

It was Siobhan's turn to grin at her friend's discomfiture. "Oh, really? Do tell."

"Well, there's this thing he does with rope . . ."

FOUR

"Charlie?"

He looked up from his laptop with a frown as his office assistant, Nance, poked her head into the room. Usually, Nance buzzed him on the phone or via IM when they had a client, or simply yelled through his perpetually open office door when just staff occupied the area. "What is it, Nance?"

"There's someone here to see you," she informed him in her most professional tone, which immediately raised the wariness flag. Her dark eyes sparkled behind her red cat's-eye glasses. "I think she might be a potential client."

That was always welcomed news. He'd moved his business beyond the point where he needed to do cold calls, but he didn't turn away walk-in business no matter how much he preferred to do research before making his sales pitch. He reached for one of the general information packets that provided background on their complete suite of services. "Did she say what company she represents or which of our services she's interested in?"

"No, but she already has a packet," Nance answered. A grin

split her face and scrunched it to pixie proportions. "She seems like my kinda people."

Nance's kind of people were either lesbians or flamboyant retro fashionistas. Since he hadn't asked anyone their sexual preferences since half-past never, that left the retro fashionista. "Blonde?"

His assistant made a big deal of arching her pierced brow. "Yes. You holding out on me, boss?"

Charlie ignored her by concentrating on the silent surge of satisfaction that swept through him. "We shouldn't keep a potential client waiting," he told her. "Please show her back."

Nance left, and Charlie took a moment to rein in his brain and his libido. Siobhan had come to him to talk about the proposal. That had to be a good sign. If she didn't want to do business with him, she would have called instead—and he would have used every weapon at his disposal to change her mind. If she still said no, he'd respect the decision and not push—for a while, anyway. Sure, he wanted the café's business. He wanted Siobhan more.

He shot to his feet as a beaming Nance entered his office and said something—he wasn't sure what. His entire focus shrank down to the blonde woman who'd entered his office behind Nance.

Once again, Charlie was struck by Siobhan's lush beauty. She walked in like the reincarnation of a fifties Hollywood starlet. The red-and-white polka-dot sundress fit her breasts and waist like second skin before billowing out into a full skirt. The short-sleeved white sweater about her shoulders was probably the only thing that had prevented a traffic jam on the square. Red wedges encased her feet, and good Lord, her toes were painted the same bright red as her dress and her lips.

"You need to be shot."

Her eyes widened as she froze. "Excuse me?"

"I mean, professionally," he hastened to add, ignoring Nance's snort as she exited, closing the door behind her. "It would be a terrific marketing campaign."

One perfectly arched eyebrow rose toward her hairline. "Are you talking about a photo shoot?"

"Of course." He circled the desk to shake her hand, though he wanted to do more. So much more. Instead he guided her over to a small conference table, pulling out a chair for her. She murmured her thanks as she sat down, placing her red tote bag and his proposal packet on the table. Charlie took a moment to admire the shapeliness of her legs as she crossed them at the knees. Her legs were bare, making him wonder about the softness of her skin and the color of her underwear. Though with Siobhan, she probably wore lingerie, silky pieces that showed of her assets to advantage.

She cleared her throat, capturing his attention. "That's pretty presumptuous of you, don't you think? Considering that we don't have a deal yet?"

Amusement laced her query, and he knew she was perfectly aware that he'd been ogling her. He got back to the business at hand. "Presumptuous, yes. Wrong, no."

He took the chair closest to hers, catching the faint whiff of something light and sweet and perfectly suited to Siobhan. "Would you have come over here just to tell me no?"

Her chin lifted. "What if I did?"

"I would ask you to share your concerns so that we could negotiate. I would do my level best to convince you that we'd be the perfect fit for whatever you and your business need. Our job is to ensure that you're completely satisfied with all that we have to offer."

Her lips parted, and she drew in a low, slow breath. Charlie's brain short-circuited. Did she have any clue how fucking hot she was? She had to know—those were expert moves, and he responded like he'd just discovered what his dick could do. It was almost enough to make him wonder if he was out of his league.

Goddamn, he wanted her. Wanted her so badly he'd scare her off if she had a clue. It was just her hotness, the strawberries and whipped cream lushness of her body. It was a dichotomy of care and carnality that made him want to throw her over his shoulder and stomp off to have his way with her.

"Do you think you can?" she asked then, her voice soft, her blue eyes dark with what he hoped like hell was interest in him. "Satisfy me? Give me what I need?"

Fuck yeah. "I pride myself on doing a thorough job, no matter how demanding that job may be. I have a reputation for being responsive, creative, and adaptable."

"So I've heard." After a moment in which Charlie debated whether he should press the innuendos and kiss her, Siobhan drew back. "We called a couple of your current and former clients. All of them sing your praises."

"As I said, we believe in going above and beyond for everyone who signs with us. I promise, if Sugar and Spice Café joins the O'Halloran client list, you won't be disappointed."

Siobhan opened the packet he'd given her a couple of days ago. "My partner and I have discussed the options at length. We're in agreement that you have services that we should take advantage of. The delivery service, of course, but we are also interested in the website redesign and integration as well as the social media marketing campaigns. A couple of your clients mentioned to us that those really helped their bottom line."

He tensed. What she said was at complete odds to her body language. It seemed as if she'd bolt if he said or did the wrong thing, and that was the last thing he wanted. He sat back. "I'm sensing some hesitation. What questions can I answer for you?"

"We're interested in a short-term contract initially, with a notice of intent thirty days before the contract is due to expire."

"There may not be much we can do for you, depending on the length of the contract," he cautioned. "We can certainly add the delivery service interface, since the bulk of the work will be done on our end and we've perfected our process over numerous sites. The marketing and website redesign timelines can vary based on a number of factors. We also have a standard termination clause, which I included in the sample contract."

She nodded, then pulled her bottom lip between her teeth. Damn. His thoughts swerved off the road of propriety and ran into the ditch of unprofessional intent. "Siobhan—"

"Who would you assign to our account?" she asked quickly. "For the website and marketing aspects?"

"I would personally handle it," he said, then noticed the tightening of her mouth. "Is that why you're hesitating?"

"Considering how our conversation derailed during your sales pitch last week, I think you can understand my hesitation."

"I do. I can also assure you that business is very important to me, and my professional reputation is everything. We specialize in the small businesses in town, so word of mouth and good client relationships can make or break us. You can rest assured that while we're conducting business, the focus will be completely on business."

As long as you don't do that thing with your bottom lip again, or wear dresses that might as well have "look at my boobs" embroidered on them.

He made an attempt at schooling his features into a semblance of professionalism. *Get it together, jackass. You've been around beautiful women before—you live in a college town, for chrissakes.* He didn't want to run her off. He wanted a chance to get acquainted with her, to know her better. He wanted to discover if she wore dresses like that on her days off or for all her business meetings, or, God help him, if she'd worn it because she was meeting with him.

"So the . . . other stuff. That won't happen again?"

Was that disappointment in her voice? "I didn't say that. I'm very interested in you, Siobhan. If I wasn't before, I certainly would have been after you strolled into my office like an angelic devil. I bet you literally stopped traffic on your way over here."

"Charlie . . ."

"You're beautiful, Siobhan Malloy. It's a simple fact. Should I not tell you that? That's a nice dress made better by you wearing it. Do you think I'm harassing you when I tell you that? If so, I'll apologize and stop."

A blush stole across her cheeks. "I don't feel harassed. Flustered bordering on embarrassed, yes. Harassed, no."

He folded his arms across his chest. "I would think a woman who can rock a red dress like that is incapable of feeling embarrassment."

"You just . . ." She gestured helplessly. "You overwhelm me, and I don't know if this is flattering or completely inappropriate."

"Now you know how I felt the first time I saw you," he told her, going for broke. "And the next time, and the time after that, and every day I've seen you. If I understood it, I'd explain it. What I can do is tell you that I won't be inappropriate. Being inappropriate would be me reaching for you despite the glass walls separating us from my staff and kissing you until I'm wearing more lipstick than you. Right now we're just talking, just discussing the possibilities. There's nothing wrong with that, is there?"

"No."

Score one for the home team. "The way I see it, we have a couple of options here. You can decide not to do business with me, in which case I'll pursue you. You can sign the contract and I'll assign you to one of my employees so I can pursue you. Or, you sign the contract and I handle your business because I'm very good at what I do. And when business hours are over, I'll pursue you."

Those beautiful scarlet lips bowed into a smile. "Is there any scenario in which you don't pursue me?"

"One. I drop dead."

"Well. Okay then." She blinked. "I don't want that to happen."

"I appreciate that." He smiled. "The decision is up to you, Siobhan. I don't approve of pressure tactics. OBS wants your business. I want you. I think we can make it work, but if you're uncomfortable, we'll come up with another solution. The choice is yours."

He waited, watching in tense fascination as she thought through her decision. Her eyes, he decided. It was her eyes that captivated him the most. So much living swam behind that blue gaze, living that made her angelically sweet one moment and devilishly spicy the next.

"All right," she said after a moment. "I've made up my mind."

"And?"

"Let's do this." She held up a hand. "Business before pleasure, though."

"Of course." He smiled. "You'll find I always deliver on my promises."

FIVE

True to Charlie's word, business dominated their biweekly meetings. He explained every facet of each action he took on their behalf, including any benefits and potential downsides to the café, not moving forward on anything until he got her agreement. Siobhan found it extremely interesting and even arousing to watch him work, enjoying the way he brainstormed ideas and got excited over the smallest of concepts. The enjoyment and pride he had in his work clearly came through and was as contagious as it was sexy. Smart, good-looking men were always her weakness, and Charlie had all that plus confidence and charm to back it up. She found herself looking forward to their Monday and Thursday meetings and getting to know more about him.

"How did you get started, Charlie?" She asked him as they prepared to test the new website enhancements. "I'm curious to know how you went from a bike messenger company to providing marketing solutions and stuff."

"Crimson Bay Couriers is my first company, and it grew out of something I did during the summers as a teen," he explained. Something dark flashed across his eyes, so quickly there and gone she would have missed it had she not been staring at him so intently. "At eighteen, I turned it into a full-time business because I needed money in a hurry. I was a one-man company then, but business grew and I was able to hire on more couriers pretty quickly. As my business expanded, I identified areas of opportunity that I either learned to deal with myself or hired someone to take care of for me. Mostly I did it myself because that's just how I am."

"A hands-on kind of guy," she guessed. "So you saw a need in your own company, created a solution, then offered that solution to other small businesses?"

He flashed a smile. "Exactly. Through trial and error—and there was a crapload of error in those early days—we tested and perfected processes that we were then able to package for our clients. Word of mouth drove our success. It still does."

He shrugged. "With our expanding business expertise, we couldn't keep operating under Crimson Bay Couriers. It didn't take much to create the umbrella company of O'Halloran Business Solutions. We know what it takes for small businesses to survive because we've been through it ourselves."

Siobhan looked down at her tea, processing everything he'd told her. The man knew his business, she knew that without doubt. Everyone she and Nadia had talked to spoke of how professional he was, but also how personable he was, and how easy it was to work with him to find the solutions they needed.

None of them spoke of how hot he was, but they didn't need to. With every concept, conversation, and accomplishment he seduced her. His sharp mind lured her as much as his easy smiles and warm glances. The play of his hands on the keyboard, so firm, so sure, made her wonder how his fingers would feel cupping her breasts, teasing her nipples, thrusting deep inside her.

The way his muscles flexed in his arms and across his chest beneath his shirts made her wonder what it would be like to see him in all his naked surfer-god glory, sunlight playing across his muscles as his body flexed against hers. She wanted him. Wanted his mouth on her, his fingers on her, his cock in her. Wanted to know if he lived up to the sensual promise that burned in his eyes whenever he looked at her, whether they were talking business or just sharing tea and coffee. Even now, as she watched him test the interface between the café's website and the delivery service's point-of-sale portal, she had to press her thighs together against the burgeoning flood of need.

Yeah, Charlie didn't have to try to seduce her. She was doing a pretty good job of seducing herself.

The buildup of sexual frustration had led her to change out of her comfortable work clothes on the days she met with him and into something a little more . . . accessible. Today she wore one of her more demure Sugar Malloy outfits, a snap-front shirtwaist of pale blue with a fitted waist and a full skirt. Since she had rehearsal that evening, it was a simple matter of changing early instead of waiting until after she and Charlie were done for the day. Maybe today would be the day. She was horny enough to break her self-imposed rule about focusing on business and take a detour into pleasure.

But first . . . "I owe you an apology."

Charlie looked up in surprise. "Do you now? I'm all ears."

"I'm being serious." She took a fortifying breath against the teasing light in the sea-blue depths of his eyes. "I misjudged you."

The teasing glint dimmed. "How did you misjudge me?"

"I dismissed you when I first saw you as some young surfer-god playboy with a string of brokenhearted college coeds in your wake."

"Somehow, I don't think I'm supposed to take that as a compliment."

"I wasn't being complimentary," she admitted, noting the slight tightening of his jaw. She didn't want to anger him, but apologizing for her misconceptions was important to her. "When you started flirting with me during your sales pitch, I thought you were doing it just to get our business and not because you were interested in me. So it was easy to dismiss it, and you."

With his smile gone, his face reshaped itself into something harder, older, making her miss his teasing expression and hope she hadn't just permanently relocated herself to his bad side. "I would like to point out that I'd ended my sales pitch before pointing out how beautiful you are, but I'm still stuck on the fact that you dismissed me so easily even after that."

"I never said it was easy," she retorted. "It wasn't. Regardless, I'm sorry I thought of you that way."

He spun the task chair until he faced her fully. Though seriousness still painted his features, his body language was alert, primed. "How do you think of me now, Siobhan?"

God. When his voice dropped into that seductive burr, it was hard to concentrate. "I . . . I think you're a very capable and intelligent man who knows his business. I admire the solutions you've tailored for our company."

His gaze dropped to the pulse beating rapidly at the base of her throat, lingered on her lips, then lifted to meet her gaze as if he knew the effect he had on her. "Is that all you think, considering how not easy it was to dismiss me after all?"

A flash of irritation had her snapping out, "Are you going to accept my apology or not?"

He studied her, and she fought the urge to shift in her chair. "I'll accept it," he said, his tone serious. "On one condition."

The way he said it put her instantly on alert. "What's that?"

"I want you to kiss me," he told her, his voice blunt. "A real mouth-to-mouth kiss for at least thirty seconds."

Surprise shoved her eyebrows up. "That's one hell of a request," she said, unable to decide whether she should laugh or punch him.

"You owe me one hell of an apology."

"You want me to kiss you before you'll accept my apology?"

"I want the kiss to be your apology," he answered. "It's the least I deserve for the slight to my character, don't you think?"

She folded her arms. "I think you're beginning to prove that my initial assumptions were correct!"

"I've stuck to my promise of business before pleasure," Charlie pointed out. "We're done with everything we had on the agenda for today."

"But—"

"You stated your need to apologize, and I laid out my conditions for accepting said apology."

"You're a piece of work," she groused, unable to be mad at him. "Is everything business with you?"

"I thought that was how you wanted me." Mischief danced in his eyes. "If you prefer me some other way, just say so."

She threw up her hands in exasperation. "I'll give you points for being persistent, that's for damn sure."

"I'd rather you give me that kiss."

Siobhan stared at Charlie, feeling out of her depth. She had five years on him, dammit. She should have been the one keeping him off-kilter, channeling her inner Mrs. Robinson. Instead she'd spent days and way too many nights fantasizing about his touch, his kisses, and more. Even practicing for her burlesque performances, the one thing guaranteed to take her mind off her worries and troubles, couldn't excise him. Instead she imagined singing for him, seducing him with her striptease. Layer by layer, piece by piece, revealing to him almost everything he'd imagined and wanted.

Fuck Mrs. Robinson. Charlie was about to be introduced to Sugar Malloy.

Siobhan surprised him by pulling out her smartphone and attaching it to a small speaker on her desk. "I'm going to give you something better than a thirty-second kiss," she informed him, pushing to her feet. "When I'm done, you'll be the one apologizing, not me."

"Oh, really?"

Siobhan raised her chin, putting Charlie on instant alert. Had he pushed her too far? He didn't think so. She struck him as the type of woman who wasn't a frail, fragile flower but was still feminine, who could give as good as she got and not take crap from anyone. If she minded his teasing, he had no doubt she'd tell him so.

Instead her lips curled into a Mona Lisa "you're gonna get it now" smile that hardened his cock with anticipation. God, he needed to do everything in his power to move beyond an apology kiss and into gratitude orgasms.

Keeping her gaze locked to his, Siobhan rose from her seat, moving around the desk to face him. She wore a pale blue dress that transformed from simple to sexy thanks to the snap closure that ran the length of the front, the wide dark blue belt, and the blue-and-white polka-dot heels that showed off her legs to perfection. It was so different from what he usually saw her in that he'd been dumbstruck for a full minute when he'd first seen her. She looked as if she'd stepped out of a retro advertisement for MILFs.

"Turn your chair this way," she ordered, indicating that he face her. He shoved the armless chair around, wondering if she'd straddle his lap to deliver her apology kiss. He sure as hell hoped so, since she'd probably have to hike up her skirt, putting her sweet heat close to his aching cock. The act would fuel a few wet dreams until he could convince her to go for more.

He slapped his thighs to encourage her to take a seat. "I'm ready for my apology kiss, Ms. Malloy."

She rewarded him with a low and throaty laugh. "Anyone can kiss for thirty seconds, Mr. O'Halloran. What I'm going to give you is so much better, you'll drop to your knees in gratitude."

He raised a brow, her assertiveness flipping his switch. "You think so?"

She leaned forward, giving him a perfect view of her creamy cleavage. The scent of baked things, sweet things, and the light hint of spice that was unique to Siobhan filled his nose and drop-kicked his brain. A hunger that had nothing to do with food and everything to do with her seized him.

"*Think* so?" she echoed. "Sweetheart, I *know* so." She gave him a wink before straightening. Striking a pose that arched her back and thrust her breasts out, she reached up and pulled out the clip that held her hair up. Golden waves tumbled down around her shoulders, prodding him to reach for her and sink his hands into the sun-kissed curls.

"Uh-unh," she admonished, wagging her finger at him. "No touching. Whatever you do, don't move until I tell you to. Understood?"

"Yes, ma'am." He'd asked for the kiss because her mouth had been driving him insane for days. Natural, barely glossed, or painted fire-engine red, he wanted that mouth, wanted to know what it tasted like, what it felt like. Wanted to know if she'd part her lips under the pressure of his, let him shove his tongue inside and take her mouth. Wanted to lightly sink his teeth into that full bottom lip. Hell, he'd spent several nights with his hand around his dick imaging her mouth sucking him dry.

She was an obsession that was beginning to consume his days. He had to do something about it, if only to get her out of his system—no matter how foolish an idea that was. Prodding her for the kiss was a way to get what he wanted while giving her the control. He had a feeling that if he took over too quickly, Siobhan would freak and slam the door down between them, and that was unacceptable. So he kept his hands hanging loosely at his sides, waiting for her next move.

She danced back, a teasing glint igniting her eyes. Sitting on the edge of her desk, she reached back, tapped her phone. A soft, bluesy melody wafted into the air. He tried to place the song but all thought fled as Siobhan began to move.

God bless America. With slow, sinuous movements she slid to her feet, rolling her hips with every movement as a woman's soulful voice sang about her desire for sugar in a bowl. Her hands slid down her chest to her waist. As he watched, she unhooked the wide belt at her waist then stepped forward to drape it over his shoulder.

Holy shit, was she stripping for him? "Siobhan?"

She pressed a forefinger to his lips, then executed a spin away from him, her skirt flaring and showing more of her gorgeous legs. Keeping her back to him, she swayed, her arms graceful as she raised her arms. Then he heard *pop, pop, pop*, his mind conjuring an image of each snap on the front of her dress bursting open in perfect harmony to the bass beat of the music and the echoing throb in his veins.

The grin she tossed over her shoulder hit him with seductive heat and teasing. Then she opened the dress—still with her back to him—and did a shimmy. He leaned forward, licking his lips in anticipation of the reveal, forgetting to breathe as she slipped the dress off one shoulder then the next. Another shimmy, then she let the dress fall off her arms before tossing it onto the desk.

Fuck me.

Siobhan wore a gold and sapphire-blue waist-thingy—a corset, he recalled—with the laces revealing the line of her spine and accenting her waist. Matching ruffled panties cupped her buttocks, and little blue ribbons hung down and clipped to her thigh-high stockings. She spun in a slow circle, giving him a three-hundred-and-sixty-degree view of perfection. He had to reach down and grip himself hard through his pants as his cock strained with the urge to come.

As the music continued, she reached behind her and loosened the laces of her corset, gyrating her hips in a series of movements that boiled his blood. She spun around to face him, a seductive siren's smile on her bright red lips as she opened the corset one hook

at a time. It joined the dress on the desk, leaving her in a bra, panties, and that belt-like bit of blue lace that attached to the ribbons.

She strutted to him, and with perfect balance lifted one leg high
before resting her foot on the seat between his spread thighs. She
gestured, and it took him a moment to realize that she wanted him
to remove her shoe. He quickly slipped it off, his fingers grazing
over her calf as she lowered her left leg then repeated the move with
her right. He removed that shoe too, and was rewarded with a
wink. God help him, he'd never been so horny in his life.

He bit the inside of his cheek, using the flash of pain to blunt the
urge to throw her on the desk, drop his pants and fuck her until
they broke the desk. This was what they meant by striptease. This
was a master at work. This was art.

As he watched, she danced back to the desk and sat down on the
edge. The way she kicked her legs and smiled at him bludgeoned his
brain cells, erasing all higher thought. Posing sexily, she slid both
hands down each thigh and opened the snaps holding her stockings,
then undulated her way out of the lacy belt-thing circling her waist.
Next came the stockings, rolled down her beautiful legs one by one.

Then she did a shoulder shake, and her bra straps fell down her
arms. He was panting now, he knew it—like a dog after a female in
heat, especially when she reached for the front clasp holding her
bra closed. Her gaze locked to his as she held her bra to her breasts,
then she opened it and let it fall to the floor.

Pasties. Bright blue sparkly pasties covered her nipples and areo-
lae, but dear God, her full breasts sat up proudly and moved like they
were real. They bounced as she sprang to her feet, stuck her thumbs
into the waistband of her panties and did a heart-stopping shimmy
that dropped the lacy fabric to her feet, leaving her in what he

realized was a flesh-colored G-string. As the music reached a crescendo, she straddled his lap and entwined her arms around his neck. His dick surged against his zipper as her heat settled onto his lap.

He didn't know where to look—at the full breasts pressed against his chest, the nude-colored thong that barely hid her pussy, or the bright blue eyes that gazed at him with lust, pride, and a hint of vulnerability.

"I'm sorry," he said thickly once he remembered how to speak. "For everything I've done up to this point and everything coming after. I'm sure as hell sorry that I didn't try harder to learn what you wear under your clothes."

Her husky laugh bounced her tits and brushed her thong-covered mound against his zipper. He gritted his teeth, still not touching her though he burned with the need to run his hands up her waist to her beautiful breasts. Good things came to those who waited, right?

She sank her hands into his hair. "Apologies accepted. Now be a good boy and hold still for your thirty-second kiss."

Oh hell yeah, things were very good indeed.

SIX

Siobhan straddled Charlie's lap, more turned on than she'd ever been in her life. Performing with the burlesque troupe was a way for her to feel sexy and empowered on her own terms, but this was different. She'd never done a striptease for an audience of one before—hadn't wanted to do a private striptease before. Charlie, however, brought out that side of her she hid under layers of sweetness, that side that wanted to be very, very bad. The side that needed to be fucked in the worst way.

But first, a thirty-second kiss.

She pushed his hair back from his eyes, their pupils blown wide with lust. Pride swelled within her. It was a heady thing to know that she, with her thirty-five-year-old post-motherhood body, could arouse him like this. The thick ridge of his cock pressed against the zipper of his dark khakis, which put it right beneath her with only a couple of layers of fabric separating them. If she wanted, she could dry-hump him to glory. As strung tight with desire as she was, it wouldn't take long to reach orgasm. But she wanted more, much more.

Done with torturing him and herself, Siobhan darted her tongue out for a first taste of him. He parted his lips as her tongue swept over his mouth, the sharp spice of him bursting on her tongue and sending a bolt of lust shooting straight to her core. He tasted good, so good. She licked at his mouth again, tracing the contour of his lips before lightly taking the bottom one between her teeth and gently biting down.

He shuddered and bucked upward once, and the feel of his erection pressing against her made her want to swoon. The embers of desire flared to life as Charlie took over the kiss, cupping her face in his palms. His tongue pushed into her mouth, hot and wet and oh so perfect. Moisture seeped into her G-string as she rocked against him with an instinctive movement as she greedily took the almost punishing kiss he meted out. Nothing mattered except this feeling, this moment. This man.

His fingers sank into the hair at the back of her neck, holding her away. "Siobhan."

She forced her eyelids up, too drunk on erotic thoughts to fully appreciate the clenched jaw, the tightness about his eyes. "Y-yes?"

"A man's only got so much willpower," he ground out. "When the beautiful woman he's been lusting after for weeks strips for him, then sits in his lap, it's cruel and unusual punishment to leave him with only a kiss."

Did he really think this was the end? "No, no, no. No stopping." Kissing wasn't enough, rocking against him wasn't enough. Nothing would be except experiencing his cock plunging inside her.

His big hands slid down to cup her buttocks. Recognizing his intent, she wrapped her legs around his waist as he stood, turned, then laid her down on the desk. "More," he muttered. "I need to taste more."

He parted her thighs, staring down at the silky scrap of material that she knew she'd already soaked through. Her eyes rolled back in her head as he pressed his index finger against her silk-covered slit, his knuckle brushing against her painfully engorged clit. Her hips lifted involuntarily, craving more pressure, craving more of him.

His questing fingers followed the swath of fabric to the string waistband. She lifted her hips again as he slowly pulled the thong away from her pussy, down her legs, and off, leaving her bared to his gaze. His hands slid up her calves, the pads of his fingers almost rough on her soft skin as he cupped her knees and parted them. "You are so fucking beautiful," he breathed, his voice raw and reverent. "I'm gonna enjoy tasting you. Take my time and then I'm gonna fuck you slow."

The blunt words made her moan with hunger. She didn't think she could handle slow, certainly not for breaking her self-imposed sex-fast, and certainly not when it came to Charlie and his drugging kisses.

She heard him drag the chair closer before he sat down between her open thighs. A tremble swept through her as his thumbs stroked over her damp folds, opening her. As soon as she balanced her feet on his wide shoulders, he lowered his head to taste her.

The first warm contact of his tongue along her opening had her groaning aloud, her hands scrabbling along the desk's surface for something to hold on to before reaching for the golden thickness of his hair. His fingers spread her outer lips open as he deepened the intimate contact, tasting her fully. A fleeting thought entered her mind—her ex-husband Mike saying he'd enjoyed going down on her like this. But Charlie . . . Charlie savored her, his lips grazing along her slit in a slow exploration that sent her senses reeling and her body sizzling, her breath shortened by each pass of his tongue.

Charlie's hair tickled her thighs as he thrust his tongue deep inside her, deeper than she'd thought possible, fucking her. She moaned again, his name a breath on her lips as she ground her hips up against his mouth, wanting everything he had to give her. He devoured her as if she were his favorite dessert, swirling his tongue around her swollen clit before sweeping deep into her core then down to the rosette of her anus, laving her there before reversing his path.

He drove her high, higher, up into a lightning storm of sensation. She held on for as long as she could, wanting to draw out the pleasure, the electric brightness of balancing on the edge of coming. Then he thrust two fingers inside her, stroking, stroking as he flicked his tongue against her clitoris. In and up and deep he stroked her channel while his mouth teased her clit with licks and suckles. Good, so very good, so good she could feel her skin tightening, her body quivering as it gathered the energy to come.

"Charlie," she gasped. "Charlie, please . . ."

He knew what she wanted, knew what she needed. Fingers plunging, driving pleasure with the flick, flick, flick of his tongue before he closed his mouth over her clit and sucked.

She shrieked as her orgasm broke, her hands tugging on his hair as her thighs clamped around his head. Her back bowed off the desk, her pussy grinding against his fingers and his mouth as the orgasm barreled through her then rolled her under again.

He didn't move away from her immediately, not Charlie. Instead, he brought her down slowly with gentle kisses and touches until her sensitized flesh protested. Only then did he rise to his feet. She rose to her elbows, her desire blunted but not extinguished. There was only one thing that would take care of that.

His features tight with restrained hunger, Charlie reached into his back pocket for his wallet, opened it, then extracted a condom. Placing the foil packet on her belly, he tossed the wallet aside, then opened his khakis, shoving them and his dark red briefs down his hips.

"I want to see you," Siobhan said, voice thick with renewed desire. "Let me see you."

Without a word, Charlie pulled his shirt off over his head, revealing his gorgeous tanned torso, the light scattering of dark blond hair across his chest leading down the defined abdominals to the thickheaded cock jutting proudly. She licked her lips as her mouth watered at the sight of him.

He wrapped one large hand around his erection, a slow stroke from root to tip. "I've fantasized about your mouth on my cock for days," he told her, his voice rough with desire. "You lying there licking your lips like that's the best idea ever tempts me to make that fantasy a reality."

He cupped her mound. "But now that I've tasted you, I'm hungry for more. The first time I come with you, I want my cock to be right here, inside you." He reached for the condom, opened it, then rolled it on. "Are you ready for me, sweetheart?"

Ready for him? She didn't think she'd ever be ready for Charlie, but she was ready for this moment, ready to feel him moving inside her, ready to give him at least some of the decadent pleasure he'd given her.

"Yes . . . oh." Words failed her as he pressed his cock against her. Charlie dragged the head along her slit, then very slowly and methodically filled her. The pressure, the fullness, the inexorable charge took her over.

"Ah, fuck, Siobhan, that feels so good." He gripped her knees as he bottomed out inside her. "So damn good, better than I imagined."

Her breath caught in her throat as she watched him, watched him stand there, eyes sliding closed, pleasure breaking over his face as he savored the moment of finally being inside her. She savored it too, feeling every inch of his possession, feeling her body stretch to accommodate him, welcome him. Then he withdrew, a slow drag along her inner walls until only the tip remained inside her. Slow in, slow out, making every blood-pumping moment of it a body-tingling experience.

She sighed, her body going liquid for him. "Charlie."

His eyes blinked open and he smiled at her, a smile at once sweet and full of sensual promise. "Love seeing you like this, your beautiful body spread for me, your pussy all wet and pink like rain-covered tulips because I gave you pleasure and made you come."

"I want you to come too."

He chuckled, the vibration of it echoing down to where he connected with her. "I will, babe, I promise you that." Another slow thrust and withdraw as he gave her a cheeky grin. "Now let's see if we can make those sexy-as-hell tassels bounce."

He balanced her ankles on his shoulders as he leaned forward, hands splaying on the desk. Then he rolled his hips, his cock hitting her core in new, nerve-searing ways. He rocked into her with steady strokes, little shocks rippling through her body as her breasts bounced with each thrust. His gaze locked to hers as he completely focused on giving and receiving pleasure.

Oh, nice. Better than nice. Her inner muscles massaged his length, pulling a shuddering sigh from him. "You're trying to break my control when it's taking everything I've got to not slam into you like I'm in a demolition derby."

She dropped her legs down to encircle his waist. "It'll take more than this to break me. Slam away."

Fire blazed in his eyes as Charlie let himself off the chain. He gripped her hips and began to move, pistoning in and out of her, stroke after stroke. Siobhan teased her breasts with one hand, the other snaking down between their colliding bodies. She had never been a multiple-orgasms-in-one-session type of girl, but Charlie's masterful handling of her body demanded her response and she was powerless against it.

For a moment he just watched her fingers stroke over his cock then her clit, his mouth slack. "God, Siobhan, God," he breathed, then clamped his hands on her hips. He drove into her, spurred her higher and higher, heat and passion colliding.

The office filled with the sounds of their bodies slapping together, their mingled moans, the desk scraping against the floor. Siobhan threw her hips up, meeting each violent stroke, wild with need, her inner muscles clenching down on him, her fingers swirling over her clit, crazed with the need to come.

Her orgasm struck like a lightning bolt, throwing her over the edge. She cried out as her body tightened around him. Charlie gripped her shoulders and began to pound into her at a breakneck pace, the scrape of the desk across the floor as loud as the rush of blood in her ears. She bowed off the desk, her body blazing with the rush of his powerful strokes, his absolute possession, his delivery of the best sex of her life.

His fingers dug into her shoulders as he pulled her upright, pistoning into her faster than she'd have thought possible. She entwined her arms around his neck just before his mouth slammed down on hers. One, two, three more violent strokes, then he stiffened, his entire body shuddering with the force of his orgasm, her name a guttural groan on his lips.

Instead of immediately pulling away he gripped her ass, holding her close as he collapsed back onto the chair, still buried deep inside her. He rained soft kisses onto her cheeks, her lips, the crook of her neck before resting his cheek against her cleavage. "You are amazing. And that was the most epic apology ever."

Charlie almost tightened his grip when Siobhan attempted to lift off his lap, especially since her soft laughter made those bright blue tassels swing in a hypnotic way. Instead, he contented himself with letting his hands slide down her full curves as she regained her feet. Good God, he could revel in her lushness all damn day, but not in a spent condom. "Can I ask you something?"

She tossed him a smile as she reached for her G-string. "You just did."

"Another question then." He grabbed a tissue from the container on the worktable, then took care of the condom. After tucking himself back into his pants and retrieving his shirt, he gestured between them as she stepped into the flesh-colored scrap then the blue lace panties. "Your outfit. Those moves, the nipple covers. Were you a stripper or a Vegas showgirl before you became a café owner?"

"No." She shrugged into her bra, and he mourned the loss of his spectacular view. "For the last couple of years I've been a member of the Crimson Bay Bombshells. It's a burlesque troupe."

"Burlesque?" He frowned for just a moment, then recalled several videos he'd seen online. "Oh, burlesque. You do that?"

"Yeah." The belt went on next. "I perform as Sugar Malloy. We have a show at Club Tatas one weekend a month, but we've been talking about adding another show or moving to a different venue since our audience is growing."

A burlesque performer. Everything made sense then. The retro clothes, makeup, and hairstyle, the corset, and the sizzling striptease. "You're the gift that keeps on giving."

She laughed as she gathered her stockings, taking a seat in the chair. "Well this gift has given all she can today and is close to being late to rehearsal."

"Let me help." He knelt in front of her.

"I can dress myself, you know," she said, but held the stockings out.

"You most certainly can." One by one he rolled the stockings up her shapely legs, then took his time figuring out how to clip them into place before helping her on with her shoes. "But I'm fascinated and turned on by helping you. And this gives me the chance to touch you. Besides, you did say I'd end up on my knees in gratitude. Consider me extremely grateful."

He stood, reaching for her waist cincher. "Do you have different costumes when you perform?"

She rose. "Most of them run the frilly lacy route, but I do have a couple of specialty ones," she answered, holding the corset in place while he hooked the front, then turning so he could tighten the laces at the back. His blonde bombshell transformed into a sex goddess again. "A raincoat one, a couple of leather ones, and one I call Little Miss Lollipop that involves colored sugar. I'm also working on a multi-dancer act to 'Fat Bottomed Girls,' which is what we're rehearsing tonight."

"Good God, woman, I think you're trying to kill me." He held the dress up so she could slip it on. A mental image of Siobhan in leather holding a belt or paddle sent blood racing to his cock. So did the idea of her and colored sugar, or showing off her delectable bottom. "When is your next show?"

"In two weeks." Her brows crinkled. "Are you planning on coming to the show?"

"Would you have a problem with that?" He knelt at her feet again to begin fastening the snap closures on her dress. "Now that we've had sex you don't want me to see you dance, or would my presence impede your interacting with your other admirers?"

"Hey!" She thumped him on the shoulder to get his attention. "You really think I'd let you fuck me stupid on my desk if I were doing someone else?"

Oh, the flash of irritation on her beautiful face, her breasts rising and falling with each indignant breath fired his blood. Maybe he could make a special request and have her break out the leather. All she needed was a paddle or a crop and he'd bend over and take it like a man if it pleased her.

"I'm sorry," he said, pressing a kiss to her thigh before closing her dress over it. "Unfortunately my dick sometimes does the thinking when it comes to you."

She harrumphed, settling her hands on her hips. "Well tell him to stop."

"I'll try, ma'am." He grinned up at her as he fastened the snaps up to her waist. "But he can get awfully hardheaded at times. Maybe a little discipline would help."

Her eyes widened momentarily, then shuttered to half-mast. "You have been a naughty boy, haven't you?" she asked, her voice low and husky as she cupped his cheek. "Perhaps you do need a little discipline, especially since you look so damn hot kneeling there, helping me dress."

"I can help you undress too."

"Duly noted. Is that what you want, Charlie? To submit to me?"

"To do whatever you want, whether that's obeying a command, getting disciplined, or screwing you hard against a wall." He shifted to ease the pressure on his revived cock. "If it pleases you and I get to have you as my reward, I'll try just about anything."

"Even if I want you to bend me over the desk, grab my hair, and fuck me stupid again?"

He groaned. "Especially if you want me to do that." He paused, staring up at her. "Shall I undress you?"

She worked her bottom lip between her teeth. "I can't be late tonight," she answered, reluctance coating her tone, "but I wouldn't be opposed to continuing this discussion tomorrow. At my place, say about four?"

Her voice held a slight note of doubt to it at the end, as if she feared he'd say no. Like there was a chance in hell of that happening. Now that he'd staked his claim—and she'd staked hers, courtesy of that dance—he had no intention of letting her go easily.

Rising to his feet, he backed her against the desk until he could reach the navy blue belt and clasp it around her waist, his lips grazing her throat, her cheek, then her lips. "Your wish is my command," he whispered against her mouth. "Until tomorrow."

SEVEN

Siobhan thought she'd made it through the day without revealing anything to Nadia or their staff. Today was Tuesday, however, and that meant a session of Bitch Talk, when she, Nadia, and their friends Vanessa Longfellow and Audie McNamara got together. It was part recovery group meeting, part therapy session, and all sisterly tough love.

There were times when their weekly sessions were a lifeline. When she and Nadia had escaped from Los Angeles and come to Crimson Bay, they'd almost left when they'd discovered no support infrastructure for those in recovery from drug addiction. Instead, they had decided to establish a support group themselves, holding it on Tuesdays, their slowest day in the café. When business had picked up, they moved the support group to Saturday afternoons, with volunteers from Herscher University's psychology department occasionally leading discussions. Tuesdays, however . . . Tuesdays were sacrosanct. No matter where they were or what they were doing, the four of them gathered to unwind and unburden.

Vanessa and Audie arrived together, a study in contrasts. Vanessa was the epitome of grace and class—makeup perfectly applied to her bronze skin, not a wrinkle to her floral sundress, her dark mane pulled back into a sleek ponytail and designer shades perched atop her head. Her outward serenity hid a deep inner turmoil exacerbated by her parents' relentless belief that she wasn't perfect enough, successful enough, or just plain good enough for the Longfellow name. While Siobhan understood why her own parents had issues with her, she couldn't understand why Vanessa's parents weren't happy with their daughter as she was—a dedicated volunteer, fund-raiser, administrator at the college, beautiful, caring.

Where Vanessa was outwardly controlled, Audie was an unleashed force of nature. With red hair as vibrant as her personality, Audie was sexually liberated and proud of it. Audie's problem was that her appetite for sex sometimes led her to make bad choices in partners—though she was militant about safe sex, she didn't really care to learn her partners' names before she took them to bed. She was the queen of one-night stands, an impressive feat in a town built around a progressive college. Though she'd had a date go horribly wrong a few weeks ago, Audie seemed none the worse for it, back to her old habits as far as Siobhan knew.

Siobhan took her place at the table, her tea steeping in front of her. As always they started by reciting the Serenity Prayer. It was something Siobhan and Nadia had done at the rehabilitation facility they'd been in while in Los Angeles, and while they'd both rolled their eyes at the idea of asking God for anything—after all,

He hadn't given Siobhan her family back, hadn't kept Nadia's former manager from dying—eventually they took the intent of the prayer to heart.

"Does anyone want to start?" Siobhan asked. They very loosely followed the meeting structure they'd been introduced to in rehab, especially with Vanessa and Audie battling different addictions. The main thing was that they felt free to share.

"I'll start," Audie said, her usual coffee and muffin before her. "The district attorney finally made a decision on my assault case. Looks like we're going to trial."

"That's good news," Vanessa exclaimed, then looked at the others. "Isn't it?"

Nadia wore a somber expression identical to Audie's, and Siobhan was pretty sure hers matched theirs. One of Audie's one-night stands had gone violently wrong, ending with her making a trip to the hospital. She'd pressed charges, but it had taken weeks for investigators to build the case, a source of constant anxiety for Audie, and by extension, the rest of them.

"It is good news," Siobhan said, wanting to assure Audie as much as Vanessa. "It's a brave thing that Audie's doing."

"What she means is, it's a brave thing for someone with my reputation for sleeping around to do," Audie said, no heat in her tone. "A fact that the defense attorney will more than likely attempt to bring up, according to my counselor, which is why I hired my own attorney."

"I'm glad you're still seeing that counselor," Nadia said, concern wreathing her face. "Did you get your legal advocate through them?"

Audie nodded. "I wanted someone familiar with assault cases and victims. Though the defense can't directly put my lifestyle on trial, they'll go after my credibility when I testify, and nothing hurts credibility more than a little character assassination based on truth."

"The fact that you're a single woman who likes sex has no bearing on the fact that this bastard put you in the hospital!" Vanessa retorted.

"We all know and understand that, but a jury might not." Audie stirred her coffee. "The counselor I've been working with has been educating me on the reality of cases like this. We're thinking the district attorney is hoping the other side will plead it out."

She sighed. "The irony isn't lost on me that all of this crap occurred because I decided to not have sex with the guy."

"No means no," Siobhan said, anger burning her ears. "Turning you into a punching bag is not the way to respond. That guy has issues."

"This could happen to someone else if they let him off," Vanessa pointed out. "In fact, it may have happened before but no one's reported him."

"My lawyer thinks so too, which is why he suggested hiring a private investigator." Audie blew out a breath, mussing her bangs. "Unfortunately I can't afford a lawyer and a private investigator."

"That's why you have friends." Nadia slapped her hands against the table. "Especially a friend with a brother named Sergey who can help."

Hope flickered in Audie's eyes. "Isn't he a police officer down in San Diego?"

"He left the force and got licensed as a private investigator about a month ago. He's been doing a lot of work in LA, but I'm sure he'll be happy to help out. You guys are family after all. I'll call him tonight."

"Thanks, Nadia. You guys . . . you're the best."

Audie's voice warbled, and Siobhan had to swallow the lump in her own throat. Audie had a hard time believing that people would do things for her just because and without expecting anything in return, which made it difficult for her to accept that help, much less express gratitude for it. That just hadn't been her experience, and though Siobhan didn't know all the details of Audie's life, she knew enough to know the redhead had a long road to regaining some sense of self-worth.

"Hey," Siobhan piped up, blinking emotion away, "speaking of family, are your dads coming down for the Fourth of July holiday celebration?"

Everyone at the table perked up. Nadia's dads had become surrogate fathers to all of them over the last couple of years. Siobhan's father hadn't spoken to her since her daughter, Colleen, went to live with Siobhan's parents during her relapse, and she felt the absence keenly. Nadia's fathers had "adopted" all of them, filling a painful void. Maybe she didn't love Nicholas and Victor Spiceland as much as Nadia did, but she never missed a birthday or Father's Day in gratitude for their care and support.

Thanks to Nadia and her fathers, Siobhan had kept to her recovery, had regained the will to do better, to be better. She hadn't given up when it would have been so easy to allow loss to consume her and drive her under. She owed everything to them, and she knew it.

"The dads are coming down," Nadia announced, but Siobhan noticed the tightening of her shoulders. "Kane wants to invite people over to watch the fireworks from his balcony, so consider this your invitation."

"Sweet. We'll have an awesome view of the bay." Siobhan loved fireworks, thrilling to the sight, sound, and smell of the explosions since she was a little girl. She hadn't had much opportunity to enjoy them for the last few years, what with spending her time getting the café up and running successfully. Nadia's boyfriend, Professor Kaname Sullivan, had a spectacular condo with a killer view overlooking Crimson Bay. After seeing it during a dinner party a couple of months ago, she completely understood why Nadia would want to spend more time there than in her condo over the café. Of course, having a sexy professor boyfriend to go home to didn't hurt either. "Are we gonna barbecue and do something else?"

"Don't know yet. Or rather, I haven't decided yet." Nadia pulled her bottom lip between her teeth. "Kane's parents are coming in too."

"Oh, wow." Vanessa gave Nadia a brilliant smile. "This will be your first time meeting them, won't it?"

"I was introduced to them through a webcam chat, believe it or not," Nadia said with a shake of her head. "It was a little weird, especially since Kane and I—um, never mind. Anyway, not only will I be having my first face-to-face with Kane's parents, it'll be the first time both sets of parents are meeting each other too. And Kane wants us to cook for everyone. I have no idea what we're going to serve!"

Audie laughed. "Only you would freak out more about what to serve your parents and future in-laws than the fact that the big meet and greet is about to go down."

"Future in-laws?" Nadia paled. "Oh God, I can't breathe!"

"Oh, honey." Siobhan laid a hand on Nadia's arm. "This can't be a surprise to you. You guys obviously love each other. Where did you think you're headed?"

"Shacking up," Nadia answered. "We're still in the fornicating like bunnies stage, and testing the waters of living together. Well, he's talked about it and I've sort of gone along with it without making a decision one way or another. I've been thinking about putting the condo up for sale or renting it out. As convenient as it is to just walk downstairs five minutes after I roll out of bed, Kane's place is bigger, has that view, and a better kitchen.

"And, if you ever tell him I said that, I'll—I'll—oversalt your soup!" She glared to make her point.

"He won't hear it from me, pinky-swear," Siobhan said, hiding her smile.

"Me either," Audie said with a wink. "Sisters before misters."

"I wouldn't dare reveal what's discussed during Bitch Talk," Vanessa said solemnly. "But Siobhan has a point. You're already at his place more than you are at yours. You do love him, don't you?"

Siobhan watched as Nadia's expression softened. "More than I thought I could."

"And we know he loves you," Vanessa added. "The professor can be very strategic when he wants to. He probably has a whole 'get Nadia to marry me' plan in the works, and this holiday meet-up is part of that. He'd rather you stress about what to serve everyone than about meeting his parents for the first time."

"Devious bastard," Nadia groused without any heat.

"Thoughtful boyfriend," Siobhan countered. "And smart too. Probably why he's a professor."

Audie reached over and rubbed Nadia's back. "That man will stop at nothing to make you his—and make sure you know you're his."

"I know," Nadia answered, and Siobhan could hear so much happy certainty overflowing Nadia's tone that it was almost painful to hear. "Kane finds very interesting ways to prove we're meant to be together."

"I guess so," Audie cracked, pulling at the collar of Nadia's loose-fitting shirt to expose a band of bright red cord peeking out of her bra. "You want to tell us about your new fashion accessory?"

Nadia cheeks darkened with a flush, but mischievous delight

flooded her eyes. "Let's just say that Kane and I have extended our studies beyond *The Perfumed Garden*," she explained, "and I've reaped the benefits of our extracurricular activities."

"I guess you have," Siobhan said, glancing toward the entrance as the bell tinkled overhead. Her heart leapt as she caught sight of the Crimson Bay Couriers uniform, but a woman held the arrangement of tulips, not Charlie. "Kane obviously appreciates the way you've taken to your studies."

Nadia met the courier at the counter with a smile, a smile that widened as she signed for the ginormous bouquet and returned to the table—only to set the vase down in front of Siobhan. "These are for you."

With her blood pounding in her ears so loudly she couldn't hear her friends' ribald comments, Siobhan reached for the card tucked into the arrangement of a dozen pale peachy-pink tulips.

A small token of appreciation for my new favorite dessert. I look forward to my second helping.

The card wasn't signed, but it didn't need to be. Only one person would send her that particular note with those particular flowers. Only one person had referred to her womanly parts as tulips.

"Looks like I'm not the only one getting in some after-hours extra credit," Nadia said with a smirk.

"Cute." Siobhan shoved the card into her bra before Nadia could snatch it away. "I'm not doing any late-night anything." That wasn't a lie. She had Charlie had parted ways long before sunset.

"Uh-huh." Nadia's smile was a little too wicked. "Care to tell us about the condom in the trash can?"

"Oh, God." Heat exploded in Siobhan's cheeks. "Are you serious? I thought he got rid of—"

She broke off as the table erupted with laughter. She glared at Nadia. "You beyotch. There wasn't a condom in the trash bin, was there?"

"No." Nadia dabbed at her eyes with a napkin. "The bin was empty. But I saw what you wore to work yesterday, and Rosie told me how Charlie got all bug-eyed when he saw you. So I did some snooping when I came in this morning and found a condom wrapper under the desk."

"Siobhan?" Audie gasped, incredulous. "Siobhan did it on the desk? In the office? Here?"

"Why are you surprised by that?" Siobhan asked, indignant.

Audie held up her hands in surrender. "I'm just surprised that you did it here, instead of at your house. Despite you playing a sexpot for burlesque, you tend to be a little conservative."

"Am not!"

"You married your high school sweetheart," Audie pointed out. "And you haven't once dated anyone since I've known you, or taken home any of your admirers lining up for pictures with you after your shows."

Siobhan pressed her lips together. She had no comeback, but Audie told the truth. "Okay, maybe I am a little straightlaced when it comes to this. I'm not as casual about it as you are, and I didn't make a sexual declaration in the middle of the café like Nadia did."

She lightly stroked one of the tulips. "If you guys don't mind, I don't want this, whatever this is, to be public knowledge yet. We just had sex for the first time yesterday."

"Yesterday was the first time?" Vanessa asked, surprised.

"Yes."

Vanessa smiled. "Pay up, ladies."

Siobhan's mouth dropped open as Nadia and Audie both slapped five-dollar bills onto the table. "You guys bet on when Charlie and I would have sex?"

"Yes, and I lost." Nadia pouted. "I had you doing the deed after a week."

"And I had you at two," Vanessa said, gathering her winnings.

"For what it's worth, I had you at three weeks," Audie told her.

"Thank you," Siobhan said. "At least someone expected me to show some restraint with someone I'm doing business with."

"Come on now, Siobhan," Nadia interjected. "I told the girls how the air damn near crackles with electricity when you two are in the room together. Frankly, I didn't expect him to take that long to seduce you."

"Actually . . ." Heat scalded Siobhan's cheeks again. "I seduced him."

Audie cackled. "Pay up, ladies."

"You beyotches bet on that too?" Siobhan asked as Vanessa and Nadia handed another pair of fives over, this time to Audie.

"We were in a betting frame of mind, and no one thought you'd make the first move, considering how reluctant you were when he first started flirting with you." Nadia leaned forward eagerly. "Now that I'm broke, you can console me by sharing. What did you do? Because I gotta say, with that guy all you probably had to do was smile."

"There was some smiling going on, especially afterward," Siobhan confessed, thrilling at the memory. "I introduced him to Sugar Malloy."

"That's how you do it!" Audie said, giving Siobhan a high five. "The poor guy didn't stand a chance!"

"No, he didn't." A different kind of heat stole over her as she remembered the hungry way that Charlie had stared at her, the way he'd powered into her after licking her to orgasm. "He most enthusiastically approved of my burlesque persona."

"I just bet he did," Nadia snorted. "I'm not a voyeur, but I would have paid to see his reaction! Was he as good as he looks like he should be?"

"Yeah, even better than good."

"Woo-hoo!" Audie threw her arms around Siobhan, catching her off guard. "And he earns bonus points for sending you flowers. So when are you hooking up again? I'm assuming you're going for seconds. And thirds."

Siobhan squirmed in her chair. "He's supposed to meet me at my place at four."

"Good for you," Vanessa piped up. "Why waste time when you've got a hot young stud like that?"

"Don't remind me about the age thing. I'm trying not to think about it."

"You shouldn't be thinking about it at all!" Audie said. "There's nothing wrong with enjoying yourself with this guy. Life is too fucking short not to have fun fucking."

"What Audie's saying so colorfully is that you need to let go of the hang-ups," Nadia said. "I told you that before. You're both consenting adults. You should consent the hell out of him as many times as you can."

Vanessa gave her an encouraging smile. "What they said."

Audie raised her glass. "I for one am glad that we're all finally getting some on the regular."

"All?" Siobhan and Nadia echoed simultaneously, then turned to face Vanessa. "Have you been holding out on us?"

"I have." With a calm that Siobhan envied, Vanessa took a sip of her tea, then returned the mug to the table. "Audie and I are helping each other out. She's teaching me to be a little bit naughty, and I'm helping her to be a little more—"

"Nice?" Nadia guessed.

"I was going to say discerning," Vanessa answered, giving Audie a conspiratorial smile. "I think it's working well for both of us."

Audie and Vanessa? Siobhan sat back in her chair, completely flummoxed. "I know opposites attract, but I really didn't see that coming. Good for you, both of you."

Audie broke into peals of laughter. "We're not dating, Siobhan."

"Oh, is that what you thought?" Vanessa grinned. "Audie is a sex goddess who knows her way around the Big O. If anyone could convert me, she'd be the one. The fact of the matter is, we both like dick too much."

Siobhan spluttered into her tea. It always surprised her when Vanessa allowed a crude word to pass her lips. She should have known better. With Vanessa, still waters ran really deep.

"I'm confused." Nadia frowned at them. "Did you or didn't you? Not that it bothers me, but I can't help being curious."

"A lady doesn't kiss and tell," Audie said, her grin definitely of the shit-eating variety.

"Too bad there aren't any ladies present," Siobhan retorted. "Exactly how are the two of you helping each other out?" They were all friends, true, but she'd thought Audie, the youngest of the group at twenty-six, was closest to Nadia, the next youngest at thirty, than Vanessa, who'd recently turned thirty-two.

"We're acting as each other's wingman," Vanessa explained.

"We both have memberships at Onyx, a private club just outside San Francisco."

"What the . . ." Nadia's eyes widened like a startled character in a Saturday-morning cartoon. Siobhan would have laughed if she hadn't felt as shell-shocked as Nadia looked.

"You." Nadia pointed to Vanessa. "You bought a membership to a—to a—"

"Sex club," Audie supplied helpfully.

"It's more than a sex club," Vanessa explained. "They offer a little something for everyone. Not just anyone can get a membership either. We both had to go through a series of offsite interviews and provide all sorts of records before we were sponsored, and then approved."

She toyed with her tea. "It was worth it, though. That level of consideration was important to me. The safeguards were important. And the space is . . . it works for me. I wouldn't have considered it at all if it weren't for Audie."

"If you're happy, then I'm glad for you," Siobhan said, stretching her hand across the table to give Vanessa's a reassuring squeeze.

She turned to Audie. They'd had a minor falling out after Audie's assault, mostly because Audie had struck out against Nadia, who'd helped her during that awful night. After they'd staged an intervention of sorts, Siobhan had been the one to drive Audie home and give her the verbal ass kicking she'd needed, offering to pay for a wellness retreat to give Audie the professional support she needed. Audie had taken her up on the offer and now seemed far down the road to getting herself and her life together.

"Is this working for you?" she asked Audie.

"We've been going pretty regularly, so it's working for now."

She hunched her shoulders. "I'm not going to apologize for having sex. I'm sure as hell not going to apologize for liking sex."

"You shouldn't have to in this day and age," Siobhan said. "But you know there are people out there who don't agree with that. People who may be picked to hear your case."

"I know that." For a moment, a bone-deep sadness pulled at Audie's features. "I'm still in counseling. I'm working through things. I'm making better partner choices and my desire for sex isn't interfering with my job. I have nights at the club, and I volunteer at a no-kill shelter a couple of Saturdays a month. Who knows? I might surprise you and become a crazy cat lady."

"I don't think you'll be a cat lady," Siobhan told her, "but you've got the crazy down pat. I mean, look who you hang out with."

Audie grinned, her earlier sadness gone. "If I'm going crazy, at least I've got some fabulous company. And we look good doing it!"

"As fabulous as the company is, it's time to break this up," Nadia said. "We wouldn't want Siobhan to be late for her afternoon delight!"

"Ooh, you know what we should do?" Audie bounced in her chair. "Road trip to the naughty store this weekend!"

"That's a good idea," Nadia said with a nod of agreement. "It's like makeup. You can never have too many accessories."

"Come on, guys, this is still new," Siobhan protested. "Shouldn't I wait to find out what he's into?"

"He went after you on purpose, my dear," Vanessa said. "Not only because you have boobs for days, but because you're an experienced woman. You're good at taking the lead and giving orders. I'm betting he's more than willing to take some direction from you."

"Did someone say bet?"

EIGHT

A chime cut through the music on the car stereo, signaling an incoming call. Charlie thumbed the controller on the steering wheel. "O'Halloran."

"Hello, Mr. O'Halloran." Siobhan's warm voice filled the front seat. "I wanted to call and say that I received your flowers."

Charlie smiled as he adjusted the volume, even though Siobhan couldn't see it. "Do you like them?"

"Very much." She paused. "So did my friends."

Uh-oh. "I asked for them to be delivered at closing so that you could avoid any questions if you wanted to."

"I appreciate that, but Nadia and I have a couple of friends join us for afternoon tea and talk on Tuesdays. They were all here when the flowers arrived."

"Oh." He paused, trying to gauge her mood. He'd debated whether or not sending the flowers was a good idea and in the end had trusted his instincts. "I guess they wanted to know why you were getting flowers."

"They figured that out rather quickly. Apparently all of them, even my best friend and business partner, had placed bets on how long it would take us to do the horizontal tango. They even had a separate bet on which of us would be the instigator."

"Are you upset?" She didn't sound upset, but she was a woman and he was clueless about women on the best days.

"Amused and aggravated mostly," she answered. "If you knew my friends, you wouldn't be surprised."

Women who bet on when one of their friends would have sex? He couldn't begin to imagine what their "tea and talk" had been like. "Did you tell them about today?"

"It's the only way I was able to get out of there on time. They're enthusiastically supportive of this."

"Then I say we give them something to be enthusiastic about."

She remained silent for so long he wondered if he'd overstepped. "Siobhan?"

"I'm trying to decide if I should reward you or punish you."

His cock perked up at that. "Why not put both on the menu?"

She laughed. "I like the way you think, Mr. O'Halloran. Are you on the way over?"

"Sure am. Is there anything you need?"

"Besides the obvious?" The amusement in her voice washed over him like music. "Actually, I do need you to do something for me."

"Of course, what is it?"

"Stop at the grocery store."

The hard edge of command in her tone was unmistakable. So

was the hard ridge rising in his pants. "Yes, ma'am. What do you need?"

"Honey," she answered. "Chocolate sauce. Your choice of raspberries or strawberries. You also need to get some whipped cream, the kind that comes in the can."

Damn. His mind instantly conjured images of dripping honey across her nipples and down her belly, then taking his time licking it off. "May I ask what's for dessert?"

"You may." She paused.

Oh. Right. He slowed to a stop at an intersection. "What are we having for dessert?"

"Your favorite and mine. Us."

Thank God he was at a traffic light. He reached down to adjust himself. "I'm going to have some trouble walking around a grocery store sporting wood, Ms. Malloy."

"You're a resourceful guy, Mr. O'Halloran," came her airy reply. "I'm sure you'll figure out something short of providing relief. Understood?"

He suddenly felt lightheaded. "Yes, ma'am."

"Good. Get here in one piece, without a speeding ticket. I'll be waiting. Remember, good things come to those who wait and those who wait get to come good." She disconnected.

God. His body tight with anticipation, Charlie pulled into the parking lot of the first grocery store he saw. Jogging inside, he grabbed a basket, strategically placed it in front of his crotch, and gathered the requested items at breakneck speed, using the self-checkout to get out of the store and back in his car as soon as he could.

Siobhan. . . . He gripped the steering wheel, forcing himself to take a couple of deep breaths before he started the car and pulled out of the parking lot. Something about her taking charge and giving him orders just did it for him. Hell, everything about her did it for him. Which meant he was in serious trouble.

His fantasies of her over the last couple of weeks had been hot but basic standard stuff—her going down on him, his face buried between her thighs, bending her over while fucking her from behind. After yesterday, with the dance and the thought of her in leather, his fantasies had changed. Last night he'd dreamed of kneeling at her feet, naked, his hands tied behind his back, waiting to pleasure her however she wanted. The vision of her as a dominatrix had been so powerful that he'd awaken to find himself already stroking his cock, halfway to coming.

Now he wondered if those fantasies could become a reality. If he could dare do more than hint at discipline and straight out ask her for it. Asked her to tie him up and have her way with him. Push him to the edge, then push him over. Not every time, but once in a while would be good. Better than good.

Siobhan lived a couple of miles inland from the bay, her neighborhood a collection of bungalows and ranch-style homes with neat, landscaped yards. He pulled into the drive behind her cherry-red Ford Falcon convertible, grabbed his purchases off the seat, and jogged to the front door. With his blood pounding in his ears and his cock straining against his zipper, he rang the doorbell.

Siobhan opened her door, careful to remain out of sight behind it. Charlie stepped over the threshold, gorgeous in a navy blue shirt and gray pants. She closed and locked the door behind him after he entered, then waited for him to turn to face her.

He did, gulping audibly, and she knew she'd achieved the desired impact. She'd changed into a chiffon halter-style baby-doll in bright red, with a matching G-string, sheer robe, and her favorite marabou slippers. It was one of her favorite outfits and she wore it when she wanted to feel especially sexy. Like now.

Charlie held out the bag to her, his gaze so like a physical caress that her nipples pearled in response. "I bought the stuff you wanted."

"Thank you." Pleased with the effect she had on him, she took the bag. "I think we can save the tour for later. Follow me."

She led him deeper into the living room, full of sleek but comfortable mid-century modern furniture. She'd already prepared everything she wanted here, figuring it would be easier to clean up than in the bedroom.

"Take off your clothes and put them there," she ordered, gesturing to the sofa. "Then I want you to sit in that wooden chair."

He swallowed again, but began to unbutton his shirt. "Is this reward or punishment?"

"It depends on whether you keep asking questions or not."

He pressed his lips together, but she could see desire ignite in his gaze. Vanessa's words rang clear in Siobhan's mind. Maybe Charlie wasn't opposed to a little direction after all. Maybe he wanted more.

While he undressed, she went into the kitchen and prepared the fruit and sauces, loading everything onto a tray along with a damp washcloth. By the time she returned to the living room Charlie was naked and seated in one of her straight-backed dining chairs that she'd placed beside the sofa.

Setting the tray onto the side table, she turned to face him, her heart beating a staccato rhythm. He sat with his hands on his knees, feet spread, his cock jutting up in all its happy glory. Charlie was a gorgeous man on any given day, but naked he was a thing of beauty, his build athletic but not over-defined, skin sun-kissed and covered with a dusting of golden hair.

"You're a beautiful man, Charlie O'Halloran," she told him, loosening the sash at her waist. He tracked her movements avidly as she approached, twirling the bright red ribbon through her fingers. She trailed the slash over his shoulders, down his chest, across his thighs, then around his cock. He sucked in a breath, ab muscles flexing, his erection thickening as it bobbed between his legs.

Desire pooled low in her belly, dampening her panties. The urge to straddle his thighs and impale herself rode her hard, making her bite her lips in self-defense. Moving behind him, she let her hands roam over his neck, across his shoulders, down his back, her nails lightly scoring his skin. She smiled when he shivered in response, then leaned over to breathe in his ear.

"You got to have your dessert first yesterday. I didn't get dessert at all, so I have to punish you for that. Hands behind your back."

He complied without question, muscles flexing beneath his golden skin. She looped the sash through one of the slats in the chair, then wound it around his wrists before tying the ends into a bow. If he had wanted to get free, he probably could have, but it would have taken more than a couple of seconds of effort.

Desire flushed his cheeks and brought his eyes to half-mast as she stepped back in front of him. "Do I get to have dessert, Ms. Malloy?"

"Of course you do." She slipped the robe off, tossing it onto the sofa, then reached up to untie the halter of her baby-doll. Making a show for him, for herself, she slid her hands down her throat and over the rise of her breasts, pushing the cups of the nightie down and away until the garment fell to the floor. Charlie tracked the motion, licking his lips as she revealed her body to him.

The heat in his gaze, the obvious desire sent a raft of emotions sweeping through her—pride, need, feminine confidence. She controlled his pleasure. She would give him what he wanted, give them what they both wanted, but on her own terms.

"Do you like honey, Charlie?" Heat crept through her, flushing her skin as she reached for the bear-shaped bottle. With slow, deliberate movements she upended the bottle and squeezed a sticky-sweet trail over her left breast, paying extra attention to the puckered nipple.

"Y-yes," he answered on a rasp, his lips parting as he watched her pick up one of the raspberries. She slid the puckered fruit through the honey slicking her left nipple, circling her areola, tightening her nipple even more in the process. Keeping her gaze locked to Charlie's she raised the honey-coated berry to her mouth. The surprise and disappointment that colored his features would have been comical if she'd truly meant to deny him, but she didn't. Not when it meant she'd have to deny herself.

She held the raspberry out to him. He took it without hesitation, his tongue warm as he sucked the honey from her fingers before chewing the berry. It was her turn to moan as she watched his mouth work.

"Hmm, maybe we should try chocolate this time." She picked up the bottle of chocolate syrup then squirted a curlicue of sauce onto her right breast, shivering a little as the cool chocolate hit her lust-warmed skin.

"You're cold. I could warm that up for you, Ms. Malloy." Though his voice held a teasing note, his expression showed how desperately he wanted her to agree to his suggestion.

"What an excellent idea, Mr. O'Halloran." She stepped forward until she straddled him, the kitten heels on her slippers giving her enough height to not be awkward. Even so, the head of his cock brushed against her panty-covered mound, making them both groan.

"Maybe . . ." Charlie cleared his throat. "Maybe you'd be more comfortable if you removed that? I could warm you up from the inside too."

It was a tempting suggestion, which was why she'd kept the panties on. She ground her teeth against the pulsing need to free his hands, to pull aside her panties and plunge down on him, riding him until they both fell apart. Her hands slid down her sides to the waistband of her panties of their own volition until she caught herself. Instead, she settled her hands on his shoulders, ignoring his knowing smirk. She'd told him good things were worth the wait, which meant she'd have to wait too. But not for the feel of his mouth on her.

"Taste me now."

He leaned forward eagerly, the tip of his tongue grazing the swollen peak of her chocolate-covered breast. Just a light touch that teased them both. She stared in fascination as he licked her sensitive flesh with the flat of his tongue, taking care to get every bit of the sauce before sucking her puckered nipple into the warmth of his mouth.

Her eyes slid closed on exquisite sensation as he suckled, the pull of his mouth shooting an echoing pull deep into her core. She moaned, her hips rocking in a blind search for relief, pressing her mound against the hard ridge of his arousal.

He bucked his hips in response, trying to enter her, stopped by her panties. His shoulders jerked as he tried to reach for her, only to be stopped by the sash binding his hands. He growled as he pulled off her breast with an audible pop, only to move to her left, still covered with honey. With teeth and lips and tongue he fed on her, driving her need higher and higher.

It was almost too much. In danger of losing control of herself, of the situation, Siobhan opened her eyes as she pressed on his shoulders, moving back from his tantalizing mouth, the temptation of his cock. Disappointment slashed across his features, making her waver. She was wet, so very wet for him already. She had been from the moment she'd called him. While she knew the feel of his cock plunging deep inside her, she didn't know the taste of it, and that desire won out.

He hissed as she drizzled a thin ribbon of chocolate sauce from the base of his throat to his chest before following the path with her mouth, kissing and nipping her way down his neck to his pectorals. He groaned aloud, his gaze unfocusing as she lightly set her teeth to one nipple, easing the sting with a long swipe of her tongue before moving to the other. After lapping up every bit of chocolate she poured more, licking and biting her way down his abs until she ended on her knees in front of him.

He was panting now, chest rising and falling rapidly, arms flexing as he strained against his binding, her name a rough scrape of sound on his lips.

"Not yet," she said, as much for herself as for him. She reached for the honey. "I haven't finished my dessert yet."

His cock jerked. "God, Siobhan, I don't think I can take it."

"You can. You will." She upended the bottle.

Honey coated the head of his cock, mixing with the pre-come

there before cascading down his length. The sight of the golden liquid drenching his engorged length made her mouth water, so much so that she decided not to add the chocolate and whipped cream.

Wrapping her fingers around the base of his cock, she swirled her tongue around the bulbous head, lapping up honey and pre-come in a heady combination of delicious taste. She licked her way down the underside, hearing his harshening breath as she mouthed his testicles, laving every bit of sweetness from his skin to reveal his natural flavor.

She kissed her way back up his length, full-mouthed kisses that had him panting her name. When she reached the crown she looked at him, taking another bead of moisture onto the tip of her tongue as he watched. His eyes blazed with lust, with barely leashed demand. "Suck me down, Siobhan," he ordered. "I want to see you take my cock in your mouth."

"Yes, Mr. O'Halloran." Charlie could only be submissive for so long, she realized. That was fine with her. She liked that she could push him to a point, to the limits of control before he turned the tables and pushed back.

Gripping the base again, Siobhan stretched her mouth open over the crown and took him inside. He shuddered, her name like a curse on his lips as she sucked him in as deep as she could, careful not to scrape his thick girth with her teeth. While the honey was nice, his unadulterated taste was even better.

With a low, slow suction she reversed direction then repeated the process, going down on him again, then again. With his muttered encouragement she increased her pace, bobbing her head. The chair creaked beneath him as he flexed his hips to match her rhythm.

"Fuck me, Siobhan, that's good. Yes, baby, fuck me with that hot mouth of yours. God, you'd better stop if you don't want me to come."

She didn't stop. Didn't want to stop. Instead she stroked his balls as she sucked him deep, hollowing her cheeks to increase the pressure. His balls drew up tight beneath her fingers, his body tensed, and there was a still, breathless moment before he spurted his release, flooding her throat, and making a deep, guttural groan of satisfaction.

Siobhan swallowed every bit of him down then eased off him by slow degrees. She rested her cheek on his knee, pleased with herself as she waited for him to come back from his orgasmic high. Next time she'd definitely have to break out the whipped cream and build a sundae on his cock.

"Siobhan?"

She raised her head to stare at him. The lust burning in his eyes stole her breath and caused moisture to pool in her panties. "Yes?"

"Punishment's over. Now it's time for my reward, and I intend to take it."

NINE

"Untie me."

The command in Charlie's voice had Siobhan rising to her feet before she could process it. Her sex throbbed as she untied the sash, unwinding it from his wrists before returning to face him again.

He rubbed at his hands, flexing his fingers as he stared at her. "Turn around. I want to see these panties that kept me from getting inside you."

She turned her back to him. There wasn't much to her panties except a small triangle of fabric at the front that tapered to a thin string that passed between her buttocks to the string of the waistband. Because there wasn't much to them, she could feel her moisture dampening her thighs, the panties too minuscule to contain her excitement.

She heard his intake of breath, the shifting of the chair. Was he getting hard again? God, she hoped so. Going down on him had only made her needier. Maybe she shouldn't have sucked him until he came but he'd enjoyed it and she'd enjoyed giving him that blissed-out look.

"Bend over," he ordered next, his voice hoarse. "Place your hands flat on the coffee table and spread your legs."

For a brief second she thought about disobeying, then sanity prevailed. It was his turn to take command, and she had no idea what he'd do to punish her. Probably withhold sex. The thought made her whimper.

"What is it, Siobhan?" he asked, his voice gentle with concern.

"I was just hoping that you weren't going to punish me by not having sex with me."

His low chuckle scraped along her senses. "I'm looking at the sweetest, juiciest pussy I've ever seen," he told her. "I see how wet you are and I know it's because you want me, want my cock. I suppose it would be a punishment not to fuck you, but that would punish me too, wouldn't it?"

"Yes, yes it would," she agreed, maybe too quickly.

"You're right." She felt him behind her, her skin prickling with his nearness as he dropped a condom on the table beside her hand. "So no, sweet Siobhan, I'm not going to punish you. Not that way."

He snapped the string waistband, the pop loud against her skin. She breathed through the sting, then whimpered again as he ran his index finger along the fabric, pressing the material into her dampness. "Is this vintage?"

"N-no."

"Good." Gripping the straps with both hands, he ripped the G-string apart, sending the torn scrap fluttering down to her ankles.

When she protested, he ran his finger over her slit again. "I'll replace it. I'll be more than happy to take you shopping for pretty lacy things."

She pushed back against his hand, wanting more of his touch, but he moved away. "Charlie . . ."

"You have a beautiful ass, Siobhan." His palm stroked over her buttocks. "Seeing you in your stockings and belt yesterday made me lose my mind. I think I'd like to see you wear that again, without the panties. Just this delectable ass framed by those straps and a little bit of lace."

She thought she was wet before. Her core felt heavy with want, with desire, with need for him. "Please—"

"It will be the perfect frame for the imprint of my hand. Or maybe a paddle or a crop." He squeezed one cheek. "Of course, if I do it to you, you'd want to do it to me, wouldn't you?"

"God." Her mouth watered at the images he described. She squirmed, needing more from him.

"Is that what we're doing, sweetheart?" he asked in a silky tone. "A little quid pro quo to keep the scales balanced?"

She hadn't thought of it that way, but now that he'd mentioned it, she supposed she had been keeping a tally. This was only day two, and he already had her pegged. God, she was in trouble.

He ran a finger down her spine, making her shiver. "Does that mean I get to tie your hands behind your back while I fuck you?"

It took her a moment to speak past the lust threatening to choke her. "Didn't."

"Didn't what, sweetheart?"

"Didn't fuck you."

"You most certainly did, milking my cock with that hot mouth of yours, and all I could do was sit there and take it. Which is exactly what you're going to do." He massaged her buttocks, his thumbs dipping into the hollow between her cheeks and spreading her open. She shifted backward, a silent entreaty for more, but he denied her.

"Do you have any toys, sweetheart?"

Her core clenched on nothing, making her groan. "Y-yes," she answered, so drunk on desire that her words came out slurred. "A couple of vibrators."

His fingers dipped down to stroke along her slit, then teased back to her anus. "I think you may need to go shopping."

"My friends suggested a trip for Saturday."

He stroked her again, drawing her moisture back to her puckered opening. "Make sure you get a vibrating butt plug."

She gasped as his finger pressed against her. "For you or for me?"

For a long moment he didn't respond. When he did, it was to sink his teeth into the apple of her left buttock. She cried out, a sharp sound that subsided into a soft moan as he kissed the sting away.

"What you get for you, you're getting for me. Just like me doing this to you does it for me." He scraped his teeth along the curve of her ass. "Up on your toes, sweetness. You need a little bit of punishment before you get your reward."

She didn't know what he meant by punishment, but if it included more of those delicious bites, she'd take it. Balancing on her toes and keeping her hands flat on the coffee table tilted her ass even higher in the air, opening her up even more. She felt more than heard his sigh, his breath cool against her enflamed sex. Then his hands cupped her buttocks, his thumbs holding her open for his questing tongue.

She mewled, her core contracting at the contact as she tried to press back against him, gain more of his tongue. But Charlie knew what he'd meant by saying it was a punishment. He stoked her desire, drove up her need, pushed her toward the pinnacle without ever allowing her to reach the peak. Over and over he revved her up with his tongue and his fingers, playing her like a maestro until she was reduced to panting his name like a mantra, a curse, a plea.

"You take your punishment so beautifully," he told her, his voice scraped raw as he reached for the condom, ripped it open. "Go kneel on the couch."

She did, moving unsteadily, intoxicated by sensation. He stepped up behind her, one foot on the floor, the other on the cushion. He fit the head of his erection against her opening, then drove himself home with one powerful thrust.

The sudden fullness had her crying out, her sex clamping down on his cock. He circled his hips as his hands clamped down on her waist. "God, baby. Yes, just like that. Hang on."

He powered into her, rocking her into the couch, the impact of his body slap, slap, slapping against hers, reverberating through her sex. His fingers dug into her hips, holding her where he wanted her, where she needed to be. Then his thumb pressed against her back opening and she was too far gone to care, to worry, to do anything but crave him and the pleasure.

She tossed her head back on a low moan as he breached her, his cock and thumb filling her in tandem. Incredible sensations burst over her, slicking her skin, her sex. It arced over her, powering her up the precipice to orgasm. There was no stopping it, no holding back, she could only let go and take the pleasure he gave her.

She did, screaming his name as she came, flying apart and out and away. As if she'd given him permission, Charlie increased his pace, his thrusts almost brutal as he slammed into her. Speeding,

speeding, then he clutched her hips like a vise as he erupted inside her with a guttural groan.

For long moments he ground against her, wringing every bit of sweetness from the orgasm, slowly bringing them both back to earth. It felt so good, so damn good. She moaned as Charlie stepped back from her, then swayed as her muscles refused to obey her commands.

"Easy there," he said, scooping her up. "I've got you. Just let me know where the master bath is."

She pointed him down the short hallway to her master bedroom, embarrassment fighting with the bliss. "Sorry, I wasn't expecting all that. I thought yesterday was a fluke from breaking my drought."

"I get it. Me too. About the drought, I mean."

She snorted as he placed her on her feet. "You? In a sex drought?"

He tossed her a glance as he disposed of the condom in her wastebasket. "You know as well as I do that keeping a small business in the black takes a lot of work. I needed that to be a priority, not being wild and raunchy."

She pursed her lips as she opened the glass door to start the shower and tried not to think of how long it had been since she'd last showered with anyone. "Forgive me for being skeptical. Drought or not, you rocked my world."

"Thank you." He kissed the back of her neck as he followed her into the shower. "My sister would leave her girly magazines lying around all the time. I caught myself reading a few of them. I guess some of the information stuck."

She blinked up at him as he stepped beneath the water, watching the play of his muscles as he reached up to slick his hair back. Damn, the man was beautiful. "You have a sister?"

"Yeah. And two brothers." He guided her into the stream of almost-hot water, working his fingers through her hair. "What about you?"

Her eyes slid shut. She'd forgotten about this, about the feel of someone else's hands on her body in an intimate yet nonsexual way. Forgotten how comforting the caring touch of another could be.

"Siobhan?"

He'd asked a question, and it took her several seconds to remember what it was. "No, no siblings. I was an only child." *And now my family pretends I don't exist.*

"I have no concept of what that must be like." The scent of flowers filled the shower stall as he massaged shampoo into her hair with gentle but sure pressure, as if he'd done it thousands of times. "There was always someone being loud over some injury or argument or roughhousing. They got on my nerves sometimes—they still do—but I wouldn't trade them for anything."

Something dark and hard entered his tone at the last, causing her to open her eyes and look up at him. Concentration set his features but shadows flitted through his gaze as he cupped the back of her head to rinse the shampoo from her hair. She clutched his shoulders as he took care of her, rinsing her hair, then gently lathering her body with her favorite castile soap.

Disquiet slithered through her. Being tended to like this was far more intimate than the sex they'd had. That had been about lust, about basic need. This . . . yes, it was something she needed, something she craved deep in the dark of the night. It also required a level of openness and vulnerability she couldn't afford to indulge.

"You're frowning," he observed, his voice barely above the sound of water hitting the tiles. "What are you thinking about that's so bad?"

"You," she answered honestly, undone by him and not knowing how or why. "I don't mean that you're bad, just that I'm thinking about you."

He stepped behind her to lather her back. "And thinking about me is a bad thing?"

"Yes. No." She shook her head. "Damn, you're good at this."

"I'm good at a lot of things," he told her, as if he were simply stating the truth and not bragging. "Which thing in particular are you referring to?"

"You've had me off balance since the day you gave me that proposal. Even now, I can't believe I'm standing here in my shower with you, allowing you to soap me up like it's no big deal."

"It's not a big deal unless you make it one, Siobhan."

She bit her lip. Maybe it wasn't a big deal for him. Maybe he did this all the time, despite what he'd claimed earlier about a sex drought. If so, it would explain why he was so casual showering with her while she was still so shattered.

As if sensing that she was ready to bolt, Charlie smoothed his hands over her shoulders. "I like doing things for people I like, Siobhan," he said, his fingers lightly rubbing at the back of her neck. "I like taking care of people that I like. It's part of my nature. That's what I meant about it being no big deal."

A hot flash of guilt warmed her ears. "All right."

He ran his soap-laden hands over her breasts, taking his time, his touch hovering between sensual and casual. "Does this make you uncomfortable?"

Because she wasn't facing him, wasn't staring into those sea-blue eyes, she could be honest. "A little."

"Why?" He turned her to face him. Confusion tinged with anger lowered his brows. "Would it be easier to handle if my dick was inside you while I soaped you up? Or better yet, left you ass-up on the couch and just took off, so it's just about sex and not about caring?" He shook his head in disgust. "You need better lovers."

Like a fast-moving thunderstorm, his expression cleared and his irrepressible grin returned. "It's a good thing you have me."

She snorted, her discomfort pushed back by wry amusement. "You sure are cocky, Mr. O'Halloran."

Making sure she watched him, he slid a hand down his water-slicked chest and abs to wrap around his half-awake cock. "Yes, yes I am."

A rueful laugh escaped her throat. "I need to know what vitamins you're taking. That energy would come in handy when I'm performing."

"Performing?"

"The burlesque show." She nudged him with a hip. "Did you forget the dance from yesterday already? I suppose I will need those vitamins."

"That dance will be forever seared in my memory. I just forgot that you strip for other people." He froze in the act of lathering himself up, realization dawning in his eyes. "You're a stripper."

"Let's get one thing perfectly clear." She thumped his chest. "I am not a stripper. I'm a performer, part of a troupe of entertainers who sing as well as dance. I strip down, yes, but only to a G-string and pasties. No one's making it rain on me or stuffing dollar bills into my garter belt."

She glowered at him, hands on her hips. "If you can't handle that, this ends now."

"Whoa." He held up his hands in a placating gesture. "I'm sorry. It just hit me what that means. I didn't mean to offend you."

"I know you didn't." She took the soap from him and began to return the favor, lathering his magnificent frame with slow sweeps. "You said you might like to catch one of my shows. I think that's a good idea. We're performing two weeks from this coming Saturday. Nadia and her boyfriend will be there, and so will some other friends. You can experience the full production of the Crimson Bay Bombshells in all our glory and see what you think."

He wrapped his fingers around her wrist, stopping her from lathering his chest for the second time. "You mean, see if I can handle the audience ogling you."

She gave him a frank stare. "That's exactly what I mean. Some of the troupe members date others in the scene or leave their significant others at home because they get jealous of the fact that strangers get to stare at their nearly naked partners. You think you can get through a show without getting a complex?"

"There's only one way to find out, and that's to say yes to the challenge." He pulled her under the spray for a long, lingering kiss that left her clinging to him. "I meant to do that when I first came in, but you have a way of blowing my mind."

"As long as we're even."

A slow grin spread over his face. "If you're dead set on being even-stevens, then I owe you another orgasm." He quickly cleaned up, rinsed the soap off, then shut off the water. "How about we discover what it's like to have sex in a bed?"

"A bed?" She winked at him. "Why, Mr. O'Halloran, you do like to live on the edge."

TEN

Two weeks ago, if someone had suggested to Charlie that he'd be going to a drag club to attend a burlesque show because the woman he was having sex with was one of the performers, he would have laughed in their face. Yet here he was, paying the cover charge for Club Tatas and searching out Siobhan's friends in the most eclectic group of people he'd ever witnessed.

"Hey, Charlie!"

A brunette in a dark green corset waved at him. He did a double take as he realized the stunner was Nadia, Siobhan's business partner. He made his way to her table, front and center to the stage, where she enveloped him in a huge welcoming hug. "You made it!"

"I wouldn't miss it," he answered, breaking away from her. "This will be my first time catching the show."

"It's a great show." A dark-haired man stood behind Nadia, dressed head to toe in black. He put a hand to the back of her neck, toying with the black lace choker at her throat. Charlie didn't miss the possessiveness of the seemingly casual gesture, but he didn't need the warning. He wasn't there for Nadia.

Still, "That's a pretty pendant," he said, pointing to the gold symbol dangling at the hollow of her throat. "Does it mean something?"

"It does indeed." Kane's deep voice flowed as smooth as water and dangerous as an undertow. "It's the kanji character for 'precious.' A treasure for a treasure."

Nadia smiled as she reached up to touch the pendant. "Kane—Mr. Tall, Dark, and Possessive behind me—gave it to me. Kane, I'd like you to meet Charlie O'Halloran of O'Halloran Business Solutions. I told you about him, that he's working with Siobhan on our delivery business and they've finally progressed to seeing each other."

She reached back, thumping the man behind her on the chest. "Charlie, this is my man, Kane Sullivan. When he's not marking his territory, he's a professor at Herscher University and I love him dearly. Now shake hands so we can sit down."

They did, and Charlie took a seat next to a dark blonde woman in a shiny black bustier. She wore a collar with a leash dangling from it, the end held by another woman dressed in a three-piece suit. "Hi, Charlie," the blonde said in a deep tenor. "Siobhan will be glad to see you."

"Jas? Nadia's assistant, Jas?"

The blonde grinned at him. "Yep. I like to slip into something a little more comfortable after hours." He nodded to the woman beside him. "This is my fiancée, Tracy. And you know Rosie from the café. With her is her boyfriend, Oscar."

Charlie shook hands with all of them, wondering if he was the only "normal" one at the table, dressed in black slacks and a bright blue short-sleeved shirt, though Rosie seemed normal despite her pink and purple hair. Then again, in a progressive college town, normal was relative. His day-to-day life would probably seem boring in comparison to those gathered around him, at least on the outside. On the inside, his evolving sexual tastes had him drifting further away from normal every time he and Siobhan got together.

Not that he minded. Exploring the boundaries of what he would and wouldn't do with a willing partner just enhanced his experience with Siobhan. The fact that she didn't blink, didn't balk, and suggested things herself made being with her all the better. She was a fantasy come true.

"How are things going with you and Siobhan?" Nadia asked after he'd ordered a beer from a server.

"The quality-assurance testing on the delivery portal went well," he answered, then proceeded to bring her up to speed on the enhancements to the café's website and social media platforms. "We're ready to implement the soft launch test for your preferred customers, unless you'd rather save it until after the holiday."

She arched a brow. "I have no doubt that things will go smoothly, but you know that's not what I'm talking about."

He accepted his beer and paid the server, then took a sip before giving Nadia a level glance. "Don't you get updates every Tuesday?"

"Touché." She gave him an unrepentant grin. "Maybe I want to hear it from your point of view."

"Is there money riding on my answer?"

"She told you about that, huh?" Nadia's expression was one of thoughtful surprise. "Hmm, maybe she thinks more of you than she lets on."

He kept his expression neutral but inside he cheered that information. "She invited me to her show, right? That must mean she likes me."

"It does. I actually didn't think she would. Invite you here, I mean." Nadia paused, as if choosing her words carefully. "Siobhan's cautious when it comes to relationships, no matter what type they are."

"I can appreciate that." He did. He had his reasons for wanting to be cautious as well, reasons he had no intention of discussing with Nadia when he hadn't shared them with Siobhan yet. In fact, other than their talk about siblings, neither he nor Siobhan had shared much information about their personal histories. They were still at the early stages of their relationship, so early he wasn't sure it could be defined as a relationship.

"I like her. She seems to like me. We get along well. I plan to keep seeing her. That's where we are right now."

She leaned back against the professor, who seemed content to let her do all the talking. If Charlie had Siobhan sitting on his lap the way Nadia sat on Kane's, he wouldn't be talking either. "That's all I'm going to get, isn't it?" she asked.

"Pretty much." He gestured toward the stage. "How long has she been doing burlesque?"

"It's been about two years, maybe a little but longer. It's important to her. She loves to dance."

He filed away that information. "She wanted me to experience what it's like for her. I guess some people have issues with their partners doing burlesque?"

"Siobhan hasn't had that issue since she's never invited someone she's involved with to her shows." Nadia leaned forward. "You need to be prepared. The Crimson Bay Bombshells have a large and devoted following. They do a meet and greet after the shows, selling merchandise and posing for pictures and stuff like that. Sugar has fans and it's important to her and the troupe to interact with their fans after the shows."

He tilted his beer up before answering. "So you're warning me to not cramp her style and go all Neanderthal if guys start slobbering all over her pasties?"

"Something like that." She snorted. "Sugar can take care of herself in that regard. It's why you don't see frat boys clamoring for her autograph and pictures in the café. I'm just saying that if you want to be with her, you need to be cool."

"I can do that." He wasn't the jealous type, and he certainly wasn't going to throw a possessive tantrum in the club. If Siobhan chose someone else, he'd try to convince her to change her mind, but he'd eventually respect her decision. If Siobhan wanted his help fending off overzealous admirers, he'd crack a few heads. Happily.

"One more thing."

"What's that?"

Nadia smiled. "Siobhan is my best friend, the sister I never had. If you hurt her, I will go Sweeney Todd on your ass."

"Understood."

The house lights fell and the emcee took the stage to thunderous applause. "Welcome guys and gals to the best night of your week. Are you ready?" The crowd erupted into cheers and whistles. "All right then. Ladies and gentlemen, I present to you the Crimson Bay Bombshells!"

Charlie wasn't sure what he expected from a burlesque show but apparently there was more to it than beautiful women stripping. This was more like an old-time vaudeville show with some risqué comedy sketches mixed in with the variety of female dancers. The rowdy crowd showered whistles and applause on the performers, making the atmosphere party-like.

The master of ceremonies took the stage again. "Now here to satisfy your sweet tooth, ladies and gentlemen, give a big round of applause to Sugar Malloy!"

The crowd burst into applause as a spotlight hit the stage, highlighting Siobhan. If he'd thought of her as a blonde bombshell before, she was now elevated to goddess status. A heavy electronic bass beat pounded from the speakers as the lights rose enough to show her dressed as the most provocative ringmaster he'd ever seen.

She wore a tiny black top hat with netting atop her blonde pin curls. Her blue eyes were a smoky mystery, her lips painted a smoldering fuck-me red. A black satin tuxedo coat with tails and white cuffs hugged her breasts and waist, framing the bright red corset and matching hot pants she wore beneath. Fishnet stockings and black stilettos called attention to her gorgeous legs. A red bow tie and matching gloves completed the ensemble.

Sugar tossed a beguiling smile to the crowd as they applauded, then began to lip-sync to a song by Garbage about being queer. She teased, she tantalized, she tortured as she worked the stage, removing her hat, twirling as she stripped off the bow tie before shimmying out of the coat. Next came the gloves, each removal timed perfectly to the music, leaving her in all red from the bra to the corset to the panties and garter belt.

The ensemble reminded him of the first time he'd gone to her house, when she'd greeted him in that glorious see-through nightie. He knew it was a coincidence and not an outfit she'd chosen for him, but it still felt like she'd worn it for him. That she danced for him, stripped for him, revealed herself for him.

Desire rode him as he watched, mesmerized, caught, his blood heating and his cock hardening. He gripped his beer, forgetting about her friends seated around him, the other onlookers cheering and whistling their approval. His thoughts, his whole world centered on the woman slowly revealing herself onstage.

By the time she'd stripped to the final reveal—heart-shaped pasties and a scarlet G-string—he was burning with lust, desire clawing its way through his gut. From the enthusiastic appreciation of the crowd, he wasn't the only one.

More performers took to the stage but he only paid limited attention, his thoughts filled with memories of Siobhan and sex. Having her writhe beneath him as he slammed into her. The way her breasts bounced as she rode him like a jockey gunning for the Triple Crown. Discovering that they both preferred each other covered in honey more than chocolate or whipped cream. Her taste, her scent, the silk of her skin, and the sounds she made were an intoxicating cocktail more powerful than any energy drink.

She had one more performance with several other ladies doing a group dance to "Fat Bottomed Girls" that brought the crowd to their feet. He joined them in their appreciation, clapping and whistling loudly.

"So what did you think?" Nadia asked him as the house lights rose and he returned to his seat.

"I think I'm extremely lucky. She's amazing." He stretched his legs out, hoping to ease the ache in his cock. Popping wood was probably a common occurrence for guys attending these shows. The thought set his teeth on edge. Ogling his woman was one thing. Strangers actively lusting after her was another.

This was why Siobhan had invited him, he realized. Performing with the burlesque troupe was obviously a large part of her life, one she wasn't prepared to relinquish. If he wanted what he had with Siobhan to develop into something more, he'd have to make peace with the idea that while Siobhan might belong to him, Sugar Malloy belonged to everyone.

Of course, she didn't belong to him yet. Not officially. Two weeks of screwing like bunnies did not a relationship make. But he was greedy and he wanted to be selfish for a change. He wanted to have Siobhan, and he didn't want to share her. He wanted her to want only him, the same as he only craved her. He knew he had miles to go before he could convince her of that.

No time like the present to start, though. "Can we go backstage?" he asked.

"Not much room back there," Nadia answered, settling herself onto Kane's lap. "The troupe usually does their meet and greet on the stage. Should be another fifteen minutes or so."

He ordered a bottle of water to cover his two-drink minimum and settled in to wait for Siobhan to appear. If this was a test, he had every intention of passing it.

———

Siobhan hummed with excess energy as she finished changing into street clothes appropriate for Sugar Malloy: a black pencil skirt that buttoned up the back, sheer black stockings with back seams, a rose-colored off-the-shoulder top with a matching silk flower in her hair. A dab of ruby-red lip stain and she was ready.

"Ready to meet our adoring fans?" Lola Fontaine asked as she surveyed her own reflection in the makeup mirror. The head of the Crimson Bay Bombshells did a spot-on Josephine Baker homage that brought the house down every time. Her street clothes consisted of a tangerine-colored sheath dress topped by a black lace cincher and a silk tiger lily clip in her hair, and she looked as stunningly beautiful as usual. "We had a great crowd out there tonight."

"We sure did." Siobhan matched the dark-haired woman's grin. "Let's do this."

They made their way out of the cramped changing area and back to the stage, trusting the troupe's apprentices and stagehands to safeguard their costumes. The troupe had grown since Siobhan had joined nearly three years earlier. Now the Crimson Bay Bombshells had two sketch comics, six dancers, and three apprentices, as well as Max, the show's master of ceremonies.

All of them were younger than Siobhan, but most of the time she didn't think about it or let it bother her. Besides, they were a motley crew of misfits who banded together as their own creative family. Everyone accepted everyone, or they answered to Lola, who could out-mamma Siobhan in a heartbeat.

A crowd waited for them as usual, a mixture of men and women wanting selfies, autographs, and answers to a host of questions both personal and professional. Siobhan glanced through the crowd, trying not to appear too eager. She knew Audie and Vanessa had headed out for their club, but she wondered if the others had stayed. She wondered if Charlie was sitting out there, waiting for her. He had said he would come, but she hadn't heard from him since he'd sent a "good luck" text about an hour before the show began.

What if he had attended the show, but left? What if he couldn't handle the sometimes over-friendly fans of the troupe? What if he was too jealous, too possessive, to date a burlesque dancer?

She shook her head. If those what-ifs proved true, it meant that Charlie wasn't the guy she'd thought him to be. Better to head things off now than get more involved with him. However, if he was out there, if he had stayed . . . she had to decide what that meant for her. For them.

Setting those thoughts aside, she joined Lola and the other performers posing for pictures with their fans, signing some of the color stills and T-shirts they sold at their merchandise table. She also spent a fair amount of time deflecting any fishing questions about her sexual orientation or marital status while Max, who was six foot three and pushing two-twenty on a good day, kept the inebriated frat boys from getting too handsy.

"Ooh," Lola cooed, "looks like we have a new one tonight. He's hot. Sure hope he's not a stalker."

"Who?" Siobhan glanced out into the dimly lit audience, her gaze crashing into Charlie's. He sat at one of the front tables. Curiously, Nadia and Kane and the rest of their friends also still manned their spots. Jas and Tracy usually headed to Down Below as soon as the show was over, taking Rosie and Oscar with them.

Suddenly that didn't matter any longer. Her chest tightened the longer her gaze tangled with Charlie's. He wasn't smiling, and what called to her in that moment wasn't laughter. Promise shone in his eyes, the certainty that what burned between them was real, was hers for the taking.

Heat gathered low in her belly, her temperature rising, her breath shortened. She was grateful for the padded bra that concealed her tightened nipples, the dim lighting that hid her blush. Her idea of convincing Charlie to go dancing with her seemed ridiculous in light of the need that gripped her. Two weeks. Two weeks, and her body was already tuned to his, trained to respond to his, even from across the room.

"Sugar?" Amy's voice intruded on her thoughts, her tone indicating that she'd called Siobhan's name more than once. "Are you okay, sweetie?"

"I-I'm fine," she managed to say, trying to find her nonchalant distance instead of this weak-kneed, trembling state.

"That guy's got some serious staring mojo going on," Lola observed, her protective instinct rising. "He hasn't stopped looking at you this entire time. Do you know him or do we need to get Max to run interference for you?"

"No, you don't need to send Max over," Siobhan finally answered, her head clearing. "His name is Charlie."

Taking a deep breath, she said the words that changed everything. "He's mine."

ELEVEN

A s if he'd heard her, Charlie rose to his feet, Nadia and Kane
following. Siobhan watched him approach the stage, her
mouth watering at the way he moved, the casual confidence he
exuded.

Beside her Lola chuckled, a sexy, delighted purr of sound.
"'Bout damn time," the dark-skinned beauty laughed. "And from
the looks of things, he is well worth the wait. Damn!"

"Simmer down, Lola," Siobhan said, half-teasing, half-serious.
"Don't make me get Max after you."

"Girl, please." Lola snorted. "You've been trying to get Max
after me since you joined the troupe. He's only interested in friendship, and I'm not about to ruin our business by indulging in some
temporary pleasure."

Siobhan shook her head. Lola was a smart businesswoman,
augmenting the troupe's performances with merchandise, including
calendars and appearances at vintage car shows and other events.

Why she couldn't see how much Max wanted to be with her dumb-founded Siobhan. If she had a guy who looked at her that way, she'd—

"Ladies." Charlie stopped short of them, but though he nodded at Lola, he kept his gaze on Siobhan. "It was my first time seeing a burlesque troupe perform live, and I hope it won't be my last. Amazing show all around."

"Thank you," Lola said, then cleared her throat. Charlie's smiled deepened, but it wasn't until Lola blatantly elbowed her in the side that Siobhan realized she needed to do introductions.

"Charlie, this is Lola Fontaine, the head of Crimson Bay Bomb-shells," Siobhan said by way of introduction. "Lola, this is Charlie O'Halloran. He runs O'Halloran Business Solutions and the café is one of their clients."

"Yes, it is." Some of the heat left Charlie's eyes. He turned to Lola. "Speaking of business, one of the reasons I attended tonight's performance is because of a concept I have to advertise the café's launch of a delivery service. May I ask if the troupe is available for photo shoots and advertisement opportunities? I think it would be an excellent idea for the café to advertise their new service with photos of the troupe with classic cars or Vespas, perhaps a couple of old school bikes with baskets filled with café goodies."

Siobhan flushed as Lola gave her a look that clearly said, *What is this?* "Maybe we should talk about business some other time," Siobhan said, sure that her ears matched the color of her lipstick. "This is hardly the place."

"There's never a bad time to discuss business and this seems like a *purr-fect* opportunity to me," Lola said, easily slipping into sex-kitten mode. "Of course the troupe is available for public appear-ances and if there's a request for a particular performer, I'm sure we can make that happen. Perhaps Mr. O'Halloran should buy me a drink so that we can continue this discussion?"

Lola glanced at Siobhan. "Unless there's something else you need to do?"

Charlie faced Siobhan, question and challenge in his eyes. "What other reason besides business could I be here for?"

Siobhan parted her lips, but couldn't spit out the words. What the hell was wrong with her? Everyone standing with her already knew that she and Charlie were together. Why couldn't she say it out loud?

"Oh, for fuck's sake." Nadia took that moment to step in. "Just announce that you're seeing each other and get it over with!"

Charlie responded before Siobhan could. "This is getting awkward," he said, pulling out his wallet. He opened it, extracted a business card, then handed it to Lola. "Here's my contact information. Please give me a call sometime next week to discuss the modeling proposal. I'll get a budget from my clients and we'll go from there."

He nodded to everyone as he returned his wallet to his pocket. "Good night."

It was as if her feet were nailed to the floor. Stupid, stupid, why was she being so stupid about this? She'd already claimed Charlie to Lola. Why couldn't she say it in front of everybody?

"Siobhan," Nadia hissed as they watched Charlie head for the entrance, "surely you're not going to let him leave like that? What the hell is wrong with you?"

Nadia's words galvanized her. Siobhan hopped off the stage as quickly as her skirt would allow, then rushed after him. "Charlie, wait!"

He stopped, turned, his expression distant yet polite. "Yes?"

She didn't think. When it came to Charlie, thinking only incited her to screw things up. She acted instead, grabbing the front of his shirt and kissing him with everything she had.

To her dismay, Charlie gripped her upper arms but otherwise remained still. "Please, Charlie," she whispered against his mouth. "Please kiss me back."

"Why?" His grip tightened. "You've already put on one show tonight. They don't need another one."

Ouch. Siobhan knew she deserved Charlie's scorn, but his words still hurt. "I didn't do it for them. I did it for you."

"For me." He put space between them, his expression and tone rigid. "When we talked about me coming to watch you dance tonight, I thought it meant that you were ready to make our relationship official."

"Relationship?" Her voice squeaked. "Official?"

"Isn't that what this was about? Making this our first public appearance as a couple?"

"No." The thought made her lightheaded with panic. "No, I wasn't thinking relationship."

"Obviously." His lips twisted. "You can't even say it without freaking out. What were you thinking then? That this was the perfect time to show off your boy toy?"

She blanched. "I don't think of you that way. I haven't thought about our age difference in a long time. I just thought we were having a fling. That's all."

"A fling? I see." His expression closed. "Look, if this is only about sex for you, that's fine. We can keep it strictly physical. You just need to let me know. But if that's all this is, Siobhan, don't expect me to want to hang out with your friends when we could be at home fucking instead."

She sucked in a breath as the sharp edge of his words stabbed her deep. It would have been easy to get upset, to throw angry words back at him. But she'd created this crappy situation, and she was the one who needed to fix it.

"Charlie, I'm sorry," she blurted out. "I didn't mean to hurt your feelings. It's just—I suck at relationships. I married my high school boyfriend. We got divorced five years ago and I've spent the last four years making the café a success. That's the extent of my relationship history."

Some of the tightness around his eyes loosened. "So you're saying you're inexperienced at the whole dating thing?"

"Yes," she answered, adding a nod. "I think it's safe to say that you're better at it than I am."

His lips quirked, but she wasn't sure if it was from humor or not. "That's a given."

She waited but he didn't say anything else as the crowd thinned around them. "Since all of this is still new for me, don't you think it makes sense for us to focus on enjoying each other's company and not worry about the other stuff for a while?"

He tilted his head, his gaze steady as he regarded her. "Want to know what I think?"

Tension ramped up inside her. "I'm almost scared to ask, but tell me anyway."

"I think you should kiss me again." He stepped closer, gathered her hands and lifted them up to rest on his shoulders. "Ready when you are, Ms. Malloy."

Unsure of whether he'd forgiven her but relieved to move past their earlier difficulty, Siobhan reached up to kiss him, a tentative brush of lips. That wasn't enough for Charlie.

He switched his hold to her waist then slanted his mouth over hers, claiming her and demanding a response. Respond she did, her arms curling around his neck, her body pressing closer to his. A whimper of sound escaped her as his tongue danced with hers, making her forget where she was, that her friends were waiting. All that mattered was this man and the fire he ignited low in her belly with just one kiss.

Charlie pulled back from her, his breathing harsh as he rested his forehead against hers. "I don't want you to think I'm fetishizing you," he said in her ear, his hand dropping low on her waist, tingling the base of her spine. "But if you want to focus on the physical, fine. I have to admit that seeing you in this outfit is blowing my mind. I have a powerful urge to find the nearest dark corner and snap open the back of your skirt just enough to bend you over and slide my cock home."

"Charlie." She glanced around the club, but no one paid them any heed.

"Are you wearing the garter and stockings?"

"Yes. It's black lace."

"And are you wearing panties?"

"No." Her voice was barely a whisper. "But neither Tatas or Down Below have dark corners."

"I said I had the urge, not that I would act on it. I still have a little self-control." His lips skimmed the underside of her jaw, sending shivers coursing along her skin. "We can stay here and dry-hump each other while everyone else dances around us. Or we can race each other to your house. Last one to arrive has to come last."

She blew out a shaky breath. "You like coming last."

"What can I say? I like the feel of your pussy gripping me after you've come a couple of times. But then, I like your pussy no matter what." His hand slid down between them, but the tightness of her skirt prevented him from cupping her mound. "Shall we go get naked?"

She licked her lips, lust on the tip of her tongue as she swayed, caught between the beat and his heat. "Yes, please."

———————

Charlie gave her exactly what she wanted, and it sucked.

Siobhan sighed as she slowly came down from another orgasmic high. In the weeks following the tensions at Club Tatas, she and Charlie had focused on keeping things easy and carefree between them. It worked, and they filled their days with one pleasure after another. Well, not days exactly. More like stolen hours here and there during the week. Plenty of afternoon delights but no nights, no weekends. No invitations to spend time at his place. He'd come over, make her see stars, then leave her body satisfied but her emotions in tatters.

It didn't bother her at first. How could it? Flings didn't include plans for picnics or lazy Sunday afternoons, dinner dates or cuddling in front of the TV. Those were things people in relationships did, and she hadn't wanted a relationship. She hadn't minded until she'd suggested he stay for breakfast and head to work from her house. He'd had a perfectly plausible reason for declining that night, and the next and the one after that, but the excuses were beginning to wear thin. It was enough to make her wonder if he'd agreed to fling status so readily because he couldn't give her more even if she'd wanted it.

He slid off the bed to search for his pants. "I have to go."

"Of course you do. You say that every night." She glanced at her alarm clock. "Within thirty minutes of sex, you're headed for the door. Every time, no matter what time it is."

"Believe me, I wish I could stay." He shoved his way into his pants. "There's no greater temptation than the feel of your sexy body pressed against me. I want to stay, I really do. I can't."

"Why?" She sat up, afterglow fading. "We've been seeing each other for two months, Charlie, and you haven't stayed over once. Sure, it's the middle of the week now, but you don't even try to stay over on weekends. Why is that?"

He fastened his pants with short, sharp movements. "You told me that this is what you wanted. Something light and casual, no plans, no demands. I thought flings were about satisfying the demands of our bodies." His gaze raked her. "You look thoroughly satisfied to me."

She slid out of bed, reaching for her robe. "I didn't take you for the passive-aggressive type."

"What other type can I be when I have no idea what you want from me?" He threw his arms wide. "Do *you* have any idea what you want?"

She thought she knew what she wanted, but it seemed to change with each heartbeat. When he was with her she wanted time to slow so she could savor each moment. When they were apart she wanted time to speed up so that she could be with him again, be with him and away from the doubts that made her question herself. Question him.

"I know I don't want to fight." She shook her head, wishing she could reach for anger, but all she felt was confusion and something hovering close to hurt. "I want you, Charlie. I want more time with you, but I'm not sure it matters that I've changed my mind. You obviously need to get home to . . . something or someone, even though you said there's no one else. It's getting harder to accept that, to believe that. I'm many things, Charlie, but I'm not delusional. I'm not a home wrecker either."

"Siobhan." He stalked around the side of the bed, grabbing her shoulders. "I'm not seeing anyone else."

"All right." She didn't believe him. How could she believe him? A young stud who looked as hot as Charlie did, who owned his own business, was a prime catch. He could have his pick of women of any age. He didn't act like a man who needed to be discreet because he had someone waiting at home, but why else did he not want to stay over? "If you say so, I have no choice but believe you, right?"

His voice was a growl of warning. "Siobhan—"

"What?" A flash of anger sparked inside her. "I think it's a reasonable expectation to want my boyfriend to stay over a night or two, just as I think it's reasonable to be curious when said boyfriend refuses to do so."

His eyes glittered. "Now you want to call me your boyfriend?"

Her heart pounded against her breastbone, and not because of their sexual exertion. "I'm trying, Charlie. And you're evading."

"I'm not sneaking around." Sudden anger hardened his expression. "Just because I can't stay doesn't mean I'm going off to be with someone else."

He didn't have the right to get angry about her questioning him. "What does it mean, then?"

He clenched his jaw. Whatever his reason, it was something he didn't want to share. That had to mean it was something he was sure she wouldn't be happy hearing.

She swallowed down a shot of pain. "See? This is why we should dial this back. I won't make any claims on you. We'll be friends with an amazing list of benefits, and not worry about what each other is doing when we're not together. As long as we keep being safe—"

Breath escaped her lungs as she found herself jerked against the hard planes of his chest. She had just enough time to draw a breath before his mouth crashed down on hers. He gripped a handful of hair at the back of her head to hold her still for the most dominant, demanding kiss she'd ever received from him.

Something hot and fierce broke free inside her. She shoved his jeans down and fisted his cock. With a growl he tossed her back on the bed, fell on top of her, then entered her in one hard, thick stroke that had them both groaning aloud.

"I don't know what the fuck you're doing to me," he ground out, resting his forehead against hers. "I'm so deep into you that I can't think straight most days. I think I'm obsessed, because even when I've just had you, I want you again. I need you again. I'm always hungry for another helping of your sweetness. But you—you're always so ready to make this a casual thing when there's *nothing* casual about what's between us."

Flattening himself out above her, he grabbed her hips and proceeded to fuck her, fast and frenzied. She wrapped her legs high around his waist, biting at his bottom lip, urging him on. She loved it when he chose to submit to her, but this—this wild, domineering possession—had her mewling in the back of her throat as her body went liquid for him.

"No. One. Else," he growled with each hard slap of his body against hers. "Not for you, not for me. This is mine. Mine."

"Yes." She sank her fingernails into his back, making her own claim. "No one else."

He hissed in response, his eyes slitted with pleasure. "Fuck yeah, babe. Mark me up."

He stroked into her repeatedly, making her senseless to everything but wave after wave of sublime sensation. Up and up, conscious thought unraveling, dimly aware of her nails clawing his back as she tried to hold on, tried to contain the overwhelming pressure. All too soon it boiled up from her toes, desperate for a way out. A quick and dirty orgasm slammed into her. She bit his shoulder to muffle the scream of release as she came.

His movements grew wilder, frenzied as he grabbed her wrists, holding them over her head as he held her where he wanted her, how he wanted her for the sensual onslaught. Driving, driving, driving, his gaze unfocused, face taut with strain. All at once he convulsed then stiffened against her, a tortured groan tearing from his lips as he collapsed atop her.

After a long moment he looked down at her, trembling, breath sawing harshly past his lips. Then he rolled away from her and onto his back, covering his eyes with his arm. "Shit."

Alarm sparked inside her. Concerned, she reached out to touch his shoulder but he flinched and moved away, sitting up on the opposite side of the bed. "Charlie, what's wrong?"

"What's wrong?" He shoved a hand through his hair as he cursed again, looking back toward her without meeting her gaze. "We didn't use a condom."

"I'm protected, from pregnancy at least." She scooted off the bed to rise to her feet, pulling her robe closed. "Do I need to go get tested for other stuff?"

A frown pulled at his features as he regained his feet, fastening his pants before reaching for his shirt. "You probably should, if only so it will ease your mind that I'm not some whore-dog dipping my dick into every available hole I can."

She flinched. "I didn't put it like that."

"You didn't have to. It's what you're thinking, isn't it? You think I'm cheating on you, cheating on something you don't even want to acknowledge as a relationship."

Siobhan fisted her robe closed at her throat. "You're angry."

"Angry that you doubt me, when I've all but got your name tattooed on my dick." He stepped into his shoes. "I might even be angry that this is feeling entirely lopsided. I mean, I know that this is only about sex for you, but sometimes it seems like it doesn't matter who the guy is behind the dick as long as you get it."

"It matters." God damn, it fucking hurt to know she'd hurt him like this. "I swear it matters, it matters that it's you. You, Charlie."

She reached out, but didn't touch him. "This intensity between us is strange and scary. I'm out of my depth here and I don't know what to do about it. It was silly of me to think I could keep this light and only focused on sex. I want more with you, I just . . ."

She sighed, lowering her hand. "I'm not as together as you think I am."

His hooded gaze settled on her. "You've got a story too."

"Yes."

"Is that why you've been fighting this? Fighting us?"

Her throat closed up, so tight that she could only give him a nod in response.

"Okay." He crossed to her, gathering her hands to place kisses in her palms. "Okay, so we both have things we need to tell each other. There's something I need to do first. Give me a couple of days. I'll come pick you up, take you out to dinner. I'll tell you what's going on with me, and you'll tell me what's going on with you. We'll clear the air, I promise. And then we'll move forward."

Doubt shaded his eyes. "I need to know that we're okay, though. Are we okay right now?"

"Yes." It wasn't the whole truth, but it was close enough. At that moment they were as copacetic as the circumstances would allow. What she didn't know, couldn't predict, was where things would stand after they'd finished their talk.

TWELVE

I t was time to come clean.

Acid churned in Charlie's gut as he pulled into the garage and killed the engine. He hadn't wanted to leave Siobhan's side, her bed, but he had no choice. Responsibility was something he took very seriously. The consequences of not being responsible meant losing everything that mattered most, and he had no intention of being threatened with that level of loss again if he could help it. Pitting everything he held dear against a few stolen moments of pleasure . . . there was no contest.

His knuckles whitened as he gripped the steering wheel. God damn him, those moments were some of the best he'd experienced in a long time. Siobhan was everything he could want in a woman—smart, sexy, comfortable in her skin and the bedroom. She had no problem with telling him what she wanted from him in bed, and she sometimes didn't tell him—she just took what she wanted. Holy fuck, that was hot, and it made him want to give her whatever she wanted, whatever she needed. It didn't mean he was pussy-whipped—he took the lead as much as she did, and she got off on it just as much. Holding her hips while she rode him was just as hot as holding her hair while he fucked her mouth.

His head thumped against the headrest as his cock thickened yet again. Siobhan tied him up in knots. He hadn't allowed himself to want something, want someone, in years. All his desires went into achieving his goals and proving to everyone that he could do the impossible. His own pleasures and desires had been shunted aside. Before Siobhan, sexual satisfaction had been limited to hand jobs and the occasional one-night stand. He hadn't had a real relationship since college, and that one had dried up shortly after his parents had died and his life briefly went to hell.

Now . . . now, all he could think of were Siobhan's blue eyes blown wide with sensual overload, with orgasms that gripped his cock or his fingers so sweetly. Her soft curves revealed under his hands as he stripped her of her lingerie, her breathy moans, and the sweetest pussy he'd ever tasted. He wanted it, wanted more of it, wanted it every chance he could get it. Now that she'd finally admitted she wanted more than casual hookups from him, his chances were in jeopardy if he didn't come clean with her.

The doubt in her eyes tore at him. He'd done everything he could think of to let her know unequivocally that he didn't have another lover—everything except tell her the truth. His plan called for that moment of truth to arrive later since there were other hurdles they needed to jump over. What he hadn't counted on, though, was getting so close so fast. Hadn't counted on this intensity morphing into possessiveness, the desire to claim and take.

A cool head was what had gotten him through the hardest months of his life. Logic, methodology, planning, executing at the right time—those were the keys to a successful life and he applied those keys to every situation. Siobhan, however, wasn't a situation. She was so much more, and he had a feeling she'd challenge every single one of his hard-earned rules if he truly wanted to claim her and keep her.

Charlie stayed in the car for a while longer, contemplating his options, possible actions and reactions. Dodging and evading would only make Siobhan more suspicious. She was skittish enough already. His assurances that he wasn't going behind her back didn't mean jack shit if he continued being unable to stay with her longer than a couple of hours. He didn't want to ruin his chances with Siobhan just when the possibility of more took another step closer to reality. The fucked-up thing was, the reason for his early farewells wasn't the biggest secret he had to tell her.

The door leading from the garage into the house opened, and a dark blonde head peeked out. "Hey, what are you doing sitting in the garage? You do know that if you want to end it all you have to keep the car running and actually close the garage door, don't you?"

"Not funny, Lorelei," he said as he exited the car. "You're not getting rid of me that easily. Are the boys okay? They're not mad I missed dinner, are they?"

"The boys are fine." She hit the button to close the garage door, then stepped back so he could enter the kitchen. "I think they'll survive you missing one cheeseburger macaroni night. I gave them another hour of gaming. They're in heaven."

She stepped back so he could enter the mudroom. "What about you? Are you okay?"

"I'm fine," he replied automatically. Lorelei asked that question more and more often. Was he losing his edge, not doing as good a job as he used to in convincing her and the boys that he was okay? He was, truly. At least she didn't ask him things like was he happy, did he have regrets. He could evade, but he didn't want to lie.

Lorelei sighed. "Charlie, you forget I'm an adult now. I can drive, I can vote, and I'll be able to drink in a couple of years. You can stop blowing smoke up my ass when I ask how you're doing."

"Watch your mouth, young lady," he retorted with as much sternness as he could muster, which wasn't much at that moment. She'd busted him, which she had an uncanny ability to do lately. Something to do with deciding to be a psychology major, which meant he was going to be in serious trouble.

"I'll watch mine if you watch yours." She reached out, rubbed a thumb across the corner of his mouth. "Rose-colored lipstick. You've been holding out on me."

Well, hell. "You got me." He dropped his bag on the kitchen table then scrubbed at his mouth with the back of his hand. "I guess it's time for a family meeting. Will you go get Kyle and Finn?"

Lorelei arched a brow. "This is gonna be good. I'll be right back." She hurried off.

Charlie opened the fridge, wishing that he had an emergency beer hidden in the kitchen. Instead he decided to live dangerously by pouring a tall glass of milk. As he reached for the bottle of chocolate sauce, his mind immediately went to an image of Siobhan's breasts, her rosy nipples pearling as he dribbled warm fudge sauce over them. It was the best damn dessert he'd ever had.

God damn him, he had it bad. Already the thought of no longer having the opportunity to sample Siobhan's curves and sexual appetite made his pits sweaty. But if he wanted to keep her, he'd have to tell her the truth. He'd have to tell her that while he didn't have another woman in his bed, he did have a family.

Just as he had to tell his family about Siobhan. He didn't know which would be harder.

Taking a long pull of his chocolate milk, Charlie joined the others in the den, the room where all their family meetings took place. Most had been good meetings as they'd discussed their plans for the future, but some had been bad. Really bad, and those were the ones that had been ingrained on the boys. Sixteen-year-old Kyle looked so much like their serious architect father that it was difficult to look at him sometimes without remembering the loss. Thirteen-year-old Finn had the ready grin and happy disposition of their elementary school teacher mother. All of them were shades of blond like their parents, but the boys had their father's brown eyes while he and Lorelei had shades of their mother's blue.

Kyle stood with his hands clenched at his sides, body tensed as if ready to absorb a blow. Though Lorelei had stumbled through adolescence without their mother to help her, Kyle had taken the greatest emotional hit of losing their parents. During that first year when Charlie had had to fight everyone to keep the family together, Kyle had suffered nightmares and separation anxiety that had stolen his lighthearted personality. He'd gotten better mostly because they'd banded together, them against the world, but it didn't take much for Kyle to stress over the possibility of the family breaking up.

"What happened?" Kyle asked, his voice tight. "Is everything all right?"

"Everything's fine," Charlie assured them. "There's just something I wanted to let you guys know about."

"What is it?"

"Charlie's got a girlfriend, Charlie's got a girlfriend," Lorelei sang, breaking the news before he could.

"Ugh," Finn said, adding an eye roll for good measure. "A girl? That's it?"

"Yeah, that's it." Figures his youngest brother would have that reaction. Since he didn't want Finn to be interested in girls until his youngest brother turned thirty, Charlie could live with Finn's less than enthusiastic response. "I've been seeing her for a little while now, and I thought it was time to tell you guys."

"Finally," Lorelei said with a wide smile. "We figured something was going on when you went out on a Saturday night—twice—but you never said anything. Kyle and I thought you were aiming for sainthood or something."

His continued bachelorhood was a common joke with his sister and Kyle ever since he'd had "the talk" with them. "You guys are far too interested in that stuff. Besides, all of you are entertaining enough as it is."

"Yeah, right." Lorelei rolled her eyes. "Not as entertaining as a woman who's not related to you."

"Lorelei," Charlie said in warning, glancing at Finn. He'd yet to have the uncomfortable birds-and-bees talk with Finn and he wanted to delay that conversation for a while longer if he could help it. Like until the next millennium.

"Don't be stingy, give us the deets," Lorelei demanded. "Who is she, what's her name, what does she do?"

Charlie relaxed a fraction, smiling as thoughts of Siobhan filled his mind. "Her name is Siobhan Malloy. She co-owns Sugar and Spice Café just off the square downtown."

"Hey, I've been in there on study breaks," Lorelei piped up. "Which one is she? The blonde or the brunette?"

"The blonde."

"Wow." Lorelei sighed. "I love her style, and she's really pretty."

"I think she's beautiful inside and out."

"A looker and a cooker." Lorelei gave him a fist bump. "Good going, bro."

Kyle perked up. "She cooks?"

Kyle had taken over kitchen duties when he was twelve almost in self-defense since Charlie's repertoire was limited to heating frozen meals and Lorelei had a tendency to burn lettuce. "She does. She makes all her soups from scratch and they make their own bread and desserts too. I've done some marketing work for them. They source everything locally, so it's all fresh and delicious."

"Is she nice?" Finn asked, deciding to join the familial interrogation.

Charlie nodded. "Very nice, very friendly. I've seen her calm down irate customers with just a smile."

"Does she like kids?" Kyle went straight to the heart of the issue as usual.

"I haven't asked her about kids, so I don't know." Charlie mentally kicked himself. That was something that should have come up earlier, but he and Siobhan had focused more on the sex than asking personal questions.

"Have you told her about us?"

"That's the point of this family meeting, I wanted to let you guys know about her first. I want to tell her about you guys. If that goes over well, I thought it would be good to invite her over one night or maybe on a Saturday so you all can meet. We could have a cookout."

"A cookout would be a great idea," Lorelei said. "Less stressful for everybody."

She meant less stressful for Kyle, who'd already folded his arms about himself, his thin face screwed up in concentration, no doubt planning what he could cook to impress a woman who owned her own café.

Finn looked from Kyle to Charlie, his usual open expression pensive. "Do you think she'll like us?"

"How can she not like you?" Charlie joked, ruffling his youngest brother's hair. "You guys are great—when you're not yanking my chain, that is."

"What if she doesn't?" Kyle asked.

God, this was why he didn't date. He didn't want to get anyone's hopes up—not his, not his date's, and especially not his siblings'. It was just easier to avoid any potential heartache and hard feelings by not looking for anything beyond sex. Siobhan was different though. At least, he fervently hoped so.

"If she doesn't like you guys, I stop seeing her," he promised. "It's that simple."

"But—"

"That's not open for debate," Charlie cut in. "We're a package deal until all of you guys are out of the house and on your own, preferably with college degrees in hand. Even then, we're family. Family matters most. If she doesn't like you guys, she's not someone I'm interested in seeing long term. End of story."

His stomach churned at the thought. Siobhan had told him that she'd married her high school sweetheart but that they'd gotten divorced. Why? There was a reason why Siobhan remained single and childless at thirty-five, a reason he hadn't bothered to uncover as he pursued her. What if she didn't like kids? Was that part of the story she had to tell him?

Finn stared down at his ever-present tablet while Kyle hugged himself tighter. Even Lorelei looked subdued. "Come on, guys. We'll cross that bridge when we come to it, all right? There's nothing to worry about. She's good people and I'm sure she'll be thrilled to meet you. Now, how about we get a game in before bedtime? You guys have garden duty tomorrow, which means we all need to be up before the heat rises."

The boys groaned as they usually did, but it was halfhearted at best. Charlie lost handily, but his mind wasn't on the game. No, he had a much larger game he had to play, one with much higher stakes that he couldn't afford to lose.

"He actually got insulted when I questioned his habit of fucking and ducking." Siobhan slapped a lump of dough into a loaf shape with more force than necessary.

"Why would you question it?" Nadia asked from her side of the kitchen. "I thought that was what you wanted?"

"It is. It was. The sex, hell yeah. The evasiveness? Not so much." She beat the dough into shape again. "He claims to have a good reason for it and that reason has nothing to do with being involved with someone else. What it *does* mean, I have no idea. Maybe he needs to dispose of the bodies in his cellar or something."

"I'm pretty sure that isn't true," Nadia said soothingly as she inserted loaves into baking pans for proofing. "Besides, how many houses in Crimson Bay have cellars anyway?"

"Very funny." Siobhan slammed the dough scraper down,

dividing the dough in half. She'd come in earlier than normal because even though Charlie had worn her body out, her mind kept racing into the wee hours. "I couldn't sleep because my mind kept coming up with these outlandish scenarios, and the later it got, the wilder my imagination became."

Nadia took the scraper away. "Maybe you should stay away from edged implements for a bit, and help me stage the dough for the proofer."

"Fine." Siobhan noted the different varieties for sandwiches and soup bowls. Business had picked up post–Independence Day, thanks to the soft launch of their delivery service. Who wouldn't want to stay inside on a hot summer day and have someone else bring a meal to them? "Anything to take my mind off the thought that he's got a wife and kids at home or he's in one of those complicated deals where they're separated but still sharing the house."

"Or maybe he's Batman."

Siobhan racked a sheet of baking pans. "He's not Batman, this isn't Gotham, and you aren't helping."

"Just trying to lighten the mood." Nadia opened their proofer so that Siobhan could roll the rack of breads inside. "I'm pretty sure you have nothing to worry about."

"If it's nothing, he would have told me already, wouldn't he?" She choked her ever-present hand towel in a death grip. "Anyway, he made a very convincing argument that he's not seeing anyone else."

"I guess he did," Nadia said, pushing Siobhan's collar back to reveal a nice-sized hickey. "Rocked your world, huh? Is that gonna be faded by the time you have to dance again?"

Siobhan fought a blush. Charlie had a way of making her flustered even when he wasn't around. "I'm pretty sure they'll be gone by the time I have to perform. If not, that's what stage makeup is for."

"They? As in, more than one?"

"A couple." Siobhan shrugged. "We both got a little territorial yesterday. His back looked like he'd been flogged, poor guy. Anyway, he made his case clear. There's no way Charlie's got anything left in the tank by the time we part ways, especially when he went all alpha male claiming his woman. It was so emotional it was scary."

Nadia's expression grew thoughtful as they began cleaning their prep area. "Why is that scary?"

"It's scary because it makes me off balance. I feel like I'm a teenager again, all nervous and fluttery and giddy. I like the way he makes me feel, and that's the scariest thing of all. Then there's this talk he wants to have. Obviously it's a game changer in his mind." She sighed. "It also means that I have to have the talk with him too."

"The talk . . . ? Oh, no." Nadia's eyes widened. "You haven't told him about rehab yet?"

"Not about rehab or anything that led up to it," Siobhan confessed. "I haven't even told him about Colleen yet. I didn't tell him I was divorced until that night at Club Tatas."

Siobhan stopped scraping at the flour covering her prep counter. "When did you tell Kane about your stint in rehab?"

"The first night," the brunette said with a guilty flush. "If it was going to be a deal breaker, I wanted to know up front."

"God." Siobhan's stomach soured like fermenting dough. "Apparently I screwed that up too."

"Come on, Siobhan, don't be so hard on yourself. My situation with Kane was different. If I didn't have the cooking show credentials and the very public, tabloid-fodder flameout, I wouldn't have told him that soon."

"You wouldn't have waited two months either," Siobhan pointed out.

"I would have waited until I started having feelings for him, until the relationship was more about the person than just the sex." Nadia placed a comforting hand on Siobhan's arm. "If that's where you are, then now's the right time."

Siobhan had to face up to it. Despite her attempts not to, she was becoming emotionally attached to Charlie. After her divorce, the stint in rehab, and the deterioration of her relationship with her daughter and the rest of her family, Siobhan had given up any thought of having a close personal relationship again. Eventually she'd weaned herself off the need for that sort of emotional connection, the same as she'd flushed the drugs from her system. She'd bonded with Nadia, and through supporting each other in rehab, had been absorbed into Nadia's family. It gave her an emotional connection but she still kept a shield up out of self-preservation, not wanting to let anyone close enough to influence her heart.

Until Charlie. He was gorgeous, funny, wickedly sexy. Being with him was easy and comfortable and exhilarating. It filled a space inside her she'd long ago walled off. Everything she hadn't been looking for but secretly wished she could have.

It couldn't go anywhere, she knew that. Not long term. While her mind knew that, accepted that, other parts of her still wanted more. Those parts were the ones badgered by Charlie's reluctance to stay over, to linger in the post-sex haze that nurtured the seeds of a relationship. His secret, whatever it was, hounded her and kept her from enjoying the right-now-ness of being with him.

She'd hear what he had to tell her, whenever he decided to tell her. Then she'd tell him about her past and hope that he cared enough to want to continue being with her.

"We're meeting tomorrow night," she told Nadia. "He's going to tell me his big secret and if it's something I can live with, I'm going to tell him mine."

"If it goes south, you call me, all right?"

"Kane's taking you away for a romantic getaway, remember? I can't ask you to interrupt that to handle my issues."

"Then it's a good thing you don't have to ask." Nadia gave her a hug. "We're here for each other, through thick and thin, hell and high water, and all the other old sayings. I think Charlie's a pretty understanding guy, though. It might take him a minute or two, but I know he'd come around. Especially when you consider how gone he is on you."

"I hope you're right."

"Me too. If I have to go Sweeney Todd on him, you're going to have to use the café as collateral for bail money."

THIRTEEN

The doorbell rang at six p.m. Friday on the dot. Siobhan opened the door to find Charlie on her doorstep, dressed in a navy suit and holding a bouquet of scarlet tulips. He also wore an expression more suited to attending a funeral than going out on a date.

"Thank you," she said, accepting the bouquet and a kiss to the cheek before stepping back to allow him over the threshold. Her nerves skittered like water droplets on a hot skillet. Charlie's somber expression was so at odds with his normally ebullient personality that she knew whatever he wanted to tell her, she wouldn't like.

Her stomach bubbled. Then again, what she had to tell him was probably something he wouldn't like.

"Charlie." She touched his shoulder. "Judging by the expression on your face and the suit you're wearing, we're about to have a very serious conversation. Let's not waste the time or money going to a restaurant staring at food that we're probably not going to have the appetite to eat."

He made an effort to shake his mood, giving her a shadow of his usual smile. "It would be a shame not to show you off. You look beautiful."

She looked down at her vintage-cut navy sundress scattered with white polka dots. "Thank you. We'll just have to show off some other time," she said, hoping it was true. If her conversation with Charlie turned sour, there probably wouldn't be any second chances, and she didn't want any witnesses to their breakup.

"If you want, we can order Chinese or Thai," she suggested. "Or I could make a quick stir-fry with some of the veggies I brought in from my garden."

Charlie's somber expression didn't change, though he did loosen his tie. "I'll order the Thai so you don't have to go through any trouble," he decided, pulling out his cell phone. "At the very least, it'll make a good wine delivery system."

Siobhan paused, turning back to stare at him. Charlie rarely drank, even when they went out, and was known to nurse a bottle of beer for an entire night. "You want some wine?"

He gave her a rueful smile. "I know, right? Me, needing liquid courage. In this instance, I think it will be good for both of us. It'll also give me something to do with my hands."

"All right. I'll go put the flowers in water, then get some wine." She headed for the kitchen.

She pulled a clear vase from beneath the kitchen sink and filled it partway with water while Charlie placed their order, remembering her favorite without asking. It was those little things that lured her, made her vulnerable when she couldn't afford to be. Couldn't let her imagination run wild with thoughts of what could be. Couldn't allow that damned emotion called hope to gain a foothold.

"They said the order will be here in less than thirty," Charlie announced as he entered the kitchen. Though he still wore the loosened tie, he'd forgone the lightweight jacket. She was struck anew by how gorgeous he was, the golden-haired surfer god who could be wonderful, wicked, or both simultaneously. He made her feel wanted, appreciated, valued. He made her feel, period.

As he did now, wrapping her in his arms and drawing her close. Being hugged by Charlie was like sitting on the beach after sunset, wrapped in a blanket staring into a fire with a circle of friends gathered around. As if nothing and no one could hurt her. All illusion, she knew, but she indulged the fantasy anyway, shutting out everything but Charlie.

Murmuring her name, he kissed her forehead, her cheek, then claimed her lips in a move no less consuming for its softness. She opened for him, her body warming, her blood surging. Their tongues danced as their bodies pressed together, seeking comfort, needing release.

Still kissing, she hiked up her skirt to remove her panties while he worked to open his pants, freeing his ready cock. No words, no foreplay beyond the intoxicating kisses, he palmed her behind, lifting her up before bracing her against the kitchen island. Clutching his shoulders, she wrapped her legs around his waist as he used one hand to fit his erection to her opening, then pushed inside.

She moaned against his mouth as he filled her so sweetly, so completely, moving inside her with sure, strong strokes. Not a wild, frenzied coupling but no less world-shattering, this wasn't solely about giving and receiving pleasure. This was about giving and receiving comfort, about emotion, about connection. This was exactly what she needed, and she knew he needed it too.

Reaching between their rocking bodies, she began to massage her clit, knowing he wouldn't come until she did. He moaned against her lips, his fingers tightened on her buttocks, his eyes closed as he lost himself to sensation. In that moment he was beautiful. Her breath caught, her heart thudded, then her channel clamped down on him as an orgasm swept her up and knocked her foundation away. Swiveling his hips, he rocked against her, then stiffened, groaning her name as he flooded her core.

Torn apart and floundering, she buried her face into the crook of his neck as she tried to pull herself back from the emotional drop-off. His hand moved on her back in comforting circles. "Ah, sweetheart, what is this?"

He pulled back enough to look at her. Alarm darkened his eyes as he thumbed at the tears on her cheeks. "Why are you crying?"

"I don't know," she managed to say. "It was just so, so—"

"Yeah, I know," he said, giving her a last kiss before stepping back from her, his gaze warm on her face as he tucked himself back in and straightened his clothing. "That's how I know it's going to be all right. As long as you're with me, everything will fall into place. I refuse to accept any other outcome."

His conviction encouraged her. "Charlie, I—"

The doorbell rang. "Perfect timing. At least we came before dinner did." He gave her a wry grin as he quickly washed his hands. "I'll get the door if you want to take a moment, okay?"

His thoughtfulness almost set her off again, but she nodded, hopped off the counter, and headed for her bedroom, hope filling her. They would have their talk and they would work through it. If he believed it, she'd believe it too.

Hope, that fragile, fickle emotion, only hung around until the end of dinner.

Siobhan pushed back from the dining table, her wineglass cradled in one hand. Dinner had been good, the company was even better, but as afterglow faded, their thoughts intruded. By the time Siobhan put her fork down, two glasses of wine and a knot of nerves battled it out in her stomach. "What is it that you need to tell me, Charlie?"

He picked up his wineglass, stared at it a moment, then set it back down. His gaze settled on hers. "I have a family."

Shock punched her, followed swiftly by profound hurt then burgeoning anger. "You told me there was no one else. I asked you point-blank, and you said no. *You said no*, Charlie."

"I'm not seeing anyone else, Siobhan. Not married, not dating, not divorced." He reached for her free hand, but she slid it into her lap. "Please hear me out."

"Fine." She set her glass back down, folding her arms across her chest. "Go ahead. I'm all ears, ready to hear about this family of yours."

"I'm raising my sister, Lorelei, and my two brothers, Kyle and Finn."

She blinked, then blinked again. "You . . . you're raising them on your own?"

"Yes. Lorelei's just starting college. Kyle's in high school and Finn's in middle school. It's been just us for the last eight years."

Brothers and a sister, not a wife and children. Her shoulders re-laxed as she breathed out, and Charlie imitated her movements, his features easing by slow degrees. "What happened to your parents?"

"Bridge collapse." He tried to shrug it off, but she could see that the loss still lingered with him. "I pretty much put my life on hold so I could take care of the others."

She mentally did the math. He was thirty now, which meant he'd been twenty-two when he became the head of his family. She'd been the mother of a four-year-old at twenty-two, but her ex-husband had taken a while to adjust to fatherhood. She couldn't imagine what it must have been like for a fun-loving, gregarious guy like Charlie to suddenly have his social life impeded by having to step up to take care of his siblings. "That had to be difficult for you," she said softly, her heart twisting for his younger self.

He waved her compassion away. "I did what I had to do to keep us together. We've had good times and bad times, but we're to-gether, and that's what matters. I'd do it again, no regrets."

"So the reason you don't stay over is . . . ?"

"Finn has occasional nightmares and Kyle has anxiety issues," he explained. "When they were little, I promised them that I would always be home before they went to bed. Now that they're older and I'm running my own company, I promised that at the very least I'd be there when they wake up in the morning. I haven't broken that promise yet."

Siobhan didn't ask how he'd been able to keep that promise to his brothers. She knew, because she'd experienced it before. Early dates and dinner, then he'd leave. Either his partners had to accept it or they'd give him an ultimatum. She knew without a doubt he'd choose his family. He'd done that the day his parents had died.

"Why didn't you tell me this before?"

"Several reasons. I wanted to give us a chance. I wanted to get to know you and I wanted you to know me. You already had issues with my age, Siobhan. You probably would have thought I only wanted you because I thought you'd be a good replacement mother, instead of because you're the hottest woman I've ever seen."

"You're probably right." She gave him a rueful smile, then cocked her head. "Did you think I'd break up with you because you're taking care of your brothers and sister?"

"Other women would. My girlfriend at the time bailed right after my parents' funeral. My other attempts at dating women my age went the same. They were interested in a single, good-looking guy running his own business until they realized I wasn't going to hang out in the club because my youngest brother has the flu."

Old hurt and anger tightened his shoulders. Maybe Charlie's age was less than hers, but he had had more than enough life experience, experience that could have left him bitter. She reached for him then, wrapping a hand around his. "You're an amazing man, Charlie O'Halloran."

He gave her a searching look. "So it doesn't bother you that I'm the legal guardian for my siblings?"

"Of course not. It says a lot about your character."

"Is it saying anything good?"

"Definitely."

The smile he gave her, true and wide and relieved, made her want to do cartwheels. "I told them about you last night. I'd like for you to meet them."

Uncertainty bubbled up inside her. "Meet your family?"

He nodded. "Would you be interested in coming over this coming

Saturday for a cookout? Just a low-pressure get-together, though I have to warn you—Kyle will talk your ear off about food. He loves to cook."

"Speaking of family . . ." She hesitated. She hated this part. This was the point at which people began to look at her differently, as if she were a failure or otherwise beneath them for being so weak. She knew what she was, what she had been. She knew exactly what she'd overcome, what she'd moved beyond. Yet she also knew that sometimes people couldn't see past the failure to the success she'd earned. "It's my turn to make a confession."

He faced her, his expression open and neutral. "Do you have brothers and sisters secretly living in your spare bedroom?"

"No, I'm an only child," she answered, smiling at his attempt at a joke. "You know I have an ex-husband. What I didn't tell you is that I also have a daughter."

His expression blanked. "You . . . have a daughter."

"Yes." She ignored the twinge of pain whenever she thought of her child. "Her name is Colleen. She's the same age as your sister. Eighteen, and she just graduated high school."

She could see the wheels turning in his mind, assessing what she'd told him. "So you were pregnant when you were a senior in high school?"

She nodded, looking down at their still-entwined hands. "I had her just after graduation."

"She doesn't live with you?"

"No." A breath of a word. "My ex-husband was awarded sole custody."

Surprise lifted his brows, and she could well imagine his thoughts. Mothers were the usual recipients of a grant of custody, even in

California. Only in extreme circumstances would a father sue for sole custody and be successful at it. "Your ex got sole custody? Not joint?"

"Not joint." With her free hand she reached for her wine again, wishing it were something stronger.

He tilted his head, those blue-green eyes studying her. "Did you try to contest the decision?"

"I couldn't." She took a healthy swallow of her wine, set the glass back down, then picked up the bottle to refresh her glass. "I was in a court-appointed in-patient drug rehabilitation program when my husband filed for divorce and received an emergency grant of sole custody."

He sat back, pulling his hand free of hers. "Drug rehabilitation? You were an addict?"

He probably didn't realize that he'd put distance between them, but she did. The rejection, however unconscious, stung. "Prescription drugs," she explained, like that made it any better. "A combination of pain meds and sleep aids."

"Wait." He frowned, stunned, obviously struggling to under-stand. "You said it was court appointed. Why?"

She looked down, startled to find herself digging her fingernails into her thigh. She smoothed a hand down her skirt, trying to smooth out her nerves. This was it. This was the moment that would change things. Even a great guy like Charlie, a guy who talked about raising his siblings alone like it was no big deal, wouldn't be able to accept what she'd done. He'd get up, walk out, and she'd go back to her life while trying to console herself with the fact that at least it had been fun while it lasted.

"Siobhan." His tone was as flat as his expression. "Why was the court involved? Why did you lose custody of your daughter?"

"Because I was going to be charged with child endangerment unless I agreed to go to in-patient treatment."

He sucked in a breath but she dropped her gaze, too cowardly to see the shock and probable horror that no doubt sheathed his features. She swallowed. She knew she should explain, but explaining didn't make it better. Explaining didn't change the past. Instead she waited for him to say something, anything to indicate what he thought of her story.

"Maybe you should tell me everything."

The usual humor and warmth that lined his voice had vanished as if it never existed. She fought the minute urge to slump down in her chair and the greater urge to upend the wine bottle and retreat to her bedroom. Running away was counterproductive to her ongoing recovery. She had to face her past and Charlie's scorn head-on, no matter how painful it was.

"I already told you that I was pregnant with my daughter when I graduated," she said into the tense silence. "I married my high school boyfriend right after, then watched my new husband go off and join the army, leaving me with his parents and mine, none of whom were thrilled with the idea of being grandparents so soon."

Understatement of the year. Her straitlaced father had declared that she'd brought shame to the Malloy name and had all but stopped talking to her. After she'd become a drug addict, he wouldn't even allow her to come to the house.

"I moved in with my grandmother Mary Katherine," she continued. "The last trimester of my pregnancy was difficult and the labor was even worse. I was in constant pain, so much so that I could barely function. On top of that, I suffered postpartum depression, though everyone seemed to think it was all in my head, or that I was lonely without Mike, or I was just a hormonal eighteen-year-old overwhelmed with being a new mother. The bottom line is that I was misdiagnosed, given a prescription for pain and more prescriptions to help me sleep and to combat my fatigue. It got to the point where I needed the cocktail of pills, more and more pills just to keep up with parenting, keep up the appearances of having my crap together.

"My grandmother realized my problem, God rest her soul. When Mike came home for good I was able to get some help. With their support, I completed a treatment program and got clean."

"I thought you said he filed for divorce."

She glanced up. Charlie stared at her, his blue eyes remote. The judge who'd sent her to rehab had shown more warmth. "That was later," she explained, adding to the evidence against her. "We had seven good years. We were a happy family. My husband and my daughter loved me and I loved them. Then my grandmother died and while I was trying to come to grips with that I got sideswiped coming home from the grocery store."

She fiddled with her wineglass but didn't drink again. "I was so glad Colleen wasn't in the car with me. I wasn't seriously injured but got wrenched around a bit. I tried . . . I tried not to turn to the pills but the pain was too much. When I took them, I could function. I could be a wife to Mike. I could be a mother to Colleen. I could pretend that I was normal, that I was fine, that I wasn't crumbling on the inside. Mike and Colleen deserved the best me, and I thought the best me was found in Percocet and OxyContin."

She sighed. "You get to a breaking point though. Mine came two years later. My tolerance had increased so I needed more pills. One day I misjudged what I'd already had in my system and had another cocktail of pills with a vodka chaser while preparing dinner. I started a grease fire. Colleen managed to run to a neighbor's for help. When the paramedics realized I was a walking medicine cabinet, I was taken into custody."

Shame swamped her. "Apparently I wasn't as good an actress as I'd thought. Colleen, my sweet girl, told Mike all manner of things I wasn't even aware of. Everything came out in the open then, and it proved to be the final straw for everyone. Mike filed for divorce and full custody. The judge ordered me into a ninety-day in-patient treatment program and only upon successful completion could I have supervised visits with Colleen. Unfortunately, by the time I finished treatment neither my daughter nor my parents would speak to me. Mike would only communicate through his lawyer. The only reason I wasn't completely alone was because I met Nadia in rehab and we bonded."

"Nadia? Your partner, Nadia?"

"Yes. She and her family took me in and I will be forever grateful to them for giving me a support network. We keep each other grounded and honest and clean. She was a celebrity chef, and cooking was the one thing I was good at doing. We both needed a fresh start, needed away from LA, and decided Crimson Bay was as good a place as any. Nadia had money that her fathers had invested for her and I had a small inheritance from my grandmother that no one else could touch. We came up with the idea to open a café, got our therapist to sign off on the idea, and moved here. Four years later, here we are."

She looked at him and immediately wished she hadn't. Anger suffused his cheeks, the tips of his ears. "What about your daughter?" he ground out.

"I try. I don't succeed," she said, the simple statement undercutting the complicated relationship Siobhan had with her daughter. God, she hated to think about this, rehash this. It only brought the pain roaring back, pain she had no defense against. "The last time we were face-to-face was two years ago when I hired her to work part-time in the café for the summer so we could spend time together. It didn't go well and she hasn't voluntarily spoken to me since. I attempted to see her at her graduation a few weeks ago but I wasn't able to. I'll still try, though. She's my daughter and I still love her."

She darted a look at him. "What are you thinking?"

"I'm too stunned to think." He scrubbed a hand down his face. "This is a lot to take in."

"I know. You thought you were dating a café owner. Now you know you're dating a café owner who used to be a pill-head and likes to strip for fun. You need to decide if you could or should expose your family to that. To me."

"Yes." He looked directly at her. "Why didn't you tell me this before now?"

"For the same reasons you waited to tell me about your family. Once I realized this was serious, I knew I had to tell you."

He rubbed at his forehead. "I need some time to process it all."

"Of course." Her heart sank. There was no way he'd allow her to meet his family now. Even after he thought things through, she doubted he'd want her anywhere near his siblings.

She rose. "I guess this is as good a time as any to say good night."

"Yeah." He stood and then headed for the front door, stopping to grab his jacket on the way. He opened the door then stopped, turning to her. "You do understand why I have to think about this, don't you?"

She straightened her shoulders. "Yes I do, and if you decide this is something you don't want to expose your family to, I'll understand. We'll still be friends, and you can send someone else to wrap up the delivery portal project."

"Siobhan . . ."

She leaned over to kiss his cheek. "Good night, Charlie," she said, knowing that she meant good-bye. The way he turned and headed for his car without another word telegraphed clearly that he meant it as good-bye as well.

FOURTEEN

adia's weekend getaway lasted until Tuesday morning, giving Siobhan plenty of time to work through her breakup with Charlie without an audience. Unfortunately, Tuesday steamrolled around, bringing not only Nadia back, but Bitch Talk as well.

"So, Nadia," Audie began with a knowing smirk, "how was the weekend? Anything you want to tell us?"

"Yeah, you've been as jumpy as a cat in a room full of rocking chairs around here," Siobhan added. "I thought for sure I'd come in to find you wearing a little something-something on your left hand."

"All of you know that if I had an engagement ring, I wouldn't be wearing it while I'm baking," Nadia chided. She reached into the neck of her shirt, pulled out a glittering necklace. "I'd wear it on a chain until Bitch Talk!"

Siobhan's heart stopped. "You're engaged?" she asked, wanting to know for sure. "For real?"

Nadia's grin split her face. "Kane asked me last night. For real!"

"Oh my God!" With a squeal of delight, Siobhan engulfed her best friend in a hug. "Oh, this is awesome. I'm so happy for you!"

Laughing, crying, and laughing some more, Vanessa and Audie joined in the hug-fest. They watched as Nadia slipped the platinum halo-style diamond ring onto her left hand so they could all get a better look as she recounted the sunset proposal.

"I thought Kane was going to propose on the trip, either in Seattle or when we went over to Victoria, British Columbia," Nadia told them, bouncing in her seat. "So when we'd get to these beautiful spots, I'd wait, but he never proposed. I put it out of my mind and just enjoyed the time away, which was exactly what he'd planned, sneaky devil."

She grinned. "Instead we got home, had a romantic dinner on the balcony, and he proposed at sunset. It was perfect."

"Just like you guys are perfect for each other," Siobhan told her. "The professor's a lucky man."

"I'm lucky too," Nadia said softly, tears spiking her lashes. "This wouldn't have happened without all of you."

"You can't include me in that," Audie said, wiping at her tears. "Vanessa egged you on the first day. Siobhan helped you see how much you love him. All I did was pick a fight with you when both of you were trying to help."

"No, Audie," Nadia grabbed the redhead's hand. "That night showed me that Kane cares for my friends because he cares for me. And we're solid now, which means you don't get out of bridesmaid duty. I do solemnly swear that I won't pick anything hideous for you to wear or go all Bridezilla on you, so help me Bitch Talk."

"Don't think we won't hold you to that," Vanessa said, dabbing at her eyes as she took her seat. "I've worn enough hideous brides-maid dresses to last me a lifetime."

"Hey—I guess this means we get to throw an engagement party!" Siobhan realized, carefully blotting her mascara with a paper napkin. "I can host it at my house unless you want to have it at Kane's."

"I think having my maid of honor throw an engagement party at her house is a great idea," Nadia agreed with a smile.

Siobhan hugged her friend again. "Thank you," she managed, too choked up to say anything else.

"You're my sister from a different mister and you've been with me at my worst and my best. Of course you're my maid of honor."

"That means this bridesmaid gets to plan the bachelorette party!" Audie exclaimed, rubbing her hands together with obvious relish.

"We'll plan it together," Vanessa said with a knowing grin for Siobhan. "It'll be the perfect balance between naughty and nice."

"Speaking of naughty and nice," Nadia said, "what's going on with you and Charlie? What was the big secret he was keeping from you?"

Siobhan's throat closed up. Reluctant to spoil Nadia's day, she delayed by reaching for her tea, taking a sip. "Charlie's got a family."

Audie frowned. "What do you mean, he's got a family?"

"I mean he has a sister who's eighteen, the same age as Col-leen," she answered. "He's also got two brothers, one in high school and one in middle school. Charlie's been their legal guardian for the last eight years, ever since their parents died."

Audie whistled in appreciation. "The man is a saint. A hot saint, but you have to admit, that's pretty damn heroic."

"I think so too." Siobhan's voice warbled, and she gripped her teacup, blowing out a slow, controlled breath. "It's amazing to me that a guy who was in his last year of college would step up like that. I could clearly hear how important family is to him, how he'd do anything to protect them."

She paused. "He wanted me to meet them."

"That's great news!" Vanessa exclaimed. She paused, looking at Audie and Nadia's concerned expressions before turning back to Siobhan. "Isn't it?"

"Yes, it was a huge gesture, something he doesn't do with just anyone." Another breath in. "It would have been nice to meet them, but I don't think that's going to happen now."

Nadia reached over, wrapping warm fingers around Siobhan's chilled hand. "You told him, didn't you?"

"I had to, you know?" Siobhan squeezed her friend's hand. "We were at the point of deciding to be exclusive and serious. Once he mentioned kids in the house and how he wanted me to meet them, I knew I had to tell him about being addicted and losing my family."

Sympathy swam in Vanessa's dark eyes. "What happened?"

"I told him everything from high school to my second stint in rehab and trying to make amends with Colleen," she admitted. "I outed you, Nadia. I'm sorry."

"That doesn't matter right now," her partner reassured her. "What did he do after you told him all of that?"

"He told me that I'd given him a lot to think about, and that he needed time to sort through it all. I said I understood." She hunched her shoulders, but it didn't make the hurt easier to bear. "He left. I haven't heard from him since."

Nadia frowned. "That was Friday!"

"I know," Siobhan replied, failing to keep the misery out of her tone.

"Four days?" Audie joined the frowning. "Four whole days without a word?"

"Yeah." Siobhan blew out a breath. "So I think we can figure out what that means. I'll just chalk it up as another life lesson. I should have followed Nadia's lead and just told Charlie up front that I was a drug addict. That way, neither one of us would have gotten too invested. It would have saved hurt feelings on both sides."

Hurt and anger churned inside her, and both made her feel guilty. She was the one who hadn't wanted to get too involved, wanted to keep it just to the sex. He was the one who wanted to try the whole relationship thing. She'd thought that after he met her friends, saw her dance, and appeared to come to grips with it that he'd be cool, receptive even, to her past. He hadn't, and it angered her even though she understood it. She'd been a drug addict. She'd gotten hooked twice, gotten clean twice. Who was to say that it wouldn't happen again? Who would want her to be around their kids, even if those kids were siblings?

"Maybe he's still thinking things through," Vanessa suggested. "I can't believe Charlie would end things with you without saying anything or at least sending a text or e-mail or something. You guys have a business project together!"

"Which we've been winding down," Siobhan explained, struggling not to drown in their sympathy. "It was just an excuse to keep seeing each other. We've had four days to think things through. I can't blame him if he doesn't want to keep seeing me. He's got his brothers and sister to think about. If our positions were reversed, I wouldn't want to bring a recovering addict into my home either."

"I don't believe it!" Audie interjected. "We've all seen you two together. You guys have the same sparks that Nadia and Kane have. You can't give up on that. You're a good person who made a mistake. Everyone makes mistakes. That doesn't mean you should be punished forever, does it? You don't deserve that!"

Her lower lip trembled. "If you can't get a happy ending, how can I hope to?"

"Audie, honey, I'm no one's role model. You're young. You've made bad choices, sure, but you haven't hurt anyone. You're turning your life around and you still have plenty of time to make a go of it. You're going to get your second chance. I just know it."

"You deserve a second chance too," the redhead insisted.

Audie's support curled around Siobhan's heart, bringing the threat of tears. "I had my second chance with my husband and kid, and I ruined it," she reminded them. "I accept that, just as I accept that Charlie's got his family to consider. If he didn't, maybe things would be different. Maybe he'd be willing to take a risk, but maybe not, because we all know those of us in recovery are always a risk. Some of us are just a higher risk than others."

She managed a smile. "So I say, let's let Nadia be our role model. At the very least, we should be talking wedding plans. Have you guys even talked about the type of wedding or when you want to get married?"

"Actually, there might be two ceremonies—"

"Excuse me, are you Siobhan Malloy?"

The table fell silent as they looked at the dark blonde who approached their table. In her floral-print tank, cutoff shorts, and sandals, she looked so much like Colleen that Siobhan's heart stuttered. When the young woman locked her blue-green eyes onto Siobhan, her heart stuttered for a different reason.

"You're Lorelei, aren't you?" Siobhan managed to ask. "You're Charlie's sister."

The girl's eyes widened. "How did you know?"

"Your eyes," she answered, conscious of her friends gathered around her. And her heart skidding triple-time. "Is everything all right? Has something happened to Charlie?" *God, if I've been sitting here bitching about him not calling and he's been injured—*

"Nothing's happened to him." Lorelei's gaze darted around the table before returning to Siobhan. "Is it okay if I talk to you for a moment?"

Siobhan hesitated. If Lorelei O'Halloran knew about her, that meant that Charlie must have mentioned her to his sister. Why would he do that? When did he do that? What had he said about Siobhan? She didn't know, but she was curious enough to try finding out. "All right. Let's sit over there. Would you like something to drink? The kitchen's closed, but we can still do coffee or tea."

"I'm fine, thanks."

They sat at another quiet table, mostly out of earshot of Siobhan's friends, who were doing their best to not appear to be eavesdropping. "It's nice to meet you, Lorelei," she finally said. "What can I do for you?"

The girl tossed her purse onto the table and slung herself into the chair with easy grace. "Charlie's the only one who calls me Lorelei," she said. "Everyone else calls me Lori."

"Lorelei's a pretty name," Siobhan pointed out. "It suits you."

"Charlie says that too." Lorelei raised her brows. "I don't mind you using it either, then."

"All right. Lorelei." Siobhan hesitated. "Does your brother know you're here?"

"No. I'm going to his office after I talk to you." She stared at Siobhan with unabashed curiosity, making Siobhan wonder how her daughter would have turned out if she'd been a better mother.

"I've been in here before with friends," Lorelei said after the silence stretched. "When Charlie told us that he wanted to date one of the owners, I was hoping he meant you. No offense to the other lady, but you're pretty and you dress cool. I like your apron."

"Thank you." Siobhan smoothed a hand down her hot pink apron trimmed with a black-and-white edging printed with sugar skulls that covered her black-and-white bowling shirt and black pedal pushers. "Did Charlie tell you anything about me?"

Lorelei nodded. "Charlie called a family meeting and told us he'd met someone he wanted to date. We were so excited. Okay, maybe I was excited—Kyle was anxious and Finn can be a little meh if it doesn't involve video games. Anyway, you have to understand— Charlie doesn't date. Like ever." She rolled her eyes. "Believe me, I've asked him. He always has an excuse, saying he's too busy, the company needs all his attention, the family needs all his attention. Or that the girls in town aren't interesting enough."

Lorelei stared at Siobhan, her expression open and earnest. "So when he said he wanted to tell you about the rest of us and invite you over for dinner, we knew that meant you were special. You're different."

"I think that's the problem," Siobhan said, fighting to keep her tone free of emotion. "I'm a little too different from what he's looking for."

"What if you're exactly what he needs?"

Siobhan shook her head. She wasn't what anyone needed. "Obviously he decided differently."

"He's overwhelmed," Lorelei insisted. "He got a bum deal when our parents died. He didn't have to step up and take us on, but he did. He kept us from being sent to foster care. Separate foster homes.

He's my hero, but don't you ever tell him that. I was hoping he was finally doing something for himself."

Her shoulders slumped. "When he came home early from his date Friday and said dinner would be postponed, we knew that meant the talk didn't go well."

"It has nothing to do with you or your brothers," Siobhan interrupted, horrified that Charlie wouldn't have explained that. "I hope you believe me."

"I know." Lorelei gave her a direct look. "Charlie told me that you were addicted to pain medication."

Siobhan sat back, stunned. "He . . . he told you about that?"

"Me, not the boys," his sister confirmed. "I had to pull it out of him, though. He tends to keep things to himself, especially if he thinks he's protecting us when he does it."

Siobhan stared at the girl, trying to decide how to proceed. She wanted to know if Charlie was angry or upset. She wanted to know what Lorelei thought of her now that she knew about Siobhan's drug abuse history. She wanted to know if Charlie wanted to see her again. Those weren't the sort of questions she could or would ask an eighteen-year-old, however.

"Given all of that, I think you can understand why Charlie and I aren't seeing each other."

"No, no, I can't understand." Lorelei shook her head for emphasis. "All he's been focused on is what's important for the family, what's best for us. He's protective of us. He hasn't thought about what's best for him in years. With you, I think he's finally thinking about it."

Siobhan wanted to believe that, but it was difficult. She only had to look at her own family, remember the judge's reprimand, hear Colleen complain about having to sit through visitations with a mother who cared more about numbing the pain than being with her daughter. How her father had shut the door in her face when she'd gotten out of rehab, as if she were a door-to-door salesperson or something. If family did that, how could she expect Charlie to react any differently?

She shook her head. "Lorelei, I appreciate—"

"You messed up. People mess up all the time. People are in the news all the time because they mess up. Some people get more famous after they mess up. Besides, what you did was five years ago—that's like forever. If you were famous, no one would care!"

Siobhan pursed her lips to hold back a smile. "The thing is, I'm not famous. Even if I were, Charlie just has your best interests at heart."

"I get it. He thinks he's protecting us, but I think he's being stupid. Now that I've talked to you, I think he's being really stupid."

"I know he's your brother, but I don't appreciate you talking about Charlie that way. Your brother's a good man."

"See?" Lorelei slapped the table. "That's what I mean! You're standing up for him. You didn't have to tell him all that stuff, but you did. You're pretty and honest and nice and Charlie needs that. He needs you."

Flummoxed, Siobhan sat back, blinking at the younger woman. "Are you sure you're eighteen?"

Lorelei's laughter rang through the mostly empty café, drawing attention to their table. "Yes, I'm eighteen, though Charlie treats me like I'm eight. We all had to grow up in a hurry after our parents died. Charlie stepped up, but none of us were going to do anything that would get us taken away from each other. I know he gave up a lot, but he says he got much more."

She sighed, and for a moment looked far older than her eighteen years. "I just want him to have a chance to be happy. He deserves it."

"I think he does too," Siobhan said. "That's why—"

"You can make him happy, Siobhan. Can I call you Siobhan? I know you can make him happy, if you have the chance."

What was it with the O'Hallorans and their smooth talk? "Lorelei. First, yes, you can call me Siobhan. I'd like that. Second, thank you for coming to see me and telling me all of this. You gotta know, though, that I haven't heard from Charlie in four days. I think that tells me all I need to know about what he thinks."

"I can change his mind," Lorelei insisted, her voice hard with determination. "He's miserable without you and he knows it."

She stood, shouldering her bag. "If I convince him to call you or come by, will you talk to him? Personally, I think he owes you an apology for not calling before now."

Siobhan stood as well. "Again I ask: are you really eighteen?"

"Yep." Charlie's sister laughed again. "I'm going to Herscher University this fall, majoring in psychology with a specialty in family counseling."

Figures. "I'd say you have an amazing head start."

"Hey, I'm the only girl in a house full of guys. I had to do something to hold my own." Lorelei wrapped her in an impulsive hug. "I want you and Charlie to get together because I want to have another girl around the house. We can even the odds. Hopefully you'll be over for dinner this weekend. Wish me luck!"

Siobhan's friends swarmed her as Lorelei left. "So that was Charlie's sister?" Nadia asked.

"Yeah, a regular force of nature," Siobhan answered. "She thinks I'm good for Charlie and she's heading over to see him now. The poor guy doesn't stand a chance."

FIFTEEN

Siobhan was a drug addict.

Charlie sat in his office, his mind far away from work. All he'd been able to think about for the last four days was Siobhan and the story she'd told him. Even though he'd heard the details directly from her, his mind still couldn't make the leap from the woman she'd been to the woman he knew.

The Siobhan he knew wasn't weak. The Siobhan he knew wouldn't surrender to the empty promise of narcotics, not once but twice. The Siobhan he knew wouldn't endanger a child.

Except she'd done all of those things. Pain pills and sleep aids, prescription and over-the-counter. He'd done some online research about pain clinics and pill mills, read horror stories about overdoses and destroyed lives. Siobhan's addiction had cost her a marriage, her relationships with her parents and daughter, and very nearly her freedom.

Sure she had turned her life around, gotten clean, and established a successful business. For four years, she'd been a pillar of the Crimson Bay community, far removed from the child-endangering addict she'd been. Still he couldn't suppress the thought that slithered through his mind: what if it didn't last?

That was the question that paralyzed him into indecision. What if their relationship continued, blossomed into something more, and she suffered a relapse? What if some other trauma occurred and she reached for pills as a chemical crutch to cope? Could he accept that? Could he allow her into his home, around his brothers and sister, knowing the risks?

He scrubbed a hand down his face. He didn't know. He had his doubts and those doubts cut deep. His responsibility to his family superseded everything, even his own needs. He'd spent the majority of the last decade ensuring his siblings were protected, cared for. Working hard to preserve the remainder of his family had left no room for anything else, including intimate relationships. Truth be told, he just didn't have the desire to play dating games, had rarely indulged in more than a few one-night stands here and there, usually when the boys were away at summer camp,

He'd gotten used to being alone so much that it never felt like being lonely. Familial duties and business obligations consumed him and he'd allowed it, telling himself he didn't need anything more. Until the day he met Siobhan, and everything changed.

Meeting her, being with her, drove home the weight of the sacrifices he'd made for his family. Sacrifices he'd willingly make again, without question, without hesitation. Now, thanks to Siobhan, he wanted more. He needed more. Hungered for more. She was the only one who'd been capable of inspiring that level of need, and the only one who could satisfy it.

At least, she had been. Now he doubted her, doubted himself. Doubted that he could make the right decision for all of them. That doubt angered him.

He wanted Siobhan. He wanted to protect his family. Somehow there had to be a way to do both. Did that mean he had to remain alone, not be with anyone until Finn became an adult and moved out, leaving him with an empty nest? Could he wait that long? Would Siobhan wait that long?

"Well aren't you the picture of sunshine and unicorns?"

He looked up as Lorelei stepped into his office, and made an effort to pull his head out of his ass. "Hey. I thought you were working."

"I'm done for the day," she said, closing his office door then leaning against it. "How about you? Getting any work done, or is today as productive as yesterday?"

He looked at his laptop, the slew of unanswered e-mails, the half-formed project proposals scattered on his desk. As much as he enjoyed his company, work was not providing the distraction he needed. "I might as well be. Why don't we go get Kyle and Finn, and go out to dinner? I'll even let you treat."

"Sure, if we're going to take advantage of someone's dollar menu," she retorted, folding her arms across her chest. "Are you finally done moping?"

Crap. He hadn't done as good of job of concealing his thoughts as he'd hoped. "I'm not moping."

Lorelei simply looked at him with that combination of teenage-girl scorn and world-weary pity that she'd perfected before puberty. "You should go talk to her."

Charlie didn't waste time pretending to misunderstand. "Instead of focusing on my problems, shouldn't you be concentrating on clothes for college, chick flicks, and even, God forbid, a boy-friend?"

"I'll get a boyfriend as soon as my oldest brother makes up with his girlfriend and gets a life."

"I have a life."

The lie fell flat between them. "You had a life. Four days ago. Then gave it up when you walked out on her."

Charlie hesitated. He did his best to keep Lorelei—all of them—from growing up too fast, but she'd taken her role as lady of the house seriously from the age of ten, when she'd had to play hostess for their parents' wake while the grown-ups whispered about taking her away. He didn't like leaning on her for things that he, as head of the house-hold, should carry alone. Certainly relationship talks were off the table, unless the talks were about her relationships.

He had to correct her on one thing. "I didn't give her up."

"Siobhan thinks you did."

"What?" He jerked upright. "You saw her?"

Lorelei nodded. "I went to the café before I came here."

"Why would you do that?" he thrust his hands into his hair. "Dammit, Lorelei, I don't want you to get involved in this!"

"Too bad," she shot back, settling her hands on her hips. "I'm your sister, so I'm automatically involved. Besides, I wanted to see her."

"Why?"

"I watched you when you told us about her. You were happy. Happy in a way I haven't seen in a long time."

"I'm happy," he insisted, trying not to squirm beneath his sis-ter's assessing gaze.

"Right now you're not. Neither is she."

His heart thumped heavy in his chest. "Did you talk to her?"

"Yeah. She defended you, said she understood why you broke up with her."

"I didn't break up with her," he protested. "I just—"

"Haven't called, texted, or stopped by in four days," his sister pointed out. "After she dropped her story on you and you left, what else is she supposed to think?"

Fuck. He rubbed at his forehead. In all the time he'd spent thinking about what he'd do, he hadn't thought about what Siobhan was going through, what she had to be thinking. "I don't want to end things with her, but my first obligation is to you guys."

"You're hopeless." Lorelei shook her head. "What do you think your girlfriend could expose us to that television, the Internet, and school don't?"

Charlie groaned. "You keep talking like that, and I'll home-school all of you."

"You suck at homework, remember?" She morphed her features into a portrait of innocence. "Besides, the life lessons you teach us are far more valuable."

"Stop blowing smoke up my ass," he groused without heat. "I'm already paying for college, though I have to say I'm beginning to rethink that psychology degree."

"I chose that psychology major because living with the three of you drives me crazy. You owe me."

She pushed off the door. "I'll cut to the mushy stuff. I love you and want you to be happy. I think Siobhan can make you happy, and I think you can make her happy. If you decide to give yourself a chance, that is. And if she decides to forgive you."

"It's not that simple, Lorelei."

"Sure it is. She's human. Pretty and cool and totally rocking that retro vibe, but still human. Humans make mistakes. If one of us went through what she went through, would you turn your back on us?"

That was the question he should have asked all along. He wouldn't turn his back on his siblings. The very idea churned his stomach. He would support them, make sure they got the help they needed. They were family. One didn't turn their back on family.

So why was he considering turning his back on the woman who so sweetly gave him everything he needed?

Shit. He shot to his feet. "I need to see her."

"Yes!" Lorelei broke into a maniacal grin. "I'll help you shut down in here. You should go home and get cleaned up so you can make a good impression. Too bad you don't have enough time to buy her a present, something sparkly."

"You've got this all figured out, don't you?" Charlie asked as he shut his laptop down.

"Happy endings aren't only in books, you know," his sister said, bumping his shoulder. "By the way, I sorta invited her to dinner on Saturday, so make sure she forgives you. I can't wait to balance out all the testosterone in our house!"

Forty-five minutes and a pit stop later, Charlie pulled up in front of Siobhan's bungalow. Anticipation gripped him at the thought of seeing her again. He'd missed her, missed her so intensely that he knew he was gone on her. He had to make things right with Siobhan, had to convince her that they belonged together, that she was his. He'd done it once before, he'd do it again.

Siobhan jammed on her brakes as she spotted Charlie's SUV parked in front of her house. Whatever Lorelei had said to her brother had obviously made an impression. What sort of impression, Siobhan didn't know.

She took her time parking and getting out of her car. He approached as she opened her trunk to retrieve groceries, looking good in jeans and a short-sleeved navy shirt that set off his tanned skin and blond hair. Her body hummed to life as it always did when he was near, but her heart pounded at his serious expression. "Hi."

"Hi, Siobhan," he said, his voice polite, almost formal as he took her bags from her. "Can we talk?"

Siobhan wasn't sure she wanted to hear what Charlie had to say, but she knew she didn't want to hear it in her front yard. "Of course. Come inside."

They remained silent as she unlocked her front door, disabled the alarm, then stepped inside. After locking the door again she followed Charlie to the kitchen, tension rising inside her with every step. It wasn't until they'd placed her purchases on the island that she turned to him. "So I guess Lorelei—"

Charlie cupped her face in his large hands and kissed her. Startled, she put her hands flat against his chest, torn between pulling him close and pushing him away. He solved her dilemma by wrapping his arms around her waist, caging her in his embrace.

If he'd made it a hard kiss, a punishing kiss, or even an arousing kiss, maybe she would have resisted. But that wasn't what Charlie did. He gave her a soft kiss, an apology kiss. A kiss of hope and promise and everything nice. She opened to it like a flower to a gentle rain, needing it to cleanse away the dusty hurt of the last few days.

"We aren't broken up," he announced against her mouth, his voice edged with emotion. "We weren't broken up. You need to understand that right now."

"But it's been four days—"

He kissed her again, this time with more demand. "I'm not an impulsive guy, Siobhan. I used to be, but I can't afford to be anymore. Not while I'm still responsible for my brothers and sister."

"What are you trying to tell me, Charlie?" She pushed away from him. Needing something to do other than step into his arms again, she focused on putting away her groceries. "You want to sneak around on your family, for us to go back to being secret? Isn't that going to be hard to do now that Lorelei knows everything?"

She expected him to react in anger. Instead a slow smile bowed his lips. "She let you call her Lorelei?"

"Why wouldn't she? It's a pretty name and it suits her. She seemed cool with that."

"She hates being called Lorelei. Says it's too fluffy, whatever that means. I'm the only one she lets get away with using her full name, and even then she gives me crap about it."

"You're dodging my question." She slammed a cabinet door shut. "You wanted us to be public with our relationship, and I agreed. I won't be a secret, Charlie. If you want to pretend to your family and friends that we're broken up while you come sneaking over here for a booty call, you can leave right now."

He stepped up behind her, bracing his hands on the counter on either side of her. "Let's be clear about how we're moving forward, Siobhan," he said, his breath warm and insistent on the back of her neck. "One, I'm not pretending anything. I'm out and proud about wanting to be with you. Two, I want everyone to know about the smoking hot blonde I'm dating, because we are dating. Call me whatever you want— boyfriend, lover, partner, or that guy you're seeing. I don't care as long as everyone knows that we're together. Which brings me to three."

He turned her around, cradling her cheeks in his hands. "I hurt you, something I never want to do. I should have called you, but I'm used to thinking things through and making decisions on my own."

Standing so close to him like this, soaking in his warmth, the promise in his eyes urged her to give in, to agree to any- and every-thing he wanted. "If we're going to do this relationship thing, then you have to realize that you're not on your own anymore."

Something flared in his eyes, something so stark that she palmed his cheeks in concern. Then he smiled. "I like the sound of that."

He gave her a quick kiss then stepped back. "I owe you a proper apology. Let me take you out to dinner, then we can come back and have makeup sex."

She arched a brow as she took in his attire. "If you want to give me a proper apology, we need to go somewhere with a different dress code. Then we'll see about the makeup sex."

His cocky grin returned. "I have a suitable change of clothing in the car. Wasn't going to push my luck by bringing in an over-night bag before I convinced you that we're not broken up."

"Overnight bag?" Charlie wanted to stay over?

"I'm going to be exhausted after giving you a very proper apology," he explained. "You wouldn't want me driving home late at night too fatigued to concentrate, would you?"

"No, that wouldn't be right." She couldn't stop her smile from forming. "It would be rude of me to kick you out after an epic apology. Of course, I might discover that you snore, or that you're a bed hog."

"Hmm." He made an attempt at looking thoughtful. "Well then I suppose I'll have to make sure you're too tired after accepting my apology to do anything other than fall asleep."

"I do love the way you think," Siobhan said, the last of her worry falling away.

"Good. Then I think you should go freshen up and slip into something with a skirt, a garter belt, and no panties. I'll put away the rest of your groceries, get my stuff, then call the homestead. The bratlets are waiting for me to report in. By the way, Saturday dinner with the family is back on. Sound good?"

"Sounds better than good. I like the way your plans come together, Charlie O'Halloran."

"Good." He sent her a scorching look. "Because there's going to be a lot of coming together in our future."

SIXTEEN

"How did you get involved with the Crimson Bay Bombshells?"

Siobhan glanced at him before dropping her gaze to her water glass. Charlie had taken her to a small upscale seafood restaurant and charmed her with stories she was sure his siblings would be horrified about her knowing. Though it was still early, the restaurant was dark and romantic, and the hushed atmosphere only heightened the intimacy. A candle danced merrily in a cut crystal holder, its light darkening Charlie's blue-green eyes but also underscoring the temptation, intent, and heat in every glance he gave her. If she'd been trying to resist him, she would have failed miserably.

"There's a dance studio to the east of the square, called Motions. They offer a bunch of different classes, and I registered for beginner's yoga. I was looking for something that would occupy my free time—not that I have a lot of it—and help with my flexibility. I thought yoga would do it, and I'd get the benefit of calming my mind as well."

"Do you still do it?"

"No." She laughed. "I hated every moment of it, which upped my stress instead of eliminating it. Didn't last a week. Lucky for me there was a pole dancing class going on at the same time and I decided to sign up for that. That's where I met Lola."

Candlelight accented the delight in his eyes. "You pole dance too?"

"Easy there, tiger. I haven't danced on a pole since that class. At the end of it, Lola asked me if I'd be interested in learning burlesque. I went to one of their shows and got hooked. The rest is history."

She twirled the stem of her wineglass. "I've been doing it for a couple of years now and I love it, but I think it's about time for me to look for another hobby."

"Why would you give it up?"

"For me it's just a hobby. A very expensive hobby, but a hobby nonetheless. I'll always love vintage lingerie and fashion, but the Crimson Bay Bombshells is Lola's business and Sugar and Spice is mine. The café takes priority, which means I'm not always available for some of the things Lola wants to book for the troupe. Besides, if I step down, Lola can give my spot to one of her younger apprentices."

He bristled. "Is Lola asking you to step down because of your age?"

"No, she'd never do that."

"Then I don't get it. What does your age have to do with your ability to dance?"

"I'm thirty-five, creeping up on thirty-six," she reminded him gently. "Also, I'm not flat-chested."

Her nipples pearled as Charlie's gaze dropped to her cleavage, lingered. "You most certainly are not, thank God."

She deliberately drew in a slow deep breath before exhaling. "The girls aren't going to defy gravity forever. I've been lucky that they've stayed as perky as they have for as long as they have."

"No, I'd say I'm the lucky one. Me and everyone else who watches you perform."

"You're the luckiest and you know it. After all, you get to go home with me."

"That I do." Masculine pride filled his answering grin, and she again had to look away.

"Hey." He reached over, gathered her hand. "Are you afraid I'm going to hypnotize you or something?"

"What are you talking about?"

"You look at me, then you look away quickly," he explained. "We both know you're not shy. Either I have something stuck in my teeth or you're suddenly afraid to look at me. Which one is it?"

"I'm not afraid." Heat seeped into her fingers from the warmth of his hand, snaking up her arm to curl up inside her chest. "Sometimes though, when you look at me—I feel myself slipping."

"Slipping into what?"

"I don't know. I also don't know if I should hold on tighter or let go and if it should bother me that I don't know the answer to that. It's like you're hypnotizing me, putting me under some kind of spell."

"Really?" He turned her hand over, tracing his fingers over the staccato beat of her pulse. "Does your pulse start racing? Do you feel as if you've just run as far as you could for as long as you could and your heart's threatening to burst out of your chest? Do you feel like there's a static charge building up along your skin, and all it will take is one small touch to set off sparks?"

"Yes," she breathed, her heart pounding at the branding touch of his fingers. "How do you know?"

"Because I feel like that whenever I see you. That first day when I delivered those flowers for Nadia, I felt like I was at the top of a roller coaster looking down this long drop where you waited. I knew I was in for the ride of my life and I was going to enjoy every twisting, turning, exhilarating moment of it."

His hand tightened on hers. "So look at me, Siobhan. See me. I can't put a spell on you when you already hypnotized me."

"Charlie . . ."

"I like when you say my name like that, like I'm balls-deep inside you giving you everything you want."

He looked at her, and everything fell away, leaving nothing but him, her, and the connection that hummed between them. "I can, you know."

It took her a moment to swim up from the depths of his eyes. "Can what?"

"Give you everything you want."

A tremble swept her and for just a moment, just for one heartbeat, she allowed herself to believe that. That Charlie could take every one of her hopes and dreams and wild fantasies and make them all come true. She allowed that hope to live for just one shining moment, then locked it away, buried it deep. Hope was a dangerous thing, as seductive as drugs and just as deadly.

He sat back, the potent atmosphere seeping away and leaving her floundering. When he glanced her way again, mischief had replaced the ferocity in his eyes. "However, if it's dessert you want, I suggest we postpone that until we get home."

"Oh?" She arched a brow, recovering her footing. "Are you thinking of serving up something with chocolate sauce or honey?"

"It's possible." He signaled for the check. "Do you mind if we make a stop before we head home? It won't take long."

"Of course not. Where are we going?"

"You'll see soon enough."

After paying their bill, Charlie guided her out of the restaurant to the valet stand where his SUV already waited. He waved off the valet's eager help to hand her into the vehicle himself, then crossed to the driver's side.

Siobhan fastened her seatbelt, then settled back against the leather seat. "The poor guy was just doing his job," she said as he closed the door.

"A job that doesn't entail slobbering down your cleavage." He shifted into gear. "That job belongs to me, and I intend to be employee of the month from here on out."

Siobhan hid a smile as Charlie left downtown and made his way to the interstate, heading southeast to the suburban sprawl that had surrounded Crimson Bay like a besieging army in the past few years. She'd never admit it or encourage them, but she liked his casual displays of possessiveness. Liked the fluttering feeling he caused in her belly even as it made her nervous.

She shook off her thoughts as Charlie turned into a parking lot that fronted a nondescript whitewashed building with no windows. The only indication of what lay inside was the purple-blue neon that wrapped the door.

"This is your detour?" she asked in surprise.

He grinned as he shut off the engine. "You don't mind, do you?"

"Mind? No. I'm just surprised that you not only know this place exists but how to get here."

"You mentioned visiting here with your friends, so I figured we could make a trip as well. Ready to go shopping?"

"Shopping in an adult novelty store with my boyfriend?" Siobhan unbuckled her seatbelt. "Why the hell not?"

They made their way inside the brightly lit store. "You brought us here, any particular area you'd like to start?"

He grabbed a shopping basket, handed it to her. "Let's start with something easy, like the flavored lube section. How do you want to proceed? Like kids in a candy store or more Masters and Johnson?"

Siobhan smothered a laugh. "You are not going to make me snort in the middle of a sex shop," she warned. "You do, and you'll owe me two apologies."

"All right." He winked at her, but did nothing to erase the wicked glint in his eyes. "Well-behaved kids in a candy store it is."

They started their exploration in the lubrication section. "Flavored lubes," Charlie said, holding up two brightly colored bottles. "Should we go with bubble gum or tropical punch?"

"That depends on where you plan to use it." She gave him the side-eye. "Exactly where do you plan to use it?"

"Good question." He leaned close. "You get more than wet enough for me and I love the way you taste on my tongue. Lately though, I've been fantasizing about that gorgeous ass of yours."

She drew a slow breath, trying to regain some of the equilibrium he constantly upset. "I'm an anal virgin, at least when it comes to cock," she informed him. "Given the award-winning caliber of yours, I'm going to need some practice before I'm ready for the main act."

He reached for her, then clenched his hand into a fist. "Dammit, Siobhan, we're twenty minutes away from your house in light traffic. You can't say stuff like that to me when I can't do anything about it."

"Poor baby," she cooed. "What's the matter? Can't handle your own game?"

"Cock tease," he shot back, the curve of his lips blunting the edge of his words. "Would you like me to slip my hand up under your skirt to see how wet you are right now? Maybe we should sample the bubble gum lube instead. Do you think the salesclerk would blink if I ask you for a taste test?"

"He's probably ready to record it to save to his spank reel," she pointed out. "I'm just letting you know that we're going to have to work up to a little what-what in the butt-butt."

He looked insulted. "Please don't refer to my what-what or anything else as little." He tossed both lubes into the basket she held, then added another water-based warming one that touted its slickness. "I have to say, I'm looking forward to warming you up. Should we add some edible body paint to our basket?"

"Only if you let me toss in glow-in-the-dark condoms."

"Sure. You've got a high fence around your backyard. As long as we keep the moaning and groaning to a reasonable level, they won't even know we're out there."

Sex outside using glow-in-the-dark condoms. Siobhan tripped over her own feet. Charlie grabbed her elbow, concern darkening his eyes. "Are you okay?"

"I'm fine. You've had sex outside before?"

"There's a first time for everything." The heat in his gaze would have melted her panties if she'd been wearing any. "I'd have sex with you anywhere."

It was a line, she knew it was a line, but the glint in his eyes combined with the low sexy timbre of his voice enticed her to take a dare to see how far he would go, how far he would take them.

Charlie leaned forward and Siobhan parted her lips, ready for his kiss, ready for his touch, ready for everything. Disappointment swamped her when he leaned past her to reach for something from the rack behind her.

He noticed her pout. "There are cameras everywhere, goddess, and I don't want to give McSkeevy a floorshow no matter how good a discount he can give us. Think you can wait until we get home?"

"If I have to," she said with a long-suffering sigh.

"Or you can wait until we get back to the SUV, and you can break this out." He held up a slender rose pink vibrator. The naked brunette bent over on the package left no doubt of its intended purpose.

"Hmm. I suppose some training will do me good. If we add this to the basket, though, we'll need to add this too." She handed him a vibrating cock ring.

He looked at the package, his lips curving in a slow smile. Then he stretched his hand down to his groin to simulate palming his cock, then compared the circle of his fingers to the ring. "Does it stretch to fit?"

"I'm sure it will, but you know it's supposed to be snug, right? Increased satisfaction for me, delayed gratification for you."

He tossed the ring into the basket. "I'm sure if my circulation gets cut off, you'll nurse me back to health properly. In fact, I think I see a nurse costume on the rack over there."

"Don't need it. I already have one."

He froze, then swung to face her. "You're just now telling me this?"

Teasing him was so much fun. "Maybe I'm saving it for a special occasion."

"Labor Day? My birthday's coming up. Or how about Just Because Day?" He waggled his eyebrows at her. "I'll do something extra-special for you to earn my reward."

"How about getting us out of here and back home?" she suggested. "I really want my dessert now."

"Anticipation is part of the game, goddess," he told her, the twist of his lips telling her that he knew exactly the predicament she was in. "Let's see what else inspires us, then we'll leave."

Slipping an arm around her waist, he guided her through the rest of the store, pausing every now and then to describe in excruciating detail how he would use a particular item on her. The more he talked the wetter she became. She could feel the moisture pooling, coating her inner thighs.

"Charlie." She clutched his arm.

"What is it, sweetheart?" He asked the question as if he had no idea of the effect he had on her.

"I'm not wearing panties, and I'm about to drip all over this questionable carpet. We need to go."

"You're right. I've teased you long enough." He led her to the front of the store, where the curious clerk waited to ring up their items. The clerk tested their battery-operated devices, they declined to join the mailing list, and Charlie paid cash for their purchases.

Siobhan breathed a sigh of relief as Charlie assisted her into the passenger seat. She waited for him to pull out into the street to turn to him. "Do you consider yourself a safe driver, Charlie?"

He nodded. "Not even a speeding ticket."

"Good." She released her seatbelt. "As a business owner, I'm sure you've had to multitask often, right?"

"Of course." He darted a glance her way as he braked at a traffic light. "What's going on in that devious mind of yours?"

She bent over then reached for his zipper. "I suggest you concentrate on driving, Mr. O'Halloran."

He uttered a guttural curse but didn't try to stop her as she reached into his boxer briefs to free his erection. Moisture already slicked the head, proving he'd been as affected by their shopping trip as she had.

She stroked the pad of her thumb over the tip, spreading his pre-come. Charlie had a beautiful cock, and it complimented and complemented his beautiful body. Thick and veined, it made her swoon with the way it fit her hand, her mouth, her pussy. She couldn't have designed a more perfect cock for her body.

Leaning closer, she swirled her tongue over the head, rewarded by Charlie's low groan of approval. She loved being with him in moments like this, perfectly balanced between having him at her mercy and being directed by him.

If she wanted, she could push him, make him lose control. It was wrong to tease him like this, wrong and dangerous. He was driving, after all. Besides, she wasn't ready for him to come quite yet.

Instead she reveled in the taste of him, the feel of him in her hand and in her mouth. Lapping up every bit of his essence, she licked her way down his length as far as she could go before kissing her way back to the tip. Once more she swirled her tongue around the tip, then parted her lips to suck him in. Down, down, stretching over his thickness, slowly filling her mouth with his length then slowly backing off before repeating the movement.

His loud groan filled the quiet cabin. "That's it, sweetheart," he encouraged, his voice gravel-rough as he caressed her hair. "Slow and deep just like that. God, babe, I love the way you do that."

Pleasure burned his words, sparking a simmering hunger inside her. Making him feel good hit one of her needs, echoing through her and ramping up her own desire. Pleasing him pleased her, especially when she knew she'd be the recipient of his sensual attention soon.

Dimly she became aware of the vehicle slowing to a stop. Had they arrived at her house already? She hadn't made him come yet and the need to do so gripped her hard. Wrapping her hand around his shaft, she increased her pace, bobbing her head as she drew him in. She reached her free hand into his briefs to cup his balls, her middle finger teasing along the soft skin behind them.

"Babe." Charlie's voice, scraped raw with restraint, filled the cabin. "I'm almost there, almost ready to come. I wanna flood that sweet mouth of yours. Do you want that, sweetheart? You want me to come down your throat?"

God, he had a way with words. She hummed in answer, unwilling to pause long enough to vocalize her agreement.

"Good." He killed the engine then sank both hands into her hair. "Suck me hard, babe, then drink me down."

Hollowing her cheeks, she sucked on him, taking him as far down as she could go. Whispering soft words of encouragement, he rocked his hips up, the seatbelt restricting his thrusts, preventing him from wildly fucking her mouth. He was hot and hard in her mouth, so impossibly hard she didn't think he could blow.

She should have known better. His thighs tensed as his hands tightened in her hair, his balls drawing up beneath her fingers. Her name fell like a curse from his lips, a split-second warning before he flooded her mouth.

As he'd instructed, she drank him down, swallowing his come and licking along his shaft until he drew her away. She sat up, lightheaded with pleasure and need and want, ready, so very ready for him.

"My beautiful, sexy girl, what you do for me." He cupped her cheek and even in the dim interior she could see his wicked smile. "Now I get to do for you."

SEVENTEEN

B reath rushed from her lungs in a whoosh of sound. When she reached for his still-hard cock, he grabbed her wrist. "Go inside, sweetness. Get ready for me. When I come in I want to find you in the middle of your bed, naked and spread, waiting for me."

Lust thickened her throat, making it difficult to swallow. "How . . . how long will you be?"

That grin again. "Why? Thinking about masturbating to take the edge off? Don't."

She hadn't thought about relieving herself, not really, but now he'd put the idea in her head . . . She needed to come, badly. Masturbating would blunt the edge of her need but that would be an unsatisfactory cheat, like going for a burger when a perfectly grilled rib eye sat next to it. It would be better to come with his cock filling her, or his tongue on her clit. Her fingers could get the job done, but Charlie could make her see stars.

"I won't," she finally promised, too horny to play games.

"That's my girl." He leaned over to kiss her, a soft and gentle press of lips that she felt all the way to her toes. "Go on, goddess. I'll be right behind you, and then we'll play."

God. It took two tries for her to open the door. She got out, then stumbled her way to the porch, her legs wobbly from need. Fumbling, graceless, she managed to unlock her door, disarm the alarm, then make her way to her bedroom. The bed beckoned her but she bypassed it in favor of going to the bathroom. A cool shower was sure to dampen her overheated senses. Otherwise she'd go up like a match as soon as Charlie touched her.

How was he able to affect her so completely? She shook her head in disbelief as she slid the glass partition open to step beneath the shower's lukewarm spray. Something in the combination of his touch, his smile, and the heat in his eyes pulled at her as no one else had before. In moments like this, when the need to be filled by him drove her crazy, thoughts of their age difference and her past were far from her mind. Then he was just a man, she was just a woman, but together they were magic.

Charlie was more than just a man though. Her body came alive in anticipation of his nearness. His eager, focused reaction to her made her feel beautiful, desired. Appreciated, even—things she hadn't felt in years, hadn't felt for far longer than she cared to remember.

She knew could become addicted to those feelings. She was in danger of caring more than she should, of wanting more than she should. It was a danger she didn't want to avoid. This addiction wouldn't be destructive, wouldn't chew her up and spit her out. Wouldn't cost her everything she'd worked so hard to regain over the last few years. Charlie wouldn't tear her down, wouldn't hurt her. She already trusted him with her body. It wouldn't be difficult to go one step further and trust him with her heart.

No, it was too early to think things like that. They were only two months into whatever this was. They'd just agreed to exclusivity, and she still had to meet his family, a step that could go horribly wrong or blissfully right. Better to take one day at a time, one step at a time. Better to not hope for more than she'd ever gotten before.

Using the honeysuckle bath gel Charlie liked, Siobhan lathered up, biting her bottom lip to help resist the urge to stroke herself off. As she rubbed the towel over her skin, anticipation soared, heating her blood again. Her eyes slid closed as she imagined Charlie sliding his hands over her, using the fabric of the towel to tease and tantalize her. That dangerous mouth of his would follow the path of his hands, stoking the embers of her desire until the spark became a fire and the fire burst into an inferno.

Now desperate for him, she padded into the bedroom only to find it empty. Her heart thudded in alarm. Did he leave? Had the reunion and dinner and trip to the adult store been nothing more than some kind of revenge game to pay her back?

No. She shook her head. This was Charlie. He wouldn't do that to her. He wanted her, his desire plain to see. He wouldn't trick her, not about this.

Siobhan talked herself back to logic, but her pounding heart didn't ease until she heard the front door open, then close and lock. She quickly pulled back the bedcovers and got in but balked at lying spread-eagled for him. The position made her vulnerable and she already danced on the edge of vulnerability tonight.

Instead she reclined on her side, body angled toward the open door, head propped on one hand, the other draped across her belly. Still completely naked, just not as exposed. Hopefully he'd approve.

It seemed like an eternity passed before Charlie appeared in the doorway, their bag of toys dangling from his hand. He paused there, his eyes glittering in the dim light as his gaze raked her body. A slow and sensual smile curved his lips. "Did you miss me?"

He obviously meant it as a tease, but Siobhan's heart still constricted in reaction. "Yes," she admitted, emotion welling up and threatening to choke her. "Yes, I missed you. I thought you'd left."

"Leave, when I know I have a beautiful blonde goddess waiting for me? Nothing could keep me away."

Her eyes shuttered as her emotions warbled again. This was easier when it was just about sex, when all she had to worry about was taking and giving pleasure. Charlie wanted more and now she was thinking about more as well. It scared her.

"You were gone for four days," she said, the words pulled out of her. She opened her eyes again, blinked rapidly. "I thought we were done. It was hard, harder than I thought it would be."

His smile vanished as he dropped the bag then crossed the room in two large strides. Concern filled his eyes as he knelt beside the bed, framed her face in his large hands. "We're not done. I'm here now. If you want me, you've got me."

As much as she wanted to accept that promise, she knew it wasn't one he could or should make. Not yet. Not until she met his family. "But tomorrow—"

He kissed her to stop her words. "Tomorrow will take care of itself. I'm not going anywhere. You and me, we're going to work. All right?"

When he looked at her like that, resolution shining in his eyes, she had no choice except to agree. "All right."

He drew back. The devilish light returned to his eyes. "You weren't spread-eagled for me. I wanted to come in and see that sweet pussy of yours wet and ready for me. Why were you hiding?"

"I wasn't hiding," she denied, though that was exactly what she'd done. "I'd just gotten out of the shower. I was here and ready, naked. Waiting."

"Naked and waiting, yes." He nodded. "Ready, no. We've still got some trust issues, don't we?"

She drew in a slow breath. His gaze dropped to her breasts, causing her nipples to instantly pebble as she let the breath out. "I trust you, Charlie."

"I appreciate you saying that, sweetheart." He lifted her hand, kissed her knuckles. "But I'm a show-not-tell kind of guy."

"How?" She licked her lips. "How do you want me to show you?"

He stood, retrieved the bag, then returned to her. "I want you to feel. Just feel. Put your pleasure into my hands."

He reached into the bag, pulled out a scrap of fabric, and placed it on her stomach. Tilting her head up, she realized it was a black satin blindfold. "We didn't buy that."

"I did," he said with an unapologetic grin. "I thought it would be fun."

She arched a brow. "I suppose you want to tie me up too?"

"Now that you mention it . . ." His grin widened. "I want to have my way with you. After all, we do have a sack full of goodies to try out. If I do something you don't like, just tell me to stop."

Her nipples tightened to painful points. "Stop? No special safe words or stuff like that?"

"I don't know much about whips and chains and all of that except for what I've seen on the Internet, but I do know that stop means stop and no means no. I'm all for keeping it simple." He slid a hand up her belly, her ribs, then up to circle her right breast, smaller and smaller circles until his forefinger outlined her nipple. "Faster, slower, wait." He pinched her nipple between two fingers. "Harder."

She gasped as a spark of lust flared from her tit to her clit. "Softer."

"See?" He eased the pressure on her nipple, then leaned over to soothe the sting with a slow tease of tongue that left her shuddering. "Simple is easy. We communicate well together."

"We'd communicate better if you were naked."

"I'll decide when it's time for me to get naked." He picked up the blindfold, using the tip to trace around her nipple. "Are you ready?"

Excitement filled her as she gazed up at him. A faint shadow of beard darkened his jaw, giving a rugged edge to his sun-god looks. Hunger, appreciation, and command burned in his eyes, daring her to surrender to him, to trust him.

"I'm ready."

At least, she thought she was. She sucked in a breath as Charlie leaned over her to secure the blindfold, her fight-or-flight instincts clawing to the surface. Tense, she waited for his next move, only to realize he was waiting for her. "I'm okay."

"Your body says otherwise." He skimmed his fingers down her throat, resting his hand atop her frantically pounding heart. The heat of his fingers sank into her skin, holding her like an anchor. "Who do you trust, Siobhan?"

"Nadia." Theirs was a friendship forged through enduring their darkest days together. The sister she'd never had, Nadia was the only one other than her grandmother whom Siobhan had ever trusted, the only one she was certain would have her back no matter what.

Irony crashed down as she lay there, blindfolded and naked for him. "You," she added, her throat dry. "I'm trying to trust you, but—"

"I haven't made it easy for you," he cut in, regret ripe in his tone. "I want to fix that."

"No, that's not what I meant." She wanted to reach for him but dug her fingers into the sheet instead. "I meant that, after everything that's happened with me, trust isn't an easy thing. I'm working on it, though. I want to trust you, Charlie."

His hand lay heavy on her heart. "Do you want me to remove the blindfold? We can play some other time."

He would remove it, she knew. Then they would have fantastic sex and she'd get to discover what it was like to actually sleep next to him. They were trying to have a real relationship, and although that was part of it, trust had a larger share. "I want to keep it on. I know if I really need you to, you'll take it off for me."

"I will. Just say the word." He kissed her forehead. "Thank you, sweetheart."

Her heart constricted as she sensed him moving away. This was as important to him as it was to her, she realized. That fact enabled her to travel away from anxiety to anticipation. Time seemed to slow as she listened to his movements, listened to the thrumming of her blood.

She felt the electric change in the air as he approached the bed again. Her breath shortened again as he brought her hands together above her head, then wrapped her wrists with what felt like satin ribbon. A sash from one of her robes, maybe.

"It's not tight," he told her, pressing the end of the sash into her palm. "You can loosen it and release yourself anytime you want."

He'd given her a bit of power back. While she appreciated the gesture, she knew that wasn't the point of the game. "You can tighten it. I'm all right."

"A test for both of us, I think." He drew her hands up until her fingers touched one of the headboard spindles. "There's enough give in the sash so you can lower your arms a bit—or turn over. Try to keep your hands on the headboard if you can. Now lift your hips."

She immediately complied, and he slid a couple of pillows beneath her, elevating her hips. The bed gave as he regained his feet. She wondered if he stood beside her, wondered what she looked like, naked and waiting for him.

She didn't have to wonder long. "You have no idea how beautiful you are right now," he told her, his voice almost reverent. "Your lips are parted, your nipples are hard and dark pink, and your pussy is this deep, lush, wet rose. For me. It's all a feast for me."

She fell beneath the spell his words wove. "Yes, for you. It's yours, baby."

"Remember your words, goddess," he ordered, hunger scraping his words raw. "Go, stop, more."

"Now," she demanded.

The bed dipped as his low laughter skated over her senses. "I'm going to please myself by pleasing you until you come. And then I'm going to do it again."

He kissed her, a sweetly soft kiss that took her by surprise. Then he nipped her bottom lip, making her gasp. His tongue slipped into her mouth, the sweetness pushed out by spicy heat. As their mouths melded and mated he brushed his bared body against hers, reawakening the desire that never seemed far from the surface.

Slowly he made his way down her throat, alternating between open-mouthed kisses and suckling love bites. Each suckling pressure sent a bolt of lust shooting through her body and stabbing deep into her core. She arched against him wanting more, needing more.

When his teeth closed over one nipple she cried out, instinctively tugging at her bound hands in an effort to touch him. He raised his head, and when he spoke, his tone was guttural with lust. "Do I need to stop, sweetness?"

"No." She shook her head to underscore her need for him to continue, her body on fire for Charlie and the delicious sensations he created. Thankfully he lowered his head again, his mouth closing over one nipple for a powerful suckle that seemed to be on a direct circuit to her pussy. His nimble fingers plucked her right nipple, the roughened pads scraping her sensitized flesh as he rolled the distended tip between his thumb and forefinger before pinching down.

"Charlie!" She bucked against him as her senses short-circuited on the pleasure-pain. He didn't relent, just switched so that his wicked mouth suckled the tight bud already stroked to fullness.

She writhed against him, trying to settle him atop her, to cradle him where she needed him most. Instead, he continued his slow, suckling meander down her body, over the rise of her belly, detouring around her core to lick and kiss and bite his way down her legs before reversing course.

Caught up, helpless, she waited with breathless anticipation for the touch of his tongue against her clit. He denied her. She moaned a protest, only to be rewarded with a knowing chuckle. "Meanie," she complained. "This is the real reason why you tied me up, isn't it?"

"You got me."

His breath warmed her belly button, but he still denied her the touch she craved. "You're enjoying yourself, aren't you?"

"You have no idea." Deep masculine satisfaction rang through his words.

She bit her lip, torn between pique and passion. Though he was pleasing her, teasing her, focusing on her, he seemed to enjoy himself. She appreciated his teasing, appreciated that he could lighten the heavy emotion that had spun around her when she'd thought he had left. Appreciated that he could make her laugh even while he made her body sing.

Charlie moved away from her. Over the pounding of her heartbeat she could hear little sounds that told her that he had opened their bag of sensual tricks. Her fingers curled around the straps as she waited, helpless, to discover what he would use on her first.

She jumped when he placed one large hand low on her belly, his thumb perilously close to where she ached for him. "Breathe," he admonished in a low whisper. "You'll miss all the fun if you pass out."

"Don't even think of having fun without me," she retorted.

"That's just it, goddess. It's not fun without you."

She waited for his chuckle but it didn't come. He was serious, she realized. Emotion welled up again. It wasn't fun without him either. Before Charlie, sex had been good, it had been not so good, and it had even been great. What it had never been was fun, but Charlie made it that way. Fun, explosive, heady, thrilling.

His words triggered a question she'd been meaning to ask him.

In a strange juxtaposition, being bound and tied by him made her brave enough to ask, "Why do you do that?"

"Do what?"

"Call me goddess."

For a long moment, he didn't reply. When he did, he rocked her to her foundation. "Because you make me want to fall at your feet and worship every beautiful inch of you. Because being in your arms is like a blessing. Most of all, when I'm deep inside you and you have me on the verge of coming, I can close my eyes and almost touch heaven."

Tears pricked her eyes as a wave of emotion crashed down on her, threatening to pull her under. "Charlie . . ."

"I know, it's completely sappy." He stroked the back of his hand along her jaw. "Doesn't make it any less true."

"I want to hug you and kiss you and have my way with you," she told him, her chest too tight to push out more than a whisper. "Unfortunately, I'm a little tied up at the moment."

"Then I suppose it's up to me to hug and kiss and have my way with you." He covered her, the hard lines of his body branding hers as he captured her mouth with his own.

Gasping at the heady contact, she wrapped her legs high around his waist, thrusting her body up against his in a desperate urge. His need was obvious as he devoured her mouth, the thrust of his tongue against hers as intoxicating and amazing and wonderful as the thick cock sliding against her outer lips.

"You make me forget myself, sweetness." Regret filled his voice. "As much as I want to be balls-deep inside you right now, that's not the plan."

"Fuck the plan." She tugged on her bonds, but didn't loosen them. "Fuck me instead."

"No."

She nearly howled as he pulled away from her again. "Wait." She lifted off the bed. "I just—I just need—"

"Something like this?"

A low buzzing sound split the air a moment before she felt the vibrator touch her left breast. She cried out, arching off the bed as rhythmic waves of sensation spiraled out from her breast and swept through the rest of her body.

He ran the tip of the vibrator around her areola, causing her nipple to bead up in near-painful tightness. "I think you like this," he murmured, his voice deep with approval. She felt his other hand slip lower down her belly and over her mound until his thumb rested against her clitoris. "Do you want more?"

"Yes," she huffed out. She always needed more with Charlie. More sensation, more play, more pleasure. He was making her insatiable in a way she had never experienced before. "You make me greedy for you, Charlie."

"That makes two of us then." He moved the vibrator to her other nipple, laving the other sensitized tip with warm strokes of his tongue even as his thumb dragged across her pulsing clit in maddening circles. "I always want more of you, no matter how much of you I have. More of the sounds you make and the responses you give, especially when I have more of this sweet pussy."

He slipped the vibrator down the valley between her breasts, slowly trailing the pulsating device down to her belly button. Her stomach clenched in response, in anticipation, in desperate need. "Take it," she burst out. "Whatever you want, you can have it."

"Not yet," he answered, surprising her. "I can't have it yet, but I will."

Before she could ask what he meant, the buzzing intensified. His thumb against her clit began to vibrate. He must have placed the vibrator against his hand, and the result was magic. She mewled, spreading her thighs open wider, needing as much of the sensual ripples as she could get.

He obliged her, running the stimulator over her clit in a maddeningly light stroke. Her sex clenched, empty and aching. "Charlie."

"Yes, goddess?"

"More."

"Yes, goddess."

He stroked the humming device along her outer lips, once, twice, then again. Just when she thought she'd have to beg, Charlie pushed the vibrator into her waiting sex. Her body, already brimming with pleasure, flooded with delight. She gasped, then sank into a purr as Charlie fit his mouth to her. He suckled her clit, teasing strokes, tantalizing sweeps, tender kisses that promised to shatter her.

Sparks shot through her, leaving her moaning, gasping, breathing his name. He called her goddess but in that perfect moment his name was a prayer on her lips.

"That's it, sweetness," he crooned against her. He slid the stimulator into her slick channel again and held it there, thrumming reverberations echoing through her core. "Show me how much you like what I'm doing to you."

His tongue thrust into her already slick folds as he began to slowly fuck her with the vibrator. A guttural groan escaped her, her fingers tightening on the headboard as he continued the sensual onslaught. Higher and higher she careened, Charlie expertly working her body as if he'd long ago learned what would drive her crazy and make her scream. She writhed on the sheets as Charlie drove her toward bliss with fast, slow, circular strokes and the eager sweep of his tongue. Her body hummed in time to each thrust, each taste, each magical movement. A flick of his wrist and the vibrator surged to a higher setting. Charlie pressed it in and up, then sucked her clit between his lips.

She shrieked, catapulted into orgasm, bright white sparks dancing behind her closed and blindfolded eyes. Her thighs clamped together, holding him in place as she rode out the powerful wave. Finally, limp and spent, she collapsed.

It was a long moment before she could separate her higher functions from the purring contentment spiraling through her body. When she did, she became aware of him moving, taking away the pillows, making noises she couldn't discern the meaning of. Then he touched her thigh. "Lift your hips, sweetness."

She obeyed, then lowered herself back down at his soft command. He'd placed a towel beneath her.

Trepidation blunted the edge of her euphoria as he pressed a gel-slicked finger against her anus. "Uh, Charlie, I don't know about this."

He paused. "Are you worried, sweetness? I'll be gentle."

"That's not the part I'm worried about." She felt embarrassment burn her chest. "This is either going to be really satisfying or really embarrassing."

"I have two younger brothers," he reminded her with a chuckle. "Believe me, I'm not afraid of farts."

"I don't want to think of farts or your brothers while you've got your finger in my ass," she complained.

He laughed, damn him. "Allow me to give you something else to think about then."

She settled back with a loud sigh of surrender. "Okay. Don't say I didn't warn you."

"You've warned me but you didn't say your words." He paused, the tip of his finger firm against her bottom. "Do you want me to stop?"

Despite her worry over this uncharted territory, her body wanted more. She wanted more. "No, I want you inside me."

"I'll let you set the pace, sweetheart. Remember, if you want to stop, just say the word." He kissed her, a slow, thorough kiss that fogged her senses and fueled her desire. When his finger teased over her rear opening, she lifted her hips eagerly, wanting him everywhere, wanting him to claim her completely.

Pressure, then his finger slipped inside her back entrance. Warmth spread. "Ah. Wow."

"I used the warming gel." He trailed kisses down her throat. "Do you approve?"

"Wholeheartedly."

"That's my sweet girl."

He continued to kiss his way down her body as he worked his finger deeper, lubing her rear entrance and preparing her to accept the vibrator. By the time he kissed his way back to her sex again, she was ready for more. "Now, Charlie. I want it now."

He pressed the tip of the vibrator against her back hole, the slick gel and tapered tip making the breach somewhat easier to bear. She shifted her hips to impale herself, then stopped at the first flash of pain.

"Siobhan?"

"It's definitely not the same as your finger."

"Okay. We'll try again some other time."

"No, don't move. Just let me breathe through it." It took several stops and starts but then somehow her muscles relaxed and the vibrator slipped inside. Flashes of pain were forgotten as more of that delicious heat spread through her.

He thrummed up to a faster setting. "Good?"

Tingles swept through her, delicious rolling sparks. "Oh, yes."

"Maybe I can make it even better."

He fit himself to her entrance, then pushed slowly inside. She moaned as his thickness filled her, competing with the vibrator thrumming in her rear channel. Blind, bound, she was helpless to do anything but accept the dual invasion and revel in the pleasure of it.

"Yes." He shuddered as he bottomed out. "Holy fuck, Siobhan, that feels good."

He withdrew, then reentered her on a long, slow glide that had her arching up again, drawn to him, drawn to every bit of pleasure. God, he'd used the warming gel on his cock, sending more of that heated sensation spiraling through her as he found the perfect rhythm. They'd definitely have to order another bucket or two of the stuff.

"Charlie, Charlie," she chanted, the sensation almost overwhelming, driving away rational thought, memory, language. She gathered enough wits to beg. "Need you. Need to see you. Please let me see you."

His weight settled on her, heavy yet oh so welcoming, then he pushed the blindfold up. She blinked as his features came into view, her breath catching at the back of her throat. His jaw worked with the effort to maintain control but his eyes blazed as if she was everything that he needed to survive. "Hands?"

It took her a moment to realize what he meant. "Yes, yes, please."

He reached up to loosen the sash binding her hands. She immediately tunneled her fingers into his hair, dragging him down for a fierce, unfettered kiss. Wrapping her legs high around his waist, she rocked against him, his name a chant on her lips.

Her wildness triggered his own. Groaning her name, he powered into her repeatedly, the thickness of his cock pressing against the pulsating solidity of the vibrator filling her ass, making her helpless to everything but the pleasure that steamrolled through her, obliterating everything but him.

"Charlie, Charlie, I'm gonna come," she warned him, not wanting to go without him.

"Go, babe, I'm right there with you," he said huskily, his hips slamming against her. She shoved one hand between their colliding bodies, so wild, so wet, so ready that it only took one stroke to overload her senses and rocket her to an earthshaking release.

Charlie buried his face into the crook of her neck as he pummeled into her in pure masculine ferocity. He stiffened, tossing his head back, mouth open in a wordless groan as he jetted deep inside her. They collapsed together, spent, drained, and utterly satisfied.

EIGHTEEN

Much later, Siobhan traced her forefinger across Charlie's pecs as they lay together in a tangle of sheets and limbs trying to fall asleep together for the first time. "Do you think they'll like me? Your brothers, I mean?"

"Absolutely. In fact, they're more worried about making a good impression on you. Kyle knows you own the café, and since he loves to cook he's been stressing over some elaborate dish to impress you. Finn will ask you if you can play video games, but since he's got a car fixation, he'll be a goner as soon as he sees your vintage convertible."

Siobhan pursed her lips as she thought about how to best relate to Charlie's family. "If he likes classic cars, I can get you guys passes to the Crimson Bay Classics auto show that's coming up at Tidewater Park in three weeks. The Bombshells are going to make an appearance. With Kyle, I can certainly talk food, and maybe we could even cook together."

"The boys will love that. You'll have them wrapped around your finger in no time."

"I'll be happy with them not actively disliking me. The only thing I want to be wrapped around is you."

He huffed out a laugh. "Noted. I do have to say that it sounds like you've got each one of us pegged already."

"Not all of you," she admitted. "I have no clue what to do with Lorelei. My track record with girls Lorelei's age—well, that's mostly been centered around trying to get my daughter to stop hating me, which means it sucks. All I can do is try though. I'll just follow her lead."

"Lorelei already likes you, as proven by the fact that she lets you call her Lorelei," Charlie pointed out. "She told me so when she came to read me the riot act for taking so long to get back to you. I think it's safe to say that all you'll have to do is show up Saturday and not be frightened off by the O'Halloran clan in all our loud, obnoxious glory. In fact, I may just tie you to my bed or the couch or something until we're done brainwashing you."

"I don't think you need to do anything so drastic," she said. "I'd rather you do other things to me when you tie me to the bed."

"I'll make sure to put that into the rotation often then."

She settled against him, enjoying the comforting bulk of his body next to hers, the steady beat of his heart beneath her ear, and the weight of his arms around her. She could get used to this, she thought. No, not used to it, because she didn't want to take anything with Charlie for granted, but moments like this, spent lying entwined together sated and exhausted, were gloriously precious.

Aided by Charlie's slow deep breathing and his hand resting on her waist, Siobhan edged toward a contented sleep. She'd thought

Charlie was already asleep until he shattered her contentment with a quiet question.

"Why do you think your daughter hates you?"

Siobhan cringed. She didn't want to talk to Charlie about this, not here, not now. Not when things were going well between them. Even though her past was still and always would be a big part of her life, she didn't want to remind Charlie of what she had been. She did want him to understand though, if only so he'd realize that the place she was in now was better than where she was.

"I know Colleen hates me because she told me to my face that she did. This was two years ago, when I thought having her work in the café with me would bring us closer together. It didn't go as well as I'd hoped."

"Tell me again what happened to you," Charlie said, running his hand down her back.

Siobhan froze at the soft request. "Why?"

"Because I want to know," he said into the silence, his voice low but no less determined. "I'm having a hard time understanding why your family treats you the way you say they do, especially your daughter. Especially when everything I know and see and experience with you makes me like you more every day. Who could hate you?"

She pressed her face against his chest, the warmth from his words colliding with the chill of old memories. "I had to talk about it in rehab. I had to talk about it with my therapist. Talking about it brings back the pain, and I don't want that pain to come back."

"If it's too difficult for you, we don't have to talk about it." He dropped a kiss on her forehead. "Let's get some sleep."

She could almost feel him withdraw. "Charlie." She spread a

hand on his chest, over his heart. "I want to tell you. I need to tell you. I just . . ."

He seemed to understand. Lifting her hand, he gave her fingers a gentle kiss. "Tell me what you want, when you want. I'm here to listen."

"Okay." She sighed, then turned her back to him, needing the slight distance to give her the courage to speak. "Pain is what started it. People will tell you there's this endorphin rush after you deliver the baby that takes the pain away. I didn't get that rush, just more pain. It was everywhere and it weighed me down.

"I wasn't nursing so they prescribed Vicodin. Everything was fine for a while, but the pain returned and it hobbled me. Mike was serving overseas at the time and Colleen and I were living with my grandmother. I was supposed to help her and keep her company, but I think it was more the other way around. She was my lifeline but I still felt like I was failing everyone—my daughter, my husband, my family—and that added to the pain. I would have done anything to keep from disappointing them more than I had already."

"How did you disappoint them?"

"My parents, my father in particular, weren't happy that I got pregnant during my senior year of high school. Good Catholic girls don't do that, and certainly no daughter of theirs would let herself be used that way. That was the main reason I went to live with my grandmother."

She hunched her shoulders. "I felt a lot of pressure, especially after my grandmother died, but I was failing at life. I couldn't fail at motherhood too. So my doctor put me on OxyContin. The pills dulled the pain and when I doubled the dosage, they got me back to happy. They got me to a place where my family liked me. My relationships with my parents and Mike's parents improved. I could play with my daughter the way she needed me to since she was an only child. I was able to be there, be in the moment for all of them even though there was this soft focus over everything. It seemed like everyone liked me better when I was stoned."

"You can't mean that. Did you have a completely different personality when you were high?"

"No. I don't think so, but the memories of those years are mostly fuzzy. Obviously, I was able to function well enough, be myself enough, that no one suspected anything for a long time, or they simply believed that motherhood agreed with me. But my tolerance went up, which meant the amount of pills I took each time went up. Then it was pills with a glass of wine."

She gripped the sheet in a trembling fist. "Sometimes it makes me wonder what would have happened, how far I would have gone if I hadn't set the kitchen on fire."

His hand slid over her waist, then splayed across her belly. "Sometimes the worst things can become good things with a little time and distance. You got the help you needed. Your family should be happy about that."

She shook her head, not to deny his words, but the memories they evoked. "I embarrassed them. Worse than that, I disappointed them. Malloys are made of stronger stuff than that. I was in treatment for ninety days and by the time I got out, they'd made up their minds. I got served divorce papers the day I was released. Mike had put my things in storage, moved to the other side of the county, and my daughter and parents wouldn't see me."

She remembered that day with crystal clarity. How hopeful she'd been, thinking the future was bright, thinking her family would be there ready to welcome her back. That none of them had visited her during her stay she'd chalked up to a tough-love approach. Instead of her husband waiting for her, a process server had delivered a thick envelope with divorce papers, a custody judgment against her, and keys to a storage unit, along with letters from her mother, Mike, and Colleen explaining why they were kicking her out of their lives. Devastated, she'd retreated to her room and refused to leave, knowing that as soon as she left the treatment facility she'd be truly alone.

"That day was the worst of my life because I had nothing. I'd gotten clean for them, endured withdrawals and baring my soul because I knew they were waiting for me. Instead they abandoned me. I had no family, no place to stay, and I didn't have the chemical cocoon the pills gave me. That pain . . ." She stopped, breathed deeply several times before continuing. "That pain nearly did me in. If not for Nadia and her fathers, I don't know what I would have done."

She did know, though. She'd had nothing and no one. Her life had been over, and in her mind being clean and sober hadn't been worth the price she'd paid. If Nadia hadn't invited Siobhan to stay with her, Siobhan doubted that she would have survived the day.

"That was the worst day. And the worst night, the biggest temptation to say the hell with it all and let go. Then I swear I heard my grandmother ask me, did I truly get clean for them or for me? If I failed, I'd be proving them right, proving that they were right to cut me off. I realized I had a choice to make, and I chose to prove them wrong. I chose to succeed. I chose to move on with my life. And I did. Mostly. But I still want to reconcile with Colleen and my parents if I can."

His arms had tightened around her while she told her story. "I hope you can. Family means everything."

"I know," she whispered. "I hope so too."

"What do you do for pain now? If you get a headache or stub your toe or have cramps, how do you deal?"

"Homeopathic remedies," she answered. "Teas, hot or cold compresses, or a TENS unit—transcutaneous electrical nerve stimulation—usually does the trick. I put in that large jetted tub when I bought the bungalow, and soaking in it is a dream. I've been lucky that I haven't had to deal with anything more severe than sore muscles since I got clean. I don't do medicine of any kind."

Charlie remained silent behind her and she wondered if she'd have to say good-bye to him again. Wondered if he'd finally realize how much baggage she brought with her. Their sex was phenomenal, but was it worth dealing with her issues?

"I'll be right back," she said, sliding out of bed. "I need to go pee."

The dim nightlight in the master bath caught the sheen of tears on her cheeks, her runny nose. Not wanting Charlie to come after her, she did her business, then turned to the sink, wetting a washcloth but leaving the cold water tap on full blast to muffle her sniffles.

Dammit. She should have had this conversation with Charlie when he'd first arrived, instead of being distracted by his kisses. Should have clued him in to the reality of her life, her recovery, her fucked-up, nonexistent relationship with her family. She should have turned him away at the door.

"Siobhan."

She kept her face hidden in the washcloth for a moment before lowering it, then opened the door. Charlie stood in the doorway but the darkness made his expression unreadable. The way he'd called her name, heavy and low, flooded her stomach with apprehension.

"Whatever you're thinking, it's okay," she said, wanting to give him an out. She injected lightness into her tone. "I knew when I told you all this that there was a real possibility that I wouldn't see you again. I mean, I can't get my own daughter to acknowledge my texts and e-mails, and my father hasn't said anything to me other than 'get out' in almost a decade. Because of that, I don't expect anyone to be forgiving or nonjudgmental."

"Is that what you think I'm doing? Judging you?"

She tightened her grip on the washcloth. "Not today, but you did before. I understand, and I'm sorry."

He moved then, taking the facecloth from her and tossing it onto the counter before circling his arms about her waist. Resistance gripped her for a brief moment but her body betrayed her, seeking the comfort of his warmth, his arms. He pulled her snug against his chest, tucked her head beneath his chin, and simply held her. It was the best feeling in the world.

His voice was a deep soothing rumble when he finally spoke again. "You've got nothing to apologize to me for."

"I should have told you earlier." She swallowed the lump in her throat as she surreptitiously wiped at her eyes. "You should have known before we got involved so you could have cut your losses. I'm sorry I'm not what you thought I was."

"I thought you were a beautiful and sexy woman who's slightly bent. I still do." He kissed her shoulder. "As for cutting my losses, I wish I could say that I wouldn't have done that, but the truth is I don't know what I would have done."

"You would have done what you thought best for you and your family, just like you did this time," she answered. "I know I've got a big black mark against me. I know some people can't look past that.

I'm a recovering drug addict almost five years clean. While I think I'm in a good place and I've managed to carve out a good life with friends who support me, I knew it wouldn't be fair to continue seeing you and meeting your family while concealing a major part of who and what I am."

He stroked a hand down her back. "It was brave, what you did."

His praise warmed her, though she hardly felt as if she deserved it. "Maybe bravery means doing what needs to be done because you feel as if you have no choice, as if the other option is worse, as if the consequences of not doing it are far worse."

She cradled his hand between the valley of her breasts. "Maybe you're being brave too if you plan to keep seeing me."

"I'm not being brave." He tightened his hold on her. "I thought about the risks and benefits of being with you. Then I made the decision—with a little help from my sister, of course—to be with you."

"Yes." She moved against him. "It would be hard to walk away from this."

"I agree, but that wasn't why I made the decision I made."

"What was it then?" she asked, tensing despite the desire not to.

"Actually, it was a realization more than a decision. I realized that you are worth it. Being with you is worth it. Having you meet the rest of the family is worth it. Seeing where this goes, definitely worth it. But most of all, you, Siobhan Malloy, are worth it."

Siobhan closed her eyes as a tremble coursed through her. She couldn't tell him how much his declaration meant to her. Discovering her self-worth had been a long arduous process and she'd had several emotional setbacks during the crumbling of her familial relationships. While she knew she had worth, had value, it was still powerful to hear it from someone else.

"Thank you," she whispered, her voice thick. "I'll do my best not to expose your family to any of my drama. And I swear, if I think there's a chance that I'm going to hurt you or your brothers and sister, I'll walk away."

"No one's walking away from anyone else," he said, retrieving the washcloth to dab at her cheeks. "That's not how we O'Hallorans roll. Now come back to bed so I can hold you while we fall asleep."

"All right," she agreed, not wanting to argue with him now that they'd committed to their relationship. Still, she knew that she had a responsibility to protect Charlie and his family from her past and not let it impinge on the present or the future. She'd have to be even more diligent against moments of weakness now. If she'd been strong enough, selfless enough, she wouldn't have allowed him in the house, much less back into her bed.

She couldn't bring herself to do that. The past two months with Charlie were some of the best she'd had since she'd opened the café. He made her heart race, her body sing. He made her laugh and sigh and scream with pleasure. She wasn't ready to give that up yet. She wasn't ready to give Charlie up.

Tucking her head beneath his chin, emotionally and physically exhausted, she settled against him, then relaxed into sleep.

NINETEEN

"Will you stop peeking out of the window?" Charlie demanded for the umpteenth time. "You're going to give Mrs. McGowan a complex."

Lorelei dropped the edge of the curtain but didn't step away from the window. "Are you sure she isn't lost? Did you give her the right directions? Maybe you should text her again."

"She said she's on the way," Charlie pointed out, again for the umpteenth time. "That means she's on the way. Now will you please back away from the window? You're freaking people out."

He meant Kyle, who was in the kitchen checking on the food. Again. Kyle had gotten progressively more anxious as the weekend approached, planning and replanning the menu as if it were a state dinner. Charlie finally had to put his foot down. He knew Siobhan would be happy with whatever they served, just as he knew she was equally as nervous about meeting them as they were about meeting her.

Nobody was as nervous as he was. Keeping up his outward calm was automatic, something he'd had to do since he became head of the family. Inside, though, his stomach roiled with anxiety. He wanted this introduction to go well. Needed it to be smooth. His family meant everything to him, but Siobhan was coming to mean more to him every day. Spending the night with her, waking up pressed against her softness . . . nothing could beat that. He wanted more of that. He wanted everything Siobhan wanted to give him. If he could have it all . . .

"She's here!" Lorelei bounced from foot to foot. "Oh, my God, she's got an awesome convertible. She's looks like a movie star!"

That brought Finn to his feet and Kyle in from the kitchen. The plan was for Charlie to greet Siobhan outside, help her with any packages, then bring her in to meet his siblings in the family room. That had been the plan.

"I'm gonna see if she needs help." Lorelei yanked open the front door and stepped out. Finn followed, leaving Charlie staring at Kyle's questioning face.

"Come on, bro," Charlie said, clapping his brother on the shoulder. "Might as well show her how we O'Hallorans roll."

He stepped through the open doorway just as Siobhan stepped out of her vintage cherry red convertible looking every inch the retro movie star, with large sunglasses hiding her eyes and a blue and white scarf covering her hair. He was almost disappointed that she wasn't wearing one of her trademark sundresses, but the form-fitting navy crop pants accentuated her curves as did the sleeveless red and white blouse. Damn, she was a beautiful woman.

Glad he wore an untucked shirt over his khaki cargo shorts to hide his now-expected reaction to seeing her, Charlie stepped forward to kiss her cheek. "Hello, beautiful."

A smile bowed her scarlet lips as she removed her scarf and sunglasses, revealing hopeful eyes. "Hey, yourself. I'm sorry I'm late."

"You're not late." He slipped an arm around her waist, turning her to face his siblings. She tensed, the only indication of her nervousness. "You already know Lorelei."

Genuine warmth flooded Siobhan's tone. "Hi, Lorelei. It's really good to see you again. Feel free to come by the café anytime. Your next drink is on me."

"Thanks," his sister answered with a huge smile. "I'll do that."

"And these are my brothers," Charlie said, silently noting how Siobhan leaned against him. "The tall one is Kyle and the short one drooling all over the hood is Finn."

Finn looked up from admiring the car. "Is this a fifty-seven Falcon?"

"It's a fifty-six, actually."

"Cool. Can I get in?"

"Finn, can you at least say hello before you start asking for rides?"

Finn ducked his head. "Hi, Siobhan. It's-nice-to-meet-you-can-I-get-in-your-car?"

"I don't mind, but it's up to Charlie." She looked at him so sweet and serene that it was difficult not to kiss her again, a real kiss. They were outside though. Mrs. McGowan stood on her porch openly gawking, and his siblings were poised to bark at any affectionate displays. Proper kisses would have to wait until they were alone.

Finn turned pleading puppy dog eyes to Charlie. Normally

Charlie was made of sterner stuff, but this was the best possible ice-breaker for Finn. For all of them. "You can get in. But don't touch anything."

Finn rolled his eyes. "I have to touch stuff to get in. Duh." At least he took his time slipping into the driver's seat.

Siobhan turned to Kyle. "Charlie told me that you like straw-berries."

Kyle darted a look at Charlie, and his Adam's apple bobbed be-fore he answered. "Yeah, I do."

"I made a strawberry cake for you," she said, slipping out of Charlie's hold to reach to the backseat floorboard. "I'm not much of a baker—I leave that up to my partner, Nadia—so if you don't like it, we'll chuck it and go with something else."

Kyle's shoulders relaxed as he accepted the cake container from Siobhan. "I bet it tastes great."

Charlie breathed a sigh of relief. So far, so good. "Okay. Let's head inside before Finn asks you to go for a ride."

"Aww," Finn groaned, apparently about to do just that.

"Maybe we can go for a drive after we eat," Siobhan suggested. "As long as Charlie says it's okay."

"We'll see," Charlie said, herding them all toward the door. "Siobhan, welcome to the O'Halloran homestead, also known as Crazy Town. Lorelei, how about giving our guest the five-buck tour?"

Charlie hung back, watching as Siobhan interacted with his siblings. A week ago, having her here in their space seemed like an impossibility as he'd reeled from the story she'd told him. Even now he had moments of disbelief that the beautiful goddess of a woman currently charming the pants off his family had at one time nearly burned a house down around her and her child because she'd been stoned out of her mind.

Lorelei quickly led them through the upper floor, where she, Finn, and Kyle had their bedrooms—the boys' rooms flanking their shared bathroom, and Lorelei's suite, because she refused to share a bathroom with her brothers. Charlie had the house remodeled a few years ago to give his siblings an opportunity to create space for themselves and as a way of moving forward. Changing his parents' master suite into his private retreat had been harder than he'd thought it would be, especially since he'd had to convince Finn and Kyle that he wasn't trying to erase their parents' memory. They'd kept the family room almost the same, with their father's recliner having a spot of honor and their mother's hand-knitted afghan draping the back of the massive sectional. The room flowed into the updated kitchen and the bright breakfast nook with sliding doors that opened onto the lanai and the backyard.

Siobhan stepped through the patio doors. "Oh, you have a garden?"

"Our mom loved to garden," Lorelei said as they made their way to the fenced-in patch of vegetation. "We keep it up to honor her memory."

Siobhan blinked rapidly, her hand over her heart. "Can we go see it?"

"Sure," Charlie answered. "Kyle?"

Kyle led them across the yard to the fenced section that got plenty of sunlight. Orderly rows of drought-tolerant vegetables formed the bulk of the raised beds, but they also had a couple of fruit trees, berry brambles, and a grapevine that had seen better days. Between the shed and the fence sat a bench Lorelei had decorated with butterflies when she was twelve. Beside the bench stood a sun-catcher mobile, with bright crystals in the shapes of suns and trees.

"I found a local artist to make that for us," Charlie said as they gathered around it. "It's another memorial to our parents. I'll come out here sometimes and talk to them." Much better than going to the cemetery and staring at their gravestone. That wasn't how he wanted to remember them, cold and still underground. His mother was sunlight, brightening the day with her laughter and love. His father was a tree, providing shelter in his wide-open arms and keeping them all grounded.

"I talk to them too," Lorelei admitted. "I feel close to them here."

"Me too," each of his brothers added.

Siobhan slipped her arm around Charlie's waist, giving him a comforting squeeze. "What a beautiful tribute," she said, her voice shaky. "I can feel the love here."

Lorelei and his brothers shared watery smiles as they stepped closer to her. The moment seared itself into his memory, the moment they all connected. He tripped, skidded, and fell headlong into something that could have been love but was definitely more than lust. Siobhan fit with them, fit with him. He'd do everything he could to convince her of that.

"This is wonderful," Siobhan said, easing them out of the emotional silence. "And it looks like you have a nice variety of things growing."

"Kyle's the garden captain since he uses a lot of the stuff when he cooks."

"Stuff?" Siobhan repeated, one eyebrow raised. "You mean herbs and vegetables?"

Recognizing her teasing, Charlie shrugged. "You mean the stuff that tries to overwhelm the meat on my plate? Yeah, that stuff."

"That stuff is good for you," she protested. "Your body needs that stuff."

"I try to tell them that," Kyle volunteered, surprising Charlie. "Then they ask if they can have it covered in cheese."

"Cheese?" Siobhan recoiled in mock horror. "Why do you want to smother a poor, defenseless vegetable like that? What did it ever do to you?"

"It decided not to be meat," Charlie joked, which earned him a snort and a slap on the shoulder.

"You're lucky your charm outweighs your eating habits, mister," she teased him as she stepped inside the fence. "Wow, you guys have done an impressive amount of work with your garden. I think I'm jealous."

"That's all thanks to Kyle, our future engineer," Charlie told her, not holding back his pride. "He came up with this drip installation system and a rainwater collection system. He also fabricated a way for us to repurpose some of our wastewater."

"Wow." She turned a high-wattage smile in Kyle's direction. "Maybe you could come over and help me design a system for my garden."

Kyle's ears burned deep red as he dipped his head and hunched his shoulders. "I don't know if I could do that."

"Well, we'd make sure Charlie was okay with it, but this is pure genius." She squatted down beside one of the plants. "If you're not already, you should totally think about being an agricultural or horticultural engineer. You'd be great at it. Now tell me what you're doing to make your lettuce grow so full."

Charlie watched as Kyle—shy, anxious Kyle—knelt beside Siobhan and began to talk. Quietly at first, Kyle grew more confident in his responses until he led Siobhan about the garden, talking animatedly about growth cycles and fertilizer and other things that usually made Charlie's eyes glaze over.

"I like her," Finn said in his usual abrupt way. "She's nice to Kyle. Do you think she likes to play video games?"

Charlie had to take a moment before he could speak past the lump of relief in his throat. "It wouldn't hurt to ask her. We'll play some after dinner and see if she'll join in."

"Cool."

"Hey, Finn," Siobhan called. "Can you come help us? Some of these veggies are ready and we could use an extra hand."

"Okay." Finn scurried off to join them, leaving Lorelei and Charlie alone.

Lorelei crossed her arms. "I'm not going to say I told you so, big bro," she said with a smug smile. "Let's just say that I know that you know I did, and we'll leave it at that."

"Remember who's paying your tuition, young lady."

"The best brother in the world," she shot back, her tone saccharine. "The guy I want to be happy more than anything. So don't screw this up."

"I don't plan to screw this up," he answered, ignoring the twinge of trepidation her words caused. "If everything goes according to plan, you guys will be seeing a lot more of Siobhan."

"I hope so," Lorelei said, leaning against him in her version of a hug. "Just remember, life doesn't always go according to plan. We know that better than anyone."

He did know that, was painfully, perfectly aware that life didn't always follow the plan. Not that he'd had much of one when he'd become his siblings' guardian, a fact others had tried to use to wrest them away from him. Plans were the key to success, to survival. To achieving his goals. Siobhan was a goal that he very much wanted to achieve, and he'd plan and scheme and plot to make her his, no matter what life threw at him.

Dinner was a delicious, loud affair. Siobhan acted as Kyle's sous chef as he prepared pasta with vegetables from the garden, topped with grilled chicken and served with crusty garlic bread that everyone dug into. The O'Hallorans held true to their Irish roots and kept Siobhan entertained with stories, most of them centering on Charlie's parenting skills or lack thereof.

After dinner they adjourned to the family room with slices of the strawberry cake she'd made. Finn challenged Charlie to a video game duel. Realizing it was a game she and Nadia played during their Saturday night hangouts, Siobhan convinced Lorelei to join her team and take on the boys. After spanking the boys in the best of two out of three, they switched to board games so Kyle could join in. Siobhan had never laughed so much in her life as she did adapting to the O'Halloran cutthroat method of playing.

When they brought out the monster movie DVDs, Siobhan decided it was time to take her leave. "Guys, it's been a great day. I think I'm going to take off now."

"Why?" Lorelei asked as a collective wail of disappointment went up from the O'Halloran boys. "Didn't you bring an overnight bag?"

"I brought a change of clothes in case we went to the beach,"

Siobhan explained. "I wasn't planning to stay the night, so I left it in the car."

"You should spend the night," Kyle announced.

"Yeah," Finn echoed. "Stay the night. That way you'll already be here for breakfast."

"Well, um, I . . ." Flabbergasted, Siobhan turned to Charlie for help.

"I understand if you need to go, but we'd all like for you to stay. It's late and you've got to be tired." A lopsided smile curved his lips as he draped an arm over her shoulders. "Besides, this is a monster movie marathon night. The last one to fall asleep wins and gets their favorite breakfast made."

"We usually let Charlie win," Finn piped up, "because he's bad at breakfast."

"Finn!"

"You burn oatmeal. Every time," Finn said, tossing Charlie under the proverbial bus. He turned back to Siobhan to loudly whisper, "Charlie's breakfast is us getting to pick out our own cereal."

"Who's the best at breakfast?" Siobhan wondered.

"Kyle," everyone said in unison, and the middle brother ducked his head in awkwardness.

"His blackberry pancakes are the best," Lorelei added, "but the apple crumble thing is a close second."

"Blackberry pancakes and apple crumble too?" Siobhan grinned. "I need to taste this for myself. I promise not to steal your recipe for the café."

"So does that mean you'll stay?" Charlie asked.

Siobhan looked at their hopeful expressions and gave the only answer she could. The only answer she wanted to. "Of course."

"All right!" Charlie clapped his hands. "Before the marathon begins, I want everyone showered and in their pj's."

Lorelei and the boys headed upstairs, leaving Siobhan and Charlie alone for the first time since she'd arrived. He turned to Siobhan and the private look he gave her brushed heat across her cheeks again. "I have shorts and a T-shirt you can borrow, sweetheart. Why don't I go get your bag while you take a shower?"

She bit her bottom lip. "I don't know about this, Charlie."

"I do." His hands settled on her waist, drew her closer. "I know I want to see you in my bed. I know I want the scent of you on my pillow, my sheets."

"The kids—"

"Are a floor away," he cut in. "Us being together in my bed is going to happen eventually. It might as well be tonight."

"Doesn't it seem too fast, though? I just met your family and I'm already spending the night!"

"Too fast for who? Our timetable is ours. We do what's right for us, not anyone else." He cupped her cheeks, his intense gaze capturing and holding hers. "I'm not asking you to run through the house naked. I'm not even asking for sex, though I wouldn't turn it down. I'm asking you to sleep in my arms in my bed so that you're the first thing I see when I wake up in the morning."

His words slayed her. She wrapped her fingers around his wrists, needing to touch him as he touched her. "God, Charlie, how am I supposed to be strong enough to say no to that?"

"You don't want to say no." He grinned with satisfied triumph. "You don't want to go, and I don't want to let you go. So, you're staying and we're having breakfast in the morning then spending the afternoon at the beach. Sound good?"

Her resistance melted, as it always did in the face of his determination, his charm, his everything. "It sounds perfect."

He kissed her then, a slow, soft kiss that had her clutching his shoulders to keep to her feet. "Been needing to do that all day, goddess," he whispered against her lips. "Do you know how hard it's been to keep my hands off you?"

"I have a pretty good idea," she replied, feeling the ridge of his erection pressing against her belly. "Are you sure staying over is a good idea?"

"It's the best idea I've had all day."

"It wasn't your idea," she pointed out, "unless you put the others up to it. Did you?"

"Nope." He shook his head for emphasis. "As much as I wanted it, they came up with that pile-on all on their own."

"Fine. I'll give you the benefit of the doubt this time. Which way is the master suite?"

Charlie led her back to the main room, then past the stairs to the back of the house, pausing just inside a set of double doors. "See? Nice and private. The linen closet is just inside the bathroom door. Should be some spare toothbrushes in there too. I'll be right back."

She stepped deeper into the suite as Charlie left. It was much like Charlie's personality, bright and warm and comforting. A king-sized bed sat beneath a wide window, draped with bedding in shades of blue. The furniture was contemporary and functional dark wood. A low-slung chair sat beside a large window, a book open on its seat. A desk and chair were tucked into one corner. Pictures festooned the wall above the desk, photos of Charlie and his family, most of them at the beach surfing, sunning, or playing in the sand. Several shots depicted an older smiling couple who must have been their parents. In every picture the O'Hallorans seemed to be enjoying life to the fullest, laughing, playing, loving one another. These pictures were probably what drove Charlie, what served as his inspiration and his motivation.

She crossed to the master bath, closed the door, then braced herself against the sink, lowering her head and breathing deep. Emotions roiled inside her, struggling to break free, but she forced them back one breath at a time. She couldn't let them out, couldn't let Charlie and his family get the wrong impression if she suddenly burst into tears.

Family. Charlie had a loud, laughing, loving family. Something she had always dreamed of, even growing up. Something she'd hoped she'd have with Mike and Colleen. Charlie and his brothers and sisters had it, had that easy, loving, boisterous camaraderie. Their closeness was obvious, their affection for each other undeniable. They were what she'd always thought of when she thought of family.

She wanted it. God help her, she wanted what they had. No. She wanted to be a part of what the O'Hallorans had with each other. She wanted to be part of their family. She wanted to work in the garden with Kyle, play video games with Finn, and talk boy stuff—but not Charlie stuff—with Lorelei. She wanted more days like this, hanging out and happy with people who were glad she existed, who were happy to see her.

Her shoulders bowed beneath the weight of a crushing, biting loneliness. She missed her family. Missed her parents, missed Mike and Colleen. Missed being part of a family even though it had been built on a lie, the lie of how they thought she was. They had loved her when she was high, when she'd used drugs to cope, and once that truth had been revealed, they had stopped loving her. They hadn't loved the recovered, clean her, which made her wonder at times if they'd truly loved her at all.

Composing herself, she pulled open the bathroom door only to jump as she spotted Charlie sitting on the edge of the bed, waiting for her. "Oh, you're back. Did you let up the top on the car?"

"I did." He didn't smile. "Are you okay? I didn't hear water running. I thought maybe we gave you food poisoning, or family overload."

"Don't you dare suggest the food was anything other than excellent. Kyle did a terrific job on the meal."

"He'll be relieved to know that." His gaze searched hers as he rose to his feet. "So it's the family overload, then?"

"No, not in the way you mean." She buried her face against his shirt, curving her arms about his waist. "I really like your family. Thank you for inviting me over and letting me meet them."

"No, I'm the one who should be thanking you. You have no idea what you did for Kyle today. For all of them, and for me. I'll never be able to repay that."

"Then it's a good thing I'm not asking you to repay anything."

He tilted her chin up to kiss her. Though slow, there was nothing gentle and everything hungry about the way their mouths melded, the way her body responded to his. His hands slid down to cup her buttocks, pressing her against the ridge of his arousal. Drunk with desire, she tightened her hold on him, heedless to everything but this man and what he did to her.

With a reluctant groan, Charlie backed away from her, unhanding her one finger at a time. The blue of his eyes gleamed brightly with unsatisfied hunger, his need for her so obvious it left her lightheaded.

Without taking his eyes from her, he backed into the dresser, opened a drawer. "Shirts. Shorts are in the drawer beneath." He sucked in air through his nose. "I'm gonna go jerk off in the upstairs shower."

"Charlie!"

"Taking the edge off is the only way I'm going to be able to get through the movie marathon," he told her, his tone unrepentant. "When you fall asleep, I'm bringing you back in here. I'm going to shut and lock my bedroom door for the first time in eight years. Then I'm taking off your shorts and putting you in my bed, right where you should be. Even if I don't get to make love to you tonight I want to feel you against me, here in my space."

Her body heated. "Who needs wine when she has you?"

He gave her that wicked grin that promised nothing but good times ahead. "You think I'm intoxicating?"

"You certainly aren't modest."

"You wouldn't want me if I were modest. You also know that I don't need to brag, because I deliver." He winked at her. "If you need me to, I'll be happy to remind you."

She exhaled deeply as he sauntered through the door. It was going to be a long night.

TWENTY

Siobhan looked up from making a smoothie as the bell tinkled over the café door. Lorelei breezed in, fresh and summery in shorts and a billowy, blousy top, looking as hippie as her name. "Hey, Lorelei. Are you here for lunch or you just stopping by?"

"Hey, Siobhan." Lorelei leaned against the counter. "I'm just stopping by for a little bit. Can I have a green tea lemonade?"

"Of course." Siobhan passed the smoothie to the salesclerk Rosie, then gathered the tea ingredients. She darted another look at Charlie's sister. "Something on your mind?"

"No." The young woman shook her head, then sighed. "Yeah. How did you know?"

"You're biting your lip," Siobhan pointed out. "What's up?"

"Charlie's birthday is coming up," Lorelei announced. "He usually doesn't like us to make a big deal about it but I thought since you guys are dating we could have a party, invite some people over."

Siobhan considered it as she poured a fifty-fifty mix of green tea and lemonade into a shaker. "A party sounds like a great idea. Not a surprise party though."

"You're right. Big bro's not too keen on surprises. We'll just tell him we're having a cookout at the O'Halloran homestead, but invite everyone at Charlie's office and your friends from the café."

"I suppose I could do that." The time she spent with Charlie got better with each passing day, and it was made even better by the time she spent with his family. That first weekend she'd gotten up early, not wanting the kids to find her still in bed with Charlie, as silly as that was. Kyle had been in the kitchen, already, starting coffee and his signature blackberry pancakes. They'd spent a companionable time making breakfast together, the delicious aromas bringing everyone else to the kitchen. When it came time to take her leave, they'd been as reluctant for her to go as she'd been to leave.

Three weeks later, she was coming to think of the O'Hallorans as hers, as her family. Charlie and the boys had surprised her by showing up at her place before the car show and giving her vintage Falcon a complete detail before they all headed to the event. Finn had grinned his way through the entire show.

They'd even fallen into a routine for the last couple of weeks in which Charlie stayed over on Friday nights. On Saturday mornings the whole crew showed up at the café for lunch then they all either headed to the beach or a movie or back to the O'Halloran home to hang out. They capped the weekend with a big Sunday breakfast before Siobhan left to meet up with Nadia to plan the café's menu. It was the best routine of her life, and she enjoyed every minute of it.

"A party would be nice for Charlie," she said, pouring Lorelei's drink over ice and placing it on the counter. "As long as it's low-key.

He's been putting in some serious hours, considering that most businesses around here are slow for the summer."

"I know." Lorelei paid for her drink. Siobhan liked that the girl didn't assume it was on the house. "That's the main reason I want us to throw him a party. It'll give him a chance to chill. I'd also like to invite Stephen."

Siobhan raised her eyebrows. "And Stephen is?"

Lorelei answered through her straw. "A really nice guy that I've been seeing."

"I think we need to move this conversation to a more comfortable area." Siobhan made her way around the counter and sat down with Lorelei in a pair of plush chairs with a small table between them.

Siobhan folded her arms and regarded the younger woman wearing the all-too-innocent expression. "So you think by giving Charlie a birthday party and inviting friends and coworkers over he'll be forced to be nice when you spring your boyfriend on him. And you think that if I'm involved or organize it, he'll be more accepting." She shook her head. "Have you met your brother? The man's got a serious protective streak where you guys are concerned."

"I know, but I'm eighteen now. I can vote. I have a driver's license and a job. I'm going to college in like a month. I should be allowed to have a steady boyfriend and a later curfew." She blinked puppy dog eyes at Siobhan. "Can't you talk to him? He'll listen to you."

"Oh, no you don't." Siobhan held up her hands to fend off Lorelei's request and a rising panic. "I don't have a say in how your family does things. Don't go putting me in the middle of that."

"But—"

"But nothing. You're still living at home and Charlie's paying your tuition. That means that you're still under his rules. Charlie's the head of your household and he's done a damn good job of raising you by himself. Considering how all of you have turned out, I'd say his rules aren't so bad."

"They aren't, but he still treats me like I'm ten!"

Siobhan knew Lorelei was only ten when their parents died. "I know, sweetheart, just as you know there's a good reason why he sees you like that."

"Yeah, I know, but still . . ." Lorelei pouted. "You could have a say if you wanted to. You mean a lot to him. He would listen to you."

Lorelei's conviction warmed Siobhan's heart, but she wasn't about to let her private hopes color her perception, or give in to Lorelei's wants. "What makes you think that I wouldn't agree with Charlie?"

The younger woman's eyes widened with surprise. "You don't think I should date either?"

"I didn't say that. If that's what you want to do, though, you need to approach your brother as the adult you say you are and not the kid who just complained to me." She smiled to reduce the sting of her words. "Your brother is a show-don't-tell kind of guy. You have to show him that you're an adult."

Skepticism underscored her features. "How am I supposed to do that?"

"For starters, don't spring your boyfriend on Charlie at his birthday party." Siobhan arched a brow until Lorelei nodded. "Tell Charlie about your guy tonight over dinner. Ask if you can bring him to dinner soon. Honestly though, if this guy is really boyfriend material, he would be picking you up at your house for dates."

"I've been meeting him over at my friend Tamryn's house," the younger woman mumbled through her straw.

"Lorelei."

"I know, I know!" The young woman had the grace to look sheepish. "I just really like him, you know? I don't want Charlie to scare him off or tell me not to date him."

"Then you need to be up-front with your brother. He'll appreciate the honesty. Besides, has he ever denied you anything really important?"

"Never. At least, not without a good reason."

"Exactly. If you're serious about this guy, you need to let Charlie know. After all, he told you guys about me when he got serious about me." Siobhan paused. "Are you serious about this guy?"

"I think so."

"Think so?"

Lorelei blushed. "I am."

Concern grew, kicking Siobhan's maternal instincts to wakefulness. "How serious is serious, Lorelei?"

A blush stained her cheeks. "We haven't had sex yet, if that's what you're asking."

Siobhan rubbed at her forehead, knowing that she'd willingly stepped into the deep end with this conversation. Now she had no choice but to tread water. "Yeah, that's what I was asking. You're thinking about it though, aren't you?"

Lorelei sighed again. "Stephen's such a good kisser. And he's funny, and hot, and twenty." She straightened. "Charlie will kill me if he finds out. When we had the talk he only said seven words: 'You have sex, I'll strangle the guy.' I don't think he was kidding."

"Knowing Charlie, he probably wasn't." Siobhan reached across the table. "As you said, you're an adult now. Talk to Charlie about this the way you talked us back together. Ask for adult rules and negotiate without reverting to your thirteen-year-old self."

She squeezed the young woman's hand. "If you need to talk about protection options or have a buddy go to the clinic with you, just let me know. Some things need to be just between us girls."

"You are awesome!" Siobhan found herself engulfed in an enthusiastic bear hug. "Thank you. Thank you!"

Flustered, Siobhan extricated herself from the younger woman's exuberant embrace. "Just talk to Charlie, all right? Just because I believe you should be protected doesn't mean I think you should keep this from your brother. Besides, you should know I don't plan to keep anything from him if I can help it, and I have no intention of picking sides. So, if you want to be treated as an adult, you need to put on your big-girl panties and deal. Got it?"

"Loud and clear." Lorelei gave her a bright grin. "I knew talking to you would be a good idea."

"Glad I could help," Siobhan said softly, pleasure wafting through her. "I'm glad you felt that you could come to me."

"Well, you're almost like a female version of Charlie," Lorelei said with a light laugh. "At least your brain is. You're way prettier than he is, though."

"At least I have that going for me," Siobhan murmured, her voice wry.

"You know what I mean. Charlie's our big brother, and if things keep going like they're going, you'll be our big sister. You already know Charlie well enough to know how he'd react and you gave me good advice because of it."

"Maybe, but I'm still learning." Siobhan forced herself not to focus on what Lorelei had said about becoming her big sister. She and Charlie were nowhere near that, and she wasn't sure if the idea terrified or comforted her. "I'm sure there's more to uncover. For instance, I'd like to do something nice for him for his birthday, but I don't have a clue what to get him. I'm sure Kyle has the cake covered, but I can't think of anything that I know he'd really like. I'm not getting him a tie or a gift certificate for the café. I'm open to suggestions."

"You're kidding, right?" Lorelei laughed. "This should be easy."

"If it was easy, I wouldn't be asking for help. You should know his favorite food. Is blue really his favorite color? Is there anything he'd like for his office? Does he have another hobby besides surfing?"

Lorelei leaned forward. "There's only one thing that Charlie wants from you for his birthday. You."

Heat singed Siobhan's ears. "Um, well. We're already dating, so I think he's already got me in that respect. I don't think there's anything I can do more than that—and certainly not anything I'm going to tell you."

"Ewww. Can you say *gross*?" Lorelei made a face at the thought, then her expression dimmed into seriousness again. "I'm not buttering you up when I say you're the best thing that's happened to Charlie in a long time. You're good for him. Keep on being good to him. That's the best present you can give him."

Siobhan lowered her gaze, not wanting Lorelei to see anything she wasn't ready to reveal. It couldn't be that easy. She doubted she was the best thing to happen to Charlie, just as she doubted that she was good for him. Not in the long run. Sure, they had good times together, and the sex was way off the chain. Yet she knew she hadn't been good for anyone in a long time, and despite the changes she'd made to her life, her failures reminded her that that wasn't going to change anytime soon.

"Siobhan? Are you okay?"

"Yeah." She dredged up a smile. "I still want to give Charlie a present. A real present."

The young blonde released a long-suffering sigh. "If you don't like my first suggestion, you can always make him a meal. Charlie loves to eat, so you can always cook him a birthday dinner over at your place before coming home for the cookout. Anything with meat in it will work. Or . . ."

"Or what?"

"You could do one of your dances for him. You know, in private."

Siobhan could only manage a blank stare. "What?"

Lorelei snorted. "I'm not so self-involved that I don't know what the Crimson Bay Bombshells are about. You guys do more than car shows. I can't wait until I'm old enough to get into Club Tatas. Maybe I could—"

"Absolutely not."

"You don't know what I was about to say," Lorelei pointed out, frowning.

"I don't need to know what you were going to say. You're not going to say it. We're going to pretend this part of our conversation never happened."

Lorelei rolled her eyes. "Geez, you sound just like Charlie."

"I'll take that as a compliment."

"I didn't mean right now anyway," Lorelei said, descending into a pout. "I meant like after college. I'll be twenty-two then. Maybe I'll even have a chest by then."

"How do you do that?" Siobhan wondered.

"Do what?"

"Switch from eighteen to twenty-eight, then back again." Siobhan shook her head slowly. "You give me whiplash, young lady."

Lorelei bestowed her with an innocent smile. "It's a gift." She glanced at her watch. "I'd better get going. Will you at least think about the dance idea? I think that would blow Charlie's mind."

"I'll think about it," Siobhan promised. She'd never tell Lorelei that a private striptease had kick-started her relationship with Charlie. She still wasn't comfortable with the idea of doing the do in their house, even with a floor separating them from Lorelei and the boys. "You think about what I said too."

Lorelei rolled her eyes. "Yes, Mom." She waved and left.

Blindsided, Siobhan sat back in her chair. She knew Lorelei had meant the words to tease but they still hit her hard, leaving her momentarily floundering.

Regret exploded in Siobhan's heart. Lowering her head, she gripped the corners of the table, the sharp edges digging into her palms erecting a barrier against the emotional pain threatening to devour her. This was how she and her daughter were supposed to be, sitting here in her café on a beautiful summer day, laughing and bonding over boy talk. Remorse boiled over into excruciating guilt, sadness, and for a moment, blinding loneliness.

Pulling out her phone, she thumbed to her contacts then dialed Colleen's number. She'd bought a smartphone for Colleen the summer her daughter had come to work at the café, the summer she'd believed things were finally turning around.

As usual her call went to voicemail. "Hi, honey, it's your mother." She drew a ragged breath. "I haven't seen you since your graduation and I just wanted to call you to see what your plans were for the rest of the summer and after. Call me when you can. Love you."

She disconnected the call, thought about placing one to her own mother. She quickly discarded the idea. As much as she appreciated

222

the details her mother shared about Colleen, Mary Malloy made her only daughter do backflips for each nugget of information, and Siobhan didn't want to choke down the serving of guilt that came with every conversation with her mother.

She was in danger of using Lorelei as a surrogate daughter. That wouldn't be fair to Lorelei or to Colleen. Charlie's sister would never be her daughter, no matter how close Siobhan and Charlie became. She'd probably gone too far, presumed too much in her conversation with Lorelei.

She wasn't the girl's mother. Nor was she Lorelei's older sister. She had no right to insert herself into family decisions, especially if they went counter to what Charlie thought was best. She'd have to come clean with him and hope it didn't upset him. Then she'd have to manage the family's expectation when it came to her presence in their lives.

"Hey, that's not the expression you should be wearing right now."

Audie slid into the chair that Lorelei had recently vacated. "Hey, Audie, what are you doing here in the middle of a non-Tuesday?"

"A follow-up with Sergey about my case," the redhead explained. "I'm supposed to meet with him as soon as he's done moving in upstairs."

Audie cocked her head, her expression quizzical. "It looked like things were going well with you and Charlie's sister, so why are you sitting here looking like you were one number off on winning the lottery?"

"I'm having a difficult time looking at Lorelei and not comparing her to Colleen," Siobhan confessed. "They lost their parents eight years ago, but she hasn't let that turn her bitter or angry. Maybe she has Charlie to thank for that. As for Colleen—she was a few years older than that when the accident happened but we'd had a good relationship up to that point. At the very least she didn't hate me then like she does now."

She shook her head. "I know I was in a drug-induced stupor that day. I know that I caused a lot of damage. What I haven't been able to wrap my mind around is, what happened that day so unforgiveable for her that she hates me so intensely? It was an accident—a horrible, terrible accident, but no one died. No one got hurt. The fire didn't even cause significant damage from what I understand. So why can't my daughter stand the sight of me?"

"My mother hates me because I'm a reminder of a very bad moment in her life," Audie said, her usual bright personality dimmed. "I'm the cross she bore, literally and figuratively. Nothing I did, nothing I tried could change that. Now, I think maybe she felt that way because she had no other choice, that her response was what was expected of her because of the environment she lived in. Eventually that became the only way she knew to relate to me."

Siobhan considered Audie's words. "So you're saying that Colleen hates me because everyone else in my family does."

"Fuck, I'm sorry." Color raced across Audie's nose and cheeks. "That's way harsh when you put it like that. Think about it though. Your ex was certainly furious about what happened, furious enough to file for divorce and full custody, right? And your parents, especially your dad, are something else. From what you've told us about them in our Tuesday meet-ups, I wouldn't put it past them to turn Colleen against you."

Siobhan wanted to protest, but didn't bother. Not when the same thought had crossed her mind more than once. "I thought reaching out to her would help, but it hasn't. She was even hostile when I went to her graduation. I don't know what to do."

Audie rubbed her shoulder. "Yeah, you do. You just don't want to admit it."

Plopping her elbows on the table, Siobhan covered her face with her hands. "I can't give up on them," she moaned. "They're my family."

"I know. More than anyone else, I know." Audie squeezed her shoulder, then released it. "I also know that you reach a point where you have to get off the merry-go-round and say you're not going to let them keep spinning you around like that. They're your born family and you can't change that. No one's asking you stop loving them. I'm just saying maybe it's time to take a step back and stop allowing them to keep hurting you. Maybe it's time to focus on your chosen family."

Siobhan shook her head again. "I don't think I can do that. I'm already in danger of viewing Lorelei as a surrogate daughter. It wouldn't be fair to try to substitute Charlie and his family for my own."

Audie gave her a knowing smile. "I was talking about me, Vanessa, Nadia, and the rest of your friends, not just the O'Hallorans," the redhead said. "Since you brought them up, I noticed that you and Lorelei seem to be pretty close now. How long has it been since you officially met the family?"

"Almost a month."

"You didn't ask me, but I for one think they're good for you. I think you need them. I also think they need you. Obviously Lorelei appreciates you. That was some prime-time bonding going on right there."

"I care about them, all of them. I'm spending almost every weekend with them." Siobhan blew out a breath. "I know it can't be all hearts and flowers forever, but right now, it's good. It's really, really good."

"Maybe that should tell you something."

"Like what?"

Audie held her gaze. "Like you're not the one with the problem."

Shock jolted through her. For years she'd known she was the problem, the reason why her family had rejected her. The reason why her father hadn't spoken to her long before her last rehab visit, the reason why Mike and her mother ignored her or made her guilty, the reason why Colleen hated her. For years she'd thought it was her fault for being the failure. Years. So many years it was hard to believe anything else, any way else. She couldn't make that leap.

"I hear what you're saying, Audie, and I thank you for saying it. I'll think about it, but I'm not ready to turn my back on them just yet."

"I understand," Audie said, the sheen in her eyes conveying that she actually did know. "Giving up on family is hard. I do think that you should focus on what you have here in Crimson Bay, though. Friends, friends that are like family, and a great relationship with a great guy and his siblings. Isn't that the type of life you wanted when you got out of rehab?"

Siobhan eyed the redhead, wondering when they'd done a role reversal. "You've really changed in the last couple of months."

"Getting the shit beat out of you has a way of putting things into perspective," Audie said, then flashed her trademark cheeky grin. "So does therapy. I'm making better choices when it comes to sex. I'm surprised how well that's working out."

Siobhan smiled with relief. She'd long worried about Audie's penchant for one-night stands without vetting her partners. If the redhead was getting her needs taken care of in a safe environment, Siobhan wouldn't ask for more. "I suppose Vanessa's still helping you with that?"

"She is." Another cheeky grin. "You'd be surprised at how much of a naughty streak Ms. Prim and Proper has. But that's not my story to tell."

"Maybe she'll get around to letting us in during one of our Bitch Talk sessions. Personally, I think it's good that all of us are getting some in a safe way." Siobhan was curious about Audie and Vanessa's Girls' Night Out trips to a private sex club. She'd even thought about joining them a time or two. At least she'd considered it before a certain blond sex god made her see stars on her desk.

"You're looking mighty flushed there, Sugar," Audie teased. "What are you thinking about? Or should I say, *who* are you thinking about?"

Siobhan fought her blush. "Lorelei told me Charlie's got a birthday coming up, and I'm wondering what to get him."

"How about you and a container of frosting?" Audie suggested. "Or maybe you could whip up a sexy birthday cake outfit for your burlesque show?"

"Not you too?" Heat burned Siobhan's ears as she remembered the fun she and Charlie had experienced with honey and chocolate syrup. "Other than fixing him a good meal, I don't know what else to do."

"Trust me, Siobhan, that man would rather have you for dessert than any meal you could whip up. I say you do a special routine for him during one of the Crimson Bay Bombshells shows, then take him home for some extracurricular activities. I'm sure he'll think it's the best birthday present ever."

"Okay, so that's two votes for food and sexy times." Siobhan shook her head ruefully. "Well, at least those are two things I know I'm good at."

"Well, there you go." Audie straightened. "Looks like Sergey's here. Let me know if you need help planning your present. I may have a sexy cheerleader outfit you can borrow."

"Thanks, I think I've got costumes covered." Siobhan pulled out her phone as Audie and Nadia's brother took an out-of-the-way table in the nearly empty café. It was nearly closing time, and their regulars always seemed to wrap up half an hour before closing, giving Siobhan plenty of time to set things to right in the back while Rosie and Jas took care of the front of the shop.

Thumbing through her contacts, Siobhan quickly found Lola's number and connected. "Hey, *chica*, what's up?"

"I need help creating a special one-off routine. Can I swing by the studio later?"

"You can swing by the studio whenever you want," the troupe leader answered. "Tell me about this special routine."

"Charlie's got a birthday coming up and I'd like to pull him on-stage for a special dance." She hesitated, then plunged ahead. "I think it will be a great way to end Sugar's stage career."

"Aww, honey. I had a feeling you were thinking about it. I just didn't think you'd pull the trigger so soon." Disappointment filled Lola's tone.

"I hadn't planned on it, but this is as good a time as any. We've been going easy on my routines and practices, but my recovery time is getting longer and longer. And since I'm not going to take anything to manage the pain . . ."

"Not only that, but you've been finding other ways to get your exercise in," Lola observed, then burst into her trademark bois-terous laugh. "I guess this means things are getting serious."

"Yeah. I think so. It feels like it."

Lola squealed in delight. "Then if this is Sugar's swan song, we'll have to do it up right. Do you want to drive him crazy or just give him something sweet?"

Siobhan gave it a second's thought. "It's his birthday. It should be over the top, don't you think?"

"That's my girl." Lola laughed, mad genius style. There was a reason the Crimson Bay Bombshells performed to packed houses, and Lola's savvy was it. "Poor Charlie won't know what hit him."

"Should I be afraid?"

"Yes. This will be one Club Tatas will talk about for years to come."

TWENTY-ONE

After closing the café and reconciling the books, Siobhan made her way across the town square to Charlie's office. The late summer air swirled along the sidewalk, the shade hinting at the cooler weather to come. Soon the lazy days of summer would give way to returning college students and the uptick in business the café thrived on, though she had to admit Charlie's idea of a limited delivery service was a success, adding much-needed revenue to their slim summer bottom line.

She needed to admit to a lot of things when it came to Charlie. He was a balm to her battered psyche. Charlie had given her so much by letting her into his family circle. He'd given her back a sense of belonging that went beyond what she had with Nadia and Nadia's family.

"Hi, Siobhan," Charlie's assistant, Nance, greeted her as she stepped into the outer office. "Charlie's on the phone but he won't mind you going on back."

"Thanks, Nance." Charlie's staff always greeted her warmly whenever she visited, which she tried to limit as much as possible. Like her, Charlie had a business to run and he took that business as seriously as she took hers. They didn't need to distract each other when there was money to be made.

Speaking of distractions, Charlie had his back to her, offering an excellent rear view. Years of surfing had honed his body and she was the one who got to reap the benefits.

Siobhan leaned against the doorframe and watched her man work. She didn't shy away from the phrase this time and acknowledging it didn't bring on the panic it should have. Maybe because her mind finally realized what her body already knew: Charlie was hers just as she was his.

He paced behind his desk, an earbud perched on his right ear, which freed his hands to gesture as he talked. He focused completely on his conversation. His ability to concentrate like that was one of the main things she loved about him—when he sharpened his attention on her, he made her feel as if no one and nothing else existed.

She loved him. The knowledge washed over her like the warmth of his smile, enveloping her. Charlie gave her something she'd been missing for years: comfort, confidence, acceptance. In that moment she believed she deserved the happiness that brimmed inside her, happiness that began and ended with Charlie.

He turned the corner of his desk, then stopped as he spotted her. The smile he gave her animated his entire face, making her feel as if she was the source of his happiness. It humbled her even as it tripped her heart into overdrive.

Charlie ended his call, then tossed the earpiece on his desk before crossing to her. "What's that look for, sweetness?"

Heat curled inside her, sparked by his tone, the endearment, and his nearness. "What look?"

He draped his hands on her shoulders, sliding them down and leaving tingles of awareness in their wake. "It's like you're noticing something for the first time and you're surprised by what you see." He cocked his head. "Is it that I'm wearing a purple shirt?"

"No." With her realization still freshly echoing through her, Siobhan wasn't ready to share. She settled on another truth instead. "I'm really happy to see you."

His gaze cleared as he brought her hands up to kiss. "I'm happy to see you too. It's been nearly twenty hours since the last time I was able to do this."

He kissed her, brushing his lips across hers once, twice, then again. Desire and passion lit her up, fueled by her newborn realization. Entwining her arms about Charlie's neck, she yielded to the kiss, yielded to him. He groaned his approval, his hands dropping to her waist to pull her closer.

After a long moment he pulled away, resting his forehead against hers. "It's also been about twenty hours since I was last inside you. Now seeing you in that dress is making me wonder if you're wearing panties."

"You're going to have to keep wondering, mister," she teased, laughter lining her words. "After all, you're the one who decided on an office with glass walls."

"A décor choice I've regretted every day since I've met you." He stepped back but kept his hands on her waist. "I guess we've put on enough of a floorshow for my crew. When I'm with you I have a habit of forgetting everything else."

Siobhan toyed with his collar. "Maybe I should get you some sort of reminder tool for your birthday."

He stepped back as if she'd shocked him. "How did you know about my birthday?" he demanded, then immediately shook his head. "Let me guess. Lorelei."

Siobhan crinkled her brows, curious about his reaction. "Yes, she might have mentioned it. Is there any particular reason why you wouldn't want your girlfriend to know about your birthday?"

He gave her a pointed look. "Besides the fact that it will remind you of our age difference?"

"Ouch." She placed a hand over her heart. "Okay, I know I had issues about that at the start, but to be honest I don't think about it so much anymore. When I'm with you, all I can think about is you and me and how good it is."

"And when you're not with me?"

She smiled. "I'm thinking about how many hours there are until I see you again, not how many years are between us."

His gaze bored into her. "Are you sure it's no longer an issue?"

There were a plethora of issues all on her side of the bed, but their five-year age difference wasn't one of them. "I'm sure. So can we celebrate your birthday?"

He shoved a hand through his hair as he paced away from her. "I don't like to make a big deal out of it," he finally confessed, turning back to her. "I do for the boys' and Lorelei's birthdays, and they seem to think I should have a party for mine too. If I had my way, I wouldn't celebrate it at all."

"Really?" That surprised her. This was Charlie, who called every day they saw each other "Siobhan-day," his favorite day of the week.

He celebrated everything large and small and nonsensical. "Why not?"

Warmth seeped from his eyes. "My parents died shortly after my birthday. It's hard to think about one without thinking about the other."

"Oh God, Charlie." She wrapped her arms around him. "I'm sorry."

"You didn't know. You understand, though, why I don't want to throw a party or whatever else Lorelei put you up to?"

"She wanted to have a cookout at your house with family and friends." She stroked his cheek, wanting to smooth away the tension in his jaw and the clouds in his eyes. "Maybe it's time to create some new memories. From what you and the others have told me about your parents, they were overjoyed to welcome each of you into the world. They wouldn't want you to only associate that day with their deaths. If anything, they would want you to celebrate your life, their lives, and all the good you've all shared. So if you don't want to celebrate your birthday, maybe you should make it O'Halloran Day, and celebrate your family."

Emotion flared in his eyes, so burning and intense that she had to look away. "Not that it's any of my business," she hastened to add, retreating, "but that's what I would do if I were in your shoes."

"You're wrong."

She shot him a glance. "Which part?" she asked. "I want to be sure I get angry over the right thing."

Laughing, he approached her again. "You're wrong that it's none of your business. How I celebrate my birthday is something you should definitely be a part of and have an opinion on. As a matter of fact, I think your idea is perfect."

He cupped her cheeks, warmth lighting his eyes again. "Thank you, Siobhan."

The kiss, so sharply sweet, sliced through the last shreds of doubt and hesitation she had. Charlie was everything she wanted, everything she needed. Why should she continue to stare into the storms of her past when the future was so clearly bright with Charlie?

"Hey, what is this?" He stroked his thumbs beneath her eyes. "Why are you crying?"

"Nothing bad," she assured him, blinking back the surprise tears. "I think I'm PMS-ing."

"For most guys, that would be bad."

She choked on a laugh. "Good thing you're not most guys then, right?"

"True enough." He studied her, then smiled. "Sounds like I need to ply you with chocolate. Since my favorite café is closed, should we stop entertaining my employees and head to the ice cream shop down the walk for brownie sundaes?"

"You always know the right thing to say," Siobhan said, threading her arm into his. "Lead the way, Mr. O'Halloran."

Charlie studied Siobhan as she dove into her chocolate brownie sundae with extra hot fudge on top. The fact that she wasn't being deliberately erotic made her enjoyment of the decadent dessert even more so. Remembering the way chocolate sauce slid across her beautiful breasts hardened him with hunger, but not for the dessert melting in front of him.

"Don't tell Nadia that I'm cheating on her with this," Siobhan said as she licked chocolate sauce from her spoon. "Or how much I'm enjoying it."

"If it means I get to watch you do more of that, your secret's safe with me." He shifted in his chair. "Tell me you're coming over tonight."

She froze, the spoon halfway in her mouth. "Um, I wasn't planning on it."

Was that a guilty flush staining her cheeks? "You know you don't have to wait for a formal invite, right? You can come over anytime. I'm pretty sure the rest of the clan would love to have you over for dinner every night if you can stand that high a dosage of O'Halloran charm on a continual basis."

"Thanks." She swirled her spoon in the ice cream. "I'd love to have dinner with the family, but I think tonight needs to be an all-O'Halloran affair."

Desire abated as he pondered Siobhan's words. "Does this have something to do with Lorelei?"

"It does." She returned her spoon to the bowl, then pushed the dessert aside. "She came to see me earlier today."

"I'm guessing you talked about more than my birthday."

Siobhan stared at him, a debate waging over her features. He cocked his head, giving her a quizzical stare. "What is it?"

"I'm trying to decide if the girl code trumps the significant-other code," she said honestly. "Our relationship is important to me, but I want Lorelei to know she can trust me. It . . . it touched me that she felt she could come to me for advice. You know she'll go to you with anything important, but sometimes we need woman-to-woman talk."

He exhaled a slow breath. Lorelei went to Siobhan for advice. That had to mean that his sister considered his girlfriend someone trustworthy, someone to confide in. On the one hand, he wanted them to grow closer, wanted Lorelei to have someone like Siobhan to go to. On the other hand, Lorelei went to Siobhan because she didn't want to talk to Charlie about something that bothered her.

"You think I overstepped." She sat back with a sigh. "Hell, I thought I went too far when I talked to her. I did tell her that I didn't want to get between you two and that I wouldn't keep anything from you. I didn't want to assume authority where I don't have any."

He tangled his hand with hers, not liking the worry in her eyes, worry he'd caused. "I'm glad Lorelei chose to come to you. It's just that there are only a few things she knows I'd flip out about, and one of them is sex."

He steeled himself. "Is my baby sister having sex?"

"Your baby sister is a legal adult, Charlie," Siobhan informed him, her voice soft with understanding. "She's also a very level-headed, responsible young woman."

A cold knot of panic and anger formed in his gut. "I know. I know. She's still my baby sister. I fumbled my way through her puberty without grossing myself out or her killing me. I don't want to think about her having sex."

"She's not." Siobhan tugged at their hands, making him realize he'd clutched hers a little too tightly. "Lorelei wants you to treat her like the adult she is, which is why I told her to talk to you at dinner tonight."

"A dinner you don't think you should attend, when we've both put you in the middle of this?" Charlie shook his head. "Sorry, babe. You're part of the family now. You might as well see the warts as well as the rainbows."

Her beautiful blue eyes fractured with unshed tears, but she smiled at him. "Thank you. I'll take your warts any day."

His heart thumped hard. Good God, this woman had become as necessary to him as breathing. She was everything he'd stopped hoping for years ago, a reward he almost felt like he didn't deserve. He was too greedy, too damn needy to refuse it though. Now he just had to get through his birthday and make sure that Siobhan really didn't have a problem with their age difference. If she did, he'd find a way to convince her to give them a chance. No matter what, he wasn't going to let her go.

TWENTY-TWO

The Friday before Charlie's birthday found him at Club Tatas waiting for Siobhan and the rest of the Crimson Bay Bombshells to take the stage. Nadia and her fiancé were at the usual table, as well as Siobhan's other friends and staff. Though he and Siobhan had already had a pre-performance celebration, he was ready for the show to be over so he could take Siobhan home and make love to her until he went shouting her name.

He was in deep and he knew it—so deep he didn't think he'd ever get out. Not that he wanted to. Siobhan's sweet curves were matched by her sweet heart. The patience and affection that she displayed with his siblings would have won him over even if nothing else had. The boys and Lorelei flourished under her attention, a maternal instinct that was as natural and automatic to Siobhan as breathing.

It bothered him that her relationship with her own family was so strained. They were missing out and he felt sorry for them. Their loss, however, was his gain. He didn't want to push her, didn't believe she was ready, but he'd meant it when he'd claimed she was already a member of the O'Halloran clan. Soon, very soon, he'd convince her that she had a permanent place in their lives.

Nadia fairly bounced with excitement. "Are you ready for the show, Charlie?"

"Do you know something I don't?" Charlie asked, half-teasing, half-concerned.

Her grin deepened into something downright suspicious. "I think you're going to have a good weekend, birthday boy."

The houselights dimmed before he could respond. Max, the lone male member of the burlesque troupe, who served as bouncer and emcee, stepped to the microphone. He got the crowd ready and eager, then the performers took the stage one after another. Four acts in, still no Siobhan.

Charlie fought his impatience as the first half concluded without Siobhan making an appearance. Normally she did at least two sets each night, one on each side of the musical interlude. Why hadn't she taken the stage yet? *Has she been injured?*

He rose to his feet. "I'm going to go ask Max what's going on."

"Easy, tiger." Nadia grabbed his hand, tugged him back down. "Good things come to those who wait."

Charlie stared down a Siobhan's partner. "What aren't you telling me?"

The brunette had the nerve to grin. "You'll find out soon enough. Looks like the second half is about to start."

The lights fell as Max stepped back on the stage. "Ladies and gentlemen! Have we got a special surprise for you. Tonight, for one night only, Crimson Bay Bombshell Sugar Malloy will present a very special up-close and personal performance!"

Charlie sat up straighter as the crowd whistled their approval. What the hell did "up close and personal" mean? Was she going to bring someone onto the stage?

"That's right, Club Tatas," the master of ceremonies said as if in answer. "One lucky son of a bitch is going to sit onstage while Sugar performs her one and only number of the night. Things are about to get really sweet up in here!"

What the hell? Was Sugar about to give someone a lap dance? He thought burlesque performers didn't do that sort of stuff. Charlie clenched his jaw, wondering if he could sit through Siobhan entertaining someone else. Hell, no. If she was going to break the rules, it should be with him. It had better be with him.

Max grinned into the crowd. "Of course, this guy is already lucky because he gets to have a little sugar every day. But he's celebrating a birthday this weekend, so Sugar wanted to give him an extra special present. Charlie, come on up here!"

A spotlight hit him in the eyes. Charlie blinked, rising to his feet as the crowd erupted with applause, cheers, and a couple of jeers. He didn't blame them. Hell, if he weren't the one getting a special Sugar show he'd be jealous too.

He made his way to the stage, where two bombshells guided him to a chair. He sat down as Max continued to work the crowd. "I know, I know. It's not fair that our lovely bowl of Sugar is off the market, but you've got to have a special kind of sweet tooth to capture her attention. But have no fear, ladies and gentlemen! If you're lucky, you might just be able to catch the eye of the rest of the Crimson Bay Bombshell beauties, including the fabulous and oh-so-lovely Lola Fontaine. Watch out though—that tigress will chew you up and spit you out!"

The crowd whistled its approval as Max walked over to Charlie.

The big man covered his microphone as he leaned over. "Don't give these guys any ideas, all right? Keep your hands to yourself while she's dancing unless she specifically asks you to move or help her with something. Got it?"

Charlie clamped his hands to his knees then nodded. When Siobhan went into Sugar mode, his higher functions vanished as all his energy went straight to his cock. He was powerless against her while his body raged with the need to fuck her. Now she wanted to put all of that on view for this crowd of half-drunk partiers? This wasn't a gift. This was torture.

"All right then. Ladies and gentlemen—are you ready? Then hold on to your tatas, because here. Comes. Sugar Malloy!"

The crowd clapped as the lights fell. Charlie tightened his grip on his knees, anticipation grabbing him by the balls as he waited for the music, waited for her. Electrified silence filled the club, stretching the tension tighter than a guitar string. Then the opening riff of "Pour Some Sugar on Me" thundered through the speakers.

Charlie sensed movement behind him. A spotlight hit the stage and the crowd roared and whistled. He craned his head, then felt his mouth drop open as he caught sight of Siobhan standing in the spotlight, dressed as the naughtiest biker babe he'd ever seen.

Shiny black high-heeled boots laced up her long legs, stopping just above her knees. A black leather miniskirt barely covered her buttocks, concealed by cotton candy pink ruffles. The black leather look continued with the cropped motorcycle jacket she wore over her voluptuous curves, gloves, and a leather cap pulled low over her eyes. Good God, she held a riding crop clamped between her ruby red lips.

Holy fucking hell. Blood raced to his cock, hardening him to the

242

point of pain. Sugar Malloy was a goddess, his goddess, and she was going to be the death of him. He was sure to die a very happy man.

A wickedly sexy smile graced her lips as she accepted the raucous approval of the crowd as her just due. She strutted across the stage with an exaggerated sway of her hips, slapping the crop against her booted shin with a loud snap that had Charlie's tongue lolling out of his head. She passed in front of him in a swish of woman and leather and perfume, and he had to dig his fingers into his knees to prevent himself from reaching for her.

Then she spun to him, the tip of the crop landing lightly over his heart. He sat up straight, his entire being focused on her and her next move. Facing him, she rested her right hand on the back of his chair. With the grace of a ballet dancer, she raised her left leg into an impressive showgirl kick right in front of his nose before lowering her leg to rest her foot on his knee. She speared him with a glance that clobbered him with the urge to drop to his knees and worship at the altar of her sexiness, sacrificing whatever she wanted.

He blew out a breath as she spun away behind him, only to feel his balls draw up tight as she repeated the crop-kick-pose maneuver on his other side. This time she ran the crop up her leg to flash the crowd a hint of upper thigh before spinning away again, allowing him the chance to draw a steadying breath.

Sugar tossed the crop behind her, then pranced to the front of the stage, her hands going to the zipper of her jacket. With a teasing smile she jerked down the zipper in time to the drumbeats, opening the front to reveal a frothy pink lace and satin bustier. The combination of black leather and candy pink lace blew his mind.

Sauntering over to him again, she held out her arm. He didn't need to be prodded. He grasped the hem of her sleeve, holding on as she pulled her arm free. She slipped the jacket off her shoulders then swung it over her head before tossing it toward the back of the stage. Striking a pose, she tipped her hat to the crowd before whipping it off and sending it flying backward.

Ignoring the crowd frothing beyond the spotlight, Charlie followed her every rhythmic movement like a hawk, all the while knowing he was her prey. She had captured him with a glance, with a saucy smile, with the bounce of a curl and the sway of her hips. Whatever she wanted, whatever she needed he would get it for her. He'd slay dragons, tilt at windmills, ram through barriers—

She flicked her gloved hand before his eyes. He glanced up at her, at the imperious gleam in her eyes and her fingertip pressed against his bottom lip. Obediently he opened his mouth, allowing her to stick the tip of her gloved finger between his teeth. At her raised eyebrow he bit down and she stepped back, pulling free of the elbow-length black glove. She grasped the glove, sliding it over his chest to drape over one shoulder. They repeated the process with her other glove, draping it onto his other shoulder.

Sugar shimmied in a circuit around the stage, playing to the crowd before sashaying back to him. She thrust her hip toward him, then gestured to her waist. Charlie dutifully popped the snap on the skirt, then held on as she spun away slowly. Layers of the skirt unraveled to reveal Sugar as a cotton candy vision in pink ruffled panties, matching bra and waist cincher, and thigh-high black boots.

Hot damn.

He must have reached for her because Sugar wagged her finger at him, then stepped in front of him, blocking his view of the crowd. As he sat there, raging, tormented, she loosened the stays on her waist cincher, rocking her hips from side to side as she pulled the garment away from her smooth, creamy skin.

The cincher went flying as she turned back to him. A sexy, teasing smile bowed her lips and fired his blood. She leaned forward, hands balanced on his knees. His gaze dropped to her glorious cleavage before returning to her face. Her smile deepened, then she shook her ruffled ass at the audience.

He growled. She blew him a kiss then straightened. Hooking her fingers into the waistband of her sexy panties, Sugar did that shake-shimmy thing that drove him wild, and the panties slid down her thighs and over her boots, leaving her in a nearly flesh-colored thong. Another series of undulating moves and she whipped off the frothy bra, leaving her in shimmery pasties.

Two stagehands slid what looked like a kiddie pool in front of him, helped Sugar into it, then one of them handed her a bottle. As the song rolled into its last bridge, Sugar shook the bottle. The lights shifted to black light, making Sugar's thong and pasties gleam a purple-white and the bottle of liquid neon pink. The crowd roared its approval. As if following the singer's instructions, Sugar held the bottle high then poured the liquid over her exposed skin, sending rivulets of neon spilling down her luscious curves.

Holy. Fuck.

The lights went out as the song ended. Amid thundering applause, Sugar grabbed his hand, pulling him to his feet. "Come backstage with me," she breathed into his ear.

"Hell yeah," he agreed, his need for her overriding everything else.

After accepting a large towel from one of the apprentices and wrapping it about herself, she led them through a flurry of performers, props, and equipment to the smallest dressing room he'd ever seen. He'd seen bigger bathroom stalls. It had room for a chair, makeup table, and lights. A hook held the black wrap dress Siobhan had worn to the club. There was barely enough room for them, but the size of the room no longer mattered as Sugar turned and planted the hottest openmouthed kiss on him he'd ever experienced.

"I wanted to do something special for your birthday," she breathed against his lips. "I didn't want to pick the wrong surfing thing or guitar thing, and I didn't know what else to get you."

She kissed him again. "So I decided to give you me."

His vision burned red. Sinking his hands into her hair, Charlie crashed his mouth against hers, holding her where he needed her. The urge to claim her rode him hard. "You're mine," he growled against her mouth. "Not theirs, mine."

"Yes," she agreed, the towel slipping down her breasts. "I danced for you, Charlie. Only for you."

He reached down with one hand, parting the towel to cup her mound. She was already wet. "I need to fuck you," he ground out, stroking his finger over her through the skimpy fabric. "If you don't want that, you need to kick me out now."

Her eyes slid closed on a moan. "Can't," she breathed. Her eyes opened again, revealing desire glowing in their depths. "Can't kick you out. I need you too much, but I'm covered in neon sugar."

"I don't care." He jerked the towel free, tossed it onto the chair. Clumsy with need, he fumbled his fly open then pulled out his aching cock. The flesh-colored G-string Sugar wore proved a flimsy barrier to what he wanted, what he needed, what he craved with every pounding beat of his blood. He spun her around, parted her thighs, then slid home.

"Yes." She groaned her approval, her channel already slick with her arousal. She braced her hands against the wall, thrusting that beautiful ass back against him. "Hard and fast, baby. Please, I need to come so bad."

He couldn't have gone slowly if he'd wanted to. Clamping one hand on her shoulder for leverage, he slid the other over her hip, his fingers spearing her tight, damp curls. She groaned again and that was all the permission he needed. Need burned through him as he pounded into her, needing to claim her, needing to fill her, needing to make her come. Need so hot, so damn intense he could already feel it boiling up along his nerves, tightening his balls.

Fuck, he wasn't going to last. Gritting his teeth, he slammed into her, stroking her heat with his cock and her clit with his fingers. Mindless to everything but her heat, her curves, her soft moans, he drove them up, up, chasing down the ecstasy that only she could give him.

Her inner muscles clamped down on him as she came with a muffled cry. Unable to hold back he pounded into her wild and unfettered, then erupted, his vision going white-blind as he jetted deep inside her.

TWENTY-THREE

Leaving the club, Siobhan and Charlie headed to her house in a silence thick with sensual anticipation. The quickie in the club had only blunted the edge of her need; by the way Charlie's knee bounced, he was ready for more too. Good. Performing for Charlie at the club was only part of what she'd planned to give him for his birthday weekend.

Once inside she stopped in the hallway, gently turning him toward the guest bathroom. "If you'd like to freshen up, I put some things in the guest bath for you."

He gave her a mock pout in answer, his expression almost boyish. "Shouldn't the birthday boy get to wash the neon syrup off his girl? Or at least lick it off?"

Um, licking. "No." She shook her head for emphasis. "Your girl has something else in mind. You can come in as soon as you're done."

She covered his heart. "Trust me?"

He stared down at her, his blue eyes serious. "I do trust you, sweetness." He caught her chin to give her a kiss so soft and lingering it rocked her to her toes. "Be with you soon."

She blinked at his retreating back several moments before making her way into her bedroom. She'd already set the scene for a romantic night by fitting black silk sheets on the bed and arranging candles about the room. After lighting the small votives to bathe the room in soft light, she checked to make sure their naughty supplies were ready, then made her way to the en suite bath.

Thoughts of Charlie filled her mind as she stood beneath the warm spray, sluicing away the colorful syrup residue. Should she tell Charlie how she felt about him? She wanted to—the emotion bubbled up every time they were together and even when they weren't. Doubt still crawled through her, cautioning her to keep her burgeoning feelings to herself for a while longer. Not doubts about how she felt—there was a certainty, a rightness to it that she felt in her bones. What she doubted was whether or not Charlie wanted her to love him.

She knew a large part of her was being irrational. Charlie had pushed for a relationship from the beginning. He demonstrated his desire for her every day in ways both large and small. Confessions of love, though . . . that signified a deepening of the relationship that she wasn't sure Charlie was looking for, a level of commitment she wasn't sure either of them was looking for.

The sex, however, was definitely in demand, she thought as she smoothed scented lotion over her skin. Besides, Charlie was a show-don't-tell type of guy. She could safely let him know how she felt about him without saying a single word.

Finishing her preparations, Siobhan slipped into a blush pink sheer baby-doll gown strategically trimmed with marabou feathers, then pulled on the matching robe before stepping into her vintage slippers. It was one of her favorite sets but she'd bought it thinking she'd never have the occasion to wear something so overtly sexy and intimate. Then along came a sexy marketing consultant who'd swept her off her feet. Now it was her turn to sweep him off his.

Charlie waited for her in the bedroom, lounging on the bed wearing nothing but the bottom half of the royal blue silk pajamas she'd bought for him. He'd slicked his damp hair back from his eyes and they widened with appreciation as she strutted toward him.

She danced back when he sat up, swinging his legs over the side of the bed to make a grab for her. "Do you like your present?"

"Are you talking about my outfit or yours?"

She pirouetted slowly, the feathered hem swinging against her thighs. "I mean yours."

He ran a hand down his silk-covered thigh. "I like the pajamas. I've never slept in anything so nice." He leaned back, propping himself up with his hands and displaying the generous erection tenting his pants. "Then again, I don't plan to sleep in them tonight either."

She laughed. "I didn't think you would, Mr. Au Naturel. I wanted you to have something comfortable that you could slip into when you're staying over. I also made some space for you in the dresser and the closet."

The pleasure in his eyes deepened. "You're the gift that keeps on giving, goddess. I'll do my best to be a worthy recipient."

The dark promise in his tone pulled at her. "You already are," she told him as she approached, unable and unwilling to stay away from him. "I want to make sure you have the best birthday ever."

She straddled his knees, then launched into her impression of

Marilyn Monroe singing the birthday song. His large hands warmed her back through the gossamer fabric of her robe, and she entwined her arms about his neck. With every breathy note she sang she lightly ran her mouth over his cheeks, his throat, that gorgeous, giving mouth. As soon as she finished the tune, she kissed him.

What she'd intended to be a soft kiss immediately burst into more. Charlie fed on her mouth, devouring her like a starving man breaking a fast, as if she were the only source of sustenance he needed. In turn she fell into his kiss, fell into him—then literally fell as he turned, pinning her beneath him. He dragged his mouth over her cheeks, her throat, the rise of her breasts, scorching her with the heat of his desire.

"Do I get to unwrap my favorite present now?" he asked, his eyes gleaming with mischief and sexual intent.

"You can, if that's what you want." She stared up at him, her heart dancing in her chest. Six months ago she wouldn't have dared believe that she'd be in a position like this, with a man beautiful inside and out gazing at her as if she held the answer to everything. It was both heady and terrifying, yet as imperfect as she was, she wanted to be those answers for him, wanted to be the goddess he'd named her. "Is there anything else you want, Charlie?"

"Besides you naked?" He thrust against her, leaving no doubt of his intent. "No, sweetness, I've got everything I want."

The thickness of his silk-covered erection pressing so sweetly against her core almost distracted her. "Everyone wants something," she answered, emotion throttling her voice down to a whisper. "Surely you do too."

Shadows pooled in his eyes as he balanced on his hands above her. Then he blinked them away with his trademark devil-may-care grin. "What is there to want? My brothers and my sister are healthy, happy, and safe. My company's doing well. I met Lorelei's boyfriend and he survived the encounter."

He pressed against her again. "I have the sexiest, most beautiful woman in Crimson Bay beneath me. I'm the luckiest bastard in town and I know it. I don't have the right to want anything else."

Of course he'd say that. Charlie wasn't selfish—taking care of his siblings for the last eight years proved that. He probably hadn't done anything just because, just for himself, in ages. He was a caregiver, a natural leader, a protector. But who protected him? Who took care of him?

That was the true gift she wanted to give him. At least one night in which he could let go and do nothing except accept what she offered.

"Okay, maybe not a want. What about a wish?" She reached up to cup his cheek. "It's your birthday weekend. If anything could happen today, something I could do for you, what would you wish for?"

His eyes slid closed. When he opened them again, need blazed so stark and obvious even in the candlelight. Need so deep and profound she doubted she could conquer it. "Charlie."

Once again he hid behind a smile, this one mocking. "Don't ask the question if you don't want the answer, Sugar," he chided. "Once that door opens, there's no going back."

"I know," she whispered softly, her thumb stroking along his beard-roughened cheek. "I'm not turning back. I want to walk through that door. Please tell me—what do you want?"

His gaze sharpened, focused like a laser. She felt his presence pulling at her, drawing her entire being to him. She went willingly, wanting to surrender to him, wanting to give him what he wanted.

"I want you," he ground out, his voice guttural and deep with unchecked desire. "All of you. No hiding, no holding back. Tonight I'm going to break down that damn door."

The demand in his voice coursed through her like premium tequila, heating her insides and urging her to agree to everything he wanted. "Okay."

He froze above her, his body tense, his eyes frosted with disbelief. Clearly he hadn't expected her to agree. "Okay?"

"Yes, I'll give you what you want." She framed his face with both hands. "On my terms."

"What terms are those?"

"That I also get to give you what you need."

He snorted. "What do you think I need?"

"You need to be able to let go," she answered. "You need a place where it's okay for you to not have to do and be everything to everyone. Where you can relinquish control and trust that you'll be taken care of."

She didn't think she was saying the words the way she'd planned to say them but she hoped he understood her intent. "I want to give you everything you want, but in return I'd like to have your trust. At least for tonight."

For a long moment he simply stared at her as if trying to decide whether she meant it or not—whether he could agree or not. She knew it would be a big step for him. Being in control was a necessary part of Charlie's life. He couldn't have run a successful business and raised his siblings otherwise. Giving up that control to her, even in the bedroom, was probably more than he could handle. Yet he needed to let go just as badly as she needed him to trust her to catch him.

She kept her expression open, hoping her eyes could communicate what her words couldn't. Just when she decided to give up and just let him fuck her stupid, he leaned down to kiss her. "Okay, goddess, tonight I'm at your mercy. What do you want me to do?"

She huffed out a relieved breath. "Just lie back on the pillows. I'll do the rest."

He rolled off her, then settled against the mound of pillows heaped against the headboard, his eyes dark and expectant. She straddled him, stretched his arms out, then quickly secured his wrists with the straps she'd attached to the headboard.

He lifted a brow. "Now I see why you didn't want me to have an advance peek," he said, flexing his arms to test his bonds. "Is this pleasure or punishment?"

"It will be what I decide to give you," she said sternly, lifting away from the distraction of his body. "You are mine to tease how I want. If I am pleased, you will be rewarded. Understood?"

His expression grew hazy. "Yes, goddess."

"If you want to tap out at any time, say *cotton candy*," she instructed, slipping off the robe before tossing it to the foot of the bed. The nightie followed, her breasts spilling free. "Understood?"

His gaze lingered on her breasts, her nipples tightening in response to his hungry expression. "Yes, goddess."

"Good. Now taste me." She leaned forward, brushing her left nipple over his lips. He caught it eagerly, lapping at her with his tongue, the pull of his mouth sending electric currents of pleasure straight to her sex. The sensation intensified when she guided him to her other breast, the warmth of his mouth spreading heat through her.

She pulled away from him reluctantly, her sex pulsing with need. "Your mouth is dangerous in more ways than one, Charlie O'Halloran."

He gave her a cheeky grin. "Come sit on my face and I'll show you just how dangerous my mouth can be."

Drawn by the promise in his gaze, she actually shifted forward only to catch herself, bracing her palms on his chest. "Stop distracting me, or I won't give you what you want."

"I want to taste that sweet pussy of yours." He waggled his brows at her. "Are you going to give me what I want or not?"

"Yes." She sank her nails into his chest, just enough to make him hiss. "But not if you keep distracting me. So I guess I'll have to distract you."

She nipped at his bottom lip. He responded with a soft groan, making her smile. Taking her time she nipped her way down his chin and throat to his chest, biting kisses that allowed her to taste him and leave her mark on his skin. With turnabout being fair play, she flicked her tongue across his nipples, relishing his reaction from each sucked-in breath to softly uttered curse.

Her sensitized nipples skimmed over the planes of his abdomen as she meandered down his body, removing the pajama bottoms so that she could trap his cock in her cleavage. The hard length of him burned into her soft skin but she cupped her breasts together and rocked, sliding his erection against her décolletage. His hips thrust up, his abs contracting beautifully as he began to plunder her cleavage.

"Siobhan," he ground out, his expression tight with lust. "God, woman, that feels . . . good."

"Maybe I can make it feel even better." She scrunched down enough to swirl her tongue over the plump head, teasing the slit with gentle swipes. He groaned his approval, body arching upward in a physical demand for more. More she gave, taking him into her mouth. Losing herself in the sensual exploration, she licked and suckled along his shaft, his balls, the soft skin behind them until he writhed beneath her, her name a constant refrain on his lips.

She came up for air, smiling at the blissed-out expression he wore. "Still with me, birthday boy?"

He gave a breathless chuckle. "Mostly."

"I know I said I'd keep you from making decisions tonight, but there's something you need to decide."

"What's that?"

"You get to choose how you want to come. I can keep working you with my mouth or I could tit-fuck you until you give me a pearl necklace. I could ride you until you flood my pussy, or . . ." She let her voice trail off.

He focused on her. "Or what?"

"Or I could have your cock replace this." She turned around then bent over, giving him a clear view of her ass.

"You're wearing an anal plug." His voice was deeper than she'd ever heard it. "Have you had that in all night?"

"I put it in after my shower," she told him. "I've been practicing every day for a couple of weeks, and I did some prep work for tonight."

"You've been planning this for a couple of weeks?" His cock jerked in her hand, a dollop of pre-come beading on the tip. "You've been walking around wearing a butt plug for the last couple of weeks?"

"Yes. I wanted our first time to be easy, if you decide that's what you want."

"God." He thumped his head against the pillows. "You're gonna be the death of me, woman. At least I get to come when I go."

"So which will it be?" she asked, even though she already knew the answer. "How do you want to come?"

The look he gave her told her how ridiculous he thought her question. "You know what I want. I want to fuck your beautiful ass, fuck you until I come and fill you up."

She shivered, loving the crude words, the roughness in his voice. Anticipation gripped her as she reached into the nightstand drawer to gather everything she needed. Watching his features, she stroked warming lube onto his cock, pleased when he whispered a curse and pushed himself into her hand.

He grinned when she held up the vibrating cock ring so that he could see it. "I like the way you take control, goddess."

"I certainly hope so," she said as she stroked the thick ring down his engorged cock. "Are you ready for the main event?"

"I'm ready if you are." His ab muscles stood out in stark relief as he tensed. She stood, her gaze locked to his as she reached to remove the plug.

"Wait."

She paused in surprise. "What?"

"I want to know," Charlie said, his voice the consistency of gravel.

"Know what?"

"Did you masturbate while wearing it?"

Her breath caught, but Charlie's intense gaze demanded an answer. "Yes."

"Show me. I need to see."

Heat flushed her skin, her breath shallowing as lust rose. Her hand skated down her belly to her sex. Charlie's eyes tracked her movements, his lips parted, his cock so fully aroused it looked painful.

Her eyes slid closed as her fingers parted her sex, stroking over her clit. She gasped at the electric sensation, ramped higher by knowing that Charlie watched her. She was so wet and needy for him.

"Goddess."

Her eyes snapped open. "Yes?"

"Did you fuck yourself with it?"

"Yes."

"Did you enjoy it?"

Staring at him, her nipples painfully tight, her body on the brink, she answered with an honest whisper. "Yes."

The headboard rattled as the restraints thwarted his attempt to grab her. The hungry gaze and low growl of need caused her nipples to bead up and her sex to juice even more. She focused on the loose straps draped around his wrists and realized he'd topped her from the bottom, so smoothly she hadn't noticed or minded.

"I'd lie in bed, on my back," she told him, keeping her voice hushed. "I would push it in, imagining that it was you filling me in a slow, smooth glide. Once it was in all the way, I'd imagine you ordering me to stroke myself. I would but then I'd realize it wasn't enough, so I'd have to ride the plug. But then . . ." Her voice faded.

"Then what?" he demanded.

"Then I needed more, so I'd put a condom on the vibrator, wishing it was you. Needing it to be you."

"I need it too, sweetness. Give us what we both want. Give us what we both need."

She clambered onto the bed, facing away from him to straddle him. Bending over, she reached back to remove the plug from her well-oiled rear. Charlie groaned, his tone somewhere between pain and plea. Not wanting to delay any longer, Siobhan reached between her thighs, wrapped her fingers around Charlie's thick erection, and guided it to her back opening.

He was so hot and thick that she momentarily wondered if she'd adequately prepared. At least he wasn't trying to help her by thrusting, instead allowing her to control the sensual invasion. Pressure as his cock head stretched her then breached. Blowing out a breath, she sank down on him in measured increments until she was fully seated.

"Siobhan." He groaned, shuddered. "God, sweetness, you're so hot and tight."

She glanced over her shoulder to find him fixated on where they joined. His blissful expression made her smile. She wasn't close to being done with him.

She rocked against him then leaned forward, knowing she gave him a perfect view. Knowing also that her position made it easy to stroke his balls as she rode him. He groaned his approval, gently thrusting up to match her rhythm.

Then she turned on the vibrator in the cock ring.

Charlie shouted, the headboard hitting the wall as he bucked. "Don't move! For the love of Pete, don't move."

Siobhan froze. "You okay?"

"Trying not to come," he ground out. "Trying to think about taxes, promo campaigns—anything but your sweet ass gripping my cock."

She remained still until his choppy breathing evened out and his thighs relaxed beneath her. Only then did she begin to ride him again, pleasure shooting sparks through her each time she bottomed out against the vibrating ring. Focused on his satisfaction, she balanced on one hand, using the other to cup and stroke his balls, the soft skin behind, and beyond. Tension gathered in his thighs again, his breath breaking and choppy as she rocked on him, determined to propel him to ecstasy.

"Siobhan." His voice was a hoarse rumble. "I need, I need—"

"What?" She sank onto him, turned enough to look at him over her shoulder. "What do you need, Charlie?"

"My hands free. So I can make sure that it's good for you too."

Even when it was supposed to be all about him, Charlie had to make sure she was okay too. Her heart melted. "Okay."

He pulled his hands free of the restraints—she'd kept them loose more for the show of restraining him than the actuality—wrapped his hands around her waist, then rolled her until she lay facedown on the sheets. Still throbbing thickly inside her rear channel he pushed her thighs farther apart until she crouched on her elbows and knees. Draped over her like a living blanket, he began to move inside her, one hand teasing her nipples while the other plundered her empty pussy, his thumb swirling over her slick nub. The vibrations from the ring at the root of his cock rippled through her each time he bottomed out and circled his hips, and oh, didn't that do wonderful things.

She moved with him, lost to the rhythm, lost to sensation, lost to him. Good, so good that she couldn't hold back, couldn't silence the mewling noises, couldn't stop the orgasm that skittered up her back like water droplets on a hot skillet and burst from her on a long groan, her sex clenching with pleasure.

Her name broke from him like a curse as he shuddered. His arms tightened around her and he began to drive into her all the way out then back in, taking her from empty to full over and over. She tightened around him, desperate whimpers clawing up her throat in counterpoint to his ragged breaths. Faster, faster, and then his nimble fingers pinched her clit. She screamed as her brain short-circuited, her body clamping down. She heard Charlie's guttural groan as his orgasm hit him, flooding her. He ground against her, milking every drop, then carefully eased out of her before collapsing on his back beside her.

When they could move again, they made quick work of cleaning up, then extinguished the candles before returning to bed. Charlie pulled her back against his chest, spooning her. One big hand splayed across her belly with a sweet possessiveness that thrilled her. It made her feel as if she belonged, belonged to him. That he would care for her and protect her no matter what.

His fingers traced nonsensical patterns on her skin and she realized he was still awake. "You're still awake?"

"Yeah. Just thinking."

She tensed. "It wasn't too much was it?"

"My beautiful girl," he murmured, his lips grazing her ear. "You—that ring thing—I've never come that hard and long in my life. This whole day was exactly what I needed. Best birthday present ever."

His hand grazed her hip. "Are you okay though? I tried to go easy but you clamped down on me and my brain exploded."

Relieved, she turned in his arms to kiss him. "I'm good. I'm glad I could make you happy."

"You make me happy all the time. Every damn day."

"Good to know, since you make me happy too." She sighed against his chest. "What you do for me, what you give me—I can never thank you enough. That you do it because you want to, because you like to, that makes it even more special."

"When you say stuff like that, it makes me think—" He broke off with a shake of his head. "Never mind."

"What?" She rested her palm over his heart. "Makes you think I want you? That I'm falling for you? Well, you'd be right. I wouldn't tell you though, so I won't have to hear you say I told you so."

"Are you?" His question was a low whisper in the dark. "Falling for me, I mean?"

"No. I'm way past that." She kissed his chest, right over his heart, then tilted her face to his. "I love you, Charlie O'Halloran."

For one sharp moment he froze. Then he pounced, covering her body with his. Breath whooshed out of her just before he claimed her lips in a kiss that seared her synapses. Before she could register the need for air, he'd kissed his way down her body as she'd done his earlier, his touch gentling as he reached her sex.

Her thighs automatically parted for him, wanting what he wanted, needing what he needed to give her. She drew her knees up and back, offering herself to him just as freely as she'd offered her heart. He thanked her with kisses and deep strokes of his tongue, sending her up, up and over. When she trembled and gasped his name he relented, but only long enough to fit himself to her entrance.

In the darkness she couldn't see him, but she didn't need to. She cupped his face in her hands as they kissed, tongues dancing and sliding in counterpoint to their bodies. With a roll of his hips, he hit all the right spaces, making her sing and cry and moan his name. Hooking her ankles behind his back, she rocked against him, swelling with love, swelling with pleasure until she burst, taking him with her.

TWENTY-FOUR

Charlie watched Siobhan sleep, so deeply peaceful he didn't want to awaken her. Sunlight spilled through the large window, flowing across the bed. It caressed her golden hair, giving her a halo. His angel. His goddess. She was everything he hadn't dared hope for, everything he'd dreamed of those few times when he could push aside the guilt of wanting something for himself. Someone for himself, who'd take care of him for a change.

God. A shudder swept through him. How had she known—how had she read him so thoroughly, uncovered something he could barely admit to himself, and only acknowledge deep in the night, when he was completely alone with his thoughts?

Some days he was just fucking tired of the daily grind of managing his company, of bearing the thousands of responsibilities for his employees and his siblings. He did it because he wanted to, because he had to, and because he gave orders far better than he followed them. When his world had spiraled out of control eight years ago, he'd had to take control in order to keep his family intact. Discovering his inner control freak hadn't been a bad thing, it had actually been just in time. Without tapping into that need to control, to be in charge, he would have lost everything.

But now . . . now there were days when it was almost too much. When he wished that he could ease his vise-grip on control and just let someone else be in command for a change, let someone else make the decisions. Let someone else take care of things, take care of him, for just a little while. Because he had balls he couldn't share that, couldn't confess that desire because that would make him appear weak and real men don't do weak, they just swallowed down the bullshit and tried not to choke.

Somehow Siobhan had known. As promised, she'd given him what he'd wanted and needed. Then she'd put the cherry on that perfect sundae by telling him that she loved him.

He closed his eyes as the knowledge washed over him. Last night Siobhan had given all of herself to him without hesitation. Even caught in the passion and the explosive sex as he'd been, he'd noticed the difference, noticed the openness. Felt the connection that had deepened between them. She was a part of him now, filling up all the empty spaces he hadn't realized he had.

He wanted her and he needed her. He couldn't go a day without seeing her, touching her, kissing her. It scratched the edge of obsession but he didn't care. Having her in his life made every bad moment that had come before worth it.

Sunlight kissed her cheek, causing her to stir. She blinked slowly, her smile soft and warm as she caught sight of him. "Charlie."

"Good morning, sweetness," he said just as softly, liking the sound of his name on her lips. "Did you sleep well?"

"Of course I did. You wore me out." She stroked his arm as if she needed to touch him. He liked that too. "How long have you been awake?"

"Not too long. I was watching you sleep and had just started counting my blessings when you woke up."

"Was I one of your blessings?"

"One of them? You were all of them."

Her smile widened. "Wow. Now I'm counting my blessings." She stretched as a yawn overtook her, only to break off with a groan.

Concern shafted through him as he leaned over her. "Are you sore?"

"A little bit stiff," she admitted, pink staining her cheeks. "Doing that reverse cowgirl after performing was too much for my thighs. And my back. And other parts."

"Can I get you some aspirin or something?" He stopped short, breathed out a curse. "Christ, I just offered you painkillers. That was stupid of me. Sorry."

"Don't be." She slid closer to him. "I kinda like that you forgot. It makes me feel . . . ordinary."

"You'll never be ordinary." He kissed her forehead, then ran a reassuring hand down her back when she stiffened. "What do you usually do when you're in pain?"

"Depends on the type of pain," she answered, her face tucked against his chest. "Topical stuff mostly. Hot or cold compresses, herbal teas, and I try to meditate. But nothing beats having a glass of wine and a good book with a superlong soak in the tub."

"It might be a little early for wine, but would you like me to run a bath for you?"

She pulled back to look at him, yearning clear on her face. "Do we have time?"

"We have plenty of time," he assured her. "I want to make sure you're all right."

"I'm supposed to be taking care of you, not the other way around," she complained without heat. "It's your birthday weekend, not mine."

"Taking care of you takes care of me. It's what I do." He grinned at her. "Besides, you took care of me last night."

"Charlie . . ."

"I'll even throw in a massage."

"Ooh. So not arguing anymore." She settled back with a sigh. "Thank you."

"It's always my pleasure, sweetness."

Kissing her again, he climbed out of bed and made his way to the bathroom. It was a modern layout at odds with the mid-century feel of the rest of the house. The shower was large and tiled, and a large free-standing soaker tub took up the spot beneath a frosted picture window.

Turning the taps on, he adjusted the temperature while mentally kicking himself. He couldn't believe he'd offered Siobhan painkillers. She'd handled it well but he still felt like an idiot for suggesting them.

It made him wonder, though. It was almost second nature for most people to pop a couple of aspirin for everything from cramps to headaches. How did she fight the urge to slip a bottle into her shopping cart while at the grocery store? Did she go out of her way to avoid pharmacies? Was every day a battle in a country that had a pill for everything? How was he supposed to explain Siobhan's aversion to medicines to his brothers and sister?

"Did the bathtub make you mad?"

He looked up to find Siobhan standing in the doorway, gloriously naked. "No, why?"

"You were frowning at it. What are you thinking about?"

"Nothing." He gave her what he hoped was his most convincing smile. "Do you need to use the john?"

"I went down the hall." She turned to the vanity, piling her sleep-matted waves atop her head and securing them with one of those claw-teeth things Lorelei had a habit of leaving all over the house. "That's a whole lot of frowning for nothing type of thoughts."

"I'm thinking the water isn't as hot as you probably want it," he said, which was a truth but not the answer.

She paused, watching him in the mirror. Her gaze traveled to her own reflection. Something flashed in her eyes before her expression went blank. "All right," she said, her voice calm as she accepted his lie. Wrapping her arms about herself, she turned away from the mirror without looking at him.

"How do you do it?" he blurted out. "Deal with the pain and people offering to ply you with pills when they don't know any better?"

"I politely refuse," she answered, crossing to the tub to check and adjust the water temperature. "If they're curious, I usually tell people that I prefer homeopathic remedies. Most of the time they accept that at face value. This is California, after all."

She opened a jar on a glass shelf above the tub and poured a handful of granules into the tub. "The best way is to not put myself in situations where I could be tempted. Not that I've been tempted. I've been doing my best to live my life as positively as I can.

She held the jar close. "It's muscle-relaxing and stress-relieving bath salts," she explained, swirling her hand in the water. "Nothing too girly."

"You should make it as girly as you want, and take your time."
He headed for the door. "Would you like some coffee?"

"You're not going to join me?" she asked, surprise coloring her
voice.

"I thought you'd prefer some alone time." The excuse sounded
lame to his ears, and he knew Siobhan must have heard it.

"I've been alone long enough," she said, her voice barely audible above the gushing water. "Maybe it's time to get a cat."

She shook her head as if to clear it, then flashed him a remote
smile as she shut off the faucet. "Thanks for starting the water for me."

Turning her back to him, she carefully stepped into the tub
then slowly sank into the water. She rested her head against the rim
of the tub then closed her eyes, a deep sigh seeping from her. Shutting him out, which he deserved.

Crap. He'd hurt her feelings and she'd responded by shutting
him out. Not the best way to start the day after the woman you
wanted more than your next breath said she loved you.

"Are you still there?" she asked after a moment.

"Yeah."

She didn't open her eyes, just sank down until the water reached
her chin. "Why?"

He went with the truth. "I'm trying to figure out how to apologize to you."

She huffed. "Do you even know what you'd be apologizing for?"

"Ruining the best gift I've ever received?"

The water rippled as she hunched her shoulders. "Maybe I'm the
one who should be apologizing for ruining your birthday weekend."

That surprised him. "You didn't do anything."

"I dropped the L word," she reminded him. "You were supposed to not have to think about anything and I gave you a whopper to think about. To be honest, I'd thought about not telling you but I got caught up in everything last night and just couldn't keep it in."

Dread slid an icy hand down his back. She couldn't have regrets already. What was he going to do if she had regrets? Change her mind, that's what. "Scoot up, I'm getting in."

Not waiting for an answer, he strode across the tiled floor then climbed into the prickly hot water, settling in behind her. He pulled her back against his chest, trying to ignore his burgeoning cock that apparently wanted a repeat performance of last night's festivities. Though she didn't resist he could feel the tension in her shoulders. Tension he'd put there.

He dribbled water along her tight shoulders, seeking to lighten the mood. "Hey, the whole point of this is to relax and loosen your muscles," he reminded her, "not cause others to tense up."

"I know. I'm trying."

Hoping to get her to relax and open up to him, he focused on massaging the back of her neck. "Why would you not tell me how you feel?"

"Because." She sighed. "That takes things to another level. You have to consider what it means to have a recovering addict in love with you, what it means for you and your family. And I have to wonder what it means when you say nothing is wrong immediately after we have a conversation about my addiction. Because 'nothing' is almost always something, and it's usually something unpleasant. Especially when a guy who kisses me every time he walks away doesn't this time."

Shit. She was in tune with him in a way he'd never experienced with someone else and she must have thought he was rejecting her because he never passed up an opportunity to kiss her or be naked with her. "I'm sorry for that. Does it help if I tell you that saying nothing's wrong is an automatic reaction from when people questioned my ability to take care of my family?"

"That sucks." She tensed again, but this time he knew it was indignation and not directed at him. "And yes, it does help. A little."

"I'm really sorry I put you off like that." He kissed the back of her neck as he curled his arms about her. "Last night, you said you were giving me what I want and what I need. Did you mean that?"

"Of course I did."

"Then how could you think that I wouldn't want you to tell me that you love me?" He rested his chin on her shoulder. "Or that I wouldn't need to hear you to say it?"

"Because of this . . . distance. Because things are fine when you forget what I went through."

She half turned to him. "Does it weird you out? Remembering that I'm a drug addict, I mean?"

He copped to it because she already knew the answer. "Sometimes."

She flinched. "I thought it still bothered you. I should have known." She pulled herself upright to climb out of the tub. "I need to shower off the bath salts and wash my hair."

"I'll scrub your back for you," he offered, "then give you that massage I promised."

"That's not necessary, Charlie," she told him, her voice politely distant. "I can manage on my own."

"I know," he said quietly, fighting the urge to pull her back down into the now tepid water. "I want to."

"All right," she said in a tone that told him the exact opposite.

Without waiting for him, she padded over to the shower, slid the door open, then started the water before stepping inside.

The longer he waited, the more solid the wall between them would become. Somehow he had to prevent that. He wasn't about to lose her due to his own stupidity.

He joined her in the shower after getting out of the tub and opening the drain. She stood beneath the spray shampooing her hair, the water temperature just as hot as the bath. It must have been her go-to setting to manage her pain. "Do you use a heating pad too?" he asked as he lathered up.

She didn't open her eyes. "Yes, but not with you here. Obviously." A frown flashed across her face. "I didn't want you to see proof of how old and decrepit I am."

"Decrepit my ass." He rinsed off, soaped his hands with her shower gel, then began to rub her back in slow circles. "I don't know any woman who can run a café, perform with a burlesque troupe, and still have energy left over to rock my world. You did all of that yesterday, I'll remind you. If that's the power of tea, I'll have to start drinking."

A brief smile bowed her lips. "There goes that tongue again. You always know what to say."

"If I always knew what to say and how to say it, I wouldn't have to apologize to you right now." He stroked his hands down her back, keeping his touch comforting. "When you asked me if I was weirded out, I was. Just not in the way you'd think."

He paused, hoping he wouldn't make things worse as he searched for the right words to say. "When you caught me frowning earlier it was because I was wondering how hard it must be for you doing things I take for granted like walking into a pharmacy or reaching for ibuprofen when I have a headache. How you handle people making asinine comments about getting high or drunk or any other addictive thing. And I wondered how you're managing it alone."

Siobhan pressed her palms against the wall and lowered her head, allowing the water to cascade off her hair and down her back. "I'm not alone, Charlie. Nadia and the others are part of my support network. Nadia and I, since we went through rehab together, have the same mentor. I also have a therapist. I can call either of them whenever I need to vent or be talked back from the ledge. With that support and hard work, I haven't slipped. I don't intend to slip."

"I believe you." He said it as simply as he could so that she'd know he meant it. "More than that, I trust you. I trust you with me, with my family, and with being in our house. Just like you're working through accepting our age difference, I'm working through being what you want and need."

A tremble swept through her as she breathed out a long slow breath before turning to face him. With her hair slicked back and her face makeup-free, her vulnerability was clear to see. "You are what I want and need, Charlie. I don't think about our age difference anymore—probably because when I'm with you, you make it difficult to think at all. I love who you are, not what you are."

"It still stuns me to hear you say that. Maybe this is one long dream and I'm caught up in a fantasy."

"You're not." She tweaked his nipple. "You shouldn't be surprised either. After all, hasn't that been your plan all along? Making me fall for you?"

"Yes." He gave her an unabashed grin as he ran soapy hands over her shoulders, throat, then slowly across her chest and belly. "What I didn't expect was for you to beat me to the punch."

She sucked in a breath, but he couldn't tell if it was in reaction to his words or his touch. "What?"

Instead of answering, he knelt down to run his lather-covered hands over her legs, fingers working at the tight muscles. She tugged on his hair. "Charlie, you better answer me."

He laughed, the tightness easing from his chest as he rose to his feet. "You beat me to the punch, sweetness, telling me you loved me before I could confess my undying devotion to you."

She arched a brow. "When was this alleged declaration of devotion supposed to take place?"

"Tonight after the birthday party, when I had you draped over me in my bed." He palmed her rump, bringing her closer. "I was going to tell you how beautiful you are, how happy you make me, and that I love you. And I do. I love you, Siobhan Malloy."

She stared up at him for what felt like an eternity, her blue eyes blown wide. Then she smiled and damn if his heart didn't seize in his chest. He'd never seen her more beautiful than she was at that moment.

The hot water chose that moment to cool down. They hurriedly finished the shower, bundling into thick, oversized towels. "It's still early, isn't it?" Siobhan asked as she pulled her hair back into a braid.

"I'm pretty sure it's still morning and no one's expecting us until the afternoon. What's on your mind?"

"You owe me a massage," she informed him, her gaze heating as she dropped her towel. "I expect you to be very deep and very thorough."

"Yes, ma'am. I always try to exceed expectations."

Judging by her moans, he did just that.

TWENTY-FIVE

It was a beautiful day for a birthday party on the O'Halloran deck. Bright sunlight, an endless blue sky and balmy temperatures were the perfect backdrop for the festivities. What was supposed to be a small and intimate gathering had burgeoned into a loud and boisterous party, but Siobhan didn't mind. Charlie was a different story.

"I can still ground her, can't I?" he groused as he stacked burgers for the grill. "I know she's eighteen and all, but she's still my dependent until she graduates or moves out."

"Lorelei's intentions are good," Siobhan said, adding mint to a gallon of fruit-infused water. "She just wants you to be happy."

He grunted. "What would make me happy is if I were naked in bed with you right now."

"Charlie!" Laughing, she darted a quick look around to make sure they were alone. "Haven't you had enough for today? You should be worn out!"

"I am," he replied, his tone unapologetic. "That's why I want to be in bed with my girl as soon as possible. Sometimes it's not about sex." Then he grinned. "Sometimes it is."

"You're impossible." *And charming, and sexy. And mine.*

"You love me though."

He paused as if he needed confirmation. Or reassurance, or both. It was kinda cute. "How could I not love you? You literally charmed the pants off of me. I'm powerless against you. So yes, I love you. Not that you need the ego boost."

"I'll never get tired of hearing that." The smile he gave her, so unabashedly happy, made her giddy. *I did that. My loves makes him happy.*

He grimaced as he finished arranging the platter of meats for the grill. "Instead of cuddling my woman on my lap, I'll be manning a grill to feed the horde on the deck."

"That horde is our friends and family, and business family," she reminded him. "Besides, I thought all guys love manning the grill. Your nuts get bigger or your chest hair grows or something."

"Um. Fire. Meat. Good," he grunted in passable caveman style. "Last chance, love. We can hop in the convertible and head up the coastal highway, visit wine country."

She wavered with temptation then bumped him with her hip. "It won't be that bad. Remember, today is about making new memories, good memories about your birthday."

His gaze sparked with electric intent, causing a current of awareness to sweep down her spine. "You've already given me that, sweetness."

Flustered, she busied herself with washing her hands. "Yeah, well, if you behave yourself I'll give you more good birthday memories."

"Deal." He joined her at the sink, washing his hands. "Let's go face our guests—and hope they leave sooner rather than later."

Soon enough, a sizable gathering filled the deck and spilled into the backyard. Audie and Vanessa arrived together, with Nadia and Kane showing up soon after. Though Siobhan attempted to maintain her spot as just the girlfriend of the birthday boy, Lorelei was more than happy to cede hostess duties. That probably had a lot to do with her boyfriend—a pleasantly smart young man named Stephen—than anything else.

"You look different," Vanessa observed as she accepted a glass of lemonade from Siobhan. Vanessa was impeccably dressed, as always, in a sleeveless sheath sundress and freshwater pearls gracing her ears.

Siobhan patted her hair, smoothed back into a thick braid. Her one concession to her usual style was the blue artificial hibiscus clipped over her right ear. "I didn't have time to do my usual style this morning."

She and Charlie had lingered in bed after their post-shower kiss and makeup session. He'd loosened her muscles and tightened their emotional connection in the process. With every touch, every kiss, every whisper she had fallen deeper and deeper still. She knew she belonged to him, with him, in a way that she'd never been with her ex.

"This had nothing to do with your fashion sense and everything to do with girl sense," Audie told her, eyes twinkling. "You're in lurve!"

Her friends circled her, waiting. They probably expected her to deny it or get flustered. She did neither. Instead she smiled. "Yes, I am. We are."

As her friends squealed with delight, Siobhan looked toward the deck where Charlie manned the grill and talked with some of his employees. She hardly noticed the others. All she could see was Charlie, his casual skill and grace, his easy presence, the sex appeal so intrinsic to his nature it was like a second skin. Dressed in a bright blue polo shirt and khaki cargo shorts, he still managed to exude a level of confidence and magnetism that rivaled any guy in a power suit.

As if he felt her gaze, Charlie turned and locked eyes with her. Her breath caught, her senses humming with desire, emotion, and need. Her hindbrain recognized him on an instinctive involuntary level that sent shivers racing along her nerve endings. He smiled then, a smile that promised everything—every comfort, every pleasure. Everything she could want. She smiled back.

Even with the distance between them, Siobhan could feel the warmth of his stare on her skin, warmer than sunlight and just as necessary. When he tilted his head toward the driveway where her convertible waited, she actually took a step toward him until Nadia caught her elbow.

"Whoa there," her best friend chided. "This is your party, remember? You can't go running off for a quickie in the middle of the party."

"I know. I was just—" She broke off. What could she say? "It's Charlie."

"Yeah, we got that." Nadia shook her head, but grinned. "I think I got a contact high. That was some serious intensity going on."

"Now you know what it feels like to watch while you and Kane get into one of your stare-downs," Siobhan retorted, struggling to steady her breathing and focus on her friends instead of the idea of driving off into the sunset with Charlie. Though her parts were still too tender to entertain the idea of having sex, she still wanted to go off for some quality skin-to-skin time with her man.

"Damn, woman," Audie breathed. "Both of you. Is it always like that?"

"Yes."

"No."

Siobhan and Nadia looked at each other, then laughed. "Not always," Nadia admitted. "Though it's easy to forget you're in the middle of a crowd sometimes."

Audie turned to Siobhan. "When did you realize you had the feels for Charlie?"

"Two weeks ago."

"Two weeks!" Audie shrieked, then immediately quieted. "You went through two Bitch Talk sessions without sharing this news?"

"I couldn't tell you guys until I told Charlie," Siobhan pointed out. "That wouldn't be fair. I told him after the show last night, and he told me his feelings this morning."

"I'm so happy for you, Siobhan." Vanessa smiled. "So do we need to plan a double wedding?"

The question flustered Siobhan. "Ah, no. No. I'm nowhere near thinking about stuff like that."

"Are you still hung up on the fact that you're a cougar?" Audie teased.

"No," Siobhan answered honestly. "Besides, I'm not a cougar—we're both in our thirties. Five years isn't a big deal."

"So if you love him and aren't bothered by your age difference, why are you hesitating?" Audie wanted to know.

"It's only been a few months that we've been together," Siobhan pointed out. "I'm still trying to come to grips with staying over at his place and doing you-know-what while the kids sleep a floor above us. Besides, it's not like I was so good at it the first time around."

"Is it his family?"

"Charlie's family is great. I love his brothers and sister as if they were my own. I mean, think about it: they could be my own. It's not Charlie's family that's the problem."

Nadia's eyes softened in understanding. "It's yours."

Siobhan stared into her glass. "Of course. I haven't heard from Colleen all summer, not since I saw her at her graduation. I've left messages . . . I'd really like her to meet Charlie and his family, especially Lorelei. I'm hoping Lorelei might be a good influence on Colleen."

"They're the same age, aren't they?" Vanessa asked.

Siobhan nodded. "My relationship with Lorelei is completely different from my relationship with my own daughter. It's not fair to compare them, but I do. I get along great with Charlie's sister and it makes me feel guilty."

Nadia pursed her lips. "What you should feel is the realization that maybe your issues with your family aren't your fault."

Siobhan sighed. It was an old argument between them. "Maybe they're not entirely my fault, but I have to shoulder some of the blame for what happened, for the inability to mend fences with my parents and with Colleen."

Remembering her hostess duties, she left her friends to check on the other guests, then headed inside. The estrangement from her family still haunted her, and would continue to do so. Sure, her therapist was helping her manage the guilt but it hadn't disappeared. She knew the issues with her daughter and her parents would always be a dark spot in her future happiness if she couldn't resolve things one way or another.

Unsurprisingly, she found Kyle in the kitchen overseeing the last of the side dishes they'd prepared together. "Kyle, are you making something else?"

He inspected the array of dishes on the kitchen island. "No, everything's ready."

"Good." She pointed to the patio doors. "Get out."

"What?" His eyes rounded.

"You heard me. There's a swarm of people in your backyard. Finn's got a bunch of them tossing a Frisbee around. Join them."

"But—"

"Kyle." She put her hands on his shoulders. "It's a beautiful day. Go enjoy it."

His Adam's apple bobbed as he swallowed. "You sound like Mom. She was always making us go outside, whether it was working in the garden with her or dragging the whole family to the beach. Twice a year we even went camping. She'd say, 'The day's too pretty and my kids are too cute to be stuck inside.' I haven't thought about that in a long time."

Kyle threw his arms around her for a tight, impulsive hug. "I'm glad Charlie found you."

He made a break for the patio doors before she could respond. Not that she could have spoken past the lump in her throat. Kyle brushed past Charlie and she spun around, not wanting him to see the sudden tears that had sprung to her eyes.

"Hey." Gentle hands turned her around and she found herself staring up at Charlie, his blue eyes bright. "Looks like I'm not the only one you're giving good memories to. Thank you for that."

"I wasn't trying to," she confessed. "I just didn't want him to be in here stressing out."

"I know." He stroked his thumbs beneath her eyes, capturing her tears. "That makes it even better. If I didn't already love you, that would have kicked me over."

"Charlie." Her heart trilled at the ease with which he spoke.

He shook his head ruefully. "There are so many things I want to do and say to you right now. Instead, I'll tell you that it's time to feed the horde. After that I'm sending the boys to the movies and Lorelei on a date so I'll have you all to myself."

She kissed him once then again, pulling away before she could slip into that sensual place he could always put her. "Looking forward to it."

They set the food up on the kitchen island buffet-style and soon everyone had an overflowing plate and had found a spot at one of the tables scattered on the deck and in the yard. Siobhan sat next to Charlie at the picnic table. Though she made small talk with the others, she was hyperaware of Charlie beside her, the brush of his thigh against hers, the low rumble of his voice. She realized she was exactly where she wanted and needed to be, surrounded by friends and family. The day couldn't get any better.

When everyone had eaten all they wanted, Charlie climbed to his feet. "First of all, I'd like to thank you all for coming. Celebrating my birthday isn't something I like to do. Eight years ago we lost our parents pretty close to this day, so it seemed wrong to have any sort of festivities. Two very special ladies convinced me that this was the year to rethink it. So a toast to my sister, Lorelei, for suggesting this party—and talking to my girl about it. They're the reason you all are here today."

He turned to Siobhan, his smile spreading as he pulled her to her feet. "Another toast to Siobhan, the best birthday present a man could hope for. Thanks for the new good memories, love, and here's to many more."

A collective "aww" filled the air, followed by applause as he kissed her. Tears stung her eyes again as emotions buffeted her. Luckily Charlie was there, anchoring her, her shelter from any storm.

"Happy birthday!"

Siobhan stepped back, flushed with need and chagrin. They turned as Lorelei slid the screen door open to allow Kyle to step out. He balanced a huge chocolate cake on his palms. The crowd broke into a decent rendition of the birthday song as Kyle proudly delivered the massive sheet cake to their table.

Shock slapped her as she registered the numbers on the cake. "Charlie?" Her voice quavered. "Is this some sort of joke?"

"Siobhan," Charlie began, but Lorelei's laughter cut him off.

"Joke? There's no joke. Charlie's twenty-six."

Twenty-six?

Good God. There weren't five years between her and Charlie. There were ten.

TWENTY-SIX

Siobhan stood at the sink, elbow deep in suds. She'd held it together during the cutting of the birthday cake, smiling even though those damned number candles mocked her every time she had to look at them. She'd even laughed when her friends threatened bodily harm to Charlie on her behalf.

"Siobhan."

Her shoulders tightened at Charlie's voice, but she didn't turn around. "Is everyone gone?"

"Yes."

She hurriedly continued before he could say anything else. "Lorelei and the boys are gone too?"

"Yes, we're alone. We can talk now if that's what you want."

She rinsed suds off a dish, then thunked it into the drying rack before going to work on another. She didn't want to talk, didn't want to think. Didn't want to sort through the maelstrom of emotions threatening to choke her. So she did as she'd done with her family, swallowed the pain down and pretended that everything was fine.

He edged closer. "If it makes you feel better, your friends threatened to take my balls and beat me over the head with them."

Her friends. They'd been outraged on her behalf, though they'd toned it down for her sake. He'd duped them too, but they didn't feel the embarrassment and hurt she labored with. How could they?

"Sweetheart, please. Say something. Talk to me. Yell at me. Get mad."

She finally turned to face him, drying her hands on a towel. "I'm not going to yell at you, Charlie. I'm going to finish the dishes, then I'm going home."

He rocked backward as if she'd hit him. At least she wasn't the only one hurting now. "You said you were okay with our age difference, sweetheart," he reminded her. Though softness filled his tone, she heard the hurt loud and clear. "I thought you meant it."

"Ten years, Charlie," she said, because she needed to hear the words out loud. "There's a ten-year age difference between us. Oh God, you're closer in age to my daughter than you are to me!"

"So?"

"So?" she echoed, stunned. "That's all you have to say? So?"

"What do you want me to say?" he demanded. "This reaction is exactly why I didn't tell you. If you'd known I was only twenty-five when we started dating, you wouldn't have looked twice at me. And I wanted you to look twice."

"But you lied to me!"

"I did." Misery and determination gripped his expression. "I'm sorry about lying to you. I can't be sorry about the lie itself."

She shook her head, incredulous. "Why do you feel that you had to?"

He reached out to her but stopped when she drew back. "Why didn't you tell me at the beginning about going to rehab?"

She flinched. He grimaced but pressed on. "Why didn't you tell me from the start, Siobhan? Why didn't you tell me before I fucked you on your desk? Why didn't you tell me that first time I saw you dance at Club Tatas?"

"You know why." She dug her nails into her palms, needing the physical pain instead of avoiding it. "That's different."

"Is it?" He gathered her hands in his own, preventing her from hurting herself further. "You wanted me to think of you as you, not as a recovering drug addict. It took time for you to come to grips with a five-year age difference. If I'd told you my true age, you would have blown me off. Full stop. Are you going to tell me different?"

She couldn't, and they both knew it. She'd been concerned about dating him as it was thanks to their business relationship. Upon discovering that a decade separated them, she would have squashed her infatuation and gone on with her life, and missed out on some of the best months of her life.

"I wanted you to know me," he ground out. "I wanted you to like me. I wanted you to want me. Not my fucking age."

"I do like you, Charlie," she answered. "But—"

"No." Anger flashed in his eyes. "Not like. Love. You told me that you love me."

She pulled free of his grip. "That was before I found out you're ten years younger than me!"

"So that changes everything? I'm still the same person I was last night. I'm still the same person I was an hour ago. Can you really turn your emotions off like a switch?" He shook his head. "I can't. I love you too much."

"Charlie." Tears clogged her throat. "How can you possibly know what love is?"

His expression hardened. "How does anyone? I watched my parents flirt and laugh like teenagers around each other. My dad called my mom his angel, because he said she was a blessing from above. My mom would pinch Dad's butt when she thought we weren't looking. They still held hands when they walked together, up until the day they died. Neither one of them was perfect but they got each other in a way that was amazing and inspiring and stuck with you."

He thumped his chest. "That's how I know. Are you telling me that you knew what love was when you got married at eighteen?"

She hadn't had a clue, even though she and Mike had dated for a year before she'd gotten pregnant. Her parents had never openly displayed any affection for each other, so what she knew of love was what she'd read in the romance novels she'd snuck into the house or seen on television. What she'd thought was love for her ex had been hormonal puppy love. She'd had to grow into it, and even now she knew that what she'd felt for her ex-husband was vastly different from what she felt for Charlie. Still felt, despite the shock that numbed her.

"I know, Charlie. But . . . a decade? It's hard to get past it."

"A decade. Ten whole years. Almost three thousand and seven hundred days, and who the hell knows how many minutes. What difference does any of that make?"

"It makes every difference! You should be with someone your own age."

"Someone my own age." He snorted. "Someone right out of college thinking the whole world's ahead of them like a CW television show? Oh yeah, they're really going to want to date a guy who's still raising his brothers and too busy working to put his sister through college to give a flying fuck about her brand of shoes or what movie star is dating what rock star."

"Is that why you picked me? Because I'm not fresh out of college?"

He reached for her hand again. "I didn't pick you. I walked into your café with a bouquet of flowers for Nadia and I couldn't see anyone else but you. You in that sexy apron that hugged every dangerous curve and those amazing blue eyes that were happy and sad at the same time. I saw you and I was done. I wanted you and I wanted a chance to get you."

"But people—"

"Do you think I give a crap about people?" Anger hardened his face. "People were all sympathetic when my parents died, then started spreading gossip. People offered their condolences and promises to help, then tried to split us up. People thought I was too young to take care of Lorelei and the boys—Finn was five when we lost our parents, after all. People thought they knew what was best for us, and tried take my brothers and sister away from me and convince me my life would be easier without them. I was eighteen, had just buried my parents, and people wanted to take the rest of my family away. So fuck people."

"Charlie—"

"Fuck. People!" He stepped back, scrubbed a hand over his face. "I don't give a damn what people think about me, about us. Why do you?"

The question stopped her in her tracks. Why did she care what people think? She didn't. She'd been raked over the coals by the people she'd loved most because of her two stints in drug rehab and it left her with little room to care what anyone else thought about her. But Charlie was a different.

"I don't care what they think about me," she told him, honesty stripping her voice bare. "I care what they think about you."

"Why?"

She wrapped her arms about her middle. "People will wonder why you're with me. People will say that you could do so much better than me."

"What is that supposed to mean?"

Acid bubbled in her stomach. "Maybe you had your choices and chances taken away when your parents died, but not anymore. Lorelei is an adult. Finn and Kyle are almost grown. Your legal guardianship will be officially over in a few years and you'll be free to put yourself first for a change. Free to discover what you want, who you want to be and where."

"Why couldn't I discover those things with you?"

"I'm not good for you Charlie. I'm not good partner material or good parenting material. If you're looking for a substitute mother, you need someone better than me."

For an electrified moment, he just stared at her. Then he broke into laughter—great, stomach-clutching peals of laughter.

"What the hell is so funny?"

"For one thing, this is California. No one looks their age here. Two, this is Crimson Bay, home to a liberal arts research institution and college. The town's skewed too young to care. Three, you're Sugar Malloy. Every male between sixteen and seventy wants you.

They're all jealous, because they can want you all they want. I'm the one who has you. And I'm not giving you up."

Her heart leapt in her chest. "You're . . . you're not looking for some sort of mother figure, are you? Because I suck in that department."

He stepped closer to her. "Sweetheart, I don't have an Oedipus complex. When we're together, doing what we do so fucking well, the last thing I'm thinking about is motherhood in any capacity."

He slapped his hands down on either side of her, trapping her between him and the sink. "I'm thinking about this sweetness right here, and how soon can I get my mouth on it and my cock inside it."

"Charlie."

"I think about shoving my dick between your tits, and how gorgeous you are wearing my pearl necklace." He ground his hips against hers. "And I think about how your pussy is my favorite dessert, and how hungry I am for it. All the time."

"Dammit, Charlie." She was wet from his words alone.

His expression softened. "I also think about what it would be like to have sex with you at midnight, as the sun's coming up, just before dinner, and after the boys have gone to bed. I think about how precious your laughter is and how it makes me feel when you gift me with one of your smiles. I don't think about what other people think, Siobhan, because all I can think about is you."

She covered her mouth with trembling fingers, unable to do more than whisper his name. He kissed her hand, eyes sliding closed as a shudder rocked him.

"I know I made a mistake, Siobhan," he said softly, his breath warm against her ear. "I'll make it right. I'll earn your forgiveness.

I'm not afraid of working hard for what I want, especially when what I want is worth it."

She sighed. "The problem is, I can't stay mad at you for long. Even when I was working up a good head of steam thinking about the fact that you lied about your age, I did the math and realized you were eighteen when you became head of your family."

She cupped his cheeks. "Same age I was when I had Colleen. At least I had time to plan for parenthood. You—you had it thrust on you with no warning, and yet you've managed to raise some amazing kids. That says a lot about you and your will and your character."

"I'm not a saint, Siobhan," he murmured, leaning against her. "I was an eighteen-year-old jerk who suddenly became not only man of the house, but head of the household. Hell yeah, I had issues. I was fucking angry at everyone. I needed somebody to talk to so I wouldn't explode, so I went to a grief counselor. Lorelei and the boys needed me to keep my shit together, and I needed to keep them together. So I did what I had to do."

"Act now, ask for forgiveness later?"

"That's the family motto."

Releasing her, he sighed. "You asked me yesterday what my birthday wish was. I didn't want to answer you because I don't make wishes. I haven't wished for anything since my parents died. Wishing didn't bring them back. Wishing didn't stop people from trying to take my family from me. Wishing didn't help me keep them fed and housed and emotionally sane. Wishes haven't done anything for me."

He turned back to her, and the raw vulnerability in his eyes brought tears to hers. "Then I met you and I started to wish again. I started to want things for myself again—things that involved you.

You asked me what my birthday wish was," he said then, his voice low as he folded her in his arms. "There's only one thing I wish for. I wish you would stop looking for reasons why we shouldn't be together and start seeing the reasons why we should."

Was that what she'd been doing, even after she knew she loved him? She'd been ready to leave instead of talking this out with him. Ready to walk out on a man she professed to love. What did that say about her?

Charlie had had a huge responsibility thrust on him at a time when most men his age would have been trawling for the next pretty coed and keg party. He'd done it because he'd believed it was the right thing to do and because his three siblings needed him. She'd had one child to raise alone while Mike was in the service and she'd had her hands full. She couldn't imagine having to shoulder the obligation of taking care of three children.

"You're an amazing man, Charlie O'Halloran," she said, her voice thick. "A woman would have to be a fool not to want you."

"What about you?" he asked, hope flaring in his eyes. "Do you want me?"

"I could tell you," she answered with a smile, "but I hear that you prefer to be shown. So why don't I show you how much of a fool I'm not?"

She kissed him then. A desperate kiss because it had been hours and she needed to show him, show herself that they were still connected. With a groan of pleasure, he palmed her butt and hefted her up. She locked her ankles together around his waist, her tiny skirt and teeny panties a flimsy barrier to the imprint of his erection against his fly.

Hungry, she gave herself over to the kiss, over to him. He

grabbed her braid in one fist, holding her where he wanted her as he plundered her mouth, whispering apologies with every breath. Tiny zings of delight sparked through her body as he kissed her, his free hand tunneling beneath her blouse to cup her breast.

It wasn't until he sat her on the island that she partially came to her senses. "No. Open. Kids. Soon."

He frowned for a moment. "Oh. It's too open and the kids could be home soon. It probably wouldn't be good if they caught us having sex in the kitchen when they get home."

"Not enough eye bleach in the world to clear that up," she agreed.

He stepped back from her. "We probably shouldn't anyway. You're still sore."

She pouted, but she wasn't sure if the tingle in her sex was joy or dread at the prospect of having sex. "We'll take it easy and be inventive. You're a creative guy, right?"

"That I am." He scooped her up again then pivoted for the master bedroom.

"Oh, wait! The dishes."

"Leave them for the kids. I'm going to show you just how creative I can be."

TWENTY-SEVEN

"I don't care how much you beg, Finn, you're not getting me on a surfboard," Siobhan vowed. "Not going to happen. Besides, isn't it too cold to get in the water?"

"Oh, come on," Finn cajoled. "We'll get you a wetsuit so you'll be warm enough. It'll be fun."

"Fun, he says." Siobhan turned to Charlie. "Do you hear the words coming out of his mouth?"

"I do." Charlie tried and failed to swallow his smile. "I happen to agree with him."

"Trying to teach me to balance on a surfboard at my age wouldn't be fun," she pointed out. "I could break something."

"It wouldn't be that bad," Lorelei chimed in. "There are plenty of people older than you who go surfing."

"Yeah, people who've been surfing since before they could walk," Siobhan retorted, leaning back against the hard wall of Charlie's chest. "Does no one remember the paddleboard incident? I was stiff for days."

She wasn't really complaining. How could she? Charlie, his brothers, Lorelei, and Lorelei's boyfriend had come into the café after the recovery group meeting had ended to place an order for a picnic at the beach, ordering enough for a small army. She soon discovered that small army included Lorelei and her boyfriend, Nadia and Kane, and many in their extended circle of friends. The thought touched her in ways she couldn't describe. After they closed down the café, she'd get to spend a lazy Saturday afternoon at the beach with the man she loved and her chosen family. The day could not get any better.

She suppressed a pang of regret. The only thing that would make the day better would be for Colleen to be with her. Siobhan had called her daughter several times over the last few weeks, hoping to encourage her to come to Crimson Bay for a visit before Colleen went off to college. If Colleen's intent was to go off to college. Siobhan wasn't sure, and attempting to communicate with her ex or her parents was worse than getting a root canal.

As her therapist has encouraged her, she set aside the worry over circumstances she couldn't control and focused on the here and now instead. "I think I'm a little too old to be trying something new."

"Oh, I don't know about that, sweetness," Charlie drawled, his fingers tracing a light pattern on her arm. "People try new things all the time. Sometimes they even find they like those new things."

Siobhan fought a blush as Lorelei stared at them in mock horror. "You better not be talking about what I think you're talking about," she warned.

A chuckle rumbled up from Charlie's chest, vibrating through Siobhan. "I'm talking about getting my girl into a bikini," he said, his tone entirely too innocent. "What are you talking about?"

Seeing as how Siobhan had been on beach trips in a bikini more than once, she knew Lorelei wasn't buying it. Sure enough, Lorelei stuck her tongue out. "Don't be gross, Charlie."

"What's gross?" Lorelei's boyfriend, Stephen, chimed in. "She's hot for an old chick. Like, you're a smoking thirty."

Charlie stiffened behind her. "Unless she's sweating next to a barbecue grill in the middle of a heat wave, I don't want to ever hear the words *smoking* and *hot* coming out of your mouth in reference to my woman ever again."

Poor Stephen nearly swallowed his tongue apologizing, until Siobhan and Lorelei burst out laughing. "Don't let Charlie scare you," Siobhan told the younger man. "The fact that he's letting you come to the beach with us means he likes you well enough. By the way, you got a brownie point for saying I'm thirty, but you lost it by calling me an old chick. We'll let you off the hook this time, though."

"As a matter of fact," Charlie added, "why don't you guys go on ahead and scope out a good spot? We'll be along as soon as we close up the café."

"Well, well, well. Isn't this a cozy picture?"

Surprise and joy shafted through Siobhan as she looked up into her daughter's tight features. She extricated herself from Charlie's hold and surged to her feet. "Colleen! You came!"

"Colleen?" Charlie interrupted, holding on to her hand. "Your daughter, Colleen?"

"You know about me? That's weird, because I know nothing about you." Colleen folded her arms across her chest, stepping back as Siobhan reached for her. Her hard gaze raked over Charlie and the others before swinging to Siobhan. "Is this what you've been lighting up my phone about, Mother? Wanting to introduce me to your replacement family?"

Siobhan stepped between her daughter and the O'Hallorans, conscious of the curious gazes of her last few customers focusing on her corner of the café. Conscious of Charlie's family staring at her. She could understand Charlie's disbelief. Colleen was her father's daughter: tall, slender, dark-haired. The only hint of Siobhan in her daughter lay in the thick wave of her hair, the creamy skin, the blue of her eyes. Though she was always beautiful to Siobhan, Colleen would be a definite stunner if she got rid of the sullen teenager demeanor.

Siobhan hadn't seen Colleen since the night of her graduation. Before that it had been two years since she'd last attempted a reconciliation. Colleen had been sixteen, and Siobhan had given her daughter a job at the café despite Nadia's objections. Colleen had done little to assist customers, and her sour attitude had driven some away. Siobhan's relationship with her partner had taken a hit, especially after they had discovered that Colleen had skimmed money from the register.

"It's hard to tell you anything when you won't return my calls," Siobhan pointed out. "Why don't you come back to the office so we can talk?"

"Why? Afraid I'm going to embarrass you?"

Siobhan tightened her hold on her patience, not wanting to escalate things and cause a scene in front of her customers. "I've got nothing to hide, Colleen. I was hoping you'd finally decided to accept my invitation. Unless you wanted to talk about something else. Did you come up here by yourself?"

"Yeah. Dad got me a car for graduation." She shrugged one bony shoulder. "It's how I got up here."

"Oh, good. You'll be able to drive it to college then." What teenager wouldn't be thrilled with getting a car? She didn't bother asking how Colleen was going to pay for the gas and insurance on a car. Obviously her father wouldn't have given Colleen the car if he hadn't made plans to cover the upkeep. Throwing things at Colleen was Mike's way of apologizing for having Siobhan as a mother.

"I'm not going to college."

"What?" Siobhan asked. "Why not?"

"Because I don't have to go if I don't want to." Colleen folded her arms across her chest. "Like you care," she added with a mutter. "Dad's fine by the way. Donna's pregnant again. Grandpa and Grandma are doing fine too. I'm living with them now."

More proof that they got along just fine without her and had for the last five years. Her family didn't need her. What was now painfully clear was that they didn't want her.

Charlie climbed to his feet beside Siobhan, and it was only then that she realized she held his hand in a death grip. "Colleen, this is Charlie O'Halloran. We're dating. This is his sister, Lorelei, and her boyfriend, Stephen, and these guys are their brothers, Kyle and Finn. Everyone, this is my daughter, Colleen."

"Hi, Colleen," Charlie said at his most charming, sticking out his free hand to Colleen. "It's a pleasure to finally meet you. We're heading out to the beach after Siobhan closes the café. Why don't you come with us?"

"Oh, you totally should," Lorelei chimed in before Siobhan or Colleen could reply. "We were just getting ready to head out and stake out a spot. If you didn't bring a suit with you, we can pick one up on the way. It'll be fun!"

Siobhan's heart clanged. The O'Hallorans were trying to make space for Colleen just as they'd made space for Siobhan. She squeezed Charlie's hand in silent thanks before turning back to her daughter.

For one heart-stopping, blindly hopeful moment, Siobhan thought Colleen would say yes. That her daughter would set aside years of hurt and anger and accept an olive branch of reconciliation.

Hope died a quick death. "You've got them all fooled, don't you?" Colleen asked, incredulous. "They have no idea what you are or what you did to me."

"Colleen, please—"

"I think your mother had the right idea," Charlie cut in. "Maybe you two need to talk in private."

Siobhan knew Charlie was only trying to help. While she appreciated it, his assistance would only make Colleen angrier. God, less than ten minutes facing her child's sullen anger and she was already wrung out from the beating her emotional shields were taking.

Colleen snorted. "What's to keep private? That she abandoned her only child to drugs? That she almost got me killed?"

A rush of blood pounded in Siobhan's ears, drowning out the gasp of shock that rose in the café. She knew saying anything would only goad Colleen but she couldn't stop herself. "You know that was an accident—"

"You were strung out on pills," Colleen screamed. "You chose drugs over me twice! You're nothing but a drug addict. Everyone needs to know that!"

Pain blossomed in Siobhan's chest. The scene began to take on a surreal quality. It felt as if she were dreaming, but Siobhan couldn't wake herself up. *It's just a nightmare,* she thought. *I'll wake up and find myself wrapped in Charlie's arms. I'll open my eyes and everything will be okay. This isn't happening.*

She released Charlie's hand even though she wanted to cling to him, wanted to hold on to the comfort he provided. "That's enough!" Siobhan shook with anger, hurt, and a bone-deep sadness. "You have issues with me, fine. I get it. But you're an adult now, and it's time to act like it. You don't come into my place of business and insult my friends and customers. I won't stand for that."

"You think I care what you want?" Colleen seethed. "You need to be reminded of what you did. Everyone needs to know what an awful mother you are, especially your picture-perfect new family! They need to know that what you did to me, you'll turn around and do to them!"

"How dare you!"

Siobhan blinked in surprise as Lorelei shot to her feet. "How dare you come here and speak to her like that!"

Colleen drew back, then sneered. "What gives you the right to say anything to me?"

"Our mom died eight years ago," Lorelei said, her voice loud in the electrified silence. "I was ten. There's not a day that doesn't go by that I don't miss her, that I don't wish she was here. I can't get my mom back, and your mom is right there."

Lorelei pointed to Siobhan. "She's right there and you're treating her like shit when I would give anything to have one more day with my mom, just one day. If you can't understand how lucky you are to have a mom who wants you even when you treat her like this, I feel sorry for you."

"You don't know what she did!" Colleen shot back.

"I don't need to know what she did," Lorelei countered. "You're holding a grudge over something that happened years ago. Something that happened when she was ill. I know her now. I know she loves my brother. I'm pretty sure she loves us. I know she's a nice woman with a big heart who really wants her daughter to be a part of her life. There's room for you here, if you want it."

Colleen surveyed the united front of O'Hallorans. "You're all pathetic," she hissed. "You think I want to be here? You're as high as she was. Why in the hell would I want to be with a drugged-out excuse for a mother?"

"Leave her alone!" Kyle jumped to his feet, standing in front of Siobhan as if to protect her from Colleen. "You shouldn't talk to your mom like that. She's your mom!"

"Yeah, if you don't want her, we'll take her!" Finn declared, standing beside his brother. "Stop being a-a bitch!"

Siobhan wasn't sure what actually happened next. Colleen took a step forward, one hand raised. Siobhan surged in front of the boys. Shoving ensued, then a loud crack split the air. Colleen stumbled back, her expression slack with shock as she cupped a cheek blossoming red from the impact of Siobhan's hand.

Horror churned the acid bubbling in her stomach. "Oh, God, Colleen—"

The vulnerability vanished beneath a sneer. "You want to replace me? Fine, go ahead. It's not like you've done anything for me since I was a kid. There is nothing you can do for me. I hate you!"

Colleen slammed her way out of the café, leaving Siobhan to face a shop full of shocked customers and Charlie's family. She wanted to run after Colleen, wanted to apologize and make sure her daughter was okay, but she couldn't leave. Couldn't breathe, couldn't move, couldn't speak past the pain that shackled her.

Charlie placed a hand on her shoulder. "Siobhan—"

Embarrassment flooded her, heating her skin from the neck up. No. She couldn't face him yet, couldn't face his family.

Instead she turned to the last few customers in the café. "I apologize for subjecting all of you to that and ruining your dining experience. Our regulars can attest to the fact that we've never had a floorshow like that before, and we never will again. If you'll step to the counter, we'll give everyone a refund or gift card that you can use on your next visit. I'm sure you'll understand that we need to close early. I apologize for the inconvenience."

Rosie already manned the counter. So did Jas. Shoving her shame down deep, Siobhan focused on customer service, apologizing to the customers and accepting their pity and curiosity in return. Nadia and Kane arrived as the last customer left. Unfortunately, a police officer arrived with them.

TWENTY-EIGHT

Her daughter had called the police.

Charlie sat in the visitor's area of Crimson Bay's downtown precinct, fighting to control his rage. Siobhan had told him that things were bad with her daughter, but he'd had no idea of the depth of the dysfunction until the officer had arrived at the café and informed them that a warrant for assault had been sworn out on Siobhan.

Remembering Siobhan's stricken expression when she'd received the news squeezed his heart in a chokehold. Her knees had buckled and he'd had to catch her before she hit the floor. When she recovered she had admitted to hitting Colleen but hadn't offered an explanation, hadn't attempted to defend herself. It was as if she blamed herself for her daughter's behavior and wanted to take the punishment upon herself.

He and the others had set the officer straight on the details before Siobhan had been arrested, but Siobhan had still been requested to take a trip to the precinct. Now he sat in the visitors' area with Nadia and her fiancé, Professor Sullivan, waiting for Siobhan to finish. It had been more than an hour and she was still giving her statement to the officer. Thank God, Nadia had had the presence of mind to call their lawyer. Siobhan needed someone to look out for her interests since she seemed incapable where her daughter was concerned.

Charlie shoved his hands through his hair, needing to do something, anything to help Siobhan. He wanted to take her pain, take her sorrow, then take her someplace where nothing and no one could hurt her again. She deserved that happiness. She deserved that peace, not a daughter who couldn't look at her without sneering.

Nadia reached over to give his hand a reassuring squeeze. "It's going to be all right."

"Is it?" he wondered. "Her daughter wanted her arrested. Her own daughter!"

"I know." Nadia blinked rapidly, leaning back against Sullivan. "But we have a good lawyer, lots of eyewitnesses, and the closed-circuit video. She'll be done soon."

"Will she be okay, though? After what her own kid just did to her?"

Nadia's eyes watered. "I hope so, but I've never seen Colleen do anything this bad before."

"Why does she put up with it?" Charlie burst out, then quickly lowered his voice, remembering he sat in a police precinct. "Why hasn't she cut her losses before now? She doesn't deserve this kind of abuse. No one does."

"You're right. I've told her that a thousand times, but she believes she deserves it, that if she just keeps taking what they dish out, they'll eventually forgive her."

"Siobhan told me the story. Yes, it was horrible, and yes, Colleen had a right to be hurt. Still holding on to that level of anger now, after all these years?" Charlie shook his head. "I don't think

Siobhan's daughter plans to forgive her anytime soon. Colleen's attitude is just too over the top for an incident that happened years ago."

"I agree. I've wondered about that too. Colleen has been mad for years and seems to get angrier every time I see her."

"Do you think someone like Siobhan's ex poisoned their relationship on purpose?" A few "well-meaning" relatives had tried the same thing on Lorelei and his brothers, trying to convince them that he wanted to give them up. What he'd thought was grief had been their fear that he didn't want them. It had taken a showdown with his extended family and months with his siblings to mend that emotional trauma.

Charlie clenched his hands on his knees. He'd had friends become collateral damage in nasty divorces. If Colleen's father had tainted her relationship with Siobhan, Siobhan didn't stand a chance at mending things with her daughter. Maybe it was time to find out where her ex-husband lived and pay him a visit.

"I don't think it's Mike," Nadia said as if reading his intent. "He's remarried and his wife is expecting their second child. Maybe Colleen's feeling like she's getting pushed out because of that."

"At the café she mentioned she was living with her grandparents."

Nadia's lips flattened. Sullivan ran a hand down her back and she relaxed again. "Siobhan's parents. Talk about pieces of work."

Charlie's gut churned. "She told me they were strict and that her father basically disowned her after she got pregnant."

Nadia nodded. "I've only seen them once, when Siobhan and I drove down to Colleen's graduation back in May. If it's possible to dislike someone on sight, that's how I felt about her parents. I didn't care about how they treated me but they treated her like less than shit, like she wasn't related to them at all. Like it bothered them that she breathed the same air. To hell with all of them."

"Nadia." The professor wrapped an arm about her shoulders.

"I mean it. Siobhan's a good person. She's like a sister to me and I want her to be happy. She doesn't deserve to be treated the way they treat her!"

"No she doesn't," Professor Sullivan agreed. "We'll convince her of that."

Charlie ground his teeth with impotent frustration. Siobhan's ex or her parents had had years to convince Colleen that Siobhan was evil and deserved to suffer. A few visits here and there wouldn't stand up against that. He knew she'd try, though. She'd keep trying to work things out with her daughter because that was the kind of person she was, the kind of heart she possessed. She'd hurt herself before she'd deliberately hurt someone else. How many times could Siobhan throw herself against that level of coldheartedness before she broke? What would happen to her when she did?

Nadia reached over to squeeze his hand again. "Please don't give up on Siobhan. I know this seems bad and like it's too much to deal with, but she needs you and your family to balance out the crap she gets from her own."

"I'm not giving up on her," Charlie swore. "I told her that she's worth it, and I meant that. My brothers and sister love her as much as I do. As far as I'm concerned, we're her family."

He shot to his feet as soon as he spotted Siobhan, dimly aware of Nadia and her fiancé doing the same. Siobhan looked . . . devastated and diminished, as if every bit of vitality had been sucked from her bones. When her gaze tangled with his, she stumbled to a stop. He moved toward her, stopping only when she gave a single sharp shake of her head.

A uniformed officer said something to her and her lawyer

before walking off. As Charlie watched, Siobhan gathered herself, straightening her shoulders and schooling her features into a pale semblance of serenity. The lawyer said something to her, nodded their way, then walked off, leaving her alone.

Nadia rushed forward but Siobhan held up her hand. "Can we please get out of here? I need some air."

Charlie looked to Nadia, who shrugged helplessly. Charlie wanted to give Siobhan space if she needed it, but only so much. He wasn't going to let her shut him out and suffer the pain alone. Maybe it was time to show her what family—especially chosen family—really meant.

He snagged her hand as they made their way out of the precinct to visitor parking. Alarm shot through him as he felt the iciness of her fingers. He hauled her into his arms. She initially stiffened, then collapsed against him, minute tremors shaking her frame. "I'm here, sweetness, I'm here."

"You shouldn't be," she whispered as she clung to his shoulders. "But I'm so glad you are."

"Like I could be anywhere else." He held her tight, hoping that if he could give her some of his warmth, some of his strength, he could chase some of the desolation from her eyes.

"Are you okay, Sugar?" Nadia asked when they parted, wrapping Siobhan into another hug. "What did they say?"

Siobhan stiffened again, as if donning emotional armor. "They're going to keep the investigation open."

"Why?" Nadia demanded, her voice high with indignation. "Everything they needed to see was on the tape we gave them."

"I know." Siobhan shuddered, and Charlie pulled her close again, the need to protect her almost primal. "Based on their questions, Colleen must have unloaded all of my dirty laundry and made a bunch of accusations. She also said that I was harassing her and had placed her under emotional duress and that's what led to our altercation. They said it's going to take some time for them to sort through everything before they prepare the report for the district attorney's office."

"The district attorney? For what?" Nadia shook with outrage. "They can't seriously be thinking of charging you?"

"Sam asked the same thing." Siobhan leaned against Charlie. "He reminded them that I'm a business owner with a spotless record in Crimson Bay. They reminded him that I've been in drug rehab twice, then began to question me about any stress I've been under, any financial problems or disagreements with you, Nadia. At that point Sam decided it was time to end the interview."

Charlie's anger surged. "Son of a bitch."

Siobhan flinched. When she spoke, her tone was brittle. "They're probably going to interview you all again and bring up my drug use. I'm sorry for that."

"Don't be," Professor Sullivan told her. "It's not the first time any of us have talked to the police."

"You don't need the publicity." She looked up at Charlie. "None of you do."

"We'll handle it," Nadia assured her. "You know we've got your back."

"I know. Sam says they're just digging because they can, and he'll do what he can to put a stop to it. I'm just . . . I'm sorry for what I'm putting you guys through."

"Don't you dare apologize!" Nadia seethed. "None of this is your fault. This is all on Colleen!"

"Nadia." Both Charlie and the professor spoke simultaneously, but only Charlie's tone held a warning. Yes, they all knew that Colleen was the instigator, but Siobhan didn't need to have that point dumped on her on top of everything else she'd endured over the past few hours, even if it was her best friend doing the dumping.

"I'm exhausted," Siobhan said with a soul-deep sigh. "I want to go home."

"Of course," Nadia said, giving her a quick hug. "Get some rest, sweetie. I'll see you tomorrow for our regular planning meeting. We can discuss what to do then."

Siobhan nodded, but Charlie felt her sag. She must have been running on fumes. "Let's get you home, sweetness."

He guided her toward the convertible and into the passenger seat, more than ready to take her away. By the time he slid into the driver's side, she was slumped down in her seat, head tilted back, her sunglasses firmly on her face. The message was clear: she was done talking. He let her have the silence, the need to get her home more important than the need to talk.

The silence deepened as he drove, worried, and planned. He was relieved he'd sent the kids home immediately after Colleen had left, relieved they'd missed the arrival of police. He'd called Lorelei and told her they were at the police station for routine stuff, but he had no idea how he was going to explain the ongoing investigation and follow-up interviews. He certainly wasn't going to let the police talk to his siblings if he could help it.

What the hell had Colleen told the police? He couldn't believe they would bring up Siobhan's past drug use, treat her like she'd done something wrong when he knew the tape clearly showed that Colleen had shoved her mother first. He wanted to make sure that Colleen could never get close to Siobhan again, but he knew that wasn't his right, nor was it Nadia's right. Siobhan would have to come to the realization on her own that her blood family was toxic. All he could do was make sure he stood beside her through it all.

Siobhan finally stirred, sitting up as she pushed her sunglasses to her forehead. "Where are we going?"

"I'm taking you home."

She looked out the window. "This isn't the way to my house."

"I know. I'm taking you to our house."

"What? No." Her hand clutched the door handle as if she wanted to jump out. "No, Charlie. I can't go to your house. I can't be with the kids."

Ice slid down his neck. Surely she only meant at that moment and not forever. "Of course you can," he said, keeping his tone light with effort. "The kids will want to make sure you're all right. Besides, I don't want to leave you alone right now."

"Why? You think I'm going to break out my secret stash of drugs?"

He bit back the instant retort that would have escalated the fight she clearly wanted to instigate. "Sweetness, I'm having a hard time here. You're hurting, and that's making me want to smash things. Since I can't do that, I have to get you someplace I know you'll feel safe and happy. The kids will want to make sure you're safe and happy. That's why I was taking you home."

"I'm not ready to face them and try to explain this," she told him, her voice warbling. "Not now."

"Okay, we'll head to your place." Not wanting to upset her, he changed direction, pointing the convertible toward her neighborhood. The rest of the drive passed in silence steeped in misery. He fought to swallow down his anger. His woman was hurting, dammit, and he wanted to go break down doors and burn bridges to make it better. Instead he could feel the wall going up between them brick by brick.

She remained silent until they made it into the house. "I'm sorry, Charlie," she told him, her voice hollow. "Sorry for everything."

He closed and locked the front door with precise movements. "You have nothing to apologize for."

"Yes, I do." She pressed the heels of her hands against her eyes, her fingers trembling. "I promised you that I wouldn't expose the boys to my issues. Now we've got to explain things to them we never intended to explain."

"I'll talk to them," he told her, not wanting to subject her to reliving her altercation with her daughter. "We can talk to them together. It'll be like the birds-and-bees talk."

She shook her head. "Everything about me went into the police report, Charlie. Everything. The altercation is sure to make the local news. In a small college town like this, if nothing else newsworthy happens quickly, they're going to run with it until they beat it into the ground. Nadia will get pulled in because she used to be on TV, then Kane will get pulled in because of who he is and what he does. I can't let them pull you in too. I can't. It could hurt you, hurt the kids, and I promised you that I wouldn't do that."

He remembered her promise, he just didn't want to face it. "So what are you saying?"

"I'm saying . . ." She took a deep breath. "I'm saying that we should spend some time apart, a couple of weeks maybe, until this blows over."

"No."

"I told you." Her eyes glittered with unshed tears. "I told you that if my past became an issue, I would walk away."

"Hell no."

"Charlie, please. If you think about it, you'll see that I'm right. We have to think of the kids. You have to protect your family."

He gently slipped his arms around her waist when what he really wanted to do was tie her down and never let her go. "I want to protect you too."

She closed her eyes then, a single tear slipping down her cheek as her composure cracked. Somehow she managed to wrestle it back. "I appreciate that, but the kids come first. That's rule number one. I'll be okay."

Maybe she would. He doubted he would be, though. He brushed his thumb across her cheek, capturing the tear. "You love me," he told her, daring her to deny it.

She jerked then froze, as if she'd break if she moved. Then she raised her gaze to his, a heartbreaking smile curving her lips. "I love you, Charlie O'Halloran. With my whole heart I love you."

He kissed her then, kissed her because he couldn't not kiss her, because she was right, because he had to stay away from her for two weeks when all he wanted was to never leave her again. He kissed her because he needed it, she needed it, and at that moment nothing else mattered.

Siobhan moaned as he drove his hands into her hair, holding her by the grip on her hair, the press of his lips, the weight of his body. Her hands slid into his back pockets, dragging him even closer, her mouth moving greedily against his.

"Charlie, please," she whispered against his lips. "Take the pain away, even if it's just for a little while. Help me to forget everything but here and now."

TWENTY-NINE

For one wild, charged moment, she thought Charlie would refuse. He gripped her shoulders, holding her away so he could read her eyes. She had no defenses against him and knew he could see how destroyed she was. She just hoped the love and the need she had for him overrode everything else.

"Please, Charlie," she whispered again. "I need something good today, and you're the only good thing I have. Take me out of my head for a little while. Please."

His fingers traced a slow path over her lips, down her chin and throat, leaving fire in their wake. She took a deep breath as the heat of his hands seeped into her heart. Holding her gaze, he gripped the collar of her blouse then jerked, sending buttons flying.

Yes. She nipped at his bottom lip to goad him on, needing the roughness. Needing to forget everything but this moment, this pleasure, this man. She crushed her mouth to his as her shirt went flying, tunneling her hands beneath his shirt to sink her nails into his back. He hissed in approval, his mouth branding the curve of her neck, the rise of her breasts.

He ripped her bra off next, cupping her breasts so that he could feast on them. She gasped as his teeth closed on her nipple, shooting sparks of delicious sensation through her. He knew, he always knew what she needed and how she needed it, stoking her desire with an expert hand.

His lips and tongue and teeth scorched her skin as he kissed and bit his way down her body. He scraped kisses along the soft expanse below her navel, biting kisses that echoed in her sex. Drowning in need, she held her breath as he made short work of her capris and panties, finally, finally leaving her bare.

He looked up at her, his gaze tangling with hers. So much emotion spun across his gorgeous features that she couldn't speak, could only drink him in. Then she felt his touch, warm and sure, glide over her folds then press inside. She sucked in a breath as his fingers filled her, her head thumping back against the wall. Widening her stance, she opened to him, to the magic he wove.

Again he positioned her as he wanted her, her right leg over his shoulder, opening her farther. The sweep of his tongue on her clit had her clutching at his shoulders, his name slipping from her lips on a groan as her body went liquid for him. He buried his face between her thighs as if he couldn't get enough, would never get enough, tongue and fingers driving her higher and higher in a relentless ride.

All too soon she could feel her orgasm building, coiling deep inside her as Charlie continued plundering her, his fingers stroking up and in as he licked and suckled her clit. Her hips undulated, taking as much as she could, taking more until the coil of desire snapped and took her screaming into ecstasy.

Boneless but still wanting more, she slid to her knees as he rose to his feet. With frantic movements she worked his shorts down, his cock spilling hot and hard into her hands. She licked and suckled him eagerly, savoring his taste, his feel, his heat and hardness.

He snagged his fingers in her hair. "That's it, sweetness. Fuck me with your mouth. Just like that. God, yes, like that."

He held her hair in both fists, keeping her still as he rocked his hips, driving his erection into her mouth. She hollowed her cheeks and took his thrusts, her fingers teasing his balls, eager to give him every bit of pleasure he'd given her.

With a soft curse, he slowed his pace to savor each thrust until he stopped. She reached for him but he withdrew, then pulled her to her feet. "I need to be inside you. Bed or wall, your choice."

"Bed." She wanted the scent of him on her pillow, her sheets, in her most private space. She'd need that last bit of him to last her.

He scooped her up and made his way to her bedroom. Depositing her on the bed, he made quick work of the rest of his clothing, then joined her. The wildness roared back as his body slid against hers and she clutched at him, craving every touch, every taste. They rolled together in a desperate tangle of limbs and a clash of mouths, engaging in a sensual warfare.

He rose above her, his features taut with desire, with anger, with the inevitable parting. "You're mine, Siobhan Malloy," he said as he sank into her, filling her. "Say it."

"Yours," she agreed, groaning as he slid into her to the hilt.

"You'll always be mine, no matter what." He withdrew completely, then sank back into her again with a slow, eye-rolling glide of pleasure. "You know that, don't you?"

"Always, Charlie," she vowed, knowing it was true. "I love you."

A flash of pain arced across his face and he closed his eyes against it. Then he stared down at her, his gaze dark with intensity. "Say it again, sweetness."

"I love you." Her back arched off the bed, the physical pleasure and the emotional pain almost too much to bear. She wanted him to know that she loved her, wanted him to feel it in every kiss, every thrust of her hips, every score of her nails down his back. "I love you, Charlie."

"You're my heaven, my goddess," he told her, moving into her with slow rolling strokes. "I need you to remember that. Remember that I love you."

"I will, I swear," she promised, tears clogging her throat. "I won't forget."

He hooked her legs over his arms, sinking deeper, so deep he'd always be a part of her. He stared down at her and she couldn't look away. She met him stroke for stroke even when he increased his pace, reaching between their colliding bodies to stroke her clit so that they could shoot off into the stars together.

Afterward they lay entwined, sharing soft kisses. She didn't speak and neither did he, knowing there weren't any words, wasn't anything that could be said that would make everything all right. She could feel the minutes ticking by and though she wanted to hold on, she knew she had to let him go.

Every day she missed Charlie. Every day hurt. Every day she had to convince herself that she had done the right thing, that she couldn't return his calls, couldn't see Lorelei when she stopped by the café, couldn't stalk them on social media or stop by Charlie's office even for professional reasons. Eventually she became numb, burying the pain down deep in order to function.

It took three weeks for the local media fervor to die down. The café staff and Siobhan's friends had banded together and when the media got no response to their questions from anyone associated with the café or the burlesque troupe, they had thankfully grown tired of the speculation without substantiation. The good news was that there were enough issues in other parts of the state to keep Crimson Bay from gaining too much attention. The bad news was that Siobhan's personal and professional business had spread like an oil slick through the town, forcing her to spend most of her time in the kitchen or office instead of on display behind the sales counter. Not that she'd minded—she just didn't have it in her to smile and pretend everything was all right when very little was.

The police investigation had been as subtle as a bull in a china shop. They had raked through her entire life, unable to believe that a former drug addict and burlesque dancer could be an upstanding contributing member of society. The one saving grace was that she was positive she'd been successful in keeping Charlie and the kids from getting dragged deeper into the morass of her life. She'd had to carve her own heart out of her chest and quit them cold turkey, not answering phone calls or texts from anyone remotely connected to the O'Halloran family.

"I was told yesterday that the investigation is finally over and no charges are going to be filed," Siobhan told her friends. Their Tuesday Bitch Talk sessions continued, but they'd moved upstairs to Nadia's condo away from the curious and the well-meaning.

"About damn time," Audie said, curling up in one corner of the couch. "They knew they didn't have a case. They just wanted to give you a hard time."

"They saw a lot of smoke. They just wanted make sure there wasn't a fire." Siobhan cradled her tea in her hands, but didn't drink. Doing the simplest things took too much effort. All of her energy went into cooking for the café and presenting a calm façade to the world.

Siobhan did her best to move on with her life and prove that she'd accepted everything that had happened if only because she was so damn tired of everyone asking her if she was fine. No, she wasn't fine. She wasn't going to be anything close to fine for a long time.

"The only fire was the one started by Colleen," Audie pointed out. "Is there any sort of blowback on her for filing a false report?"

"She didn't file a false report," Siobhan reminded her. "It was obvious that I slapped her, something that I regret every day."

Nadia finally broke her silence. "You were defending Finn and Kyle. Don't regret facing off with a bully."

"Colleen's not a bully," Siobhan protested. "She's just—"

"She's not misunderstood, if that's what you're going to say," Audie cut in. "She's an adult now, the same age you were when you had her."

"Yes, and I didn't know my ass from my elbow back then. At least I had my grandmother Mary Katherine and Mike."

Nadia voice was gentle when she replied. "She has her grandmother, and Mike's her father."

"Yes, but her grandmother is my mother." Siobhan sighed. "I know I need to let it go. You guys aren't saying anything my therapist hasn't already suggested. Asking me to give up on my only child—it's not easy."

"Sometimes you have to walk away," Audie said, her tone hard. "Sometimes the family you choose is better for you than blood family."

Siobhan knew Audie had left her family as a teenager. "Don't you have regrets? Don't you sometimes wonder what it would be like now?"

"It would be hell." Audie wrapped her arms around herself. "It was hell then and it would be hell now. Even living on the streets was better than being in that house."

Vanessa reached over to rub Audie's shoulder until the redhead relaxed. "Sorry about that," Audie said, blowing out a breath. "I don't like having those memories in my head."

"Siobhan, when are you going to call Charlie and tell him the dust is settled?" Vanessa asked, not bothering with subtlety for her segue.

Siobhan stirred her tea, then looked at Nadia. Her best friend pursed her lips but remained silent. She already knew the answer, though Audie and Vanessa didn't. Yet. "I'm not. We broke up. Permanently."

Audie's mouth dropped open. "Oh, Siobhan. Why?"

"Because he got a visit from Child Protective Services, that's why."

Shock rolled through the room. Even Vanessa's usual composure faltered. "What?"

"Lorelei stopped by one afternoon and told me that they had a request for a welfare check from a concerned citizen," Siobhan explained, her tone level. She'd been cold inside for days, ever since she'd said good-bye to Charlie. Any hope she'd harbored that they could get back together had died with Lorelei's panicked visit. "Apparently the social call was instigated because Charlie had associated with known unsavory characters, namely me."

She gave up the pretense of drinking her tea, setting it down on the coffee table. "Charlie had nothing to hide, but from what I understand, he didn't take the visit very well. I haven't heard anything from him or any of the kids since. It's for the best."

"The best for who?"

"For him. For the kids."

"I thought you loved him," the redhead said, her tone ripe with accusation.

"I still do, Audie. Sometimes love isn't enough. If it were, my daughter wouldn't have tried to have me arrested."

She curled her hands into fists. *No, don't go there. If you do, you'll open the door to pain that needs to stay locked away.*

"What are you going to do?" Vanessa asked, her voice soft with concern.

"The only thing I can do. Live my life." She gave them a smile she didn't feel. "You only fail if you don't try, right? I'm learning to live without drugs. I'll learn to live without Charlie too."

She had a feeling that it was going to take much longer to get Charlie out of her system.

After Bitch Talk, she went back to the office to run the numbers. Nadia had done much the same when she had broken things off with Kane. The difference was there hadn't been children involved. There hadn't been a police investigation to endure. And Nadia and Kane had gotten back together.

"You know we love you, right?"

Siobhan looked up from their inventory management program as Nadia entered the office, a cupcake peace offering in her hand. "I know."

She accepted the confection, placing it beside the keyboard. "I know you guys want what's best for me, and all of you think I'm making a mistake with Colleen and with Charlie. Yet you can't deny the fact that he'd have been better off if I had stopped things before we got started."

"You can't mean that."

"Of course I do." She saved her entries, then closed the program. "Charlie will do anything to protect his sister and brothers, and their worst fear has always been the fear of being separated. Having Child Protective Services contact him—even if they found nothing—had to have been a nightmare for them. He'll make sure they don't have a reason to visit him again. That means staying away from me."

It hurt to say it, but it was true. She was a liability. Charlie would realize that eventually, if he didn't already.

"Do you want to go grab an early dinner?" Nadia asked. "Or you could come and have dinner with us."

Right. Nothing would make her feel better like being the mopey third wheel with Kane and Nadia. "No, but I appreciate the invite. I have a couple of phone calls to make, then I'm heading home."

"Siobhan . . ."

"I need to know that she's okay," Siobhan said, trying not to sound defensive. "I'm not going to try to call her directly."

Nadia frowned. "You're going to call your mother."

Her best friend's tone telegraphed her opinion of the idea. "I have to. If I don't, I'm going to keep worrying. I need one thing that I can stop fretting over."

"You'll keep it short and sweet and to the point?"

Siobhan managed a smile. "Promise. I don't want to talk to her longer than I have to."

"All right." Nadia patted her shoulder. "I'm going to do a final check out front and in the kitchen. We'll walk out together."

"Don't you have to be here early?" Siobhan wondered. "You don't live upstairs anymore."

"Wednesdays are my late days," Nadia reminded her. "Jas has the early shift. Be back in a bit."

Nadia left. Siobhan blew out a long breath, then reached for her cell phone. She placed a call she knew she'd regret, but she needed to know how Colleen was doing. Since she couldn't contact Colleen, there was only one other person she could call.

THIRTY

"Hello?"

"Mama?" She clutched the handset so hard her hand shook. "It's me. Siobhan."

"Just a moment, please." Her mother's voice twanged over the connection, accompanied by the muffled sounds of movement. "Okay, now I can talk. Are you in trouble?"

Siobhan gritted her teeth. Why did her mother immediately assume the worst when she called? Yes, there had been bad moments in her life when she'd called her mother, but she'd been clean for years. She owned her own business, was an upstanding member of the community. But to her mother, and especially her father, she'd always be a fuckup.

"No, Mama, I'm not in trouble, despite what Colleen did. I'm doing good, and so is the café."

"Are you sure?" Her mother's voice thinned with worry. "Colleen told me about your argument."

"Argument. Is that what she called it?" Siobhan asked, ignoring the stab in the vicinity of her heart. "She shouted me down in my own restaurant, in front of customers. She wanted to have me arrested for assault!"

"Oh, Siobhan, can you blame her?" Her mother sighed. "You abandon her for years, and then when she tried to reach out to you, you shut her out. Then you slapped her."

Blood pounded in Siobhan's ears. "I shut her out? She's the one who demanded I not attend her high school graduation, but I attended anyway. I called her for weeks trying to get her to come see me. Then she tried to get me arrested, but somehow I'm the bad guy?"

"Why are you trying to make this Colleen's fault? You abandoned your flesh and blood for another family."

Ice pellets churned in Siobhan's stomach. "I did not."

"Colleen told me about the girl and the two boys who came between you two. She said they seemed very protective of you." Anxiety ripened her tone. "Oh, Siobhan, do you really think it's a good idea to get involved with someone, especially someone with kids, given your troubles?"

Siobhan suppressed a sigh. "Mom, my 'troubles' were over years ago. I'm clean now. I'm living right."

"You've said that before," her mother retorted. "You promised us your troubles were over before. Then you relapsed. You broke Mike's heart, and mine, and Colleen's, your father's. It was a good thing you grandmother wasn't alive to see how far you fell."

"Mom." The edges of the phone dug into her hand as she tightened her grip to keep herself grounded, keep her emotions in check. She'd had enough emotional upheaval over the last few weeks to last her a lifetime. "I'm sorry about that. I'm sorry for what I did to you and Dad, and to Mike and Colleen. I've already apologized over and over for my failings and shortcomings. Are you ever going to forgive me?"

This time her mother sighed. "Can you swear that you'll never use again?"

Pain and disappointment shafted through Siobhan and she closed her eyes against it, fighting to keep it in. "You know I can't make that promise, Mom. No one with an addiction can. All I can promise is that I'll try and I'll fight to stay clean."

Silence filled the distance for a long moment before her mother spoke again. "You know what you need to do, Siobhan. You can't let that man and his family go on thinking that you're something you're not."

Her mother's words stabbed her deep, deep where hope dwelled, where love lived. Deep enough to cause a mortal wound. "You don't have to worry about that. After the stunt Colleen pulled, I had to break up with him."

"That's for the best, don't you think? You don't need to hurt them the way you hurt your husband and daughter."

Emotions churned inside her, fighting to claw their way out. "So I'm supposed to spend the rest of my life alone? Am I supposed to keep on hurting because none of you can forgive me?"

"That's not fair, young lady," her mother reprimanded her. "You hurt a lot of people through your careless selfishness."

"I was hurting too!" The words bludgeoned her throat as they escaped. "It wasn't selfishness, you know it was—"

"All about you, as always," her mother cut in. "You need to think about more than just yourself. You owe that to us. At the very least, you owe that to Colleen."

Gravel filled her mouth as Siobhan drew in a breath and spoke the hardest words she'd ever uttered. "I don't owe Colleen anything anymore. I've done my penance. I've turned my life around. I know I can never make up for lost time with Colleen, but I've tried to be part of her life. She came to my place of business, provoked an argument in front of my customers, then tried to have me arrested when I slapped her. She told me that she wants nothing more to do with me than to watch me suffer, and I will not give her that. I am done suffering for past sins."

"How dare you turn your back on your daughter like that!"

"I could ask you the same question, Mother," Siobhan answered, her heart in her throat. "Why can't you give me the same chances you want me to give Colleen?"

"We gave you every chance. People reach a limit, Siobhan, where they simply can't take any more."

"Exactly, Mom." Siobhan choked down the knot of grief lodged in her throat. "I love you, all of you, but I can't do it anymore."

Thick silence. "Well." Her mother breathed a shaky sigh. "If that's how you feel, then I suppose there's nothing else we need to say to each other. Colleen is better off without you. I hope your friends will be there for you when your life falls apart again. You take care of yourself."

"Mom . . ." Siobhan began, but the line went dead.

She lowered the phone, her mind and heart numb. That wasn't right, she knew. She was supposed to feel something, something other than this gaping, cold emptiness that seemed delicate yet voracious. Maybe, maybe this was what it felt like when hope and love died.

The phone clattered to the desk as she shot to her feet. She had to find a way to distract herself. Something that required concentration so that she wouldn't think about the joy of numbness, the sweet haze of feeling nothing, like wrapping herself in layers of cotton batting to insulate herself from the rest of the world, from the pain that, if she let it, would warp and surge and metastasize into something dangerous and deadly and unstoppable.

Her mind immediately filled with thoughts of Charlie. Charlie, with his teasing grins and welcoming arms. Charlie, with his ability to make her forget everything but being in the moment with him. Charlie, who had made her happy. Charlie, who had everything she wanted and wanted to share it with her.

She couldn't take it, couldn't reach for it no matter how much she wanted it, no matter how much she loved him and had come to love his siblings. While her mother wasn't right about her being selfish, Mary Malloy was right that Siobhan couldn't risk destroying another family.

Her heart thumped once, hard, and suddenly the emptiness collapsed beneath a tidal wave of agony. Her back bowed under the weight. A dying animal sound ripped from her throat, followed by another. She clamped her hands over her mouth to hold the cries in, an ineffectual dam against the flow.

Arms swept around her, squeezing tight, preventing her from being swept away. Siobhan hung on to Nadia as waves of grief battered her, knowing she needed to excise it, needed to swim through it and make it across because holding it in, trying to bury it led to trying to numb it, led to popping pills to inure herself to pain that never completely vanished. "Nadia. I . . . they—"

"Shh. You don't have to say anything. I heard enough." Anger laced her partner's voice, but Nadia's hand was tender as she brushed at Siobhan's bangs. "Do you need me to call Anne?"

Siobhan sucked in a breath, held it, then sucked in another one. The emptiness remained, and she knew she should worry about it but couldn't seem to muster the care needed. "No, I'm not on the edge," she answered. "I don't need therapy talk."

"How about friend-and-partner talk then?" Nadia gave her another squeeze. "I know it hurts to think about it, sweetie, but you have to let your mother go. You have to let Colleen go. You can't keep letting them hurt you like this."

"I know." She did. She bled from a thousand cuts daily thanks to throwing herself again and again against her family's sharp-edged refusal to forgive her. Despite four years being clean, despite owning her own business, they would forever see her as the strung-out woman who'd endangered a child and killed her marriage. "I know, but they're my family."

"They're your blood, I get it," Nadia said into her hair. "But you have chosen family too, and your chosen family loves you like crazy. Come upstairs with me."

"You don't live there anymore. You live with Kane, and he's probably waiting for you."

"Kane will understand. I'll call the girls over and we'll have a night in. Or even better, I'll call my dads and have them come down. You haven't had a kitchen battle with Victor in a while."

That brought a smile to her face. She and Victor Spiceland were cut from the same cloth in that regard: if someone was unhappy, you comforted them with food. Granted, some of Victor's concoctions scared you out of your sadness, but his intentions were good.

"You're so lucky, to have your family support you unconditionally. To love you like that."

Nadia hugged her again. "I know. Just as you know they consider you part of the family too. If that's not enough, there's another family that would be happy to have you as their heart."

Her gut clenched at the thought of Charlie and his family. "I can't. I can't risk it."

"Every day is a risk," Nadia pointed out. "We take a risk whether we get out of bed or hide beneath it. You remember those early days when we first got out of treatment and had to function on our own? How scared we were?"

"Scared shitless, wondering how we were going to cope." Actually, she'd been scared shitless, knowing that she'd be alone, truly alone, for the first time in years. Compared to Nadia, whose family had rallied around her, Siobhan had been on a countdown clock to relapse or worse until Nadia's family had made room for her.

"Thanks, Nadia," she said, hugging her friend. "I think I'm going to go home and crash instead. I'd be shit for company, even with your dads. Maybe we can go visit them this weekend. A change of scenery will do me some good."

"I'll hold you to that." Nadia studied her. "Don't do anything stupid."

"There's a new soufflé recipe I want to try," she answered, deliberately avoiding Nadia's statement. She couldn't promise that she wouldn't do anything stupid when she had a record of stupid mistakes trailing behind her.

"All right, then. I'll call you later."

Siobhan agreed, knowing that if she didn't, Nadia would follow her home and probably camp out outside her door, just to make sure she was okay. She was anything but and far too emotionally exhausted to fake it to her best friend the entire night.

With another hug from Nadia, she made her way to her car and headed home. She could feel her scarred-over wounds cracking, threatening to split wide again. Keep them covered, keeping the pain buried deep was a necessity in order to survive but the will to do so eroded with each breath she exhaled. She was an emotional masochist. Why else would she keep reaching out to her parents, reaching out to Colleen? Why did she keep hoping that they would forgive her, welcome her back?

Let them go. That was Nadia's advice, but even though Nadia knew her better than anyone she couldn't understand this pain. Nadia's parents and brothers hadn't turned their backs on her. Nadia had been afraid of disappointing her family, but they'd rallied around her instead. Siobhan had not only disappointed her family, she'd been disowned by them.

Why was she bothering? No matter how successful she was, she would forever be a failure at the most important things. She would always be an addict who had endangered her daughter. Once people knew, that was all they saw, all they could see. Even Charlie had had doubts and she'd convinced him to overlook her past. She shouldn't have, not when her past was so determined to make her suffer in perpetuity. Why pretend to be other than what everyone thought she was?

The words slithered through her mind as an insidious whisper. *Why bother? You're not normal, you'll never be normal, so why bother trying? What makes you think anyone would want to take a chance on you again? You need to resign yourself to the fact that you're going to spend the rest of your life alone and miserable.*

That voice. She white-knuckled her steering wheel. She'd heard that voice so many times over the years. Telling her that she wasn't smart enough, thin enough, *enough* enough. Sometimes the voice sounded like her mother. Most of the time it sounded like her stern father. The only thing that silenced that voice, even for a little while, was taking pills.

Pills. Her mouth watered and her stomach cramped with the thought, proving that she wasn't cured, would never be cured. She wanted the pills. She *needed* the pills. Without them she wouldn't be able to get through her day, wouldn't be able to manage the pain that constantly beat at her, wearing her down. She had to work. Nadia depended on her to manage her share of the café. Their staff looked to them for their livelihoods. They needed her to be capable, and she couldn't be capable if she allowed the pain to cripple her.

She'd be doing it for them. Just a few pain meds to start, so she could appear normal, so they'd stop worrying about her. Just a few, so she wouldn't disappoint them.

No. No, she couldn't think like that. Couldn't even allow an aspirin to pass her lips. She knew it wouldn't be one, or ten, or two dozen. She'd take them until she was numb, until the pain stopped or she did.

No, she thought again, as she turned onto her street. Her mother was right, Colleen was right. She deserved the hurt, deserved to suffer. It was the only way to pay for her sins, and she'd just have to resign herself to a lifetime of payments.

She frowned as she caught sight of two towheaded teens on bikes near her mailbox. She lived in a low-key neighborhood, but it was almost fall and bored teenagers were a fact of life. As she approached, one pointed toward her. The other slammed her mailbox closed, then hopped on his bike to pedal away.

Recognition flared, pushing her misery away. "Oh, no you don't," she muttered, accelerating and honking her horn.

They slowed to a stop as she approached. Charlie's brothers looked tired, scared, and sad. What the hell was going on?

"Kyle, Finn, what are you doing here? Why are you wearing backpacks?"

"Uh . . . " Kyle's Adam's apple bobbed as he glanced around nervously. Finn kept his eyes downcast, but misery telegraphed itself through every line of his body, bowed beneath an overstuffed backpack. "We just came by to leave you a note, asking you to go see Charlie. We'll take off now."

"No, you won't. Not until you tell me what's going on." She threw the car into park, then killed the engine. "Does Charlie know you're here? Why is Finn upset? Did you guys get into a fight?"

Even as she peppered him with questions, her mind jumped to the only logical conclusion for both of them to be on their bikes with backpacks, far from their house or the school, and Finn's tear-streaked face. Oh God, they were running away.

"Come inside," she ordered, getting out of the car. "We'll talk."

Kyle shook his head, and she wondered if she'd have to chase him down the street. "We gotta go. You should go see Charlie."

Dear God, please let me find the right thing to say. "Kyle, Finn's tired from pedaling all the way over here. I think he could use a break. Why don't we go inside for a little while? You and I can talk while Finn has something to eat."

Kyle looked at his younger brother, indecision twisting his features. Then the O'Halloran family bond won out, and he nodded.

Siobhan breathed a sigh as she escorted the boys up the driveway to her front door, relieved that she'd said the right thing to get him to agree. Now she had to hope that she continued to say the right things to keep the boys from running away and breaking Charlie's heart.

THIRTY-ONE

Kyle squared off with her once they made it to her kitchen. "You gotta promise not to call Charlie."

"You know I can't promise that," Siobhan answered. "He's got to be frantic that you're not home. He's probably already called the police."

"He doesn't know yet." Kyle eyed her warily as he built a massive sandwich for himself and a matching one for Finn. "I left a note explaining things, but he's been working late a lot. He probably won't get home until after dark."

God, by nightfall they could have been out of town, on a bus, or picked up by random strangers. The thought made her stomach turn. "And Lorelei?"

"She's working late tonight too."

"So you planned this out," she said, her dread growing when he nodded. "Why, Kyle? You know this will hurt your brother."

"Charlie's being mean," Finn announced. "He yelled at me."

Concern gnawed at her gut. Charlie being mean to his brothers? Yelling at sweet-natured Finn? "Why would he do that?"

"We had a fight."

"Who had a fight?" Siobhan wondered. "You and Charlie?"

Kyle nodded, but Finn said, "It was my fault."

"No, it wasn't," Kyle insisted, but his younger brother ignored him, turning tear-filled eyes to Siobhan.

"I had a nightmare about Mom and Dad. I hadn't had one in a while, but stuff got bad, and I got worried and then . . ." He shrugged, hanging his head.

Kyle took up the story. "I went to Finn's room to make sure he was okay. Charlie ran in and instead of making Finn feel better like he usually does, he yelled at him."

Siobhan sank onto a barstool, disbelief weakening her knees. "Charlie yelled at Finn?"

Kyle nodded, his face pale. "Charlie told Finn to shut up and deal with it, that life's not fair. He said Finn wasn't a kid anymore and Charlie wasn't going to be around forever, so he needed to grow the eff up."

"Oh God." Shock slid down her back like ice, followed by a heated blast of anger.

"So I pushed him," Kyle said. "I told him to shut up and leave Finn alone. He . . . it was like he woke up or something. He apologized to Finn, then to me, and then he just walked out of the room like a zombie."

"He isn't the same no more," Finn said, sniffling. "He acts like nothing's wrong, but you can tell."

Kyle swallowed hard as he fought for composure. "Charlie misses you. He sleeps on the couch every night. He works late, and he— He fake-smiles at us like people did after the funeral. He hasn't been the same since you broke up with him. And then those people came."

"People?"

"Like the people who came after Mom and Dad died," Finn explained. "Asking us if we were all right but making it seem like something was wrong."

God, he meant the child welfare people. Pain stabbed at her, so sharp and deep she couldn't breathe. "I'm so sorry, guys. I'm sure Charlie didn't mean to lash out at you like that. He's just—he's got a lot to deal with right now."

"He could deal with it if you were there," Kyle told her. "You make him happy."

"Can't you get back together now?"

The hope in Finn's eyes cut her to her soul. "No. We can't."

"Because of your daughter?" Kyle asked. "Because of what she said?"

Siobhan knotted her fingers together. "I made a lot of mistakes a few years ago. Bad mistakes. I had problems and I tried to fix them with pills. Doing that hurt my family. I'm still trying to make it up to them."

"But you apologized, right?" Kyle asked. "You said you were sorry. You said you wouldn't do it again."

"That's right," Siobhan confirmed. "I apologized to my family and I got help so I wouldn't make those mistakes again."

"Then it's not your fault that they won't forgive you," Kyle pointed out. "If they can't see that you're a good person, that's on them, not you."

"We don't care what you did before!" Finn declared. "We know you now. We like you now. We want you to marry Charlie and live with us."

Misery spread like smoke through her body, infecting everything. "I can't do that, Finn," she said as gently as she could, her voice hoarse with tears.

Kyle nodded, as if he expected nothing more. "Because we're there. That's why you can't be with Charlie. That's why the people came. That's why we have to leave, so you and Charlie can be together."

Siobhan didn't think her heart could handle another blow. In trying to protect the O'Hallorans, she'd made a mess of things instead. She'd do whatever it took to fix things. Another family wouldn't be destroyed because of her.

"Finn, Kyle, listen to me." She took their hands in hers. "Charlie loves you. You mean everything to him. It would devastate him if you ran away. It would devastate me too. I love you guys, all of you. You're not the reason why Charlie and I broke up."

"Then why?" Finn demanded. "If you love Charlie and he loves you, and you love us like we love you, why can't we all be together?"

Siobhan parted her lips to reply, but no answer sprang to mind. Why couldn't they be together? Because her daughter wanted her to be miserable? Because her mother thought she should pay indefinitely for her past mistakes?

She looked the two boys in their faces, saw their unhappiness that so sharply echoed her own and knew she had to do something. They wanted her. Charlie wanted her—or had until she'd pushed him away. Here was a family that knew what she'd been through, knew her faults and failures, and still wanted her in their lives. Why was she denying them? Why was she denying herself? To gain the approval of people who no longer had a say in her life, people who would never see her as she was now?

"I promise I will talk to Charlie," she told them. "That's all I can promise you. First things first though, we need to get you guys home before he gets off work. All right?"

"All right."

Somehow, she managed to safely load boys, backpacks, and bikes into the Falcon and headed for their house, her heart pounding harder in her chest with every mile she drove. What if Charlie was home? What would she say to him? What could she say to him?

"Do you think he's going to be mad?" Kyle asked.

"Yes," she answered honestly. "But not for long, because he'll be relieved that you're okay. He'll probably still ground you for a month, though."

"That's okay," he said, relaxing against the seat. "As long as you guys get back together, he can ground me for a year."

"Kyle." She shook her head, trying to blink the tears away. "Please don't get your hopes up, okay? I promised I'd talk to him, and I will. But . . . it's complicated."

"Adults always say that," Finn said, disgusted. "Charlie said that too. If you love each other, what's complicated?"

She didn't have an answer for that.

Her heart lodged in her throat as she pulled onto the O'Halloran's street and saw Charlie's SUV in the driveway. "I thought you said he was working late."

"He usually does," Kyle answered, slumping down. "He said he was. I think we're in trouble."

Charlie burst through the front entrance as Siobhan pulled into the driveway. The first thing she noticed was that he'd grown a beard. The second thing she noticed was his angry expression.

He stalked to the car as she shifted into park and killed the engine. The boys scrambled out and retrieved their backpacks as Charlie stopped, holding up a piece of paper. "You mind explaining the meaning of this?" he demanded, looking at Kyle.

Kyle darted a look at Siobhan, but Charlie spoke again. "Don't look at her. I'm talking to you. I want an answer."

"We thought we were doing the right thing—"

"By running away? Running away is never the right thing." Anger pinched at Charlie's features. "What are you doing with her?"

Siobhan flinched, but managed a smile when Kyle turned to look at her with a question in his eyes. "They stopped by to talk to me," she explained, proud of her blithe tone. She'd perfected her everything-is-fine act over several years of being in addiction denial; it was second nature now. "We had a good conversation and then I decided to give them a ride home."

"Charlie." Kyle's Adam's apple bobbed with a loud swallow. "Don't be mad at Siobhan. She didn't do anything wrong. I thought—"

"I know what you thought." Charlie leveled a finger at his brothers. "Finn, you're grounded for a month. Kyle, I know you instigated this, so you're grounded for six weeks. No computers or video games. Go inside."

Kyle's shoulders drooped as he slid Siobhan another guilty glance. He and Finn huddled together as they headed toward the front door but as the boys passed their brother, Charlie grabbed them both in a bear hug. "Don't you ever scare me like that again, do you hear me?" Charlie demanded, his voice breaking. "I thought I'd lost you!"

The reunion was too painful to watch. Siobhan busied herself with untying the cords holding the trunk closed so that she could take their bikes out. Better to focus on that task than the thoughts circling her brain like a slow-draining sink. *I'll never have that. Never have family who'll be happy to see me when I come home.*

She had to get out of there before she did something stupid, like begging them to give her another chance, begging them to let her be part of their family. It was a stupid wish. What could she offer them, anyway? She wasn't a good mother, wasn't a good role model. She couldn't even be what Charlie wanted and needed. She'd tried again, taken a chance again. And had crashed and burned again. There wouldn't be a third try. Her heart could only take so much.

Screw it. She'd hire someone to deliver the bikes. She fumbled with the door handle, managed to get a clammy hold on it, when he stopped her. "Siobhan."

Plucking up her courage, she turned around. "Yes?"

"You've lost weight." Accusation filled his voice to match the hurt and anger in his eyes.

"Yeah." She shrugged. "Eating hasn't been high on my priority list." She gestured toward him. "You grew a beard."

He scrubbed on hand over his chin. "Shaving hasn't been high on my priority list either."

She folded her arms across her chest to prevent herself from reaching for him. The last three weeks hadn't been easy for him, she could tell. Not only was the beard new, but she could see new lines of strain around his eyes, lines she wanted to smooth away.

"Please don't be hard on the boys," she said into the thick silence. "They know you haven't been happy the last few weeks. They thought they were doing the right thing. They—*oof!*"

Charlie caught her up in a hug so tight she couldn't draw a breath. "Thank you," he muttered into her hair. "Thank you for talking to them, for bringing them back to me. When I found that letter and realized what it meant, it felt like my world was ending. Again."

He shuddered, holding her tighter. She blinked back tears, finally returning his embrace, wanting to comfort him, wanting to take his pain. "I couldn't let them leave you because of me. I'm sorry you had to go through that, sorry you had that visit from child welfare."

He pulled away from her. "How did you know about that?"

"Lorelei stopped by the café a week ago, demanded to see me. She told me then."

"Lorelei." He snorted. "Always Lorelei. Come inside."

Her heart pounded. "I don't think that's a good idea."

"Siobhan. It's been almost a month. We need to talk. Come inside before I throw you over my shoulder and carry you in."

He looked like he meant it. Even though she knew she was making a mistake, she was too weak to resist spending a little more time with him. "All right."

She followed him into the house to the family room, but was too nervous to take a seat. "Kyle said you were sleeping on the couch?"

He shoved a hand through his hair. "I haven't been at my best for the last few weeks," he admitted. "I haven't treated them with the love and care they've needed. Apparently I'm a bitch to live with without you."

"Charlie . . ." She sank onto the couch.

"How is the investigation proceeding?"

"It's officially over. Sam gave me the news yesterday." She turned to look at him. "What about your investigation?"

"Over and done. They didn't find anything because there

wasn't anything to find." He captured her hands in his. "Are you ready to give up the idea of making this breakup permanent?"

Siobhan gasped and tried to pull her hand free, but he tightened his hold. "I know that's what you intended. I stayed away because I didn't want to cause any problems with your case and, yes, because I wanted to shield the boys. I only intended to stay away until the investigation was over one way or another. I never intended for this separation to be forever. That's the only thing that's kept me sane."

"We can't, Charlie," she managed to say, her throat clogged with tears. "I can't."

She looked at him then and knew he could see every wrecked emotion on her face. Charlie sucked in a breath. "Dammit, Siobhan, why are you convinced that breaking up is the answer?"

She shook her head so hard it hurt, but now, facing him, words wouldn't come. "I have to. Your family—"

"Want and need you here," he cut in. "Just like you want and need to be with us. Do you remember what I said to you our last night together?"

"I do." Her eyes slid closed as she swayed with the desire to be with them, with him. "You said that I was your heaven. You told me that I'll always be yours no matter what."

"No matter what, Siobhan." His gaze bored into hers. "I love you. I can't turn it off or pretend it doesn't exist. I can see in your eyes, in your tears, that you still love me. You wouldn't be so willing to sacrifice your happiness if you didn't love us so much."

"I'm not good for you, Charlie. Any of you."

"Says who? You've given my family good memories at a time that's usually full of nothing but bad. You've helped Kyle and

Lorelei." His voice roughened. "You brought my brothers back home today. How can you say that you're not good for us? You've been nothing but good for us."

Her mother's words echoed through her mind, mocking her desire for the foolishness it was. "I can't . . . I can't promise that I won't slip, that my addiction won't get the best of me. I slipped once before."

"And your family, especially your daughter, won't forgive you for it?"

She nodded, her voice too tight to speak.

He took her hand. "I'm not your mother or your daughter, Siobhan. I'm not going to abandon you or cut you out of my life because of past mistakes. I'll go with you to meetings. I'll be beside you at counseling sessions. And if you slip, I'll catch you. If you fall, I'll help you back up. Because that's what you do for someone you love."

His gentle words rang with truth, battering through her fragile composure. He hauled her into his arms, cradling her while she sobbed into his shirt. In halting breaths, she told him about her conversation with her mother. He remained silent throughout her recitation but she could feel the tension that tightened his body. "Are you okay?"

"No, I'm not," he said, his voice a tight knot of anger. "Family is everything to us. We don't turn our backs on each other, no matter what was done. When we lost our parents, we thought the world was ending. The only way we survived was because we banded together, we worked together, we survived together."

He took a deep breath. "I'm sorry to say it, sweetheart, but if they can turn their backs on their own like that, on you, they don't deserve you."

"I realize that now," she told him. "I realize I have to let go. I'll always love them and I'll always hope we can reconcile, but I can't allow them to keep hurting me like that. I can't keep looking in the past when there's so much waiting for me here and now."

He wiped at her tears. "If you mean that, there's only one solution."

"What's that?"

"Marry me, Siobhan," he blurted out. "Marry me, and we'll be your family. We'll be your home."

Her heart overflowed to bursting. "Marriage isn't necessary, Charlie," she told him. "This is where I want to be."

"Good, because I'm not letting you go again. As for whether or not marriage is necessary, I'll just have to win you over to my side."

She smiled, her sadness blown away by the force of Charlie's love. "How do you plan to do that?"

He stood, then swept her up into his arms. "I can be very persuasive when I want to be, and right now I definitely want to be."

She laughed. "Then I have to warn you right now that I'm a show-don't-tell kind of girl."

"Good, because I plan to show you all night long."

ABOUT THE AUTHOR

Seressia Glass is an award-winning author of more than twenty contemporary and paranormal romance and urban fantasy stories. She returns to contemporary romance with the sexy Sugar and Spice series. She lives north of Atlanta with her guitar-wielding husband and two attack poodles. When not writing, she spends her free time people-watching, belly dancing, watching anime, and feeding her jewelry addiction. Visit her website at seressia.com.